Chapter One

C arminia Adona stared down at her raw red hands and interlaced her fingers, praying they would stop shaking.

She'd been kneading the dough for almost a half hour. It was overboard. She knew that. But the pillowy mass hid the trembling. The little bursts that would grow in her chest and bubble up her throat? She could play those off as the grunts of a damn fine cook hard at work.

They weren't.

Although she'd never been told as much outright, Carminia felt that looking nervous in the Palace would be bad. Maybe dangerous.

It had been a mistake to visit the little stone cabin in the rear courtyard before starting the day's work. She cursed under her breath then crossed herself, smearing a bit of dough on her forehead. She left it there.

No, no.

Of course, it hadn't been a mistake. But despite the kindness—and that was all she had in her heart for those poor creatures—the sight left a dark spot on her soul that years of kneading dough wouldn't squeeze out.

Weeks earlier, her new boss had appeared on one of the countless screens around the Palace. That had been the first time she'd *met* Steve Janus, and when he'd seen her smashing away at a yellowed ball of dough, he'd scoffed. She could get help for that sort of thing.

"Like an assistant? Another cook?" she'd asked.

That had made him laugh. She was the only worker in the massive *home*, and no, that wouldn't change. He'd offered to have one of his people send over a mixing machine. In fact, she'd guessed he probably owned a company that made them.

She'd declined but had been quick to thank the man for the offer. He appeared to be the sort of man you needed to thank.

Carminia explained to him that machines made the dough too tough. And that a man such as himself deserved proper *flautas*. Made by hand and not some shoe leather, as if they'd come from a robot factory.

Not that he would ever taste her cooking. She'd never seen him in person because he never actually came to dinner and never would.

But his clients did.

"I have a Luddite for a cook, it seems. But good. Only the best shall be served to my guests," he'd said and blinked off the screen, leaving Carminia alone once again in the grand halls of the Palace.

Hardly a palace forty years earlier, it had once been the so-called *playhouse* of one of Mexico's former and most corrupt police chiefs.

How corrupt?

In a country where the average wage hovered around ten thousand dollars a year, the chief had amassed millions.

He'd built a racketeering empire extorting money—"tariffs," he'd called them—from importers.

He'd collected kickbacks from the cartel to look the other way from their drug and gun smuggling.

He'd take payments from residents—often everything they had—who were looking to flee his country. Flee the lawlessness that he, as the police chief, did nothing to quell so they might get into trucks that promised a better life north of the border.

Those people never made it to their destinations.

With all his millions, the chief had built a massive, gaudy replica of the Greek Parthenon. His secluded palace in a lifeless desert.

Still, the chief's giant home of stone had been made lush with green gardens from water stolen from the region's sole river. More than a century before, the river had been used by the residents of a convent for their bread making. The nuns were long gone. Their bread too.

The convent, now abandoned and fallen into disrepair, remained. So did stories about the souls that never left.

The chief was also gone. No one knew where, and no ever asked.

Many locals thought the Palace would have been bought by a cashed-up hotelier. Or someone with a more liberal interpretation of the Airbnb guidelines.

Kane Unchained

Wolfwere Series Book 4

Dick Wybrow

Dee Dub Publishing

It had eventually been purchased, but by whom, no one knew. And after seeing the armed guards stationed at the only road leading to the massive complex, no one ever asked.

Carminia had learned about its owner only a few weeks earlier. Just a name and the promise of a small fortune to work there. And despite the requirements of a reciprocal promise to not leave the property until the job was finished, she'd agreed.

The money had been too good. And she'd desperately needed it.

"Stop daydreaming," she muttered to herself in English, not Spanish. That had become a habit. The boss didn't like "foreign languages" spoken in his home, by which he meant anything that wasn't English.

This was the rule of all visiting guests and one strictly obeyed without question.

"Including those who speak to dough," she said and chuckled as she squeezed the squishy mass through her fingers.

Finally, the dough was ready. Well, it had been ready some fifteen minutes earlier. Finally, *she* was ready to serve up dinner to the guests waiting in the conference room.

Carminia elbowed the handle on the upper oven and pulled the door open. She sniffed inside.

"Yes." The aroma pushed aside all those troubling thoughts, as only the scents of home baking can do, and she smiled. "Yes, done."

She let the door hang open, and the hot air billowed out. Steam rose and roiled across the ceiling like spirits who'd finally broken free, stumbling over one another as they sought the whispered promise of the next life.

Dropping the dough onto the massive wooden slab—she'd asked for a cutting board and got something the size of a door—she tore the white mountain into tiny hills. She spread it out into forty tiny piles.

Tongue poking between teeth, she tried to do the math in her head.

"Seven guests," she muttered as she grabbed the rolling pin and started on the first tiny mound. "Four tortillas for each plate of *buñuelos* is twenty-eight. Plus, two more for the staff."

She smiled at the thought of sitting down to eat the sweet treat once all the guests had their meals.

Carminia had seen them walking up from the airstrip behind the property. European? Asian? Some appeared to be Californian.

They just had a look to them.

Which could mean they might forgo the delightful *buñuelos*, leaving more of the dessert for the others. People from California did not eat real food. In east LA, yes. However, it seemed people in the rest of the state liked something called "whole food" that appeared to only come in jars. The sort you must label or risk having no idea what is inside. Could be couscous, could be bird seed. Who knew?

"Probably tastes the same."

She did not know what couscous was and had little interest in finding out. If the person who'd invented the food couldn't come up with a proper name for it—just repeating the same syllable twice—it couldn't be very good.

All the tiny piles were flattened into disks in a few minutes. She hurried now since the *flautas* were done, which meant the first course was ready.

Carminia searched around for her kitchen towel but then glanced at the clock. Her heart sped up. She reached into the oven and, using her fingertips, lifted the massive porcelain boat of *flautas* out and laid it upon the stone countertop.

Leaning down, she smelled them and smiled.

She didn't have the patience to tailor each serving to the culinary desires of individual guests. If they didn't like it, they could not eat. Simple. That had been her way before, and it was her way now.

Drizzling white cheese sauce across each in a zigzag pattern, she repeated this for the other servings. She then added a thick vein of guacamole across one end then a ribbon of pico de gallo across the other.

Her eyes drifted across the plates. The rising steam filled her kitchen with aromas that nearly transported Carminia back home. Nearly.

Soon. Maybe soon.

Then, finally, she would have enough money to repair the ovens of her food truck. Restart her business.

She wheeled the serving cart over from its station next to the double fridge and lifted the first plate of *flautas*. As she stared at the food, her breath caught in her throat.

Carminia had been making this dish since she'd been a little girl. And for the first time, the five rolled-up tacos resembled fingers. The guac looked like green rot around the wrist, and instead of pico, she saw only bloodied claws.

She knew where those images had come from.

Days earlier, she'd seen one of *them*. Only briefly, just a few seconds when she caught the image on the conference room's screen, but it was a sight she would never forget. The creature had begun visiting her in her dreams.

"No dreams. *Pesadillas*," she whispered, her eyes darting left and right. "Nightmares."

A minute later, she wheeled the cart through the kitchen's double doors and down the long stone hallway. Lights flickered on as she approached, illuminating the path ahead. She crossed the Palace's open-air breezeway and felt the night's warm air cling to her skin.

The giant floating head in the middle of the conference room table turned as she entered. With a false smile, he announced her arrival.

"Ah, my Carminia!" Steve Janus said, his digital image warbling for a fraction of a second. "Your timing, as always, is perfect."

"Thank you, sir," she said, keeping her gaze on the cart of food and away from the big screen that took up most of the north wall.

She bent down and grabbed a heavy chafing dish from the lowest rack of the cart. She grunted at its weight and let out a long breath.

A man sitting in the ornate wooden chair nearest to her leaped to his feet, saying in a clipped British accent, "Why don't I help you with that?"

"Ah, ah," the boss called out. "Please sit, Colonel Maxwell. My staff is more than capable."

Cowed, the man sat quietly.

After loading the tub onto the table, she lifted the heavy lid with little effort. The guests watched as the steam cleared and revealed a massive dish of perfect rice. Woven through the grains was the yellow of corn, the red of fresh tomato, and the green of cilantro.

The Brit smiled and whispered to her, "Looks lovely. Well done, you."

She grabbed four more dishes from the middle racks—half refried beans, the others black beans. She placed them on the table as the boss picked up where he'd left off his conversation.

Their meeting commenced once again. It was as if Carminia Adona evaporated from view, much like the steam from the rice on their plates.

"If you turn to the screen, we've got a little promotional video for you," Janus said, his image projected from the center of the table. "Not a full show of the creature's abilities, but you'll get the gist of it."

"Just the one?" a woman said with a melodic accent that sounded German to Carminia. But every accent from eastern Europe sounded a bit German to her.

She placed a plate of *flautas* before this woman and moved to the next guest, serving from the right. She did not know why this was the case, but it had been the instruction from her boss. Her best guess was that he'd seen it on television.

The floating head sighed. "Yes, one will be plenty for you to—"

"Are there not others?" another voice asked, this one English but not like the British man who'd spoken to her. She couldn't place that accent either. "Are we all to bid for one single Enhanced soldier?" The man didn't so much laugh as titter, as he glanced nervously around the table.

"Oh, so much more than the Enhanced," their host said. "The earlier demonstration you saw, this was a previous iteration of our super warriors. This latest is something very special."

"Maybe, if we get outbid for this new Enhanced," another guest said, "then you will make available those earlier creatures. They looked very formidable on the video you sent. But, of course, I would expect to pay less."

Carminia placed a plate in front of another guest.

"Sadly," the boss said with no hint of sorrow in his voice, "they are no longer with us."

"You *destroyed* them?" another woman asked, her pitch rising at the end.

"No, another creature did that. A *better* one."

This drew a shaky laugh from a couple of the diners. One of them asked, "Well, is that creature not available? If one creature could destroy all of your—"

"Even better," the Administrator said. "The NextGen soldier I am about to demonstrate to you, and all of those being created at our mountain facility just up the road, are derived from the blood of *that* creature. With some"—he smiled, showing teeth—"refinements."

"You have me intrigued, Mr. Janus," the British man said. "What sort of refinements?"

Their host nodded to someone off-screen.

"My technician is queuing that video up now. I would say please no recording of what you're about to see, but I know all of your devices have been surrendered to the men who met you at your aircraft." Their host's image spun in a circle in the middle of the table. "Please understand, if anyone here has sneaked in any sort of recording device, then they will be featured in our next demonstration video."

Forks clinked against porcelain as the seven people seated around the table became extremely interested in their food and wine.

Carminia put the final serving of *flautas* before the last guest. Without another word, she wheeled the now-empty cart toward the door, her head tilted away from the massive screen.

As the light began to flicker across the wall, the German-sounding woman broke the silence.

"What happened to this other creature? The, um, father of your new Enhanced? We expect the soldiers we purchase to be the best ever created. But if there is another out there..."

The room fell quiet once again, except for the glug-glug of more wine going into a glass. Even without looking back to her boss, she could sense the man grinding his teeth over the video display.

"Not a concern," the floating head said. "He's no longer in the picture."

Chapter Two

I rubbed my forehead with my palm, hoping if I rubbed hard enough, it might dent my skull and snuff out the growing ball of fire inside my brain. Wasn't working. I rubbed harder.

"Keep that up, and you'll lose an eyebrow, Emmy," Roy said from across *my* kitchen table, his eyes never leaving the six-foot-seven French Canadian sitting to his left. "Or get one of those monobrows like your grandma."

Slapping both hands on the table, I growled at him. "My grandmother does *not* have a monobrow."

"She does," Roy said. "Same color as her mustache."

I jumped up, folded my arms, and leaned back against *my* fold-away pantry door so hard it came off the track. That made me feel a little better.

Leering at my ex, I asked, "How long have you been in *my* apartment?"

He shrugged. "Long enough to put some actual food in the fridge."

"Why did you do that?"

"Because there wasn't any food in the fridge."

I dropped back into the chair hard enough to dislodge one of the wooden dowels holding two of its legs together. It clunked to the floor. If this conversation kept up much longer, my entire kitchen would be in splinters.

"No, no, no," I said and aimed a finger at him. "You know what I mean. Why are you here? Why have you been *staying* here?"

"I got out, and I needed a place. I stopped by to, you know, see my girlfriend—"

"*Ex*-girlfriend."

Another shrug. "And she wasn't at home as per expected," he said, crossing his arms and tossing a nod at Kane. "Turns out, she's on holiday with some French dude. Going around *voulay-vooing* her *choochie* up and down I-35."

To his credit, Kane didn't take the bait. In fact, he hadn't said a word since I'd waved him inside from the jeep.

"Not true and none of your damn business, Roy," I said, feeling a serious need to jump up again. In my peripheral vision, I sensed a wicker utensil holder inch closer to the wall. "We're not together anymore, man."

"Since when?"

"Since you went to prison for six years!"

Roy laughed. "Incarceration does not constitute a relationship cessation."

"Did you *blow* a thesaurus while you were inside?" I laughed at him. Because he was a moron. A moron I used to date.

What had I been thinking?

Roy, however, did not find the line as funny as I did. "That sorta stuff is nothing to joke about."

Kane chose this moment to pipe up. "Why would someone do this to a book?" The big man's amber eyes locked on to Roy. "You would only flip all the pages. This only hampers the reading."

My ex pointed at Kane. "Is he speaking English?" Not waiting for an answer, he got back on track. "I've had an entire year to work on myself. Been improving my vocabulary."

"Yet you still don't understand the definition of breakup," I said. "Because while incarceration may not constitute a relationship cessation, remember when I said, 'I'm done with all this' and 'I'm done with you'? That is a *bona fide* relationship cessation."

I turned away, pissed, because I had to now deal with a Roy complication. Wasn't my life already complicated enough?

He'd just been there *in my apartment* after we'd gotten back from the derelict Covenant factory. St. Louis had been a delicious irony because we'd chained up one of the organization's former executives inside. Doc Hammer had previously led the Enhanced program, and now she was one of her own monsters trapped within the walls of one of their old buildings.

Much like she had once left Marata, she was imprisoned and left to feast on a diet of nothing but the Enhanced solution to keep her alive. Eventually, we would have to deal with that complication.

And Marata, if we could find her. She'd bolted in Atlanta. Maybe she'd died without access to her "go-juice"? I hadn't seen any news reports about a feral woman stalking the city. At least, not yet.

Before handling those compilations, we first had to destroy Covenant's new breed of monsters hidden at a secret location in Mexico. But not *entirely* secret. I had an idea where they were.

As I'd drifted off to Woe Is Me Island, Roy had seen me go silent. So he'd found a new target for derision.

"What's your story then, man?"

Kane stared at Roy, never blinking. "Not man."

"Fine," my ex said, then overenunciated his next works. "What. Is. Your. Story. *Kane*?"

I jumped in. Or at least, I tried. "He—"

"You are asking then for stories?" My big friend grinned, showing both his upper and lower teeth. "Book to read recommendations?"

Roy looked at me, his mouth hanging open slightly.

"A favorite of mine is *Le Petit Prince*," Kane continued. "On the surface, it is about a boy who travels through space and visits the Earth. But it is a story about love, loss, and loneliness. And how youth's purity can be fleeting if one does not safeguard it."

Turning to Kane, I asked, "I thought you struggled with reading?"

"Yes. This is a book *ma mère* used to read to me when I would go to sleep." Kane lifted his chin toward Roy. "I cannot read very well, and this is a thing that Emelda is helping me with."

Roy found this all kinds of funny. Gut-bust laughable. I knew the guy well enough to realize this was a way for him to hide his nervousness. Kane had at least six inches on him.

Taller. Kane was much taller, is what I'm saying.

"This dude never learned to read?" Roy slapped the table with an open palm like this was the funniest thing in the world. I looked at Kane, but he was stone-faced. Like he was bored. Roy wasn't done. "What? They don't got schools in Canada?"

"Of course," Kane said, grinning again. "I never went."

"Why the hell not?"

My big friend finally blinked, just once. "I am wolf."

Roy's eyes got a bit bigger, and he looked to me then back at the monstrous man next to him. He started speaking, stumbled, and finally found his words. And despite his quality thesaurus time, he faltered.

"Dah fuck what?"

I waved my hands between them. "It's a Canadian thing. He just means he does his own thing, lone wolf, that sort of idea."

"Emelda, this is not true, and you know this. I have a pack. And a wolf wife who awaits me."

The squeak of a chair across worn-out tile split the air. I looked over at Roy, who'd slid back from the table.

"This dude is insane, Emmy."

"Don't call me that, Roy!" I said. My stomach roiled with acid at the thought that *this* was in my life now. Something I would have to deal with. I decided since he was here, I might as well make the best of it. "Hey, you know people. I need a passport."

"Where you going?"

"Away," I said and frowned. "Any idea who can do that?"

He shrugged. "Sure. The DMV."

"Doesn't seem possible, but I think you got dumber inside," I said. "No, *they* don't issue passports, and I don't want to travel under my own name. If I cross into Mexico under Emelda Thorne, it might set off alarm bells where I don't want them ringing."

My ex smirked at me. "What kind of shit did you get into where Mexico don't want ya?"

Hooding my eyes, I said, "You have no idea, Roy."

"I have an idea. I was there. Not in Mexico but with Emelda over several weeks now," Kane said, almost childlike. "Emelda is very formidable."

"See? I'm formidable," I said then changed the subject because the French Canadian sounded like he was about to go on a tear. Leaning toward Roy, I asked, "Hold on. How did your six-year stint turn into one?"

Roy pursed his lips and nodded slowly. "I had a good lawyer."

"You had the *worst* lawyer," I said. "You represented yourself."

He cocked an eyebrow. "Got a better one. Or, actually, the Family got me one. And a bit of good behavior and whatever voodoo juice they got, well, I got out."

It was my turn to laugh. And I think I laughed harder than Roy had a minute earlier.

"You dumb ass. The Family does you a favor, and you think you're in the clear? You owe them now!"

"That's right," he said and leaned forward, putting his elbows on his knees. He made a bridge with his fingertips and laid his chin on them, blinking. "And if you want that passport, you're gonna help me clear my ledger."

Chapter Three

We sat outside the hardware store a few blocks away from First Avenue, which used to be one of the gnarliest, nastiest, and most perfect music venues to ever birth itself onto the streets of Minneapolis. I'd long thought about returning, a taste of those old, carefree days, but going back never rekindles that high you once had.

It was the same with ex-boyfriends.

Time is a jealous lover, and when your back is turned, she swoops in, taking your former flame in her suffocating embrace.

What was once soft to the touch feels angular and sharp.

That comforting feeling of familiarity, like bare feet on your grandmother's freshly shampooed shag carpet, is gone. It was the same carpet, sure, but now it was all crusted with cat vomit.

I didn't hate Roy, but I'd never really loved him. I think I only loved who I'd hoped he might become but never could.

Yawning because of a terrible night's sleep, I looked for street signs. I was navigating as my ex drove, hoping to get us to the hardware store quickly. The sooner we got there, the sooner I could again leave Roy behind.

Kane filled the back seat of Roy's Chevy Impala. Every time he shuffled his feet, the crinkling of discarded potato chip bags would send electric prickles up my spine.

"How we supposed to know when the guy takes lunch?" I said, trying to see past Roy's fat head as he scanned the street. Roy grabbed his phone off his belt, checked the screen, and then jammed it back into place with a click.

I laughed. "You might be the only dude left who uses a phone holster."

"I don't like putting it in my pocket," he said in his flat Midwestern drawl. "Uncomfortable. Pokes into me."

Kane offered, "This is because you have the skinny jeans."

That earned him a fierce look from Roy. My ex stared at the big guy chilling in the back seat like it was a pool lounger. His eyes were closed, and his head lay back on his bicep.

"I ain't taking fashion advice from a dude who dresses like he's just stepped out of an eighties Whitesnake video." Roy laughed, thinking this was all kinds of funny.

Peering back, I watched Kane crack one eye open and stare down at his clothes.

Black leather jacket, white T-shirt, faded jeans, and a belt thick enough you could have spanked a jacked-up pro wrestler with it.

Clicking the tips of his motorcycle boots together, he said, "Ma mère liked this look. This is how I dress."

"Who's Maymeer?"

I rolled my eyes. "It's French. His mother."

Another laugh from Roy, bigger than the first. "Wait, wait. You dress like that to make your *mom* happy? Are you serious?"

Kane opened his other eye and directed his gaze at our driver, who, I expected, could see the two blazing eyes in his rearview. Roy audibly swallowed.

"Yes," my friend said wistfully. "She is always with me, and this look is one she favors."

"What?" Roy asked, finding his asshole mojo again. Stopped at a red light, he grabbed the headset and peered over the top. "You some kinda momma's boy or something?"

The French Canadian nodded, the side of his mouth hooking upward. "Yes, I am momma's boy."

Roy glanced at me, as if looking for someone to join him in the derision. When he didn't see it, he shook his head.

"Man, you just openly admit that, huh? What a—"

"What is wrong with momma's boy? My human mother loved me. Mon père as well, yes, but a mother's love, this is special."

When the light turned green, my ex got us moving again. "Your new boyfriend is such a weird dude."

"He's not—" I started to say *boyfriend* then switched gears. "A weird dude. He's sweet."

"Ha, I hope you never, ever called me sweet to anyone," Roy said, making a left turn. Thankfully, I could see the hardware store three shops down.

"No, actually. Not one time."

That earned me a grunt as Roy reached down, unholstered his phone, checked the time, and slapped it back to his hip.

We sat in silence for at least ten minutes, watching the city go by. I had missed the simple sounds of it. Behind me, Kane softly snored.

"Man, is this guy is taking his time," Roy mumbled, staring at the store across the street. "I'm sweatin' my balls off. He's got to know we're here."

As if on cue, two wrinkled fingers wrapped around the bottom of a sign that read Open and flipped it around to show a new message.

Grabbing lunch. Back in fifteen minutes!

"Finally."

I exited the old Chevy and leaned against its rusted quarter panel. Roy jumped out of his side, and when the rear door opened, he put out an open palm to stop it. Without any effort, Kane pushed it wider and stood, towering over Roy.

Refusing to look up at the bigger man, Roy instead glared at Kane's throat. I guessed he thought this made him look tough. It didn't. He looked like a toddler trying to stare down a Great Dane.

Turning to me, he threw a thumb at my friend. "Can you tell the Wookiee to stay in the car?"

"No, Kane's coming with," I said, crossing the street. "I always know where I stand with him."

"Yeah," Roy said, running up behind me. "In the shade."

Trailing us, Kane asked, "What is Wookiee?"

Chapter Four

I suppose I shouldn't have been surprised that the man behind the counter—a guy who might have been in his sixties but looked a decade older—was indeed eating a sandwich. Part of the ruse? Or maybe the guy was just hungry.

"You didn't see the sign?" he asked, chewing casually. He watched Roy as we walked in. He blinked once, and when he opened his eyes again, they were on me. Then they drifted upward.

He stopped chewing.

"Somebody's been eating their Wheaties," he said, looking at Kane over my shoulder. He swallowed the bite.

Roy started to speak, but the man simply held out a hand, wiped his palms on a napkin, and stood. The shop owner raised a pair of glasses hanging around his neck to his face. Lifting a hinged square of the chipped wooden counter, he steeped though the gap, clipping his hip on the edge.

He didn't seem to notice.

Standing in front of the big French Canadian, he asked, "Son, do you ever do any fighting?"

"If it cannot be avoided," Kane said in a warm baritone. "Then yes."

That drew a chuckle out of the old man. He brushed a lock of stark white hair away from his eye and smiled wide.

"What about for money?" He shrugged. "Fella like you could make some good money fighting."

"The payment for fighting is blood," Kane said.

The man's eyebrows rose. "Whose?"

My friend mirrored the man's grin, only wider and with twice the teeth. "In combat, blood payment is extracted from those who are vanquished."

"Right," the man said and shrugged. "I reckon cash requires less laundering."

It seemed Roy didn't like not being the topic of conversation.

"We're here looking for an order," he said as the shopkeeper crossed back through the gap, closed it up, and returned to his perch behind the counter. "I was told to come here at, um, your lunch hour."

"I haven't taken an hour for lunch since 1967, boy," the man said, sitting back down on his stool and grabbing his sandwich again. "But since you're already here disturbing my private time, what can I do you for?"

Roy hooded his eyes, gave me and Kane a knowing glance, and nodded. "You're Whitey, yeah?"

The man blinked slowly and lifted his head slightly. On the back wall, in eight-inch letters, it read Whitey's Hardware.

He looked back at Roy.

"You must be that kid who got out last week," Whitey said with a long sigh. "Heard you might be stopping by to do some HVAC work."

I thought Roy was going to burst with joy.

On the drive over, he'd started to tell me about the code the Family had started to use. This was new. I'd helped Roy with some second-story work over the years, just enough to supplement my crap job and not lose my crap apartment, but this was the first I'd heard of any secret-code stuff.

When he'd been inside, one of the Family's other cons had gotten him up to speed.

The turf battle between them and Rosa Nieto's organization had heated up. These days, that meant less about blood on the street—although there was that—and more about using technology to spy on each other.

Trackers, pinhole cameras, listening devices.

So a code had been worked up.

"Plumbing means it's a residential job," Roy had said on the drive over. "Which is the stuff we normally do."

"Used to do," I corrected.

He waved his hand then glanced in the back seat. "I don't know if I feel comfortable talking about this with your big friend back there."

"Fine," I said, looking back at the snoozing Kane. "You tell me, and I'll tell him later."

"Whatever," Roy said, happy to continue with what he saw was some James Bond-level spy shit. "Pest Control, well, you can guess what that is.

Door-to-Door Sales is one notch down from that. Rough someone up, that sort of thing."

"Dude, I am not getting involved with anything like that," I said. "Not interested."

Roy laughed. "Tell that to the two dudes you nearly beat to death with a crowbar."

Nice. A subtle reminder of a drug-fueled lapse in judgment and one, admittedly, that Roy had taken the fall for. He was reminding me that I owed him. And I guess I did.

"But don't worry," he said. "I was told we're looking to do HVAC stuff. That's like Plumbing but at a commercial property."

"We're supposed to steal from a commercial property? You mean like a business? With monitored alarms? Guards?"

Roy had shrugged it off. "Time to step up, Em."

I blinked, realizing that Whitey was staring at me. He'd asked a question, and I had been daydreaming.

"The what now?" I said. Me, I'm a smooth operator.

"I asked you," the old shopkeeper said, sighing, "if you're the one looking for a packing slip. That's you, then?"

Packing slip? I rolled my eyes.

"Right. Yes, I need a p—" *Passport*, I didn't say. Were these guys for real? "Packing slip."

He pulled a small pad from his shirt pocket, extracted the world's smallest pencil from its ringed binding, and held the tip over a page. "In what name?"

"Uh, it…" Yeah, I couldn't go as Emelda Thorne. That had been the whole point. Before I could come up with a fake name, Kane did it for me.

"Heather Thomas." Whitey repeated it back, smiling so big his eyes squinted. "Name—Heather Thomas."

I cranked my neck back and looked up. "Do I want to know who that is?"

"She is the pink-bikini girl from *The Fall Guy* show," Kane said, slapping a large meaty hand on my shoulder.

That got a shake of the head from Whitey and a small chuckle. Without looking up, he said, "You do not look old enough to remember that show, boy."

"Was favorite of my mother."

Like he was spring-loaded, Roy pounced. "Yeah, this big bastard says he's a momma's boy! Told me on the way over, and no shame about it or nothing."

Whitey gave him a bored look. "What's wrong with that? I'm a momma's boy. I loved my mother."

"Roy does not love his mother," Kane offered. "This is quite sad."

"Jesus, is that true?" Whitey flipped his pad closed and jammed it back in his pocket. "What kind of man are you?"

"It... What? No, it..." Roy looked between the two of them. "She... She wasn't around much."

"So you were at home alone, were you?" Whitey asked, his face a mask of concern.

"Y-yes. Yeah."

The old shopkeeper nodded. "Explains why she was never there."

Kane laughed, a big booming sound that shook the metal shelves. I shot him a look. *Not helping!* His laugh faded away, and he suddenly got really interested in his fingertips.

Whitey asked if I had a photo for my "packing slip," and shot a thumb over his shoulder. Beneath the shop name was an email address. I pulled out my phone, found a photo, and sent it.

"Packing slip will be ready after the order has been filled, of course," he added. "You get me?"

I got him.

Whitey reached under the counter and came up with an envelope. He held it out to me, but before I could grab it, Roy snatched it and tried to stuff it into his pocket. He couldn't fit his hand into the too-tight jeans, so he jammed it into his waistband.

"I'm going to finish my sandwich now," Whitey said, unfolding the wax paper once again. "And I prefer to dine alone."

Without another word, Roy crossed in front of Kane and opened the door. I followed, and the big French Canadian came up behind me. Once outside, he gingerly closed the shop door, waving through the window as he did. Big dopey grin on his face.

I scowled at him. "When did you get so nice?"

"Maybe when I was the golden retriever," he said, shrugging. "Or possibly the Saint Bernard."

"Saint Bernard?" Spinning around, I whispered, "When was that?"

"This was B.E.," he said, grinning. "Before Emelda."

Kane had spent the better part of the year looking for Cal Davis before he'd literally ended up on my doorstep. But I felt a bit cheated that I'd never seen him as a big dopey dog. Maybe one day.

"Let's go!" Roy called out, hopping into his Impala. When I started heading that way, I felt Kane's gentle hand on my arm.

He was staring at the shopkeeper's glass storefront. His big smile was gone. "That man says one thing with his words, another with his expression."

Inside the beat-up Chevy, Roy was already tearing into the envelope, chucking bits of paper into the back seat.

I turned back to Kane, keeping my voice low. "Whitey is a go-between for a crime family and its lackeys, so not exactly an upstanding guy. Are you worried about something else?"

"I do not know." He frowned. "But can I offer a suggestion? A warning?"

Shrugging, I swallowed then nodded.

Kane said, "Don't trust Whitey."

Chapter Five

As he drove, Roy filled me in as Kane stretched out in the back seat like he was on a family holiday.

"It's all in code," he said. "A parts list. Conduit and wiring. Tools."

'Ugh, what is the job, then?"

Roy read through it a few times then leaned his head back. He looked at me then looked outside.

"I don't like that look." Reaching over and punching his shoulder, I growled at him. "What are we stealing?"

"Oh, that," he said. "Just some old artwork. These two metal disk things about the size of car tires. Gold and silver and worth a fortune."

"Art? Like an art heist?"

He nodded, frowning.

That was kind of a relief. I'd worried it might be guns or drugs or worse. Stealing stuff like that is bad enough. Getting *busted* with stuff like that could mean a life inside. But he'd already been told what the Family wanted stolen.

Something else had soured his mood.

He shrugged and pulled out his phone, opening the map application. Looking back to the order, he scanned his phone again. Slowly, he shook his head.

I grabbed the paper out of his hands. Like he had said, it was just a list of parts. The billing address was one I didn't recognize.

"Is that where we're supposed to break into—345 Marshall Parkway?"

He stared at the sheet in my hand, and I realized his color matched the bleached paper I was holding. He looked out the window again. "The first digit means go over that many streets. Then reverse the last digits. That's where we're going."

"Where is that, then?" I looked over at him, but he continued to stare out the window, slowly rubbing his bare face. Frustrated, I snatched his phone, thumbed around the screen, and found the decoded address.

When I plugged it into the map software, I saw a big square next to three little squares. Some industrial space.

Great.

"What's at 54 Wycliff Ave?" I asked and chucked the phone back at Roy. It bounced to the floor.

He sighed. "It's a big spread. Warehouse. One way in and one way out, except for the loading docks. But those have coded entries."

He slowed at a red light, waiting. Silently, I waited for Roy to tell me what had troubled him. Then I looked at his face.

"You know this address," I said. He squirmed. "You've been there?"

He shook his head, finally looking at me. "Nope. But I've seen it. It's a front, basically. Looks like a warehouse for those big home renovation stores."

The light turned green, but he hadn't moved. Behind us, a horn blasted. I shot a middle finger at the back window. The car behind roared its engine and went around us. Another long honk as it did.

"You gonna go?" I asked Roy, and he got us moving again, chewing hard on an already-chewed nail. Just one of the many habits I hated about him. Nail biting. Farting. Breathing.

He sighed. "The warehouse belongs to Rosa Nieto."

"What? Bullshit!" I shouted loud enough to make my own ears ring. "The *rival* gang to the Family? You know what those guys are into, Roy!"

"Of course I do," he spat, venom sharpening his words. "I spent a year inside because two of their guys got beaten so bad they ended up in hospital."

I stared ahead as the next green light went to amber. Then red again.

"But of course," Roy said, still looking at me, "you did that, Emmy. That was you."

If we were going to be able to cross the southern border, I needed that passport. To get that, I would have to help Roy break into a shop belonging to the most powerful, most well-connected gang in the city.

The warehouse job was a bad idea.

But so was getting involved with the Family again.

Chapter Six

"You comfy in there?" I shouted over the din of the cargo van's engine.

All I got back was a dull thump from beneath the floor and an utterance that sounded something like "Thank you." But, nah, I don't think Roy had said that. He'd never said those words in the three years we'd been together.

Kane sat quietly in the passenger seat and hadn't uttered a word since we'd picked up the vehicle. Since he was a big guy, I guessed you could have called that brooding. We really didn't apply that term to little dudes. When someone of short stature was quiet and sullen, we called that sulking, didn't we?

Didn't seem fair.

"You want fair, go down to the elementary playground in July," my grandfather used to say. Because that was when the fair came and set up on the school property. He thought he was being clever. And, I supposed, between warm beer burps, in his own way, he kind of was.

Not that I'd ever gone to that fair.

Mom had always felt it was a waste of money, and there hadn't been a lot to go around. Dad's mother, my wonderful grandmother, said the people working there didn't seem like the sort you would want to trust if you hoped to come out of that place with all four limbs.

Not the point. I'd been thinking about Kane brooding.

Why was I so distracted?

Probably because I was freaking out. We were going to try to fake our way into a warehouse belonging to a criminal outfit that had a higher body count than John Wick.

I'd come up with how we were going to do it.

Necessity may be the mother of invention, but desperation is the drunk uncle of batshit ideas. We'd only had a few hours, so the plan was a bit nuts.

At first, I'd felt kind of smug about it. As we'd gotten closer to the warehouse owned by Rosa Nieto, my confidence was shaking more than the cages in the back in the van.

And Kane being quiet wasn't helping.

"What's going on in that wolf head of yours?" I asked, keeping my voice low enough so Roy didn't hear. Not that he could have, hidden away inside a panel in the van's floor. He'd tried to argue that Kane should go down there, but the big fella would never have fit.

And this crew might *know* Roy on sight. He'd gone inside for bashing two of their guys and probably shot his mouth off about it.

Was it odd that the first job he got from Whitey was to steal from the crew that wanted him dead? No, not odd. A total setup.

But why?

Kane ran his meaty hand down his face and shrugged. His eyes flitted to the horizon. "Getting dark, yes?"

"Nah, we got at least another hour." I glanced down at my phone, which I'd propped up in a cup holder. "Maybe a little less."

"This is enough time to steal things?"

"It better be," I said, taking a slow turn and looking up a grassy rise to a fence line. I nodded to his feet. "Chuck the second one out here."

Kane grabbed one of the leather bags, hung his arm out the window, and arched it over the fence. When it landed, I could see its occupant was not happy about any of it.

"Just the three will work?" he asked, staring at the sprawling warehouse through the fence. I cranked the wheel to head up the short hill. I would give it a few minutes. The first bag I'd had Kane throw had gone over the fence at the other far corner.

Now to see if this would work.

Most of the day had been spent securing the van and our three *guests*. It had taken far longer than I'd hoped, but we did have an unusual shopping list. By the time we had everything we needed, afternoon was getting ready to clock out and make way for the evening shift.

I wound around the streets for ten minutes to give time for the two guests we'd chucked over the fence to head toward a nearby heat source. The warehouse.

Roy had assured me there would be just the one guard shack. One way in, one way out. But the Family's code had indicated an unknown number of occupants and that there would be *copper tubing* and *nails*.

They would be armed.

Of course.

"You ready?" I whispered to Kane, and he looked at me, a smile splitting his bearded face.

When we got within twenty feet of the rollaway fence, one of the guards came out, his hand raised. As if the big gate wasn't enough of an indication to stop.

The guy stood in front of us and looked between me and Kane, tugging on his lip. Then he took a few sideways steps to check out the business name on the side of the van. He started laughing and looked up to the passenger side. When Kane smiled at him, the dude blanched.

He came around to my side.

Grinning, I said, "Maybe don't smile with those big-ass teeth of yours."

Reaching for the last leather sack, Kane said, "All the better to greet you with."

"Not funny," I said to him. To the guard, I said, "Hi. You probably knew we were coming, yeah?"

He glanced again at the stencil on my side of the van, shaking his head. "You doing door-to-door sales?"

I laughed and, my arm hanging out the window, slapped the side of the door. On the third slap, I could just hear the thump in the grass on Kane's side of the van.

"You wanna keep that banging down?" the guard asked, frowning at me. He pointed at the van. "What's all this getup? Snakes & Adders?"

"You didn't get a call?" I asked with real attitude in my voice because I thought the name was clever. Hell, *Whitey* thought it was kind of clever. The *printing guy* Whitey had sent us to thought it was clever. I think Roy did, too, after I'd explained it to him.

Kane?

He didn't get it. Not even after I explained it.

"You making a delivery or picking up?" the guard asked, smiling and laughing at his own joke. He hooked his thumbs on his belt. Good move. He looked all casual, and now his hand was only a few inches from his weapon.

"Probably on the news by now, but there's been a breakout," I said, leaning down and scanning left to right.

That wiped the smile off his face. "Breakout?"

"At the zoo. Bull snake didn't like the brand of mice they were getting fed and voiced its displeasure by chomping into the neck of one of the handlers."

"Jesus."

"Yeah, that guy goes running off in a panic—must have been new—and leaves the gate open. When they tried to get it closed, no one wanted to go near it, so they used a Bobcat."

The guard took a step back. "They used a *lion* to get—"

"No, no. You know, one of those cute little front loaders—on wheels, got a scoop out front. Good for digging trenches and stuff."

"Uh huh," the guard said, looking around now. "Sure."

"Well, the king cobra comes up and faces off against the Bobcat, and the operator freaks out, and he's spinning around like the kid in *The Exorcist* and—"

"He puked?"

"No, no, no," I said, shaking my head. "Different scene. Anyway, he knocks the damn fence down, and the snakes all head for the hills. And you, my friend, are at the top of the hill."

The guard walked down the side of the van and stared down the long grassy hill that led into the nearby industrial area.

I glanced at Kane. *We good?*

He nodded, but the smile was long gone. Before the guard came back, I snatched up my phone and pretended to be in the middle of a call.

"Well, yeah, we can head over there now. We're just at one of the big warehouses up on the hill."

The guard came up to my side and put one hand on the open window. The other slid closer to his weapon.

"Who's that?" He nodded at my phone.

I put a finger to my lips, and he frowned. He looked at Kane then back at me. His eyes darted between the two of us.

Dude wasn't buying it.

Slowly he began walking toward the front of the van and, with the hand he'd had on my window, pulled at the radio mic on his shoulder.

"Nathan, we got something weird going on here," he said, his eyes still on Kane. The corner of my friend's mouth twitched. On his lap, his hands clutched into fists.

I cleared my throat and called out the window, "Listen, we got a sighting a block or two from here. Anaconda maybe. We're gonna—"

"Stay there," the guard said, his eyes fixed on me. Into the radio, he said, "Swing on by, would ya?"

"You got it, Camp."

I glanced at the rearview mirror as a sedan pulled up behind the van, blocking us in. The van was bigger, heavier, and I knew that if I dropped it into reverse, I could move the other vehicle out of the way.

But this wasn't a getaway vehicle.

It was a big cargo van that we'd dressed up to look like some snake retrieval unit. Cages lining the walls. A big blue tank with a sticker that read Snake Repellent. We wouldn't get more than a block.

The first guard, apparently named Camp, came around my side and stood next to me, his hand back at my window. I swallowed hard as the door to the car behind us opened.

The guy at my window looked over and said, "Hey Nate, I think—"

Camp's voice got cut off by a primal scream from the man called Nate. I turned and saw the guy scramble back into his vehicle, slamming the door onto his own ankle. He screamed again, pulled his leg inside, and yanked the door closed

With eyes wide, he locked it and crawled over to the passenger-side window. Then looked out the rear window. Then looked back at the guard next to me.

As I watched him in my side mirror, I saw him glance at Camp and hold his hands out, palms down, and wave his fingers, flopping them forward and back. The universal sign for *Dude, get the fuck out!*

"What in the hell?" Camp said, then his eyes went to the ground, and as instructed, he began to get the fuck out.

A small glimmer of hope blossomed in my chest. I pressed my luck.

"Hey, so we got to head up the block. Might be a black adder, could be a coastal taipan?"

Camp shot a look at me then stared back onto the ground, eyes growing wider with each step he took. Without a word, he pointed with his finger then drew his gun.

"Here!" he said, falling into primal monosyllabic communication. "Here!"

I shook my head.

"No, no," I said. "Don't call it over. That'll only make it angry."

The guard put both hands on his weapon and pointed it at me. "Get that goddamn thing out of here!"

Kane began to shift closer, but I pushed a hand back. This was far from the first time someone had pointed a gun in my face. It wouldn't be the last.

I turned to the ex-wolf. My expression said, *The plan, right?* My mouth said, "It looks like our friend has found a friend."

Kane shot a look at Camp, who shouted, "Come on, man!"

My big friend spun between the van's two seats and bolted to the back. Hunched over, he was still able to make the slaps of his feet ring off the metal floor. I couldn't be sure, but I thought he might have done it on purpose.

When the back doors swung open, I heard Roy mutter thorough the metal below, "*Motherfucker.*"

"Shh!"

I watched in the side mirror as Kane neared the python, which had wound itself beneath the car behind us, likely looking for a place to warm up. He leaned forward. It raised its fat head and hissed at him.

The dude in the car, Nathan—Nate, to his friends—held the steering wheel with the grip of a drowning man. He pulled himself forward to look over the hood at the snake he knew was there but could not see.

His knuckles whiter than his teeth, he shouted through the windshield, "I'll run it over!"

Kane held a massive palm out to the guy and shook his head once. "Tires cannot kill such a creature. And likely it would slither up your wheel well, past the firewall, and seek out a warm place to nest and feed. Most likely the between-legs area. Very warm. And soft tissue to consume."

"*What?*" the man screamed and pushed back from the glass.

My friend swung his head toward the terrified man in the car. "However, I think not much of a meal."

Camp stepped away from the van and looked left and right, his gun still trained on the snake.

"I can't shoot the damn thing, or it'll bring the cops and... that is not ideal."

Kane's first palm still held up to Nate of the Warm Crotch, he held up another to Camp, who looked like he might wet his pants.

"No," he said, growling the word. "I have trained in the shadow of Mount Edziza for just such a moment."

"What?" Camp asked, regaining some of his composure. "You *trained* for a fifteen-foot python twisted up under a Ford in a parking lot of a warehouse?"

"Yes," Kane said, his hands still raised, moving crablike to the side as he approached the snake. "Only trained, many scenarios. All scenarios, all day. And nights, too, because there is very little nightlife in Mount Edziza."

"I think I can—" the gun-wielding guard began to say, but then my friend leaped forward, arms wide, and launched himself beneath the car. He called out, yelling and howling.

"Dude, back it down," I muttered.

When he finally came up, he had the python wrapped around his upper torso. The thing squeezed and squeezed, snapping its head toward Kane. It hissed.

Kane hissed back, showing two rows of teeth.

The snake pulled its head away. Then squeezed tighter.

"Heather Thomas, open first cage," he shouted, and I jumped up to the racks secured to the inner walls of the van, which held stacks of glass and wire cages in all different sizes. I yanked at the handle on the crate closest to the rear double doors.

It wouldn't open.

My friend stood before me, arms outstretched as the snake slithered and twisted, seemingly trying to get away. Then I realized, no, it was trying to squeeze the life out of Kane.

This, of course, made the big man smile.

I stared at what looked like a simple handle on the cage. A piece of dull metal. The shape of a pen with a U-shaped bit near the end. I lifted the divot and tried to slide it left. Nope. Then I tried to slide it right. Nope again.

"Heather," Kane said, his smile dimming a few degrees as the snake tightened its grip.

"Shush!" I said, waving a hand at him. Maybe I had lifted the latch a bit too high? I went halfway up and tried to slide it. Still, it wouldn't budge.

A grunting sound came from my left. When I looked over, Kane's eyes looked like they were bulging a bit. Maybe because the snake had begun to coil around his neck. He raised an eyebrow at me and, only moving his lips as he gritted his teeth, made a suggestion.

"Cage would be good."

I squinted at what appeared to be the world's simplest lock. Lift and pull, right?

Two short honks of the horn. When I turned, I saw the look on Nate's face as he jammed his finger upward toward Kane.

"Goddamn thing!" I shouted, gripping it with both hands and rattling it. I flapped my elbows like a bird stuck in mud when finally, *finally* I heard a clink!

I threw the door open and waved Kane toward me. He smiled at me, his lips looking a lovely shake of blue-purple, and wobbled in my direction. Reaching over, I tried to pull the snake from his torso and got a big snaky head hissing at me.

But the guy we'd borrowed the snakes from—he had *also* thought my fake business name was clever, by the way—well, he'd assured me these creatures weren't poisonous.

"Deadly, sure. Just don't get them up around your neck like a scarf," he'd said and added a nervous chuckle to make the point.

"Hea-ther Thomas," Kane said, dutifully sticking to my fake identity. "A little help with this killer snake, yes?"

The thing was only wrapping tighter around Kane, and I couldn't get it to budge. From below my feet, I heard a squeaking sound. What the fu—

The squeaking got louder—why was Roy squeaking?—until I realized what he was trying to say. *Oh shit, I forgot about those!*

"One sec," I said, holding up a finger. Kane said something, but it was mostly all vowels at that point.

"*Mrnuuueeeaaa.*"

"Yes, yes," I shouted back, sliding over to the smallest cage the snake guy had given us. "I am hurrying." This lock? Popped right open. "Why couldn't they have put *that* lock on the big cages?"

"*Snfftnblrrrn.*"

"I'm coming, I'm coming," I said, reached in, and grabbed one of the little white creatures by its tail. It flailed and flopped, but I pinched tightly so I didn't lose my grip.

Returning to the back of the van, I held the mouse out in front of the snake.

Another squeak, but this time from the mouse.

The snake began to uncoil and, in a good-news-bad-news moment, began to move toward me. But it was enough of a release that Kane could finally take in a big gasp of air. He staggered backward for a moment, his butt hitting the car behind him.

Nate honked again, and I heard his muffled voice once more. "Don't dent the car!"

The big snake head, as large as my friend's fist, was coming right at me. Or, more correctly, the mouse dangling from my fingers.

"Whoa, shit!" I hissed at it and threw the mouse into the open glass cage. The fat head went in after it. The rest of its body followed as Kane wrestled it like he was making pretzel dough. When the snake was halfway in the cage, I heard one final squeak.

Now that the snake had its prize, it began to spin back toward the opening.

"Nope," I said, put my shoulder under its scaly body, lifted it up, and got me a cage full o' snake. I grabbed the troublesome handle again, and as I was about to pull it over, the snake smashed its head against the door, widening the gap.

Kane was drawing in deep breaths, rubbing at his neck. "I think maybe we lock the cage."

"I am *trying* to!" I said, pressing against the fat snake head until the door closed. With my free hand, I grabbed the troublesome latch and drew it closed.

Huh. Closing it was so much easier than opening it.

The guard called Camp came around and looked inside, his gun still raised. He thrust it around the back of the van like he was clearing it of insurgents. His eyes widened when he saw the size of the blue *snake repellent* tank. Seeing the snake tucked into the cage, he holstered his weapon.

He regarded Kane. "Thought you might not win that one. Does it always go that way?"

"I find it easier," Kane said, his voice a bit hoarse as he drew in deep breaths, "to bite the head off. Much less trouble to battle snake without a head."

Camp took a half step back. "You *bite* the heads off snakes?"

"In the forest, this is the way. Pack distracts while another of us tears into—"

"He's French Canadian. Hard-core. That's how they do it up in, uh," I said, stepping out of the van to the pavement, "French Canada."

Kane frowned at me. "There is no such place."

Camp's gaze floated up to the snake in the cage, which was coiled but bobbing its head, looking for a way out. It eyed the lock. Then its black gaze landed on the guard. He looked away.

"Glad you got it. I don't know if I would have known what to do," he said. "Other than run."

"No, don't run," I said, hopping out of the van and sitting on the bumper. "Boas like to chase their food. Reminds them of living in the jungles in India."

"Brazil," Kane said.

I frowned at him. *Not helping!*

"But you got it," the guard next to me said. "We're good, yeah?"

I nodded, waving Kane to his side of the van. "Got that one. Only twenty-seven more to go."

"*Twenty-seven?*"

A squelching from Camp's shoulder made everyone jump. He grabbed the radio, muttered into it, and a harried voice came back. "Hey. Um, I just saw something slither behind the backup generator."

"Are you sure?"

"Yeah,'" the man on the radio said. "Thick as my leg, man!"

Camp sighed and shook his head. "That sounds big."

"Right," I said.

"Luis," he said and motioned to vaguely to another building. "He works out, so…"

Camp did not explain what the hell that meant.

Waving my arm toward the back of the van, I motioned to the stacks and stacks of empty cages, all sizes. A fat boa sat inside the nearest one on the left.

"Could be more on one of the other properties," I said, closing the double doors and nodding back down the hill. "One of the boas was pregnant, from what I've been told. Those little ones are nasty. We're just gonna head out and check the neighboring—"

"No, you ain't," Camp said, took a few steps back, and called over to his partner in the car. "Follow these guys inside."

Nate the Brave shook his head. "No way, man."

"Leave the car there, and get in the van," Camp shouted at him then turned to say, more quietly but just as fiercely, "You've got fifteen minutes. Don't touch nothing that don't slither."

Chapter Seven

P ulling into the warehouse, I realized just how dark it had gotten already. We'd screwed around outside with the snake for far too long. Well, Kane had almost died, but all that potential dying had chewed up precious time.

The warehouse lights winked to life above as the automatic door dropped behind us.

"Is like magic," Kane said, beaming his brilliant, bearded smile at Nate the guard. "Did you do this?"

Nate laughed, shook his head, and pointed to the laminate on his belt. "Pass card. Can't get in or out without one."

As he balanced between the seats in a crouch, Kane bent down and pulled the card toward him, extending the nylon pull rope. "This is you?"

"Old picture," Nate said. "My hair was longer."

Kane held it up next to the man's face. "Better with shorter hair, I think. Makes you look rugged."

"Wife told me I had to grow up, so chop-chop," he said and laughed. Nate pointed to a series of doors to our left. "There's a couple of offices back there and an area that used to be storage. Um, it's not storage now. Best you don't go in there."

"Your call," I said, steering the van into the center of the warehouse space.

The place was half the size of a football field. One wall was all crates, stacked three high and two deep. Opposite that, a fishing boat so huge it didn't look like it could float. Multiple decks, shiny brass railings, and faux-wood strips in a long, sleek hull.

Next to that, four vehicles—all of them worth more than I'd made in my lifetime.

A green one was low to the ground and the sort of thing people bought when they didn't care about their money anymore. Maybe a McLaren?

Next to that was a motorcycle with dual headlights. All chrome and leather.

The fat face of what looked like a Humvee took up two spots. Painted in a camouflage pattern that would ensure it could be seen everywhere it went, it didn't even look street legal.

The last vehicle was slick and long. Like a giant had picked up a shiny black sedan and stretched it out. The back came down at a sharp drop, which almost made it look van-like, just squatter. The only way I could tell it was a Mercedes was the tri-star hood ornament.

"This place a part-time car dealership?" I asked, forcing a laugh.

Nate looked back to the closing rollaway door then to us. He lowered his voice. "Those belong to, um, the owner."

Kane whistled. Or tried to whistle. Another thing a former-wolf-now-human couldn't do. So he breathed out a shock of air through his teeth. "Green one is very fancy."

"No driving for you, Kane," I said then bit my lip. Maybe I shouldn't have said his name. Too late.

Kane laughed and slapped the guard on the shoulder. "Which would you like to drive, Nathan?"

"None of them!" he said, and shook his head. "The boss don't like anyone even looking at them. She worries it might scratch the paint."

"No, not to real drive. But to dream drive," Kane said, leaning in closely and pointing at the cars. "What would Nate drive?"

"I do love German cars like the Mercedes, but not that one. It's a damn hearse."

Dropping the van into Park, I snapped my head toward him, unsure if I'd heard him right.

"Hearse? Who buys a hearse?"

A shrug and another glance at the big door. "The woman who, uh, *runs* the warehouse. She's dying. Been dying for a few years now. When the time is right, that's her ride, I g—"

When I heard the thunk and saw Nate fall forward, smashing his face against the dash, I damn near screamed.

Roy leaned over the guy, a crescent wrench in his damp hand. His entire body was drenched, his hair dripping sweat onto the man.

"Goddamn, you better not have killed him," I said through gritted teeth. I reached down and found a pulse.

"Nate is not dead," Kane said. "But will have a very large headache when he awakens."

Roy waggled the massive wrench toward the big man. "And what's with you chatting up the guy like you're best pals? It was punishing enough lying under the floor but to have to listen to you guys like you were on some Tinder date? Jesus, man."

"Lay off, Roy," I said.

Kane smiled.

I checked the clock on the van's car radio. We had thirteen minutes left of our allotted fifteen. And how the hell were we going to get out of there with our chaperone passed out?

"You heard the guy," Roy said, throwing open the rear door and jumping out. "Offices there. And a storage area."

"Not storage anymore."

"Yes, yes," Roy said, sneering at Kane. "I heard him. You need to dump that dude somewhere."

"What does this mean?" Kane asked.

Roy huffed. "Find a hole or something and drop him down. We don't need that guy waking up and causing us any problems."

My ex ran over to the long rows of crates.

"Does he intend to kill this man?" Kane asked me, his voice low.

I looked over at Roy, who was searching for something that could pry open the boxes. "Yeah, I'm not into it. Put him..." I glanced out the back doors and saw an option that made me smile. "Well, he ain't dead, but put him in the hearse."

Kane picked the guy up and hefted him under his arm like he was carrying a doll. I followed behind and noticed a coat rack mounted on the wall next to the vehicles. Instead of coats, keys and key fobs hung there. I grabbed the one with the Mercedes symbol.

When I went to the car, Kane was loading him in the driver's seat.

"Why didn't you just chuck him in the back?"

As Kane shouldered the unconscious man inside, he pointed at the rear compartment of the funeral vehicle. Two huge coffins. Glossy black exteriors with gold trim. Larger at one end, tapering down slightly to the other.

"Grim. When that woman kicks, they're ready to just drop her in and go," I said. "Weird that there's two."

Kane pressed the seat back, and Nate slumped to the side, his head lolling out the door. "Maybe for a beloved servant. Like pharaohs."

"Pharaohs?"

He shrugged. "Ma mère would watch documentary shows. When pharaoh people died, they killed servants so they could serve them in the afterlife."

"Shit, really? Tough gig," I said, my stomach turning a little at the thought. "Hopefully, they got good dental."

When Kane tried to close the door, Nate's head was in the way again, so he leaned in and secured the passed-out guard with the seat belt. I chucked the key fob inside.

A clatter of wood startled me. Roy had gotten off the top of one of the crates and was working on a second. I looked down the long, *long* line of them—there had to be more than a hundred. How did they expect us to find something hidden in a place as big as this?

I smacked Kane's shoulder to hurry him along. He came out sniffing as he gently closed the door. I asked him, "What the hell are you doing?"

"Odd smell."

"Yeah," I said. "This is where they put dead people." Then I shivered. "Do you smell dead people now? Are there bodies in those caskets?"

He chuckled and shook his head. "No. No dead."

We hustled over to where my ex was working on a third crate, struggling with a crowbar. Kane walked up, wrapped his fingers under the wooden lid, and lifted it open.

Roy pushed him away. "I loosened it."

I peeked inside the crate.

"It's furniture parts. Legs and wheels to ottomans or couches or something," I said and pointed to the next one.

Kane popped that one like he was opening a Pringles canister. "Glass. Very much glass all in teeny, tiny balls."

"Some ornamental thing," I said. "You put that stuff in vases and stick fake flowers inside."

Kane nodded. "Maybe they are for the lady's funeral?"

"Jesus, man, *enough*," Roy said and took a step back. "This place probably gets rousted by police or something. Building inspectors do drop-ins, maybe. I think it's all for show."

"This is… impossible," I said, stepping back. There had to be a hundred crates. "How the hell are we supposed to find some big tin plates in all this?"

I felt something cold in my hand and looked down to see the long metal bar with a hook on the end.

"Not tin. Gold and silver, Em! It's like treasure, so start digging," Roy said. He turned to Kane, smacking him on the shoulder. "I'll check offices, and you check storage."

Jogging after Roy as they crossed the warehouse floor, Kane said, "Is not storage. This is what Nathan says."

"That's right, you and ol' Nate are besties now, huh?" Roy spun around and walked backward. "I'll tell you what it is. These guys deal in drugs, guns, and girls. Traffic them in from overseas. So it *is* a storage of a sort."

The big man frowned. "For people."

"Yeah, if you see any in there, don't let them out," Roy said, laughing. "We're looking for fancy dinner plates, not people."

I looked at the crowbar in my hand then the stacks and stacks of boxes in front of me. "Man, no way. There is no *way*. No fuc—"

"Nathan, how we looking in there?"

We all froze.

The voice was coming from the hearse. I looked at Roy, who stood there wide-eyed, frozen in his spot. Kane was running toward the voice.

"No, Kane, it's not a pers—"

I chased after and watched him throw the door open, as if ready to tear into someone.

"There's no one in there. It's the ra…" I got to the door, my voice trailing off. "Dio."

"Not good, brother. There's two of the slitherin' bastards in here, and one of them gots fangs like a steak knife."

My jaw went slack.

Kane had grabbed the shoulder radio and was speaking into it. And it sounded like Nathan the Guard's voice. Nate's voice. Coming out of him.

"We might need a bit more than the fifteen, less'en we want creepy crawlies wiggling up our asses when we go to take a dump," Kane said in an imitation of Nathan's words and speech pattern. It wasn't perfect, but I expected the low-fi radio covered up any discrepancies.

There was a long pause, then the radio crackled again.

"Five minutes more," Camp said over the radio, his voice unsure. "Any more than that, and I gotta call this in. Keep 'em away from stuff. We can't have people just wandering around in there, yeah?"

"They ain't wandering," Kane said, again mimicking the unconscious man's voice. "There's a bit of jumping and a little bit of bleeding, but they got one of them already. We'll be out in a jiff, brother."

Another pause. "Make it quick."

Kane stared at the radio for a moment then returned it to the shoulder clasp of the passed-out guard. He pushed the guy's head back inside and closed the door.

I put a hand on his chest to stop him. I looked back at the sleeping Nate.

"That's why you were talking with him so much," I said. "In case you had to do... whatever that was."

He shrugged. "Yes, I simply imitated his call sounds."

"Simply," I said and grinned at him. "Is that something you learned about training in the shadow of Mount Doom or whatever?"

"I did train near Mount Edziza," Kane said. Walking backward, he nodded toward the hearse. "However, the trick to imitate your prey? This I learned from a runaway tree ocelot in the port city of Nanaimo on Vancouver Island."

With a quirky smile, he spun away and started running for the doors on the far wall.

"I have no idea what most of those words meant," I said to myself then dashed toward the crates.

We were running out of time. I didn't have much faith in Roy finding the stupid disk things, but Kane did have an odd way of figuring stuff out.

Chapter Eight

Kane

I enter the room and find it difficult to draw a breath. Too much sensation.

The cloying air upon my skin feels oily. A sickly sweet taste fills my mouth, forcing my tongue to curl. There is no sound, and the total silence buzzes in my ears. I slam my hands over them to stop the noise.

I have not yet even passed through the short hall.

What lies beyond?

I turn the corner and shiver. Dark. Very dark.

A tiny window along one wall, high up so that people may not see in. It casts a dim latticework of light upon the floor.

Ah.

I see the bars that crisscross the rectangular window atop the cold concrete wall. At first, it appears this is to keep strangers from entering and stealing the treasures within. However, the bars are on this side of the glass.

The room has been split into two, one half of it a cage. It is clear the bars upon the small window are to keep those inside from getting out.

On the opposite wall, burdened wooden shelves sag unevenly. A storage space not for papers but for things. It is only then that I hear the door close behind me. It must be slow on its hinges from the dampness in the room.

I feel around the wall and discover the light switch. When I look at my hand, some sort of soot has blackened my fingertips.

The bare bulb hangs from wires snaking through a ragged hole in the warped wood ceiling, and it stains the room in a patina the color of smokers' teeth. Its cord swings slightly, which is odd. I feel no breeze.

Dark blemishes across the gray floor tell a story, I am sure of it. But when I take a sharp inhale through my nose, I realize that it is one I do not want to know.

The cage door is open, and mercifully, it is empty.

Maybe this was for animals? Not that this would have been better. Animals would deserve better than this stench. This rot.

I turn away.

The wooden shelves hang at odd angles with their supporting metal straps buckling under the weight of fabric. So much cloth, so many different colors. I reach out to touch the material, and part of it slides then tumbles to the floor.

My vision bends strangely. Blurs. The images before me turn fractal as I feel an anger build in my chest. And sadness. A deep bone sadness.

Not just cloth.

Staring down at the clump of material at my feet, my head swims. This appears to be a shirt or blouse, but it has been torn—so very difficult to determine. When I lift my head, two small dark spots appear, dotting on the fabric.

These are clothes. Thrown upon the shelves.

Next to the blouse, beneath the shelves, are piles of shoes. Those that should have laces do not. Many are discolored by muddy streaks of black and dark green.

I shake my head to clear it and look at the shelves again. They hold no ancient metal artifacts. No priceless disks we seek.

But this is what Emelda needs if she is to accompany me to Mexico, so I continue searching.

As I swivel my head, I realize I have once again pressed my fists to my ears. Such a troubling place. I do not wish to stay. My animal instincts scream for me to run, but I must check.

The cage.

I step over and pull its door wider, surprised when its metal hinges do not cry out. The walls somehow swallow all sound.

Much of the cage floor is covered in twisted blankets, dirty and worn. A bench at the back hangs from two short chains drilled into the wall. This looks like a space where half a dozen people could sit or stand and await whatever fate their captors decide.

However, the scent in the air tells me many more were here. So many.

Then another smell. This one less of rot but still a human odor. And it comes from behind, not before me.

I begin to turn and see Roy too late.

As my face comes around, the butt of a handgun strikes my forehead, and my world fills with stars. I lose my balance, throw my hands out, but my vision flips, and I strike the floor. Something has cushioned my fall. The vapor of tears and sweat rises from the blankets and assaults my nostrils.

I gag and squeeze my eyes together. This only makes the throbbing in my head worse.

The slicing sound of metal upon metal tells me he has locked me inside. Why has he done so? When I raise my head to ask him, he has already turned away. With a flick of his hand, the room's dull eye winks out and leaves me in the dark.

Sitting up, I try to clear my head.

But I do not have time to wait. How much of our twenty minutes have already passed?

I cannot call out, for this could alert Camp the guard. However, I doubt any sound can leave a room such as this.

Before me, there are metal bars like I am in jail in one of the old Westerns that mon père used to love. I did not like them as much but loved to watch them with him. On the old couch. Safe in their home.

It occurs to me that I should have paid better attention to the Westerns. They may have revealed how a prisoner escapes the town jail. I do remember one where ropes were tied to the bars and someone smacked a horse's bottom.

Alas, I do not have a horse.

I stare through the bars at the shoes strewn across the floor. How many of those once held captive here did the same as I am doing now? Wishing to be on the other side. Wishing to be home.

I miss my home too.

The woods. My pack. My wolf wife.

Anger grows within once again. I do not trust that Roy wishes good things for Emelda. If the stealing job was his debt, why did he seek out her to help? Something is not right. A puzzle missing pieces.

And one I cannot solve trapped in here.

Standing, I stagger, my head pounding from the blow, and I reach out to grab the bars. I pull and shake them, but they are designed to prevent anyone from escaping. Bending down, I see that the bars extend into the concrete below, deep into the foundation.

Above, a thick metal brace made from iron. Even that I could not bend.

I grip two bars on either side and try to pull them apart, but as I do, my head again begins to throb. I ignore the pain and pull harder, but the bars are too thick. They will not buckle. I can get only my arm through, but there is no key.

A padlock that hangs from a loop in the handle has been secured.

If I could get something metal, I may be able to... But there is no metal within reach.

I look around. Dirty blankets. The metal chains that hold the bunk aloft would do nothing for me.

I sit on the wooden bed and examine the bars. There is no way I can make them wider, and I could never fit through for I am too...

A spot on the floor glows brighter. It's the crisscross pattern I spied earlier, and the shape reminds me of the large books ma mère used to read to me. Seeking its source, I look up.

Has Emelda found me?

No.

It is from the barred window. However, it is not daytime but dark now. I know this light.

Once again, I look at the bars. Too small a gap for a large man.

But not so for a smaller creature.

I take a long, deep breath and lift my hand to the moonlight.

Chapter Nine

M y arms shook as I cracked into a fifth box. Gritting my teeth, I
growled at it.

"Come on!"

Like the snap of a finger, the lid popped up, but I'd been leaning so hard
onto the damn thing, with all of my weight, that I stumbled forward and
nearly cracked my empty skull. Instinctively, I threw my arm out to stop
my fall. A splinter of the wooden crate pierced my skin, and I bit down on
a cry of pain.

Not letting a stupid box get the best of me, goddamn it!

I shoved the lid aside with the other hand, and it clattered to the floor,
too loudly for what was supposed to be a robbery.

But when I looked over at crate after crate after crate, I realized something.

"It can't be," I whispered. "This is some kind of joke."

Inside the new box, shower curtain rings. Like, hundreds of them. I took
a step back. It was such a varying array of junk that it was like someone had
designed this warehouse to look like a warehouse. Which, I suppose, was
exactly what it was.

I nearly jumped out of my pricey sneakers when a voice called out from
behind me.

"Anything?"

Ugh. Roy. Listening to the slap of his shoes against the slick concrete, I
sighed and lifted my elbow to look at my arm. Great. Bleeding on my shirt.

"No, just"—I winced as I plucked out a splinter as big as my pinky
finger—"junk." I spun around to ask him how we were supposed to find
two fancy dinner plates in all this stuff when I noticed something.

"Where's Kane?"

Roy threw a hand behind him, his face a mask of disgust. "Nice boyfriend of yours."

"He's not," I said, rolling my hands into fists as I faced him. "Where the hell is he?"

My ex ran up and grabbed the crowbar from on top of the next box and tried to fit it into the gap. He leaned in and popped the top off with ease.

"Ran off," he said, digging through the packing material. He pulled out a coiled roll of extension cord. "I heard him messing with a rear door, and when I went inside, he'd bolted."

I turned to look at the door to the storage area, but Roy grabbed my chin and turned me back.

"Dude's big as an oak tree but a coward."

Squinting at him, I growled, "Bullshit."

An odd *tick-tick-tick-ticking* echoed through the warehouse space, and I tried to turn away to find its source, but Roy held me tight.

"When have I ever lied to you, Emmy?" he asked with an odd look on his face. Hurt? Sadness?

I smacked his hand away. "All the time!"

He took a few steps back and looked around the floor. Boxes upon boxes upon boxes, rows and rows of them all stacked up. If we had all day to crack them open, we would never get through them.

We didn't have all day. We were out of time.

When I turned back, he was staring at me with the coldest eyes I'd ever seen.

"Plan B, then," he said, ran over to the van, and threw the doors open.

What did he say?

I looked back to door where Kane had gone through, half expecting him to come charging out. Prayed for it.

"What is 'Plan B,' Roy?" I asked, stepping to my left, making a wide arc so I could see what he was doing in the back of the van.

He had the hidden compartment open and was pulling something out of it. A black box with red wires.

Feet back on the concrete, he slapped the box up against the big blue tank. The tank labeled Snake Repellent. That had been Roy's one contribution to my plan.

He'd filled the tank.

Then I stared as he slapped the box onto the side of the blue container. I blinked. There was no way what I was seeing was really what I was seeing.

"What the hell is that?"

Roy wiped his face and took a few steps back. Then, as if remembering something, he jumped forward and pressed two of the buttons on the side of the box. A red light began to flash.

"Roy!" I shouted. The top of my head buzzed and felt like it was lifting away from my skull. "Is that some kind of bomb?"

"No, it's a detonator. The tank is a bomb," he said and looked all around the warehouse. Everywhere but where I was standing. "Plan B."

I ran over to him, raising a fist. "Why didn't you—"

Roy spun and pointed a pistol at my face. I looked down the barrel, swallowing hard. My eyes watered. I felt a rage bubble up inside and rocket down my veins so hard I thought my hands would blow off.

It was totally surreal.

"You total prick."

Roy looked at my face, then his eyes darted away. He sighed, rubbed his mouth, and shook his head.

"It... If we couldn't find the plates, we're supposed to blow the place," he said, nodding toward the van. "There's fuel in that tank to burn for an hour if the explosion doesn't snuff it out."

I took a step back, and he raised the pistol higher.

"Are you fucking joking? Where did you get a detonator from?"

He shrugged. "The Family. This is why I got out."

"To blow up a factory?"

Roy shook his head violently, placing one hand to his ear. "No, no! If we found their disk things, then it wouldn't have to go like this. But we didn't."

My world had spun out of control. I looked at the door across the warehouse. Had he killed Kane? No way. But then why wasn't my friend *here* now?

Screaming at Roy, I ran, arms in the air swinging as if I were daring him to shoot me. Seeing if he had the balls to do it.

When I got close enough, I got my answer. He pointed the gun away. I reached for him, and he spun and slammed the pistol into the side of my head.

I fell, smashing hard to the floor, but rolled and tried to get to my feet. Stumbling, I went to a knee. I tried to clear my vision, wiping my face with my forearm. I winced and snapped my arm back when the salt got into the cut from the jagged crate.

Roy pushed me down again as he ran past.

From the floor, I stared up and saw him snatch one of the keys from the rack on the wall. He ran to the motorcycle and hopped on. Jamming the key in, he fired it up and kicked away the stand.

At the sound of the engine, I heard Nate the guard's radio crackle but couldn't make out the words.

Didn't matter. The "art heist" was over.

I just didn't know what *over* meant.

Roy rumbled toward me, and I staggered to my feet. I glanced toward the storage room door, blinking through sweat and tears and blood.

Turning, I looked back at the tank inside the van. Two tiny lights blinked. Before, there had been just the one. What did that mean?

Nothing good.

Nope, nothing good.

When I took a step toward Roy, he lifted his pistol to me and slowly shook his head.

Then it all became clear.

Wasn't that funny how your mind worked out what was going on at the very moment it was too damn late to do anything about it?

Tentatively, I took another step forward, and he lifted the hand from the motorcycle's grip and pulled back the hammer of the pistol.

Through gritted teeth, he said, "Don't, Emmy."

"No, right," I said, putting my hands out to steady myself. I felt woozy. "That's why you wanted me to come along. If this didn't work out—your Plan B—you needed someone to take the blame away from the Family."

"Not just *anyone*." Roy cleared his throat and blinked his damp eyes. "I'm sorry. It was the only way."

"Why me?" I hated that my voice sounded like I was begging. I supposed I was. "What did I ever do?"

"You?" he asked and laughed. "You nearly killed two of Rosa's crew. And I did a whole year in that place because of you!" He cleared his throat, swallowed, and shook his head slowly, his eyes burning into me. "If it came to this, you had to be here."

"So to get clear with the Family, you burn your girlfriend?"

He shrugged. "*Ex*-girlfriend."

I shuffled forward again, my legs wobbly. Someone was pounding on the rollaway door, and I could hear yelling. Camp the guard called through the gap.

"Jesus, Nathan, what the hell's going on in there?" he shouted. "Listen, assholes, we've got a crew coming from the other buildings. Whatever you guys are doing in there, you ain't never getting out!"

Shaking my head, and regretting it, I chuckled to myself.

"Plan B," I said in a tired voice. "You blow the place, and they find my body inside. You're clear. The Family's clear. Blame the crazy bitch." I nodded and looked over at the steel rollaway door as it shook. "Yeah, I can see them buying it."

Roy looked to the van then back to me. With a faraway look on his face, he said, "Think of it as destiny. Rosa's always had it in for you."

"*What?*"

"I'm sorry, Emmy." His free hand went back to the grip, and he revved the bike's engine. "Really, I am."

He took a deep breath and lifted the pistol toward me, but yeah, I wasn't into that. I leaped toward the gap behind a crate. I only made it halfway, still very exposed, but the shot missed and sparked off the concrete floor.

"Jesus Christ," I shouted and jumped up. As he swung his gun my direction, I zigzagged down the row of boxes, shots sparking around my heels. I heard the rev of an engine.

But this sounded much bigger. Not like the motorcycle.

"What the fuc—" a voice called out. It was Roy. I spun around and saw the black Mercedes racing toward him. The tire on the motorcycle spun on the slick floor as the front of the hearse smashed into his bike.

Behind the wheel, Nate the security guard flopped around as he smashed the accelerator.

How was the guy even driving when he could barely hold his head up? The vehicle turned and rolled over the bike, its tires spinning. Nate's head lolled to the side as the car rose up and went over the bike, crushing it and Roy's leg beneath it.

"Aaagghh!"

The bike shot out from beneath the tires, and the big black car careened unevenly, twisting back and forth until it hit a row of crates. Shit went everywhere as it drove through the boxes like they were fluffy clouds.

Poof! Shower curtain rings and rubber ducks.

Poof! Light fixtures, PVC pipe, and blue Styrofoam in the shape of peanuts.

All beneath a whirling cloud of wooden splinters. Plumbing parts, plastic tubs, and elbow joints flew in the air and bounced to the concrete floor with the manic crescendo of a death-metal orchestra.

Then the vehicle slowed as two boxes got jammed up under its wheels.

I hadn't even realized I'd fallen to the floor again.

Any moment, Nate was going to jump out of the driver's seat and pull his weapon.

It was over.

These guys wouldn't call the police. I looked over at the device attached to the big blue tank. Two solid lights and now a blinking third. Blinking faster.

I didn't know what the final countdown might be—hell, in the movies, there was always a convenient timer—but three is one of those universal totals. Once the third stopped blinking, it was going to blow and take the warehouse and everyone inside with it.

Running up to the car, I decided to plead with Nate. At the very least, beg him to get us the hell out, and then we could work it out from there.

But when I threw the door open, the guard was still slumped—hell, he looked dead—over to the side, his head hanging between the two front seats.

On his lap was a dog.

A poodle.

I blinked. Then I blinked again.

The poodle had both of its paws up on the steering wheel.

"Kane?"

He looked at me, fluffy tufts of fur going tense above his doggy eyes. "We must go!"

"How are you even..." I looked down and saw he was sitting on one of Nathan's legs. His ankle had shifted and lay between the two pedals.

"Please to place Nate's foot back on the go-fast pedal," he said, eyes wide. Well, he was a poodle, so they were always wide. They looked wider than before. "We must go now!"

I started to lift him out of the car. "Kane, let me drive. You can't—"

A high-pitched beeping warbled into one long, constant tone.

Oh shit.

"Forget it! The van is going to explode!" I dove into the car and rolled across the passenger seat. "Roy set a charge!"

Leaning over the passed-out guard, I yanked the door closed, dove to the floor, and smashed the accelerator with my palm. The massive hearse bucked, and the tires spun. They caught, and we launched forward.

All I could do was watch from seat level as the ceiling of the warehouse flew by. Household supplies and splinters danced over the windshield.

"Whoops," Kane said, his tiny dog mouth twitching.

Another crash, and the scaffolding tumbled down around us, the metal floor landing just beyond the driver's side window.

"Sorry," my driver said, his tiny tongue sticking out of the corner of his mouth.

"Kane, you can't drive even when you're a human," I screamed over the noise, craning my neck to look up at him. "You're worse as a dog!"

"Do not need to drive," he said as I saw lights come up and shine into the vehicle. Camp must have opened the rollaway door. "But I am very good at crashing."

He looked down at me and grinned wildly.

"Hold on to Nate the security guard," he said and pushed the wheel to the left. We swerved, and I heard the car clip another vehicle.

Just as we passed, the security guard screamed at us, "Nathan, what the hell are you doing?"

"Bomb inside," Nate said in a panicked voice as we flew past. "Place is gonna go boom!"

One hand gripping the bottom of the seat, the other smashed onto the accelerator, I glanced over my shoulder.

Of course, that hadn't been Nate but Kane, once again imitating Nate's voice. I knew this because the dude was out cold, lost in dreamland. His face was placid, but with all the bouncing, his head bobbed from side to side as if to confirm he wasn't enjoying the ride one bit.

I felt the car swerve and fought to keep my hand on the accelerator. If Kane crashed into something solid, I would probably break my neck. The huge Mercedes hopped and jumped, and I could hear tires spinning. He'd gone up onto the grass.

As we crashed through the fence, the sky lit up in a fireball behind us. I watched Kane leaning forward onto the wheel. Impossible to tell, but it looked like his little doggy face was smiling.

I heard something thunk against the right fender. We went up on three wheels then back down again, running over whatever we'd hit. A gush of water behind us told me it was likely a fire hydrant.

The poodle's eyes were shining when it looked down at me.

"I am getting much better at driving."

Chapter Ten

"Help me put in Reverse," Kane said, nodding his curly black muzzle toward the gear shift. "I am very much owning the roads."

We'd plowed into a thick hedge about six blocks away, just outside a small, long-dead shopping strip. Thankfully, Kane had hit the scraggly bush lengthwise. If he'd hit it straight on, we'd have plowed right through and I'd probably have ended up inside a busted-down Icee machine.

"Uh, no," I said and pushed myself up from the pedals. I'd had to use Nate the guard's knee to lift myself, and he twitched and groaned when I did.

Oh shit.

Running around the other side of the car, I waved the tiny dog away from the driver's seat.

"*Non.* I should give it another go."

"No way, poodle boy." I picked him up by the scruff of the neck, opened the back seat, and chucked him in. When I came back up to the driver's seat, Nate was coming around, blinking, and rubbing the back of his head.

On impulse, I got down on one knee and patted him on the chest.

"Thank you so much," I said, unbuckling the seat belt. "You're totally my hero for getting us out of there. How can we—I—ever repay you?"

"Wut?" he asked, cracking one eye open and wincing. He shuffled his feet and arms as if trying to remember how they worked. "What? It... when happened?"

Hmm. Not all there yet.

Lifting his arm over my shoulder, I helped him from the Mercedes hearse. The front end of the car was jacked higher up because we'd been stopped by the now-destroyed bushes, and I kind of lost my grip.

Nate fell to the dusty parking lot, face-first.

I *did* try to catch him with my side, but man, I'm not busting a hip over some dude. It was his fault he'd been there. He had to have known what sort of people he was working for.

Kane had his tiny claws draped over the partially open rear window. "Why have you dropped Nathan on his face?"

"Didn't mean to!" I said, grabbing the guard's jacket to flip him over. Pulling him across the skinny parking lot, I grunted. "He fell."

Kane tsked at me.

I mean, really? You don't know how low you can get until you've got a fuzzy black poodle judging you, shaking its stupid little face.

"We should take Nathan to the hospital," he said. "He has bonking on both the back and now the front of his head."

Propping Nathan up in a plastic table outside a derelict restaurant, I steadied him upright. Anyone passing by might wonder if he was waiting for the café to reopen.

When I turned, Nate fell to his side, and I heard a thunk on the dirty glass.

"Also, now a bonk on side of head," Kane said. "I think he might sleep now for a very long time."

I jumped into the big black car, threw it into reverse, and we shifted back for a quick moment. I put it in Drive and moved forward.

"I can do it," Kane said from behind me.

"No, you *can't*. You're the one who drove into a bush."

Kane whined. "Mon père would say to me, if you are going to crash, aim for something cheap. Or soft. But not people."

"Great advice."

Slamming the hearse into reverse, I gunned it, heard gravel catch under the wheels, and we flew backward.

Kane, who'd had his little rat paws up on the back of my seat, launched forward.

"*Mon Dieu!*" he shouted and bounced into the passenger-side footwell.

"Well, that answers one question," I said, rolling off the curb and bouncing into the street. "You're a *French* poodle."

* * *

Kane lifted himself from the passenger seat, tiny feet on the door, and stared out the window.

"This is not your place."

"No, it's not," I said, trying to see if there was a light on in the window. On the drive over, I'd told him what Roy had said to me. He'd heard part of it but had been busy sneaking past and into the hearse. The ticking sound I'd heard in the warehouse? Those had been his silly little poodle claws.

"Why are we not at your place?"

I sighed when I saw the curtain slide over the front window. I hadn't made up my mind to go inside, but now that she'd seen me, I guess I was committed.

Grandma was north of seventy. So a hearse rolling up in front of her house *probably* wasn't something she wanted to see.

"Roy set me up," I said, turning off the car. "If we didn't find those plate things, his Plan B was to blow the place with me inside. That way, I'd take the blame."

"Forgive me for saying this." Kane hopped off the window and stared down at his paws. "I do not think he was a very good boyfriend."

"No," I said and laughed. "But I suppose it's every girl's dream come true. You know, blowing up their ex-boyfriend."

I know that sounded stone-cold, but Roy had tried to blow me up first. I glanced at Kane, and it looked like he was frowning at what I'd said. Hard to tell on a dog.

"I can't tell if you're happy or sad with a mug like that," I said. "I guess that's just your resting bitch face."

The dog raised its eyebrows and gasped.

Me, I giggled like I'd sucked on every whipped cream canister in the 7-Eleven. "Resting *bitch* face, come on! That's good stuff, man."

"I am glad you are in a good mood," he said then bugged his eyes out with a big doggy yawn. "When the sun comes up, we must go and get your papers to cross the border."

"Papers?" I asked and slowly opened my door. "This isn't 1980s Russia, man. It's a passport."

"This is what I think papers are."

I stepped out of the car. "We were supposed to get those disk things. Gold and silver treasure for, you know, papers."

"But Plan B was to blow up, yes? The warehouse definitely did blow up."

"I guess." I sighed and leaned on the car's roof, peering inside. "I hope Whitey still honors the deal."

"I will make him, if necessary," Kane said then bared his teeth and growled. I rubbed his head, and he playfully nipped at my hand.

Over the next few minutes, I asked him how he'd gone from Kane the dude to Kane the tiny French poodle. As he spoke, any hint of regret I had for Roy getting blown up went poof.

I knew my ex had always been a selfish jerk, but assaulting Kane and leaving him in a cage? Trying to shoot me so my remains fried in an industrial bonfire?

Getting locked up had either changed Roy or revealed him to be the total prick he really was.

You never really, really knew someone until shit went bad. That was how you discovered which friends were enemies and which enemies might have been friends all along.

The poodle pulled his paws back and sat in the middle of the shiny black vinyl of the seat. He looked so small as he stared out the window at the night sky. The moon seemed to sadden at his expression, its thin crescent shape bent down in a frown.

Apparently recalling the cage back in the warehouse, he spoke in a hoarse whisper. "I could smell misery."

"That was probably Roy's cologne," I said, trying to lighten his mood. "Most of it comes out of bottles in the shape of barbells."

"He said people might have been trapped inside the storage area. I wanted to be sure they were not."

"Why?"

"Because it is not right, of course," Kane said, his bloodshot eyes lifting to me. "I had to check. I saw only what they left behind."

I let out a long breath. "People do awful things to each other. Especially to those who can't defend themselves. It's not like the animal world."

"We eat our young if they are weak."

"Huh," I said and stepped back so he could hop out. "Same."

I glanced at the house as the curtain fell back. Yep, she'd seen me. I went around to the back of the hearse, opened it, and stared at the two black lacquer coffins. At first, I thought there might be trunk space beneath.

Then, no. Of course not.

Slowly, I lifted the lid of one of the expensive tombs. A few inches up, I stopped. Did I really want to look into a casket?

"Do it!" Kane whispered.

I yelped and dropped the lid.

The black poodle had its tongue hanging out, its itty-bitty feet dangling over the back seat while it looked at me with big saucer eyes. He licked his chops, having returning to the happy-yappy dog he'd been before. At that point, I didn't know if the quick mood swings were the dog's trait or Kane's.

"Sorry," he said.

I shook a fist at him and opened the casket quickly. It was like ripping off a Band-Aid. With the chance of, you know, finding a corpse.

No corpse.

The dog hopped over the back seat into the long storage area and stared into the empty coffin. He peeked in, sniffed, and lifted his head out, tongue lolling again.

"You lick my face, and I put you inside," I said and closed the lid.

The front porch light came on. That was my cue to start explaining. First, I needed to lock the car. I didn't think anyone would break in to steal coffins—full or empty—but you never knew. Some people will take anything not tied down.

"Um, where's the key?"

Kane nodded behind himself. "In the cup holder."

"How did you even start the car up?"

"Push button by wheel. Same way you turned it off."

I nodded. "Right, but how did the key fob get in the car?"

Kane jumped down next to me onto the street and stepped up the curb onto the grass. He looked around and lifted a rear paw.

"You had thrown it inside when I put sleepy Nate into seat," he said, his leg suspended in the air. "Very smart. Planned ahead."

"Right. But no, I hadn't planned *any* of that."

He grinned at me, which was weird. "Maybe this is instinct? Wolf survives because of instinct."

Pulling the passenger door open, I leaned in and grabbed the key, which was a black teardrop-shaped fob. I closed the door and hit the button to lock it.

When I turned, Kane still has his rear leg cocked in the air.

"You gonna pee or something?"

"No," he said, dropping his paw. "But if anyone saw you talking to a dog, they would think you were encouraging me to do business."

"Good thinking." I nodded. "More instinct?"

"Only when I do number two."

Bending down to one knee, I tried to look into his eyes. I bent sideways and caught his gaze.

"Was that a pun?" I asked, and he flicked his head farther away from me, but the tiny edge of his tiny mouth curled upward. "Bad doggy. No puns!"

When I looked up to the door, I realized I'd taken too long messing around the car.

I saw my favorite person in the world standing there. She had her arms crossed, was dressed in a long, peach-colored robe, and the look on her face told me I wasn't her favorite person right then.

Probably because of the hearse.

Chapter Eleven

Despite the foul expression on her face, when my foot touched the sidewalk, with each step I took, she lightened. By the time I hit the stoop, she had a big grin and was opening her arms for a hug. I gladly took it and wiped my eyes before I let go.

"You're in trouble again," she said. It hadn't been a question.

"Can't a girl just come visit her grandmother?"

She looked over my shoulder. "In a hearse?"

"Well, it's been a while since I stopped by," I said, pushing past her to go inside. "I came prepared."

I collapsed onto the most comfortable couch in the world. She'd started to close the door when a tiny poodle slipped through the gap and ducked inside. My grandmother yelped and clutched her hands to her chest.

Leaning forward, I said, "I'll warm up the hearse."

"Shush now." She pointed a bony finger at me, but I saw the hint of a smile. She hooked the digit down to the dog. "Is she yours?"

"He, I think," I said, quickly trying to conjure up a story. "I didn't look too close because that seemed gross."

Grandma bent down and flipped Kane over. When he said, "Oof," she got a queer look on her face and put him down.

"Definitely a boy," she said, and he ran up to me and hopped on the couch. "Ah ah! No dogs on the furniture!"

The black poodle looked at me, frowning. Or maybe that was his normal face. Impossible to tell. I pointed to the pristine beige carpet. "Bad Kaney. You heard Grandma. On the floor."

He rolled his eyes but, like a good little doggy, slid off and sat on the floor.

"Where did you get such a cute pooch?" she asked, standing over him.

"Just a stray I picked up," I said, grinning down at him. Kane had been outside my window all beat to hell after some local kids had kicked him around, so yeah, that was technically true. He emitted a low growl. "Bit of a temper."

Grandma laughed. "That's the inbreeding. Makes them a bit funny in the head."

"Oh, he's funny in the head all right," I said and leaned over to scratch his ears. Kane slipped to the side, avoiding me.

"At least you've got that in common," she said.

Kane laughed.

That got a wide-eyed look out of my grandmother. I waved it off. "Hair ball."

"I'm going to grab some tea for us," she said. "I've got some Rice Krispies treats, if you want."

"Um, *yeah*," I said.

She motioned to the dog on the floor, who had his mouth open, panting slightly. "What about, um, Kaney? Don't normally have dog biscuits in the pantry."

I patted the dog on the head, getting a sideways glare.

"You got a raw steak around?"

"Raw steak?"

"He's been on the streets most of his life." I shrugged, playing it off. "It's what he's used to."

She sighed. "I may have some burger I haven't cooked up yet."

I told her that would be fine, and she went into the kitchen.

Kane put his paws on my lap and said, "I would like to try this cereal treat."

Grandma poked her head back in, eyes wide.

I growled my words as if it had been me talking in the doggy voice. "But I am a dog so very happy to have raw cow all chopped up."

She went back into the kitchen, and I pointed at him and held a finger to my mouth. He slumped on the floor and squeezed out a little toot of gas.

"My apologies," he whispered. "I have been holding that in for some time now."

* * *

For the next half hour, I chatted with Grandma on the couch like I used to when I was a kid. I got her caught up with my life. That was, I totally lied about everything I'd been doing for the past few weeks. Basically, I told her stuff that had happened up *until* the day I'd met Kane.

"You shouldn't work at that place," my grandmother said, brushing some crispy rice from her lip onto a napkin. "Bars in that neighborhood are terrible places for ladies."

"Yeah, well, the hours are terrible and the pay sucks, so it works for now."

She nodded and looked down at her bone-white plate as if it held the next question. Finally, she asked, "Can I ask about the car? That seems kind of pricey for a bar maid."

"Bar maid?" I laughed. "Just how old are you, Grandma?"

"Old enough to not want to see a hearse pull up in front of my house," she said with a sly grin. "Had to get my hand mirror out to make sure I still fogged it up with my breath."

"Did it?"

She smacked me lightly on the knee.

"You know I love it when you visit, Emelda. But when you do, it often means you're in a bit of trouble," she said, leaned over and clasped my hands in hers. "Are you?"

"I'm good. Better than I've been in... well, better than I've been in a long while."

"Okay, that's good," she said. "So how long are you planning to visit?"

"Overnight, if that's okay."

"Of course it is."

Then I realized I could make this sound like a more purposeful visit instead of, you know, secretly hiding from Rosa Nieto's people who likely wanted me dead.

"Do you have any of those old boxes from our old place? My stuff and Mom's stuff?"

She nodded. "In the garage. What are you looking for?"

"Just some old pictures that her dad had," I said. "Unless you think she took that stuff with her before she went out to California."

Grandma stood and brushed crumbs off her apron onto her plate. I heard Kane licking his chops and waved him away. The thunk from the floor, I guessed, was his dejected head landing on the carpet.

He'd gobbled down the raw meat within seconds—in the kitchen, of course, and on the floor—but really wanted some of the marshmallow dessert.

"No, she dumped all the things she couldn't sell here. I haven't driven in years, so it's not like I need the garage. Although I'd be happy to have the space back. I used to do my painting in there." She turned to me. "When was the last time you called her?"

I shrugged. "A while." She lifted an eyebrow at me. "I will. Soon."

She led me out to the garage and flicked a switch just inside the door. As we waited for the fluorescent lights to slowly flicker to life, I looked around for Kane. Not seeing the dog, I called for him.

A fuzzy black streak whipped around the corner and between my grand-mother's slippers, licking its lips. A big smile with little bits of marshmal-low between a few teeth.

Bad dog.

"I'll set up the spare bedroom and leave you to your memories," she said. Then she nodded at Kane. "Sorry, you'll have to keep the little guy in here. Dog smell tends to linger."

"That's fine," I said then saw her lift her head, staring at my neck. I pulled her locket out, and the fluorescents made the silver metal twinkle. "Yes, I still have it. I never take it off."

"Why would you?" she asked. "It's got a picture of my most favorite person in the world."

She closed the door behind her. I popped open the locket and stared at myself in its reflection. More lines in my face than I remembered. The purple tint in my hair had faded. I had no idea who I was looking at anymore.

"She seems suspicious of me," Kane said, whispering.

I sat on the floor and started going through the plastic tubs. There had to be twenty of them.

"Well, you're a weird dog."

He gasped. "I am not."

"Trust me. You are very weird."

"No, I am *not* a dog."

For the next ten minutes, I dug around, searching for my grandfather's old photos. The ones he used to pull out when he'd had a few beers. So, yeah, he pulled them out a lot.

A funny thing about looking through your old stuff. You go searching for one thing but can spend hours looking at everything but the item you originally intended. It was like those old possessions and elementary school papers and mangy stuffed animals had a personality all their own.

As if each lay in a dark, dusty box for years and years, wishing to be held one last time. And when someone finally cracked open the lid and that tiny sliver of light shone in, they vied for one more moment of attention.

A caressing hand. A warm smile.

"Remember me?"

Sniffling, I spotted the wrinkled shoe box with shaky Spanish handwriting on the side of it. I dragged it out, crushing it slightly, and popped the lid off.

Kane came up and sniffed then dramatically coughed. "It smells bad."

"That was Granddad," I said then grimaced. "Ah, that's not fair. When he had to move in with us, I don't think he ever got used to it. That's probably why he drank so much. I don't really remember him sober."

"It must have been a difficult transition for him," he said, nodding. "I am sort of an expert on difficult transitions."

I laughed and wiped some dampness from my eye then patted him on the head. He didn't even complain.

"You trying to cheer me up?"

"Maybe."

Sifting through the photos, I knew the one I was searching for but hadn't seen it in years. I hoped it was still here. Hell, Granddad used to roll his own cigarettes and mighta gotten so tanked he used it for rolling papers by mistake.

Flipping through the pictures, I saw a person's life captured in faded images. A young man, with his bride, leaning up against a car. A slightly older man fishing, flashing a wicked grin as he glanced back over his shoulder.

His face blackened, hard hat under his arm, as he came out of a hole in the ground.

Kane pressed his nose to the photo and sniffed. "Hmm. I can smell him."

"You can't smell the guy in the photo, man."

"No, of course," he said. "But this is one he looked at many times. I can smell sweat and dirt on this more than others."

I shrugged. "Tough life. He worked in the mines until he couldn't anymore. Had this crazy hacking cough, which was so gross. I didn't know if it was a black lung thing or from the smoking."

"He looks happy, though."

"Yep, that was Granddad," I said. "He valued nothing more than a day's hard work. Especially when someone else was doing it."

Kane sat back and stared at me. "For such a man to then do nothing, this must have been very difficult. To feel, maybe, useless."

"Oh, he worked a bit when he first got here," I said, nodding, lost in the echoes of my past. "But I was just a baby, so I don't remember any of that."

"There are mines in Minneapolis?"

When I laughed, I sucked in a bit of dust and had to cough the gunk out. Shaking my head and stifling another coughing fit, I said, "I think he worked in a shop for a while."

"Like Whitey at the hardware store."

"Ah, no." When I laughed this time, I covered my mouth with my shirt. "*Not* like Whitey."

I reached for a faded Polaroid and felt something hard beneath it. When I pulled it aside, the side of my mouth curled up.

"This is one of his," I said, pulling out the wood figurine and holding it up to the light. Most of the colorful paint had chipped away, but I could still make out the indentations that depicted animal features. "He used to carve these."

"Is that dog?"

"Nah, I think it's a coyote." I held it next to my face and threw my head back, looking straight up, just like the carving. "Woooo!"

Kane chuffed and went to tilt his own head back. I clamped down on his muzzle.

"You'll wake her up if you do it," I said and held the figurine in both hands, examining it. "I got one each birthday for a while but just threw them away. I thought they were ugly. I guess when he didn't see them in my room, he stopped giving them to me."

His tiny black nose sniffed at the carving. "I like it."

"Yeah, I kind of do too," I said softly. "Now."

When my eyes drifted back to the box, I finally saw what I'd initially been looking for.

"There it is!"

I fished out the photo and held it up. My grandfather stood there in a suit, a flower on his lapel. He was shoulder to shoulder with a line of others. People were on both sides of the steps. I couldn't tell if it had been for a wedding or a funeral.

I tapped my finger on the spires at the top of the church behind them.

"Those pink spikes are what you recognized when we were at the Covenant place? On the video with the floating head man."

"Exactly," I said, holding the photo at arm's length. "They were down below, so those hangar-type buildings we saw with the new Enhanced creatures must be... up on a ridge or hill or something."

"Yes, the monsters created from my blood." Kane dropped to the floor and rested his muzzle on his paws. He sighed, fluttering the black tufts of curls there.

"We're handling it, man," I said then pulled the photo closer to examine it.

All the people in the photos had been standing in a cobblestone square of some sort. In the background was a pink church with spires that scraped the sky. I flipped the photo over. In perfect, looping handwriting, were the words *Parroquia de San Miguel Arcángel*.

"What do those words mean?" Kane asked.

"I... My Spanish isn't great," I said, pulled out my phone, googled it, and read the result. "Parish of Saint Michael the Archangel. That is where we're headed, my doggy friend. Near San Miguel, Mexico."

Kane scrunched up his brow and lifted his head. His breath quickened, and I turned to look at him. With his mouth open, his tongue lolled up happily.

"What's that about?"

He closed his mouth then opened it again, nodding to the photo.

"This is a good sign. If this church honors Saint Michael," he said, grinning now, "this is good news for us."

I tucked the photo in my pocket and stood to put all the boxes back in place.

"Why is this good sign for us?" I said, imitating his French-Canadian accent.

"Ma mère taught me of these things." He sat down and lifted his head to me. "Saint Michael is powerful and good and battled a great evil. He fought Satan himself."

I shrugged. "Did he win?"

"Yes," Kane said. "Killed Satan with a flaming sword. As we will kill the abominations that sprang from my blood."

"Well, we don't have any flaming swords," I said, pushing more boxes back into place as dust rose up, tickled my nose, and stung my eyes. "But we do have a two-ton car we can run them down with."

My friend turned his head toward the garage door.

"I believe it will take much more than that."

Chapter Twelve

When we entered the hardware shop the next day, the man with the white hair who was munching on a sandwich from wax paper didn't even look up. Just another customer coming in to burn some time before they had to do something else more important. More important than buying anything.

Not that Whitey cared about that. The shop was an old-school front.

Kane stepped up to the counter, casting a shadow over the man in the morning sun blazing through the shop windows.

Whitey looked up, and his mouth hung down.

At first, I wondered if he hadn't recognized the big French Canadian. A man in his line of work, maybe he worried this was it? This was *the guy*. The one who would balance the books for the myriad wrongs he'd committed in his life. A string of sins like dark pearls slung around a demon's neck.

As he stared up at Kane, I came around from behind my friend and bumped a fist off the counter. I was trying to portray a confidence I did not feel.

"Job's done," I said.

Whitey looked to me then back at Kane again. He finally blinked. Then he gawked at the big man hovering over him. My boy was head to toe in denim.

The night before, I'd slept in the spare room, and it was the best sleep I'd had in months. I took a pillow into the garage for Kane to put his head on. He really wasn't much of a blankets guy as wolves didn't really use covers. When I got up the next morning to check on him, he'd already gotten up and headed out.

That had worried me.

I mean, sure, the guy could take care of himself. Hell, he could take care of an entire town, to be honest. But *missing Kane* wasn't my favorite of the various forms he could take.

"Oh shit." I realized that when he'd awoken, he'd have been *naked Kane*. I hadn't brought any spare clothes, and the idea of him slipping into doggy mode was becoming normal somehow. I had forgotten about what the morning would bring.

I went to the side door of the garage and opened it, staring out across the backyards of the subdivision.

"Missing, naked Kane," I muttered. "That probably wouldn't sit well with the neighbors."

Then again, the guy was in pretty damn good shape.

Hearing movement to my left, I took a half step back and snapped my head toward it. Kane stepped out from around a line of trees.

My grandmother's property butted up to a stream, pitiful thing really, but that waterway was protected. So the area around it couldn't be developed. Which meant Grandma had open woods behind her that crested up to a ridge.

Just beyond that were rows upon rows of more houses.

From where I stood, it looked like you were staring deep into the Minnesota woods. With a massive French Canadian walking toward me.

Not naked.

Naked might have been better.

"What the hell are you wearing?" I asked, covering my mouth. "You do some early shopping? I hope you kept the receipt."

He stepped up to me and stared out into the street beyond the front yard. There sat the massive Mercedes hearse where we'd left it the night before.

"This is a very kind neighborhood," he said, pulling at the bottom of his white T-shirt. "They offer clothes for people. I had many to choose from."

"And still," I said, motioning toward him with my hand, revealing my smile, "you chose that."

He looked down at his feet. "The flip-flips?"

"Flip-*flops*."

"No shoes were on offer," he said. "These I discover at the bottom of a pool."

I laughed and stepped back, raising palms up to him. "I was actually referring to this... entire ensemble."

Kane was wearing his favorite, blue jeans, or what he called "jean pants." A belt and a buckle emblazoned with a Minnesota Vikings logo. White T-shirt. And over that?

An honest-to-god jean jacket.

"How did you even find a size that would fit you?"

He looked down. "It fits fine. A bit tight around my bulging chest muscles," he said and caught my expression. "Why is there smiling? This is about me, I can tell."

"Ha," I said. "How can you tell?"

"Because you all the time laugh much at me."

"No, no, dear wolf," I said and put a hand on his denim shoulder. "I am laughing with you."

"This is same thing."

"Nope, totally different," I said and sighed, turning toward the car. "Grandma sleeps kind of late, so maybe it's best we head out before she awakes. And maybe we can stop at Walmart and get you something else to wear."

"I like this. Where I am from, this is fancy dress," he said, his beard split into a half smile. "Is called a Canadian tuxedo."

Whitey cast one more glance at Kane in his Canuck tux. Dude was just a big swath of denim nearly touching the ceiling.

"Job's done?" The shop owner repeated my statement as a question. "One version of it, I suppose." He tucked his sandwich back into the wrapper and wiped his hands with a napkin. "The job was to get the hidden treasure."

"Or Plan B, from what Roy had explained."

"Right," he said and dramatically tried to peer around Kane. "And where is that boy now?"

Not wanting to get sidetracked, I tilted my head and cocked an eyebrow. It was obvious enough.

"Right," the old man said again and looked me up and down. "But that was to square Roy with the Family. Now, I guess, he's got to square accounts with the devil, yeah?"

I shrugged. I know I should have felt worse about Roy, you know, exploding, but I felt nothing. Not even relief. Just a blank space in my soul.

Whitey rubbed his hands on his pants, as if finishing up some quiet negotiation in his head, and stood. "Got the paperwork in the back. Stay there, and don't poke around."

He lifted the partition and circled around behind us. I wondered if he was checking to see if we were armed. A nervous sweat prickled up on the back of my neck when I didn't see him exit toward the back of the shop.

"Holy hell," he said then started laughing. I tensed.

I scanned for something on the counter I could grab as a weapon. Nothing. The guy kept a tidy shop. When I looked behind where he'd been sitting, on the shelves I saw something odd. Before I could ask about it, Whitey spoke again.

"Is that Rosa's death wagon?"

I turned as he stepped up to the shop window and split the blinds with the tips of his calloused fingers. "Tell me you didn't steal her car."

He turned to me with a look of confusion and amusement. I realized he was being far freer with his words than the last time we'd been in the shop. Job done, I guessed.

"We jacked a hearse that was in the warehouse," I said. "And, yeah, two caskets inside."

He rubbed his face, leaning closer to the smudged glass. "She will not like that you took her ride into the afterlife. Not one bit." He chuckled. "But I like it."

"She can afford a thousand of them," I said, walking up next to him. I looked up and down the street, making sure the hearse hadn't attracted attention. Of course, this was north Minneapolis. I could have pulled out a shoulder-mounted Stinger missile and not attracted attention.

Expect for someone wanting to buy it.

Chuckling to himself, he pulled his hands away, and the blinds snapped closed in my face. I watched him walk to the back of the shop, laughing softly the entire time.

I elbowed Kane to get his attention. He looked down at me, but before I could say anything, the old guy was back.

Waving the passport as he walked toward us, he said, "I wouldn't take any flights with that in the next few days. Need the data to percolate through the system."

We wouldn't be getting on a plane, but that didn't mean it wouldn't have to pass scrutiny in the coming days.

I asked him, "You think it would cause any issues at the Mexican border?"

"What? No one tries to sneak *into* Mexico." Whitey chuckled again. Dude was in a good mood. "You could probably show them a Costco card and get right in."

"Now you tell me," I muttered and wanted to ask more about it. But another question elbowed its way to the front of my mind. "Hey, um, where did you get that?"

Whitey passed through the gap in the counter, secured the thick wooden slat back in place, and looked up. He traced my finger to the shelves just behind his chair.

"Get what?" he asked, approaching the chair, picking up the figurine, and holding it up. "This?"

I nodded, my mind a tempest of conflicting emotions.

He chucked the wooden carving from hand to hand, and tiny bits of bright paint drifted to his pants legs like a rainbow snowfall. Scoffing, he reached down and brushed the offending flecks away.

"Someone I know used to make figures like that," I said, swallowing hard. "Just like that."

Whitey put it back on the shelf, exactly as it had been before.

"I suppose I leave it there for luck," he said and sat back on his chair. "I'm getting superstitious in my old age. But that howling dog was here long before I got here."

"Coyote," I said, my voice unsteady. "How long?"

He shrugged, ignoring my question. "If I were you, I'd ditch that big black car somewhere that—"

"How long?" I repeated a bit louder, interrupting him. "Where did it come from?"

Whitey froze, his eyes cold. This was a man who was used to people listening and doing what he said. I saw a wave of primal anger cross his face then fade slightly.

"The guy who did this job before me," he said, enunciating each word like they were bullets spitting from a gun barrel. "He never took it when he had to clear out."

"Clear out?"

Squinting at me, he found a place for all that anger that had been swirling around his head. He could obviously see that his story was troubling me. So he kept at it.

"Yeah, he did the same job I'm doing now," Whitey said then spun his finger around in the air. "But he got busted and had to get out. From what I heard, he died drunk as a skunk on his kid's couch."

I tried to speak, but I couldn't get the thoughts straight in my head. Was he saying my grandfather had worked in the shop? Worked for... Rosa?

A gentle hand fell upon my shoulder, and I heard Kane's voice, soft as a cloud, drift over my head.

"Thank you, my friend," he said to the shopkeeper. "For all of your help."

Whitey nodded once and reached for his food once again.

"Wait," I said, my mind racing. "Kane helped out on the job, right?"

The man folded his hands in his lap and sighed. "So?"

"Well, he should get something, right?" I tried to sound as casual as possible, my eyes flitting over the wooden carving. If I could get a closer look...

"Sure," Whitey said, lifting his hands like a preacher at a tent revival and motioning to the store behind us. "Take your pick. Then clear out."

I said, "Cool," but before I could single out the carved coyote, Kane pointed at it. Had he noticed me staring at it?

"I would like that," he said, "if this is all right."

But when Whitey picked up the figurine, my friend shook his head. Whitey put it back, slid a few inches over, and motioned to a square piece of padded felt with a single piece of jewelry. Kane nodded, and the old man scooped it off the material with both hands.

"It's busted," he said with a nonchalant tilt of his head. "But it's real."

He handed it to Kane, who held it up and smiled. He looked at me. "Now I have necklace like you do."

Sure, I wanted to tell him he'd picked the wrong thing. *Get the other thing!* But it was one of the sweetest moments I could ever remember. And it was about me. Me.

Kane wanted a locket. Like me.

Whitey's hard-case facade cracked, and he smiled. Nodding toward me, he said to Kane, "Right now, it's just the oval frame. You'll need to get a tiny picture to put in there."

"I will, yes. Do they still have the tiny booths in parking lots that make pictures?"

I cleared my throat and wrinkled my brow. "What? Fotomats? No, I don't think so."

"Hmm. This is too bad," he said and held the locket up to the light. "That would seem like a place to get a tiny picture."

He turned his wrist toward me, and I examined the locket. It looked old but taken care of and well loved.

"It's a bit tarnished," I said, feeling as if the world had melted away, leaving just the two of us. "We can get some polish and make it so shiny you'll be able to see your reflection."

"When I look at this, I want to see my friend," he said and closed his hand around it. "I will put a tiny Emelda picture in this."

Speechless. I stood there totally speechless.

Kane caught my expression and smiled. He tucked it into his pocket and asked Whitey, "Why is necklace warm?"

The shopkeeper frowned. He'd had his fill of the happy, happy talk.

"It's been in the sun all day," he said, waving us away. "Are we good, now? Please? We done?"

"Sure," I said, jamming my hands into my pockets. "Unless you want to buy a couple coffins? Never been used, and I'm willing to part with them real cheap."

"Hell, no," Whitey said and pointed us to the door. We'd overstayed our welcome. "You take those far away from me. It's bad juju to have them so close by. Gives me the creeps."

He held out my new passport, and I took it. We left the shop without another word, heading toward the big black car. The moment I stepped outside, the sun fried away the warm fuzzies, and my mind started spinning about the wooden figurine. And what Whitey apparently had said about my grandfather.

Could he have really worked for Rosa Nieto's criminal outfit? How could that possibly be true?

I was standing at the door to the hearse, lost in thought. Kane brought me back.

He asked me, "What is juju?"

"I dunno," I said and opened the door to get in. "Two-thirds of a law firm?"

Chapter Thirteen

W hen we rolled into my neighborhood, I circled the block twice.
I'd contemplated making a third round but then realized if there were people looking for us, we were driving around in the most "look at me!" vehicle possible. I parked a block away from my apartment and chucked the key fob under the seat.

Within the hour, it would be someone else's problem.

Just walking away, I could feel the tension melt out of my neck and shoulders. I relaxed, took a deep breath, and smiled.

I didn't know a thing about karma or juju or any of that. I was just happy to leave the death mobile in my personal rearview mirror.

At the corner, I saw my apartment, and Kane and I stood for a moment. My front door faced the alley, and it didn't look like anyone had messed with it. The curtains were still drawn, as I'd left them the day before.

"Let's get in and out. I'm just going to grab some clothes," I said. "You get whatever you need."

He nodded. "I have only my passport wallet."

"Really? You don't want to change into something a bit cooler?"

Kane flipped up the collar on his jean jacket. "I am already very cool."

I reached up and fixed the collar. When I crossed the one-lane road, I was relieved to see my jeep was right where I'd parked it.

Sure. Still there. Just not all of it.

"Son-of-a..." I muttered and walked up to it.

"Car is lower," Kane said.

"Yeah, having no wheels will do that," I said, gritting my teeth. To add insult to theft, my back window had been smashed. I opened the door and searched around to see if anything had been taken. Someone had chucked an empty beer can into my back seat.

"Dammit," I said. "Dammit, dammit."

Sighing, I pulled the house key out of my pocket and flipped it to Kane, telling him to grab what I needed inside.

"Pull all the clothes out of my middle drawer and put them into my backpack," I said, opening the door of my crippled jeep. "Your man-be-gone serum and my slingdart's already in the pack."

"You think they will let you take a weapon into Mexico?"

"It looks like a slingshot," I said. "If anyone asks, I'll say it's a present for my nephew or something."

"Violent present," he said, frowning.

"For my fictional nephew?" I shrugged. "Yeah, sure. Noted."

"What will you be doing?"

I looked back to the street and sighed. "Well, we've got to take that beast of a car across four states to the border." I leaned into the jeep and popped open the glove compartment. "I'll pull these plates off and put them on the hearse."

He nodded, and I knew from the confident look on his face he had no idea what I was talking about.

I dug around the glove compartment for my knife—I'd always had some handy weapon in any car I drove—but came up short. They had taken my damn knife and left a crushed beer can.

"Hey," I said then stood up, but the door closed before I could call Kane back. Ducking into the car again, I grabbed the beer can out of the back seat and twisted off the aluminum pull tab.

Chucking the can back inside the vehicle, I held the tab up and examined it. *That'll do.*

I bent down to spin off the first of the license-plate screws, and it came off perfectly. Finally, something went my way. That little bit of luck actually made me smile.

Of course, I knew it wouldn't last.

Chapter Fourteen

The real test of any relationship is a road trip. A long, long road trip.

My mother's side of the family had always been religious, so before she and Dad got married, they had to attend a series of premarital church sessions. To hear her tell it, she wasn't thrilled about it.

Her dad argued that if she was going to live in another country, the classes would help her decide if the move was right.

She conceded under the condition that the church she went to was in Minnesota, not Mexico. He agreed. Then traveled with her to make sure she went.

On several occasions, I'd asked my dad what they'd been like as a couple. His response was always vague and sickly sweet.

"I woulda walked through the fires of hell to marry your momma. And, truth be told, the pastor stopped just short of that particular requirement."

Dad was a softy. For a military guy, maybe he was an outlier. But I'd met a good number of folks who'd been in the military, and despite what they trained to do, they were all kind, wonderful people.

Who could kill you with a stapler, sure.

I always had crazy fantasies about what a pastor might say to two soon-to-be newlyweds. Did they talk about devotion? Commitment? Who should sleep on the wet spot?

My mother wouldn't talk about those church classes. Her avoidance technique was usually an admonishment, "Well, you could find out if you'd stop going out with losers!"

I was so busy being angry with her being angry with me—and the welts that earned me over the years, especially after Dad died—that I missed the part where she was right. To get away from home, I moved in with Roy. And, in the end, the asshole pointed a gun in my face.

Finally, my dad's mother, my wonderful grandmother, spilled the beans on the top-secret parochial proceeding known as biblical premarital counseling.

One night, after I tipped the bottom of her Kahlua bottle a bit higher into her nightly tea, she broke.

"You didn't hear it from me," she started. I always loved that phrase because it meant the good stuff was coming.

"Of course," I said, settling deeper into her big sofa.

"But I think Pastor Swanny sorta phoned it in because he got tired of giving the same speeches years after year, decade after decade," she said, watching me over the rim of her cup. "That man was so old, he got the Book of Luke on preorder."

I blinked. Just listening.

"Well, anyway, he did not have your parents go through all the sessions as per usual. Didn't seem to help anyone much anyhow." She took a big swig of her tea and smacked her lips. "Instead, he sent them to Denver."

"Denver?"

My grandmother laughed. "Yes! He said he needed a package from a friend of his who didn't have money for postage. So your mom and dad got in the car and had to drive nearly two thousand miles, there and back. In a car for more than three days together."

She sat back with her cup and breathed in the steam. I waited for the story to continue. Grandma waited.

"That's it?"

She nodded.

"I... I don't get it."

Grandma tilted her cup back, winced, and set it down on the edge of the coffee table. She missed, and it fell to the floor. I knew she was a bit loaded because she left it there.

"If a couple can last three days cooped up in a car, the odds they can survive a relationship are pretty high," she said. "If they get into a big blowout, well, they may just call the whole thing off on their own."

In its own strange way, that made sense. And my parents had been happy until the day Dad got blown up. Still, I was confused.

"Why didn't they want to tell me about *that*? Seems innocent enough."

"Ha, on their part, it was," she said, staggering to her feet and heading toward her room. She turned back around at her door a half second after I snatched the teacup and put it back on the coaster. "Although the package they picked up for Pastor Swanny wasn't. The Denver guy hadn't been concerned about postage. He was worried about getting busted for sending a half pound of pot through the mail."

I busted out laughing. "What?"

"Yep. They carried that box, wrapped up in brown paper and a string, across three state lines," she said, standing at her door, swaying slightly. "A damn-near perfect marriage, and it all started with them becoming drug mules."

Laughing harder, I had clapped and clapped.

"But trust me, doll," my grandmother had said, getting a faraway look in her eyes. "The best things in life often have the weirdest beginnings."

The slow push at my shoulder broke me out of my reverie.

Kane asked me, "Why are you smiling?"

I rubbed my eyes and grabbed the sunglasses from the dash of the Mercedes. We'd gotten a very early start after crashing a few hours in a motel just south of Kansas City. The afternoon was making its slow roll across the sky while frying my retinas through the bug-splattered windshield.

That was the only slab of glass on the car that hadn't been darkened.

The hearse had tinted windows all around. Even the double-high ones in the back. That added an extra layer of protection when we had to drive at night. I didn't need Kane going doggy style on me.

I meant, turning dog.

In the moon's waning state, a toenail in the sky, it had transformed him into a poodle just days earlier. As it continued to thin, I wasn't sure how puny a dog he might become. I loved dogs, but the little rat dogs? Yeah, not a fan.

When night came during the long, long drive to the border, I had him wrapped up in a big blanket in the back seat as a precaution.

"We do pretty well in the car together, don't cha think?" I asked and got a blank stare. "I mean, we don't argue or bicker."

"You complain about my man smells very much," he reminded me.

"Yeah, no more raw meat for you when we're on the road. New rule."

"Okay." He laughed. "Maybe the 7-Eleven will start serving blood Slurpees."

I shuddered a bit. Sometimes I forgot that he needed blood to survive. Hell, was the dude a werewolf or a vampire?

"Anyway, we might have made a good couple, you and me. If you weren't already committed to your wolf wife," I said. "And not so damn hard to look at."

"What?" He flipped back his shoulder-length dark hair. "I am very beautiful man. You are very beautiful, Emelda. However, I do not find you attractive."

"Not enough teeth?" I joked.

"Yes, there is that." He smiled and looked ahead to the big sign over the highway that read Mexico. "And not enough fur."

I started to say something then stopped. "You know, I had at least a dozen totally inappropriate jokes roll through my mind as you said that. But I didn't say one. I think I'm maturing."

"I am very proud of you."

We slowed, waiting for the short line of cars to move forward. I craned my neck around to see what I might expect. How closely would the border guards look at my ID? Would they ask about the caskets in the back?

We had come up with a story about them. When we first left Minneapolis, I'd had half a mind to leave them in an alley somewhere. But I'd realized they might be the perfect distraction. Make people a bit nervous. Pop them open, nothing to see here, all good, move on.

Now that we were about to actually cross the border, I was second-guessing that decision. I looked in the rearview to see the two black torpedoes aimed at my back.

Ahead, the gate arm swung up, and our car moved forward one spot. Kane stuck his head out the window to get a better look.

"Don't do that. You look suspicious," I hissed, tugging on his jean jacket. He batted my hand away, hung there for a moment, then slumped back into the car, making the suspension bounce.

"Hmm."

Chewing on my thumbnail, I tried to see around the car ahead. Where was the border guard? Had they gone into their tiny shack?

"What did you see?"

Kane shrugged. "The big stick has Christmas lights on it."

"What the who?"

"Christmas lights."

I craned my neck, trying to see what fate awaited me fifty feet ahead. The entire border station looked like a huge gas station without pumps. Three lanes, yellow curbs. Two islands between each lane and fat poles holding up an overhang that blocked the sun.

We had to wait at the line separating light and shade, while the car ahead slipped into shadow and stopped at the gate. I looked to the left, where I saw a door but didn't recall seeing anyone go in or out.

The bar rose, and the car ahead drove through.

Swallowing, not easy because my mouth was as dry as the pavement, I crossed under the overhang into ominous shadow. I stopped at the gate.

A white crossbar blocked our path with seven red slanted dashes painted left to right. Despite having to grip the wheel tight to stop my hands from trembling, it felt a bit like I was simply leaving airport parking.

The cement pole to the left of the gate had two panels, both darkened. Was I supposed to show ID to it? I fished around for my passport and opened it. My face stared back with the name Heather Thomas. I snapped it shut.

Who was going to buy that? What had I been thinking agreeing to that name?

I looked as much like a *Heather* as Kane looked like a *Chad*.

We waited. And waited.

No one was coming out. Were they running our plates? Could the Mexican government run American plates?

I opened my passport, my damp fingers staining the blank pages, and pointed my picture toward the two dark panels by the gate. Were they cameras? If so, I hoped they had stabilization software because my little booklet was flapping around like I was trying to swat a deer fly.

"What do we do?" I croaked.

Kane raised his hands in the air, a big smile on his face. What did he see that I didn't?

Then the top square on the pole glowed. Not cameras after all.

It had turned green.

"Merry Christmas to us," he said and clapped once.

I snatched my arm back inside. The gate lifted, and I shifted my foot from the brake to the gas a bit too quickly and came within an inch of smashing into the rising bar.

"That was it?" I asked and spun around in my seat. "Are we in?"

"Yes," Kane said, rolling his window up and flipping the AC to high.

The road made an immediate hard left then a sharp turn right. As we rolled along, there were parking bays every ten feet.

He pointed to a car in one of the spots on his side. One border guard spoke to the driver while another dug through the contents of the car's trunk.

"That vehicle got a red light, and the man with the other man waved them over. *Criminals*," he said as if the word tasted vile in his mouth. "I bet they had fruit."

My arms began to ache, so I rolled my shoulders, trying to relax. We'd made it. We were fine. Then Kane's words wiggled into my brain like they'd been on a five-second delay.

"They had... *what?*"

"Yes, you can see, no? Shifty. They do look like fruit criminals. Especially the girl with the pigtails," he said, turning his head, gawking as we passed. "Probably a banana. Or a hidden persimmon."

My heart started banging at my throat, demanding I work out what the hell was going on.

"They busted them for fruit?"

"I would think, yes." He flopped back into his seat and made a shooing motion with his hand. "Big sign warned everyone that they will get what they deserve. If you cannot do the time—"

"*Kane, what are you talking about?*"

"Do not bring in the lime." He crossed his arms, shaking his head. "This is what I am saying."

Looking left and right, I saw cars had been pulled over for what appeared to be random inspections. Every three or four stalls had a vehicle parked within.

People were out of their vehicles, popping their trunks, while guards went through their stuff. Dogs ran around sniffing everything.

"Just to be clear, we're in?"

"Welcome to Mexico, Emelda!" Kane said and raised his hands again. "That was not so hard."

Relieved, I choked out a sob of pure joy, and a dam-break of endorphins swept my anxiety away. But that feeling only lasted a second.

"Well, goddamn it!" I said. "We went through all of that to get a passport and didn't have to show it to anyone? We nearly died for nothing!"

"Maybe not."

Spinning toward Kane, I frowned. "What's that supposed to mean?"

He pointed at the man in an official-looking uniform who'd stepped out in front of our car. His hand extended toward us in a stop gesture. His other hand rested on the stock of his rifle. With his stop hand, he motioned to a bay for us to pull into.

"Now you will be happy again," Kane said, shuffling his feet on the floor in front of him. "I believe that man will ask for your passport."

Chapter Fifteen

"That man seems very unpleasant," Kane said, his words ending in a low growl.

I searched left and right, really wishing I were back in the Jeep at that moment. The wheel stop in front of us would be just a speed bump. The long concrete walkway, my acceleration ramp.

The jeep would have been sweet.

Instead, I was staring through the bug-guts windshield of a *stolen* two-ton hearse as a mustachioed border guard casually waved around a semiauto like he might lift it and clean the glass with bullets.

For a heartbeat, I considered flooring the Mercedes to make a run for it anyhow. Then I heard the *thump thump* on the back window.

"Hmm," Kane said, craning his neck to look behind us. "More people to show your passport to."

Mustache Guard pointed at me and Kane by splaying out two fingers of his left hand and then shot a thumb in the air.

As I turned to unbuckle my seat belt, I whispered to my friend, "Don't say anything. Lemme work this out."

"Okay." Kane clicked out of his belt, opened his door, and stepped out like he was ready for the beach. The dude was wearing flip-flops.

Sliding out of my side, I watched Mustache's finger lift higher and higher as he watched Kane extend to his full height.

When I saw him look at our front license plate, I stiffened. He frowned, looked up again, and spoke to us in English. "Take one step away from the vehicle."

I did.

Kane did not.

My big friend waggled a finger at Mustache Guard. "This is a trick, yes?"

"What?" The border guard bristled and gripped his weapon tighter.

"You did not say the words, 'Simon says to take one step.' *Alors*, if I move, then I am out, non?"

Mustache took a half step toward him. The barrel of his rifle inched a little higher.

"If you do not move, maybe then I shoot," he said and flicked his head. Still smiling, Kane took one exaggerated step away from the car.

When I'd stepped away, I raised my hands in the air. Just instinct, I suppose. I'd spent so much time in the company of authorities, the motion came naturally. The border guy turned to me and saw my fingers above my head, which drew a smile to his face.

This had the slightly unnerving effect of flipping his mustache upside down. Like a fuzzy black caterpillar that flinched after dropping from a leaf onto a hot tin roof in the midday sun.

The two other men walking up approached the first guard, calling out to him in Spanish, "What's up?"

Mustache let go of his rifle to let it fall slack as he pulled out a small clipboard that had been stuffed into his belt. He tapped it. That got raised eyebrows from his two buddies.

He strolled up next to me and hip pushed my door closed. "Do you have any weapons on you?"

"No." I shrugged, my voice trembling. "Can I borrow yours?"

He shouted something to the other two, his words coming out like machine gun fire. I knew *conversational* Spanish from growing up with my drunk grandfather. As long as that conversation, of course, was a tirade of complaints and insults.

But when people spoke too fast, sometimes I couldn't follow.

The two guards rounded the front of our big black car and went over to Kane. One bobbed his rifle up and down, indicating to Kane to raise his hands.

I called over, "He doesn't have any weapons either. We were just going to—"

Mustache smacked his hand against his tiny clipboard. "Answer questions. That is what you are doing. Otherwise, please be silent." He turned to his buddies, nodding at Kane. "Check him."

One guard stared up at the massive French Canadian, holding his rifle tight enough to dent the metal. The other pulled a device like a tiny black cricket bat off his belt and motioned for Kane to hold his arms out.

The wand started at Kane's flip-flops then up both pants legs. When the guard got midway, the wand beeped in three quick chirps.

"Minnesota Vikings," the guard grumbled. "Terrible quarterbacks. No defensive line."

Then he did a quick run up the front of Kane's jacket. It chirped, single beeps, all up the front.

"Buttons! This man is wearing a jean jacket," the guard said, smiling and glancing back over a shoulder at his buddy. "Are you not hot in that?"

"According to my friend," Kane said and shrugged, "no."

"*¿Qué?*"

Wand Guard then stepped back and nodded to Kane's jeans. "Please take any change or keys out of your pockets."

Hands still in the air, Kane smiled at the man. He didn't move.

"Do you not understand what I am asking?"

"Yes."

The guard huffed. "Then please remove these things from your pocket."

"I have neither."

The guard muttered something to the man behind him, chuckled, then looked at Mustache. My guy wasn't having as much fun as those guys. While he was distracted, I sneaked a peek at the clipboard clutched in his pudgy fingers.

The page clipped to the top was a half piece of paper with a very short email that had been printed out. Just a one-line message. I recognized two words. *Coche fúnebre.*

This wasn't a random stop. We were in real trouble.

"Just do what the nice border guard says, man," I said, knowing that Kane would pick up on the strain in my voice. An urgency. He looked over.

Widening my eyes, I shot a glance down at the clipboard and did a quick shake of my head.

Kane had the ability to pick up on little gestures and tells and quirks. He'd told me many times this was the language of animals. Human words often misled and clouded intent.

Expressions revealed the truth.

He grinned at me, totally missing out on the truth that we were very, very screwed.

"*Señor*, please take whatever you have in your pocket out and place it on the ground."

My big friend grinned. "May I lower my hands to do as you wish?"

The Wand Guard laughed, casting a glance at his friend, who had chilled out and now found the big weird dude all sorts of funny. He muttered something under his breath, and his buddy laughed more, waving his rifle barrel.

"*¡Córrele!* Let's go, let's go."

Wand Guard put a hand on his hip and said in a theatrical voice, "Ah, Simon says you may lower your hands to empty your pockets and then return them over your head."

Kane smiled at the guy next to me and tapped his temple with one finger. Then he dug into his pocket and pulled out what had set off the metal detector. He raised his hands above his head again.

"*¿Qué es eso?*" asked the only guard, still holding his rifle. "What is that?"

My big friend turned to him, arms up, and, with his free hand, lifted the old piece of jewelry up by its chain. As tarnished as it was, it still glittered in the Mexican sun.

Squinting as he looked up, the guy asked, "Is it valuable?"

"Not at all," Kane said. "We got it free!"

Rifle Guy shaded his eyes with one hand. "Free?"

The locket dipped once then fell from its broken chain and landed on the blacktop. The guard bent down to pick it up.

"Yes," Kane said, his elbows bending slightly. "We got it as payment for blowing up a gang lady's warehouse."

"What?" That inquiry came from the Wand Guard. He did not get clarification.

Instead, Kane brought both of his hands down in a V-shape, and Wandy got two fists on either side of his neck. Even before the first guy hit the ground, the big man carried the momentum of his right hand in an arc and slammed it into the face of the kneeling guard.

In less than a second, they'd both gone from standing to lying unconscious on the pavement.

The guy next to me dropped his clipboard and reached for the rifle strap around his neck, but too close to the car, he banged the butt of the weapon into the door. And too close to my elbow, he got smashed in the nose.

I got punched in the side of the head for it, stumbled backward, then fell hard on my ass.

He spun toward me, the caterpillar on his lip twitching like it was being electrocuted, and he raised his rifle toward me. But it kept rising and rising.

With his body.

Kane had slid over the car, his head-to-toe denim body gliding easily across the hood, and once his feet hit the pavement, he'd lifted the guard in the air. By the rifle.

Sitting on the hot pavement in their shadow, I watched as the guard hung there suspended, his arms waving at the strap, which was cutting off his breath. If he could have reached the trigger, he might have been able to pull, but he would have only shot the sky.

Holding the man high above his head, nine feet above the pavement, Kane looked up to him.

"I could throw you," the huge man said, nodding to his right, "somewhere over there. But if I were to do this, you would be very injured or die." He shook his head, balancing the guy up there like he was holding a balloon. Zero effort. "Such a thing would trouble me. I do not want to do this."

The man gasped for breath, his face reddening.

Feet slapping against pavement, just behind me, drew my attention. I spun and saw another three, four, then five guards running in our direction. Rifles bounced against their backs and chests.

Jumping to my feet, I opened my car door and punched the big shoulder in front of me.

"We gotta go!"

Kane lowered the man closer to his face. The feet still dangled helplessly in the air.

"If I put you down, you need to run. Can you do this?"

The guy's eyes rolled, and he slumped, arms dangling like a tuckered-out kid who'd fallen asleep in Daddy's arms.

"He's out," I shouted and jumped into the Mercedes, punching the start button. "Drop him and get in."

My friend lowered the guy to the ground. Stripping off the rifle, he spun once and tossed the weapon toward the five guns running toward us. Two in front went down, and at least one more crashed into them.

By the time Kane had hopped into his seat, they were all back up and running.

Boxed in by concrete on three sides, I could only go backward toward the guards chasing after us. I dropped the vehicle into Reverse and smashed the accelerator. We lurched, and I heard grit from our spinning wheels sandblast the undercarriage.

Then the tires bit, and we launched backward.

In the rearview, I saw one of the guys go to a knee, readying to fire. Cranking the wheel, I mashed the accelerator harder then yanked on the emergency hand brake. The nose of our vehicle spun around, smashed into the kneeling guy, launching him sideways.

He was out of the picture, but through the passenger side's tinted window, another guard was already lining up his shot.

I shouted, "Get down, Kane!"

He didn't.

Instead, he turned toward the guy with the rifle, blocking my view. I heard the shot and the crack of the glass. Still, my friend did not move.

No time!

Slamming the gear into Drive, I smashed the gas pedal to the floor. Kane fell back into the seat, his eyes closed. Dude was smiling.

As we rocketed away, I heard more shots ping off the car. Kane reached up and clicked his seat belt on. "We should probably drive very fast."

I glanced at my friend, expecting to see his chest stained red with gore and blood. The T-shirt was as white as it had been when he'd put it on two days earlier.

That didn't make sense. There was no way the guard could have missed. When I looked at the window on Kane's side of the hearse, I saw only the slightest bit of grit where the slug had hit and ricocheted off.

The rain of bullets from behind had stopped. When I looked at the mirror, I saw the rear door's glass was intact.

"Holy shit," I said as I came up to a sign that read Alto and blew right through it. That earned me a symphony of melodic car horns. I cranked the wheel hard to left then right, clipping the fender of a passing car.

We skidded through the intersection. I straightened the wheel, hit the gas again, and we fishtailed down the street. "The glass is bulletproof?"

"Is a cool car," Kane said, casually rubbing the leather interior. "For a death car."

I had to weave around trucks and rusty sedans, hopping the curb twice before getting to another intersection. I hooked right.

"Where are we headed, Emelda?"

"Anywhere, as long as it's fast," I shouted. "I've driven plenty of getaway cars. If they don't catch up within a minute, we're home free."

That was when I heard the sirens.

Chapter Sixteen

I admit it. I took the corner way too fast.

That epiphany came to me in a rainbow of rotting veggies, coffee grounds, empty milk jugs, and a surprisingly large pair of off-pink cowboy boots that put a knuckle-sized dent in one of our windshield wipers.

The trash cans had exploded over the hood. The hearse hadn't even slowed.

"Watch out!" Kane shouted.

"What?" I hunched down, scanning the street. "Watch what?"

"Sorry. Meant to say that sooner," he said, one hand gripping the seat belt, the other holding the dashboard. "Trash can."

"Uh huh, not helping."

I wove between minibuses, hopped up curbs, swerved in front of vans, and cut off pickups. I decided that if we survived the next ten minutes, I would track down that old pre-marriage preacher guy with a course revision. Don't send couples on road trips.

Put them in car chases.

The tiny show in my rearview revealed not one but two—no, wait, three—vehicles with spinning lights and very determined border authorities. I banked a hard left, lost control, and ended up doing a fishhook turn.

All those cops were now in front of me.

"Whoops."

Gunning the engine, I headed straight for them then did a quick jig to the right and took, um, the road less traveled.

Kane white-knuckled the tiny handle in front of him. "This is not road. This is sidewalk."

"I know!"

"Sidewalk not for cars," he said, his words coming more quickly than before. "Is road for people."

"I know!"

Punching the horn with the heel of my palm until my wrist buzzed, I had to make a quick jerk to the left to avoid a woman walking three tiny, panicked dogs.

I couldn't help it.

"Friends of yours?" I asked Kane. He growled back.

At the next intersection, I crossed kitty-corner and got more horns, from all directions, and turned down an alleyway. My head swam, and I realized I was holding my breath.

"Very skinny road," Kane said, crouching and looking up at the brick building inches from his window. "I don't think—"

Sparks flew from the right-quarter panel, then I shifted over, and they exploded from the left. A few seconds later, both sides were shooting sparks.

Kane said, "Maybe I should drive."

We burst out of the alley like a ten-day-old pimple, my feet working the pedals as if I were trying to put out a runaway campfire with Birkenstock sandals. My black tank of a vehicle spun in a three-sixty then another half turn. Kane's head banged against the glass, which probably did far more damage to the window than his noggin.

Before we stopped spinning, I jammed my foot onto the gas again. We rocketed forward. I looked left and right at the next intersection. For the moment, the road was clear.

"I do not see the police people."

Leaning forward and shooting glances both ways at another cross street, I said, "They won't give up that easily."

Kane slowly turned toward me. "Which part of that was easy?"

Damn.

More brake lights a block ahead. I would have to find a way around. Or through.

We had a few seconds of relative calm, so I told Kane what I'd seen back at the border. "I got a peek at the guard's clipboard. Only for a second, but two words stuck out. *Coche fúnebre.*"

"This means?"

I smacked the dash with an open palm. "Hearse."

Kane rubbed his beard and pinched his bottom lip. "They were looking for us, yes?"

"Yes," I said. "Which means someone ratted us out. The only one who knew we were heading this way was Whitey. Goddamn Whitey."

"Red lights ahead," Kane said, his voice a bit shaky. "Many, many red lights under the green lights."

"Why aren't they going?" I laid on the horn. "It's a green, dumb asses!" Bobbing my head around, trying to see a way through, I told him, "Hold on."

"People road?" Kane asked.

"People road," I confirmed.

Back up on the sidewalk, I noticed the cross traffic was moving but only creeping along. Not in a traffic jam, just moving at a snail's pace. I had to take the wrong side of the road for a half block until, thankfully, one of the vehicles in the long line of cars stalled out.

I wove in front of it, joining the slow-moving traffic.

"This is more safe, yes?" Kane asked, turning around in his seat then spinning back. "We are no longer going fast."

"Who knows? Maybe they'll be searching for a speeding car and..." My voice trailed off as I looked up at the cars ahead. "This is so weird."

Kane said, "My entire existence is weird. This is nothing."

I opened the window and stuck my head out. A perfect line of vehicles all moving at the exact same speed. In fact, when we got to a red light, the line of cars didn't even slow. Didn't speed up but breezed right through.

"What the hell is this?"

Chapter Seventeen

L eandra Rios was wiping mascara-stained tears off her face, her cheeks red. Red from the flush of sadness but also from yelling for the past thirty seconds at her husband, Jorge.

"I told you to get the car fixed before today," she said in Spanish as she threw a snotty tissue at his lap. It landed and stuck to three others already there. "Of all days, Jorge! You are doing this to humiliate me, and I know this to be true!"

"No, sweetness. My cousin, he looked at it and said—"

"Your cousin is a moron," she said as the vehicle's starter ground and ground. The engine would not start. "Stop hitting the pedal. You're flooding it!"

Jorge did not respond to his lovely wife because he knew it would only cause more problems. Yes, the Buick was more than thirty years old, but he had *bought* it new. He knew his car.

In fact, he'd been with the car longer than he had been with Leandra. Of course, he knew to never say *that* to her. Jorge Rios did not have a death wish.

Unlike his wife's younger brother, it seemed. A boy who never grew into a man, despite being well into his forties. Fernando always had dreams of becoming a race car driver but only ended up in the local smash-up derbies.

Still, he had made a name for himself.

Fearless Fernando, he was called, but Jorge believed that was less about the nature of the man behind the wheel and more about the track owner's love of alliteration.

That said, Fearless had never met a foe he could not defeat. Yes, he cycled through dozens of jobs to keep his car running, but when he was in his vehicle, no opponent could best him.

And, in the end, no one did.

It had been a wall.

After hearing the tragic news, Leandra Rios only noted that, if nothing else, her dear brother died doing what he loved.

Jorge had turned to her, one eyebrow raised. "Fernando loved burning to death while trapped in his car?"

That had earned Jorge a smack across his jowls, which he'd never seen coming but should have. After two decades of marriage, he still loved his wife very much but had never worked out what exactly made her tick.

However, that was *not* true of his own vehicle. He knew his baby, his lifelong love. She didn't need spark plugs or a new distributor cap, like the rip-off mechanic by his work had claimed.

She just needed a bit of love.

A full press of the gas, wait two seconds. Then a half press. Turn the ignition, while giving it a slight love tap on the pedal. A kiss of petrol.

After she had died in the middle of the procession, the first kiss did not wake her.

"The cars ahead are all pulling away from us, Jorge!" his other love, his wife, shouted even louder than before. She spun in her seat and gasped. "We have held up the entire line."

"I know this," he said, whispering.

"Start this heap up, Jorge!"

Jorge closed his eyes and whispered, this time to the car. Another tiny kiss—tap—with his toes, so gentle. He turned the key. The car shook, rattled, shimmied and then roared to life.

Leandra crossed herself and kissed her thumb. As she looked up to thank a higher power, Jorge ran his calloused hand over the well-worn dash to thank the car.

Twisting in his lap belt to get comfortable again, he knew the line of sweat streaming down his stomach would have normally left a horrifying stain on his shirt. Thankfully, he was wearing black, as was his wife. No one would notice.

"Go, now," she shouted, waving a hand forward.

Jorge raced forward as the car just ahead, a large black Mercedes, turned the corner. He blinked at it, trying to remember if that was—

"Turn, follow!" Mary Elizabeth wailed, her words stumbling over one another as her freshly painted fingernails flailed in the air. Jorge's jowls tensed.

"Is that—"

"Follow the hearse!" she shouted, the cords in her neck sticking out, her voice strained, as she tossed another damp tissue into his lap.

Chapter Eighteen

I was second-guessing the idea of jumping into the long line of cars. At first, it had seemed like good cover, but these guys were moving way, way too slow.

The border guys knew what Kane and I looked like. And, of course, they knew what kind of car we were driving.

It was this last thought that got my brain turning down new avenues.

We'd passed a small school then the local library. Both had been named after the city.

Matamoros was not a huge town. It catered to tourists and those who might be crossing the border for cheap drugs—prescription or illegal. Or both.

According to the map software on my phone, there were three or four main arteries out of town. I could pick one and hope that the border cops hadn't covered it.

Or did they have action plans for when someone made a run over the border? Would those exit routes get covered as a matter of routine?

We would have to chance it because I suddenly realized the truth of what had triggered the hunt for our hearse.

"I don't think it was Whitey," I said and made a right turn, finally breaking away from the long line of bumper-to-bumper traffic. Thankfully, the road was clear ahead.

When I looked in my mirror, I saw a bunch of vehicles making the exact turn. Apparently, they had the same idea we did. Get out of the weirdly slow-moving traffic.

I turned my eyes back to the road.

Kane said, "Must be Whitey who said to look for the Mercedes car. He knew where we were going, yes?"

"Right, but remember the day *before* we rolled up in Roy's Chevy. Whitey would have seen that." I looked ahead to see if I could find the road labeled Mex 101. Not that we could take that because it was the most obvious route out of town. But at least if I could find it, then I could make a plan to go down and around then somehow get back to it.

"Mercedes car is much nicer," Kane said, rubbing his fingertips across the leather trim on the door. "Better than Impala car."

"Except that this one belongs to Rosa Nieto, the boss of a murder-happy crime syndicate!" I said, looking left then right. In my rearview, the line of cars behind us seemed to be growing. "There's no way the shopkeeper would think we'd be dumb enough to drive it anywhere but to the bottom of Lake Como."

"But we are dumb enough, yes?"

I growled in frustration. "*Not* the point I'm trying to make, and we didn't have any other options," I said. "But Whitey didn't know that. If he told his bosses and they gave a damn, which they wouldn't because it wasn't their car, they'd be looking for the Chevy."

Kane nodded slowly. "Maybe they went to house and saw your jeep had no feet?"

"Wheels, yeah. But that's my point," I said, my thoughts picking up speed. Then I pushed the Mercedes to pick up speed because the cars behind us were riding a bit too close. "I bet they did stop by and did *not* see the Impala."

"Because it is parked two blocks away from where we got van."

"Right! So logically they would think that if we skipped down, we'd be in the Chevy."

Kane rubbed his fuzzy chin with his thumb and forefinger then nodded slowly. "Your logic is sound."

"Great, means a lot. Thank you," I said, unsure if the former wolf could pick up the sarcasm. "Listen, Roy said that they'd had problems with rival gangs putting spies in each other's crews. Been going on since the beginning."

"This I remember."

"Okay," I said, getting excited as the pieces fell together in my mind. "Rosa's got a spy in the Family's crew. They get word to Rosa that we got a passport from Whitey and were heading to Mexico."

"And all Rosa's people know is that we have their big Mercedes car. They do not know about Chevy Impala. But the Family would know of junky car because Whitey would say this."

I clapped my hands over the wheel. "Exactly!"

"Unless spy also hears this from Whitey."

"It..." I started then tried again. "No, spy work is, you know, piecemeal. Bits here and there. Never the whole story."

"Your logic is"—Kane rubbed his chin once again—"a little bit shaky."

A pair of lights in the mirror caught my attention. We'd passed by a three-story building, which had cast a shadow onto the street, so it was the first time I'd noticed the old Buick behind us had its headlights on. It was weird. When I looked farther down the line, all the cars had their lights on.

Probably a local safety thing.

"Listen, the point is"—I pressed the accelerator a bit harder—"there'd only be one crew looking for us in a black Mercedes hearse."

Kane spun around and looked at our cargo. "The one run by the lady who owns the shiny death boxes."

"Yes," I said, scanning the road ahead as we approached a T-section. "Rosa was born in Mexico, so she'd have connections here. And, let's not kid ourselves, there's really only one local connection she might have."

Kane sighed. "Is it Amway?"

"What? No! Not—"

"They are *everywhere*. Always trying to get ma mère to buy soap, but so much soap already. Boxes and boxes in cupboards and closets. She did not need—"

"No, no, no!" At the T, I took the turn without slowing and hit the gas. "Rosa has connections to the cartels. Those guys are beyond bad news, so we need to slip this town... Is that old Buick following us?"

When I'd accelerated, the car in my mirror had matched my speed to keep up.

Kane didn't even turn around to look. "Yes."

"Is it the police?"

"I do not think so," he said, twisting between the seats to peer out the back window. "It is an old man and a woman who is yelling at him."

"Why... Why would they be following us?"

"Maybe they're leading all those cars behind them?"

I turned and looked at my side mirror. A line of dozens and dozens of cars, all matching our speed. Lights on...

"Oh shit," I muttered. "How the hell..."

Kane plunked down in his seat again, slipping the belt back over his shoulder. "What?"

"No damn way," I muttered. "We're leading a goddamn funeral procession."

He nodded and caressed the leather on the door again. "Probably because the car we are driving is a hearse."

Chapter Nineteen

I t was insanity.

What kind of mourners did they have in Mexico? I mean these people were *next level*.

It didn't matter how fast I sped up, how many corners I took without slowing down, I would lose the snaking line of vehicles for two or three seconds, and *bam!* There they were right behind me again.

"You are going very fast for side streets," Kane said, one of his flip-flops up on the dash now. "It's a good thing we have two coffins."

"Shut it, Wolfman!"

I'd already been reminded of our payload at every quick turn. Each corner I took at speed, the two slick black caskets would slide, banging into each other. This also had the effect of making my back end swing out, and while, sure, I understood some dudes are into that sort of thing, I wasn't into it when trying to keep my car on the road.

A task that I was hitting with less than one hundred percent efficacy.

"Tires are once again on people road."

"I know," I said, hitting the gas to get the rear of the hearse back onto the blacktop. I had to swerve yet again because it seemed this town's idea of road repair was putting up an Under Maintenance sign and forgetting the road ever existed.

The car bounced up and out of another pothole, the undercarriage spraying sparks as we bottomed out.

I made another sharp left and had to jam on the brakes. A line of cars paraded in front of us, and every vehicle had their lights on.

"Dammit, is that the same funeral procession following us?" I tossed a look over my shoulder. The old Buick was closing in, bouncing across the same potholes I had.

"Is like a snake," Kane said, eyes turning to slits, "eating its own tail."

"None of that is helping!"

In a gap between a battered pickup and some Euro sedan with jacked-up wheels and lights around the hood, I rocketed through, my rear fender getting a tick from the electric jalopy. Brakes squealed behind me, just for a moment, then the line following us slipped through, car for car, through the tail end of the same procession they were in.

Kane spun back.

"These mourners are persistent. This is good."

I growled in frustration. "How is this good?"

He put a hand on the dash and looked back at me again. "It is important to deal with one's grief."

We'd made it back around in a full circle, and for the moment, I was a block ahead of the man and woman in the Buick. I took another fast left and knew if I hit the gas, I would probably catch the end of the line.

But that was not what I wanted. "You got your bank card?"

Kane reached down under the seat and pulled out his passport wallet. He slipped out his card and handed it to me without a word.

I'd already passed the gas station once, trying to lose the mourners, but instead of turning down the street again, I hooked in front of a parked semitruck, bounced over the curb, and slipped between the line of pumps and a small square building.

In a bit of luck, long overdue, the semitruck sat parallel to the road I'd just left. That would help block my next move.

"Wall," Kane said, inching his butt deeper into the seat. "Big wall. Brick wall."

Twenty feet from the wall, I cranked the wheel and yanked on the handbrake. We spun in a one-eighty, facing the entrance of the square building. A car wash. I toed the accelerator, stuck my arm out the window, and was rewarded with a happy two-tone chime from the card reader.

The electronic red circle with the word Alto dimmed. The one below glowed green.

I slipped inside, and a moment later, the car wash's doors dropped in front and back with a jolt as the water began to spray us like a champagne celebration.

"Okay," Kane said. "You should drive."

"Thanks," I said, smiling for the first time since crossing the border. I saw a bubble float in over his head and realized I'd forgotten something.

"Probably should roll the windows up."

Chapter Twenty

For the next few minutes, Kane and I calmed our breathing. Or at least, I did.

He watched the bubbles on the windshield, making "ooo" noises whenever he saw rainbows form in the soap and water.

But we weren't out of the woods yet. We weren't even wandering along its edges, getting pokey burrs in our socks. Nope. Smack-dab right in the middle.

If Rosa had fired up her connections down here, we would be marked anywhere near the border.

I'd been the first of my family to be born outside of Mexico. And in my twenty-five years, I'd had opportunities to visit the place of my mother's birth, my grandfather's birth—all the births until me—but there'd never been any time.

Or at least I'd convinced myself of that.

Either way, I knew almost nothing about Mexico. Some dude in Des Moines who binge-watched *Narcos* probably knew more about my homeland than I did.

Wait, that wasn't Mexico.

Not the point.

I didn't know jack shit about eluding a Mexican cartel that would be hunting us on every street and highway for one hundred miles.

All I had were the stories my grandfather had told me. Most of which I'd ignored. Some of which I hadn't understood as he'd woven through drunken Spanglish.

My mother had told me a bit about growing up in Mexico, but most of that concerned visiting the market, or going to school, or friends she missed. Nothing about, say, how to avoid getting murdered by a cartel.

That stuff would have been very useful. Not the details about how she was jealous that Maria something or other had pretty bows in her hair that her mother had made, Mom didn't have them, and this made Mom feel bad. Blah blah blah.

She'd been raised by her dad after her mom died during childbirth. Mom was convinced that sometimes when her papa would look at her, she saw hate. That he blamed her for the death of his wife.

After living with the guy for most of my life, I can't say she'd been entirely wrong.

I told Kane what was in my head. How we needed to come up with a way to get out of the town safely and that I didn't have any idea how to do that.

"Is okay."

"How is it okay?" I leaned back against the very comfy seat. At that moment, I could have fallen asleep. Hell, we did have two fancy beds in the back. Total darkness too.

Kane shrugged and gave me one of those double-decker smiles.

"Ma mère would tell me, just when it seems there are no answers, one will present itself," he said, his eyes misting slightly. "'Open your heart, and open your eyes, Kane.' This is what she would say."

"You think we should pray our way out of this?"

He shrugged. "Whatever works."

"No, man," I said as the fogged-up exit door began to lift, rattling as it did. I didn't move right away. The damn thing sounded like it might fall off its track. Up top, a light blinked from red to green. "We need an actual plan. Not hope for inspiration."

"Open your eyes," he said softly.

"They're open. Wide open. Panic does that!"

"Open your heart."

I groaned. "I'm gonna open the big throbbing vein in your throat if you don't stop—"

He pointed ahead, but I saw nothing but the side of the long semi. I glanced to the left to see if the funeral procession was doing circles around the block, searching for our death mobile.

It wasn't.

Kane waggled his finger, and I turned back and looked at the truck. Across the trailer of the dirty white truck were the words Canadian All-Haulers.

I looked to him. Then I looked to the truck. Then back to him.

"Is that supposed to mean something to me?"

He shrugged, and I eased the car forward out of the car wash. He waved his hand downward in a "slow, slow" motion.

I turned the vehicle and parked next to the truck, which did keep us hidden from the street. Okay, that actually wasn't a bad idea. Not a solution, but it would buy us some time. A few minutes to work out a real plan.

"Fine, so— Hey, where are you going?"

Kane had opened his door, thumbed off his seat belt, and was getting out of the car. I reached for him but missed. He bent down, hanging his arm on the roof of the car and the top of the window.

"That is a long-haul truck driver. He knows these roads, yes?"

I threw my hands up. "So what? You want directions? I've got GPS, man." I grabbed my phone and shook it at him.

"When there were not buses, I hitchhiked across Canada, and long-haul truckers would often pick me up."

I cocked an eyebrow. "They would? You look like you could crush a man's skull with your hand."

"That never came up."

He rose and started to move away, and I called him back. Kane bent back down.

"Wait, wait," I said, trying to come up with some better idea. I had nothing. "Why do you think this person will help you out? They don't know us."

A heavyset man with a bright-red ball cap was crossing the forecourt, heading for the truck. I squinted and read his hat. Emblazoned across the front of it were the words Muther Trucker.

Jesus.

"He will help," Kane said. "They are kind people."

"Truckers?"

"Yes, of course," he said and started toward the truck. "But I was talking about Canadians."

Chapter Twenty-One

Since I'd met Kane, I'd learned more about microexpressions than I ever thought there was to know. A tilt of the head might mean someone was nervous or trying to bleed off some anxiety. Pursing of the lips could mean they didn't trust you or that they were holding something back.

These he'd learned from the years he'd been an animal, where seeing the truth meant the difference between eating and getting eaten. "Twitch and shift, furrow and frown" was the language of the forest.

I'd noticed that when humans touched their mouths during a conversation, they were nervous. Maybe not outright bullshitting but worried about voicing an opinion that might not be popular. Or, if they were British, concerned about just voicing an opinion.

However, when Kane sauntered back from talking with the Muther Trucker, you didn't need to be a CIA interrogator or former wolf to read that body language.

"That is smug," I said, tugging my lip. "I mean, right there, that is the swagger of smug."

Kane laughed, a big bellowing thing, tossing his head back. "I have a natural swagger. This is what makes me so desirable to all who see me."

"Nah, it's probably your modesty."

"This word," he said, coming up to me as I sat on the drying hood of the Mercedes, "I do not know."

"So that guy's gonna help out?"

"Simon," the trucker dude said as he appeared from behind Kane. Damn, my friend was so big I didn't even see the guy walking right behind him.

Tilting my head to the side, I rolled my eyes. "Sorry, I didn't see you there, Simon."

"No problem," he said, pulled his hat off, wiped his sweaty brow, and plunked it right back on. He pointed at our car and smiled. "I was going to say that if we were going to do this, you probably want to make a stop to pick up an item."

"Oh?"

He bent down, hands on his knees, and peered through the windshield of the hearse. "But you already got coffins, so you're good to go."

"It... um," I said. "What?"

Simon laughed pleasantly. "This ain't my first under-the-radar, hide-the-passenger operation. Coffin's always a good way to go. People get spooked out at the thought of looking inside."

I glanced between Kane and the trucker. I'd missed some part of the conversation.

"Right, um, good," I said, pursing my lips. "So my friend told you what's up?"

Simon tugged the brim of his hat lower over his eyes and blew out a breath. Dude was sweating buckets. So was I. Kane didn't seem to notice the heat.

The dude started walking back to his rig. "Yeah, need to work out how we're getting your big honking car in the back of my truck, but your buddy got me up to speed."

"Great, great," I said, mouthing to Kane, *What did you tell him?*

Simon laughed. "He told me that y'all are heading down to destroy a small army of monsters and that he feels responsible because they were constructed from stuff in his blood."

My mouth hung open, and I looked at Kane, who was grinning wildly. He nodded his head.

"And that he used to be a wolf, turned into a man, and that you've been helping him find the super-secret formula that can transform him back into an animal so he can return to his family." Simon stopped, now in the shade of his truck, and fluttered his shirt collar to get some air moving. "His pack, he called it."

Blinking in the sun, I stood there with my jaw still slack.

Simon turned and went to the back of his truck. Kane followed, but then I grabbed the bottom of his jean jacket and pulled him back.

"You told him that?" I whispered.

He shrugged. "Yes."

Simon unlatched the back of his rig and, with a grunt, threw the door up, which slid and banged at the top. He then waved Kane over, reaching into the bumper.

"I reckon, whatever the truth is, it can't be half as nuts as that," the trucker said, grunting and pulling out what looked like a long, rusty blade with wheels embedded on its end. "And I can tell Kane's a good man, and I don't mind a bit of company now and again, so I thought... why not?"

I looked back at our big hearse then at the interior of the truck. Tight squeeze.

"Great, thank you," I said, not looking at smug Kane. "The jury's still out on whether this big sack-o-meat's a good man, but I appreciate it."

Simon walked backward, pretty fast for a dude with a bit of a gut, and when the long, rusty rail clicked, he laid down the end he was holding. Kane saw what he was doing and did the same with the other.

Two tracks for loading.

"'Course he's a good man," Simon said. "He's Canadian."

I chuckled. "That... almost sounds like, um, reverse racism or something."

"No, no," Simon said with mock seriousness. "Being Canadian isn't a race."

"True, it is a journey," Kane added. "To a life of peace and happiness."

Simon grinned and slapped a hand on my friend's arm. "With the occasional beer strike."

They both rolled with laughter. I was standing in the middle of my family's country with a pair of dudes who had been born two borders away. Yet somehow, I felt like the stranger.

After I saw a pickup with flashing lights whip by, I hightailed to the Mercedes, fired it up, and positioned the car in front of the ramp. Staring out the windshield, I groaned and rolled down the passenger-side window.

"Won't fit," I said as Simon ambled over.

He looked at the car then at the back of his empty trailer. "Yeah, fly in the ointment there. We could tow it, I suppose, but that would defeat the purp—"

Simon jumped back as the right side of the car rose up and up. I shot my hand to the window and gripped the steering wheel with my fingers. My world tilted. I felt a scream build, but my throat had clenched so tight, the damn thing wouldn't come out.

In the window to my left, I saw the broken concrete of the gas station forecourt. The right? Clear blue sky. No clouds. And none of it making any sense whatsoever.

Simon came around to the front of the car, pulling off his Muther Trucker hat and scratching his sweaty scalp. Shaking his head, he waved me forward, taking a step backward.

I shook my head. "Are you joking? I'm on two wheels!"

The trucker moved to my left, out of my path, waving me forward. "Don't move the wheel. You're lined up."

"What?"

"Listen, I'm not sure how long your boy can hold that side of the car up," he said, calling over to me. "Hell, I'm not sure how he lifted a car like that in the first place, but if you're going to give this a shot, you need to move your rumpus, darlin'."

Darlin'? Ugh.

I eased forward, having to hold the wheel to keep myself upright. That wasn't easy because the front tire really, really wanted to turn. I gave it a bit more gas, hit the lip of the ramp, then the car eased upward.

Simon took a step back and pulled out his phone. Slowly, I moved up the ramp, the nose of the vehicle lifting higher and higher as the engine whined.

I shouted at the man, "What the hell are you doing?"

"If the car damages the vehicle, I'll need to make a claim." The Canadian trucker laughed. "If it doesn't, I'll need to make a YouTube video of this shit!"

"Emelda," a muffled voice from under the car rose up to me. "Car is heavy. Push the skinny pedal more faster."

I did.

The car lurched, and I heard Kane shout something in French, then a shuffle of flip-flops on gravel. A second later, my right front wheel gripped the upper inner wall of the trailer, bit hard, and yanked me forward.

After a few more feet, the driver's side mirror crunched against a crate. The front end of the car nosed deeper inside. I pressed the accelerator a bit more and drove along the inner wall until the blazing sun turned to shadow.

"Whoa, whoa. You're good," Simon called out, walking back from the cab of the truck. "I went to fire up the AC and heard the CB radio chatter. You're right. They're looking for you guys. We need to go."

Pulling my stiff hands away from the wheel, I exhaled a long breath. I opened the door, and it thunked on the floor of the trailer. I couldn't even get my fingers through the gap. I checked at the other door. That was leaning against the truck wall.

I looked in the mirror to see Kane brushing dirt and grit off his shoulder. The shoulder he'd lifted the car with.

He caught me staring at him and waved. I spun around and shouted, "How the hell am I supposed to get out of the car?"

Chapter Twenty-Two

W e'd only been rolling along for about five minutes when we were forced to slow behind another long line of cars. For a country with such a small population, Mexico had some serious traffic problems.

Simon put the CB radio's mic to his mouth.

"Muchos gracias, amigo," he said. "I'm on a schedule, so we'll head that way."

He hung the handset up and spun his massive steering wheel. Apparently, Simon was one of several dozen long-haul truckers looking to get the hell out of Dodge, Mexico. And through their radio network, they'd all figured out the best way out of town was the main artery, after all.

"They can't hold up traffic too much there," he said, turning the big rig down a side road. "That's a main commerce route. And if anyone were sneaking about—like you guys are—usually they'd try to find a more inconspicuous way."

Ten minutes later, yep, another line out of town. However, as our new friend had said, this was moving much faster. A few cars back from the guys with guns, Kane and I hopped in the rear of the cab and pulled the curtain, but before we could get settled in, Simon got waved through.

We hadn't eaten since early that morning, so the first place we could, we swung over and grabbed some lunch. I still didn't feel great about hanging around this close to where there were eyeballs around, so graciously, Simon let us eat in the cab.

Despite heading toward what I knew was going to be a shit show in the extreme, I was totally lost in my food. A real taco. Rice so spicy it made your eyes water and then water some more because it tasted so amazing you were weeping.

"Emelda, my food is breaking."

I put a hand up, not even looking over at Kane. He'd been digging through the greasy paper, bits of lettuce and bean and corn floating out the passenger side window.

"It's a taco, man." I took another huge bite and drifted off into bliss. "Just eat it."

When he tried to look under the wrapper, as if there might be food there, his lunch got snatched by the wind and flew out the window.

"My food has escaped," he said then sighed. "Alas, this is not the first time such a thing has happened. However, I did not expect that sort of cunning from a crunchy sandwich."

Simon laughed and wiped his mouth with a rag that dangled to the left of his steering wheel.

"Don't they have Mexicans in Canada?" I asked Kane, unable to stop the smile from creeping across my face. Our driver's laugh was infectious.

"Yes, of course," he said, dusting his hands off out the window. "But I believe we just call them Canadians."

I cocked my head toward Simon. "I never know when he's giving me shit."

"He's *French* Canadian." Our driver shrugged. "Assume he's always giving you shit."

I started getting looks from both my left and right as I licked the greasy paper, so I crumpled up my trash and put it down by my feet. I would have to remember to chuck it out later on.

Simon told us he could take us as far as San Fernando, which we would hit in less than two hours. From there, he would head east, and we would part ways.

"So, what's in Guanajuato?" he asked me.

"My grandfather was born near there. He's gone now, so I'm just looking into my roots."

"That's all?"

"Yeah."

He grunted. "So that's why the Federales were chasing you? Did you not pay your 23andMe bill?"

"It's complicated, man."

"Family always is. You know how they always say 'you'll miss 'em when they're gone'?"

"Sure, I heard that."

"Right," Simon said, waving a lazy hand toward the road ahead. "But that's not exactly true. My uncle and I never really got along. He hated the career I picked. Thought it was below me."

I patted the dash. "No way! Society would collapse without truck drivers."

"No, no," Simon said and laughed. "He's the one who got me into driving. Before, I was a lawyer."

"Oh."

"Corporate then family law. Divorces." Simon sped up to pass a station wagon that was so overloaded, I couldn't see the rear tires. "Got burnt out, and after all that nagging from Uncle Vince, I got into a truck. Haven't gotten out since."

"Sounds like he was a good dude, then."

"No, he was an asshole," Simon said, his voice rising and falling as if those words were a song. "And when he died, I didn't shed a tear."

I nodded. "My grandfather was a bit of a jerk. I sorta miss him sometimes. Not often."

"Right, right," Simon said. "But then you feel kinda bad because you don't. People say stuff like 'You never know which conversation might be the last. You'll miss 'em when they're gone.' But sometimes you just don't."

Leaning back to get comfortable—I always got tired after a big lunch—I put my feet up on the hump between the seats. "I feel ya."

"Ah, but the part they don't tell you is that sometimes, *you* were the asshole." Simon downshifted and eased back into the right lane. "More often than not, to create a real asshole, it takes two people. I mean, Uncle Vince had friends. Sorta. I guess something about me helped bring the asshole out in him."

I crossed my arms, frowning. "So you blame yourself."

"Nah, not like that. But I do wonder whether if I'd just swallowed my pride and tried to hear him instead of shouting over him, maybe we'd have gotten along better. Dude just triggered me, and maybe I wasn't mature enough to get over it."

"You do miss him, then?"

"I got regret," he said, his words getting watery. "That's much more painful than missing someone, I reckon. I *regret* I didn't try to see if we could have worked it out. In that sense... I miss missing him." Simon cleared his throat. "Missing someone means you still get to carry around that love with you. It hurts, but the love is still there. Regret is just regret."

Looking over at Kane, I saw him using his hand to do that up-and-down airplane thing. Just enjoying the car ride. Then he put his face to the wind and closed his eyes.

I leaned over to him. "If you start panting and barking, that's going to raise some questions I don't wanna answer."

Twisting his head slightly and cocking one eye open, he said, "Woof."

"The stories I'm hearing about that place you're headed?" Simon continued, grabbing my attention again. "There have always been legends and all that. Heard about *chupacabra* and all its hungry cousins since the first week I crossed the border. But these new stories are different. Whispers around town are don't go out at night. If you go in the day, don't go alone. Rumors that lights have been seen at the abandoned convent, miles into the desert, but just rumors. Place has been ready to collapse for a hundred years. No one's there."

"Rumors become legend, and legend becomes tourist brochure," I said, prodding him. "Someone saw a floating log in Scotland a hundred years ago, and that town's made millions since."

He gave me a grim smile and continued, "Hikers missing. Kids who run off to play and never come home."

"For real?" I asked, sitting up. "Or just stories to keep kids inside?"

"This is Mexico, Emelda. They want their kids outside! Too damn hot inside," he said and chuckled, but the wrinkles around his eyes had deepened. "And these are different than the old stories. I had to go through Guanajuato to Leon, dropping off carpets after a school there burned. They needed the whole place remodeled, so I went there a few times the past month."

"That's a lot of miles."

He nodded once. "First time I went, maybe three weeks back, nothing. Nobody was talking about this stuff," he said then pointed ahead at the long, empty road. "But that changed. Now, there's talk about people going missing. Sometimes that happens, and it's cartel business, but usually that's up in the city."

"Right."

"I'm back a few days later with a load of drywall. The big truck that time," he said and sighed. "Someone at the school told me they'd found the backpack of a hiker. A couple of Australians doing some YouTube thing. Going around the country. Young couple who would post every day without exception. Did that for more than two years! Then one day, they don't. And the next day, nothing."

I swallowed. "And no one has heard from them?"

"Right. At first, I brushed it off as one of them Internet pranks, right?" He wiped sweat from his brow. "Anything for attention. But some people went out for a look and came back with the backpack. Blood on it. Clothes inside stained. Phone screen cracked. The backpack was torn all up like someone had taken steak knives to it."

"Jesus."

Simon shook his head. "But the clincher was when they brought the stuff into town, they charged up the phone and turned it on. But they couldn't even get into the phone to see who it belonged to."

"Passcode protect or face recognition probably."

He pointed at me, nodding. "The thing is, though, these guys made a living off their videos. A damn good one too. So they had some setup where when they'd record something, it would auto post to their page." Simon took a deep breath and let it out slowly. "Back in town, the phone got cell reception again."

"Holy shit," I said. "It posted their last video?"

"A teacher's aide told me she saw it. Just them talking to the cam and enjoying the stars, campfire, all that. Then all hell breaks loose. Snarling and screaming."

I pulled out my phone and opened the YouTube app. "What's their account called?"

"Don't bother," he said, putting his hand on my phone. "The video got flagged. Taken down. Emelda, there was blood and, I mean, claws or something. Those screams? Nobody's that good an actor."

Kane shifted in his seat and pulled his head in, casually. But I knew he was listening as intently as I was.

"Does anyone have that video?" I asked Simon.

He shook his head. "Got scrubbed from the site, which is pretty amazing. But a kid in town, he screenshots the thing. Put it into some photo software to lighten it up or sharpen or whatever. His parents own a café right next to the old church. His mum put a pic of the thing up on the wall."

I blinked, catching what he'd just said. "What thing?"

"Caught just a frame or two in the campfire light. Blurry, but it almost looks human. But arms like a bear, mouth like..."

Kane muttered, "A wolf."

Our driver slowly turned his head toward my friend. His eyes went foggy for a moment, then he nodded. More to himself than to us.

Forcing a laugh, I wiped my hands down my pants. "Probably to drum up tourism."

"I might have thought the same thing," Simon said. "But when stories about the YouTube couple started going around, people started hearing about others. Another tourist, an old Brit who was circumnavigating the globe on foot. An entire road crew who'd gone out into the desert. And a couple of kids."

"Children?" Kane's head turned toward Simon as he said this. "Children have been taken by these monsters?"

"Monsters." Simon nodded, rolling his tongue around his mouth. "Monsters is a good word for it."

Chapter Twenty-Three

As Highway 77 came to an end, so did our journey toward Guanajuato.

There were signs pointing us toward Leon, where Simon had said he delivered supplies for the school rebuild the past few weeks. And where he'd started to hear stories about the town we were heading into.

"Not sure what kind of trouble you folks are in," he said, shaking my hand then Kane's. "But I hope it don't ever catch up to you."

I smiled at him. "You, too, Simon."

"Oh, it can't," he said, hopping back into his cab. "Why do you think I'm always on the road?"

Most of the nine-hour drive after we parted went smoothly.

For as beastly as the Mercedes hearse was, the thing drove like a dream. Of course, it ate gas like a nightmare. Kane was happy to pay for all, and I was happy for him to do it.

We grabbed some food in Ciudad Victoria but didn't stop because we started to get some stares.

When we'd parked at the tiny restaurant, I'd seen a handful of people cupping their hands to look through the tinted glass then recoiling.

If we were going to keep driving the hearse around, we would have to ditch the coffins. We didn't need them anymore, and in the end, they had done the opposite of providing a distraction.

We turned onto Highway 51 at Eliho Dolores. There we could find the church with the pink spires I'd seen in the video back at the Covenant building. From there, we would have to scan the horizon to locate the mountaintop where the three airplane-hangar-style buildings might be.

The town we rolled into looked like it had been made from white concrete and scrub brush. It felt like we were driving into a bit of a bowl with the high hills cuddling in close.

But I couldn't help but instantly fall in love with the people.

There were small stands on the side of the road, makeshift things, selling fruit, water, sodas, and barbecued meat on open grills made from oil drums. Slowly wheeling by, I saw a woman moving what looked like quarter chickens around a grill.

When she caught sight of our big hearse, she smiled. Kane had his window down, hanging his arm out. I think she may have been smiling at him. Despite how big the guy was, when he smiled, you couldn't help but smile back.

As we passed, the woman, a big bush of blond hair stacked on her head, gave my friend a salute with her barbecue tongs and went back to her grill.

Weaving around the driver of a rusted pickup who had pulled over to grab something, I leaned over and sniffed the air. "Damn. That smells amazing."

"Maybe we come back for dinner."

I laughed. "Not sure how they'd feel about you asking for a plate of raw meat."

A tiny smile tugged at his lips.

The corners of his mouth had begun to crease a bit more the last few days. The wrinkles around his eyes were more pronounced. I wanted to ask him about aging quickly but wasn't sure if he was still traumatized by nearly dying in the Covenant subbasement.

With each big moment—as a man, dog, or beast—he seemed to change a little. Like Kane was this lump of clay and every experience moved bits of the stuff around, molding him into some slightly new shape.

I suppose we were all like that. Although as we got older, I wondered if that clay started to harden. Maybe because you've built it into something strong or, at some point, you stopped bending to the world around you.

Arguably, Kane was still a baby. He'd only been human for just over a year.

I'd been at this for a quarter century, and I was fed up with letting the world mold me. I was more interested in molding my world.

When we passed the guys doing roadwork on Highway 51, I found myself scanning their faces. Like their expressions might reveal what had happened to that missing crew. Or the tourists. Or the kids.

But sweating in the late-day sun, they were just all going about their work—steam from below, the punishing sun from above.

I glanced at my map software and made the turn onto Delores Hidalgo. From there a roundabout got us onto a road called Felipe Gonzalez.

A tiny restaurant with three tables out front had a sign with a cartoon chicken giving the Okay sign with a thumb and forefinger. As if to say, "Totally cool you eat us. We're tasty!"

The homes reminded me of pictures I'd seen from Florida. Bright blues, greens, and oranges. Many of their front yards were just sidewalk.

Ah, well. Easy on the mower.

More restaurants on the other side. I would have thought this might have been too far in-country for a bustling tourism industry, but half of the people who were rumored to have been taken by the monsters had been out-of-towners.

Maybe foreigners were flavorful.

I scowled, worried I was getting too cavalier about death. At least the death of anyone who wasn't me.

Kane leaned toward me and whispered, "That man with the cumbersome hat. He is staring at the death boxes."

In the mirror, I could see the guy shuffle into the street as if he'd been drawn to the hearse. I glanced forward in time to jam on the brakes, coming within inches of a stopped car. When I looked back, the street guy was gone.

"Shit," I said. "We need to ditch the cargo."

Taking the next right, we wove around streets until we got blocked by signs declaring the road beyond had been closed. I nearly turned again but then had an idea. "Looks like there's three or four businesses down there that are shuttered up."

He twisted his head around, staring out the windshield. "The road is very crumbly. That warning sign looks old."

Made sense. They'd shut the street down and took so long to fix the street, the businesses along it had also shut down.

I checked the other three roads that led to that spot. They were clear. No one was around.

"Come on."

A minute later, I held open a gap in the rusted fence so Kane could slip through with a casket on each shoulder. Even the sidewalk looked smashed up.

The store nearest the corner had once been a boot- and shoe-repair shop. Kane smiled as we passed. "Nice smells in there."

"Yeah, leather has such a homey aroma."

"Like the scent of a day-old kill drying in the sun."

He and I had very different ideas about what "homey" smelled like.

The second building looked like it had been some sort of distillery. Big pipes stuck out of the walls where the massive stills used to sit. The only things that remained were square cement bases with dirty red rings, like rusty halos of the dead.

"In here." I waved him toward the third property. "Looks like it was a bakery or something."

Like the other two buildings, anything of value had been stripped out by the former owners. Part of me hoped they'd found another place to restart their shop. My feet crunched over busted wood panels and broken glass. On the clear parts of the floor, there was a newer-looking strip in the shape of the letter L.

"I think that's where some display case and counter might have been. You can see where the casters were." I bent down and rubbed my thumb across a divot. Then I looked up at a line of U-bolts that ran across the ceiling above where the counter had been. From two of them hung hooks, bent and rusty. "I dunno what that's about."

Kane sniffed the air and smiled. "Meat. There is a wonderful smell of raw meat here. I would have liked to have shopped at a raw meat store."

"Right. Butcher," I said and wiped my hands off on my pants. I pointed to the back wall. "Over there. That's perfect!"

I walked over to the door of a one-time walk-in cooler. It looked like the owners had taken the big "don't lock me in" handle with them.

"In there." I pointed ahead. "Hopefully they took all the old meat when they left."

Kane shrugged, which was impressive because he had massive coffins on each shoulder. After he stepped inside, I heard the double thunk of them hitting the floor. Then he came out much faster than he'd come in.

"What's wrong?"

Kane shivered. "I got spider web on me."

"You're fine."

"Is it still there?" He spun around, pointing at the back of his jacket. "Is web on me? If it is, please get it off."

I pushed the big metal door closed and piled some of the wood in front of it. I couldn't imagine coming back for the coffins, but if anyone found them it would set off all sorts of alarm bells.

Back in the car, we made our way around town, every now and then backtracking because our little detour had gotten us off the main drag. A few times, we came face-to-face with a big truck delivering food to what seemed like endless cafés and restaurants around town.

According to Google Maps, we'd made our last turn before we had to park and walk into the square. When I looked up, I could see the pink spires reaching for the heavens.

Years ago, when Granddad would pull out his photos of the region, I'd always imagined this area to be surrounded by dirt and sand.

Instead, it was a world of green.

Beautiful, majestic trees that looked like something from a fantasy movie about witches and wizards. Their lush leaves appeared to be priceless silk that some prince or princess would make finery out of.

Don't usually get to use the word finery. Pretty stoked I could wheel it out there, if I'm honest.

The sign ahead said no cars past that point, so I pulled over and parked on a side street. I wanted to do a quick recon of the church, fully aware that nighttime was aggressively elbowing out the day.

"I've been meaning to get my app to chart the moon phases on the new phone," I said. After my time with Tech Sergeant Gregor, his paranoia had rubbed off on me. I'd ditched my phone every few days for a new one. It had only taken a few seconds to find what I needed. "Cool. It even lets me set up an alarm."

Kane stepped out of the black Mercedes hearse and looked around. "This is the spot you recognized in the video?"

I shook my head. "The church is up the block. I'm thinking we go and do a three-sixty look around. Try to work out where that drone shot had come from."

The path to the pedestrian-only square transformed from blacktop to cobblestone. I thought it was kind of magical. Kane? Not so much.

"These colorful rocks are very troublesome," he said.

"I thought wolves would be used to walking across rocks."

"Rocks not so hard, no," he said, stumbling and grunting. "Walking on rocks with flipping flops, this is difficult."

"Pretend you're a tourist." I slapped his shoulder. "Go barefoot, little brother."

"This is okay?" Kane's eyes went wide, as though he was unsure if I was joking.

Hell, I didn't know. "Of *course* it is."

Kane dropped onto his butt, right in the middle of the walkway. When he stripped the shoes off, he sighed with relief.

He looked around and saw a woman sitting on her front stoop, watching him do this. Kane stood, wriggled his toes across the gritty stone, and smiled. He walked over and handed her the giant pair of flip-flops.

"I hope they serve you well," he said then glanced down. "However, these may be a little large for such tiny feet."

She shrugged, said something in Spanish so quickly that I didn't get a word of it, and disappeared inside.

Kane turned to me. "What did she say?"

Embarrassed, I shrugged.

A man walking by, pushing a wheelbarrow full of stuffed animals, said, "She says she will give them to her grandchild for the beach."

I wrinkled my nose. "Probably a bit big."

The man said, "For surfing."

Chapter Twenty-Four

The square in the expansive church courtyard was so clean it looked like if you dropped a wrapper, someone would burst out of a bush, snatch it up, and run back.

To our left, people milled around an enclosed garden encircled with forest-green park benches. Here you could sit and drink in the beauty of the magnificent cathedral. And, hopefully, spend a few dollars in countless places to buy food and drink nearby.

I dug into my pocket and pulled out my grandfather's photo and tried to position myself where the photographer had been. I got blocked by a tall metal fence that had cement poles every thirty feet to secure it. They rose up into points like the church's spires but gray, not pink.

For maybe the first time, I realized my grandfather was smiling in the photo. It changed his face so much, I barely recognized him.

"I don't think I ever saw my granddad smile," I said to Kane, who was craning his neck up to take in the massive cathedral. "How sad is that?"

"This is a very big church. Ma mère took me once as a boy to her church." He looked to the doors as they swung open. "I think her church would fit inside with very much room left."

Spinning in a slow circle, I tried to get an idea of where Covenant's drone shot might have come from. But from our vantage point on the ground, all I saw were manicured shrubs, the terracotta eaves of buildings, and sky.

Through the gate, I walked toward the open doors, tugging on my friend's arm. "Come on."

From the inside, the church didn't look as big as it did outside. A few rows of pews, like you would see in any church. Behind where the priest would stand, it looked like something out of a Rembrandt painting. Two massive tapestries hung on either side of the pulpit, which was illuminated by lights glittering off gold. Or brass. Hard to tell, and I wasn't really going to run up there and do a scraping.

The shiny metal was surrounded by foliage in a step pattern. At the top, beneath a massive chandelier, was Jesus on the cross.

Above that, I could see a railing washed in the burnt-orange glow of a dying afternoon. The sunlight streamed through a couple of huge, rounded windows. An image so enchanting, so breathtaking, I expected it to ring with soft, melodic music. "Let's go up top."

"This is okay to do?"

"Totally fine," I said, pulling at his jean jacket. He made an odd whimper noise when I unlatched the red velvet rope blocking access to the stairs.

He looked over his shoulder and whispered to me, "Does not say you are allowed to move red line."

"I'm more of an ask-forgiveness-instead-of-permission kinda person."

When I got to the top, I was winded. The stairs were steep, and by time I stomped the last few, I was making grunting sounds to get from one step to the next. The stairwell itself was skinny, so as we climbed, we had to double back four times.

I exhaled and rubbed my wrist across my forehead as Kane popped up next to me and looked down. "Is high up."

"Yeah," I said and gawked at him. "You're not even sweating. And you're wearing a damn jean jacket!"

"My body is a machine."

"Mine too," I said, walking toward the big balcony windows. "But it needs an overhaul."

We stood at one of the massive curved windows and looked down at the town. From here, we could see people going about their days. Workers, tourists, people who might be bringing their kids home from school.

Leading normal lives.

That thought both repulsed me and called to me in equal measure. Yeah, I wanted my day-to-day to *not* include monsters, super soldiers, and cartel-connected mob bosses. That would be great.

But hanging out and staring at the world? This was good.

To the left, we could see the grand square, lush grass that rolled all the way down to the main road like a shag carpet of green. It looked peaceful. The sort of spot where you might lie down and never want to get up again.

I went to the other window and heard halting whispers rise from below. From the pews, we could easily be seen. Out of the corner of my eye, I noticed an attendant staring up and shuffling back and forth.

At the second window, I found the spot.

"Out there," I said. "In the distance. You see that ridgeline? That looks like the highest point around here, and it looks down on the church."

Kane nodded. "Yes, the video was similar time of day with sun just at the top of the frame. Facing west. Sun is now behind us, so that would be the place we seek."

"Right? That's what I was saying." I hadn't even noticed the placement of the sun in the video because, come on, who does that?

I guess a dude who used to be a wolf does. The movement of the sun through the day likely affected what went on his pack's to-do list. Early in the day, go out hunting. When the sun gets low, maybe stick close to camp. Home. Whatever they called it.

Looking around the city and the tiny people below going about their day-to-day, I asked him, "Did you guys have a wolf house?"

"Den."

"Right. I knew that."

He got a faraway look in his eyes. "Necessary for the little ones. When wolves are first born, humans call this a litter, which is insulting. They think us trash."

"No, that's not... actually, I have no idea why it's called that. But, no, it's not an insult."

He grunted. "Babies do not understand predators. There is much yapping and demanding of food."

"Same."

He smiled at me. "Location to dig den is very important. Timing as well."

"Timing?"

"Um, making wolf babies timing," he said, finding something way off in the distance suddenly very interesting. "Always best they are born as other young animals are born."

"Yay! Friends!" I said with a big smile, knowing that wasn't the case. And because it would make him a little more uncomfortable.

"It is how we teach our babies to hunt. They cannot take on adults, so they eat the other children."

"Hmm," I said, shrugging. "Also same."

Behind us, a woman cleared her throat. I turned and smiled.

"Just wanted to take a look at the view," I said, sweeping my arm back. "It's stunning."

"You are American?" the woman asked, nodding as if this answered whatever her first question might have been.

"My grandfather used to live around here," I said and pulled out the photo, tapping on his image. That drew a small smile out of her. "He spoke very highly of this church."

Or, rather, he was pretty damn high when he talked about it. Old-school high from rotgut beer.

She smiled down at the photo then did a double take and extended her open hand. I gave her the photo.

"Whose wedding is this?" She stared intently at the photo, and her eyebrows bent down like arrows. "Your grandfather's?"

I laughed. "Not his. I have no idea. That's him over there on the left."

She pulled the photo closer, lifting a set of reading glasses from her pocket. Not bothering to unfold the arms, she held them up and stared through the lenses. The woman muttered something under her breath and tapped the picture. "Do you know who this person is?"

I looked down and saw a heavy man opposite my grandfather. He was beaming, hands raised in the air. Around him a small group of men cheered him on, as if it were his wedding and not that of the couple descending the stairs.

"I have no idea. Granddad wasn't one of those who writes names on the back of photos," I said. "And he never said. Or he might have said, but through the slurring, I just didn't understand."

I laughed. The woman didn't.

She pushed the photo back at me a bit aggressively, shaking it like it was about to burst into flames. I plucked it from her fingers and slipped it back into my pocket.

"You have seen the view," she said, waving to the window. "Now, it is time to go. This area is for only special occasions."

Her demeanor had switched from happy steward of the manor to angry security guard so fast, my mind started reeling. I pulled the picture back out and stared at it. "Who is that guy?"

The old woman stepped back, one arm in the air, the other waving us away from the window. "Go, please. Thank you."

Kane nodded to her. "We apologize for going where we should not. Alas, we are visitors here and do not wish to disturb this sacred tranquility. You honor the Creator with such a fine place of worship."

That renewed her smile. She looked down at his bare feet and returned the nod.

My friend walked in the direction she was waving, not looking back. I took one more glance at the photo and tucked it into my jeans.

What the hell was that about?

Chapter Twenty-Five

I was moving a bit slowly, plopping down each step like a kid who'd been sent to their room when all the adults got to stay up. Crabby about getting the boot, I was lost in thought about how weird the woman had gotten when she'd seen the photo.

The moon timer on my phone buzzed my hip.

"Okay, we gotta get our butts moving," I said to Kane, who was already halfway down the stairs. "It'll be dusk soon, and we still haven't found a place to stay."

My hand on the rail, I looked at my phone as I picked up my pace. According to the moon phase app, we were in the last day of the waning crescent. Watching my big friend take the steps below me, two at a time without effort, I tried to imagine what sort of doggy he might morph into if exposed to the smallest moon phase possible.

Hell, a few days ago he'd been a poodle. If he got nipped by moonlight tonight, I wondered if he would become one of those hairless pooches that looked like a breezy mouse fart would make them shiver.

I didn't want to find out.

When I got to the bottom, Kane was already heading out the door. To his right was the usher lady, politely waving us along.

So the old church had a modern elevator? Or she was a pedantic ghost who'd flitted down through the ceiling? When another couple came and asked her about the crying room, that idea was dashed.

As she spoke to them, I saw her glance up at me a few times.

Yeah, I'm going. I'm going, lady.

Back in the square, I knew the walk back to the car would be all of five minutes. We had a little bit of time before the moon came out.

"I saw three small hotels from the car to here," I said. "Probably should pick one and call it a night."

Kane was scanning the area, looking like he'd heard a sound I'd missed. "What is it?"

He grunted and started walking in the opposite direction from the car. I looked at my phone. As the countdown ticked down, my anxiety ticked up. "Where you going, man?"

He nodded ahead. "Simon the Muther Trucker said that there is a photo of the creature hanging up at the old café."

"Yeah, but there are ten cafés within a block of here," I said. "Maybe we scout around tomorrow. You know, when there's less chance of you growing floppy ears and a tail."

He kept walking.

Around the courtyard, lights began to flicker on, which were very pretty but also served as warning lights that it was starting to get dark.

Keeping up with a guy as big as he was meant I was half jogging behind him. I got a few odd looks from people, as if they were wondering whether we'd had some big breakup that I was taking poorly.

I turned away from a couple women repairing a filament on a dead lamp, grinning at me like idiots, and when I looked ahead, no Kane.

"Dude!"

He poked his head back around the corner. "This way."

When I made the turn, I saw his bare feet cross the threshold of a building with chipped blue paint and two tiny metal tables out front. An older couple sat at one, two guys and a girl at the other. Inside, six tables. Half of them were filled.

The interior walls appeared to serve as a history of the town. So much memorabilia, I couldn't even tell the color of the paint beneath them.

Yellowed newspaper articles had been framed. Old photos in collages that burst from the walls, all around and staggered like moon craters. One set in particular, on the far-right wall, showed the big pink church surrounded by scaffolding. Black-and-white photos of some old restoration project.

Kane stood at the counter, leaning forward to stare at the menu, which was written in chalk on a blackboard.

"How'd you know if this is the right one?" I asked and held my phone up. "Time's a-ticking, Wolfman."

A young woman popping her gum slid up off the far end of the counter, her eyes widening as she stared at my friend. She tucked a dark lock of hair behind her ear and waited for him to choose something.

What she didn't know was that Kane had no idea what was on the menu. The written language was something his animal brain could not process.

Still, he was looking intently, left to right. Searching.

"Hi," I said, and the girl blinked. She looked at me as if I'd materialized out of thin air. Her smile lost a few watts of its shine. "This might sounds like a weird question, but we're looking for—"

"Poutine," Kane said in a booming voice, grinning wildly. "A friend of ours said that you serve this."

The woman rubbed the side of her head with her nail, trying to work out the strange word he'd said.

"Is potato fries," he clarified. "Gravy and cheese."

"Oh, yes," she said with heavily accented English. "Disco fries."

Kane took a half step from the counter. He looked at me then back to her. Politely, he held up a finger to the girl and leaned down to whisper to me.

"What are those words?" He shifted his weight. "I have no time for dancing with this girl."

Laughing, I patted his big shoulder. "Different places call stuff different things."

"Okay," he said, straightened out, and turned to the girl. "I would like the Discus Flies, please."

The young woman shook her head, cocked it to the side, and then giggled. She *giggled*, for Chrissake. "You are funny."

As she walked away, I raised my hand up. "Um, yeah, just a coffee for me. Maybe a hot dog."

She leaned into a rectangular window leading to the cook station, speaking to an older guy with a paper hat. The rim around his temple was stained dark with either sweat or grease or both.

Exactly how a café should be.

Kane stepped to the left of the counter and up to the wall of photos there. He tapped his finger on a grainy screenshot printed out on an eight-by-ten sheet of paper. Held in place by a blue push pin, it looked out of place amid all the beautifully shot and framed historical pictures.

For one, it was a color photo. Or at least the best color rending the printer could pull off. And for two, while the others engendered a feeling of nostalgia, this one made my skin crawl.

As Simon the trucker had said, the image was a bit blurry. But that didn't lessen the dread it twisted into my chest, the acid it churned up in my stomach.

In the background, a campfire had been distorted by the camera's movement. The light from the fire made the sky look black. No stars. In the foreground was the fleshy palm of the creature. You couldn't make the contours out, but this was unlike any of the Enhanced we'd seen.

Two of the fingers sprouted tufts of dark hair. Like black scrub brush. The yellowed nails curled down to points, glimmering despite the fire *behind* the monster.

"They must have had the phone's light on during the video," I said, leaning in.

The face was hard to see because the two light sources had slammed the camera's iris half closed. But I could make out the glint of the eyes with its black pupils. In front of that was where things got weird.

"Is that, like, a snout?" I asked and looked up at my friend. His own amber eyes looked dark. Beneath the snout, the mouth hung open as if in the first moments of a roar.

Or howl.

"Long teeth," Kane said, his voice distant. "Larger in front, smaller in back. Those, like mine."

He looked up to the ceiling and let out a slow breath, muttering in French. I knew what he was thinking. This creature had been created from his blood.

But like the Enhanced we'd seen, it would have started as human. It didn't look like there was much left of that anymore.

"Ah, who knows," I said, shrugging and taking a step back. "You see shit like that on the Internet all the time. Hell, I could drum that up with AI in about thirty seconds."

"No, I assure you," a man said. "It is real."

The voice made me jump. I turned to see an old man standing there, rubbing his hands on his apron. This had been the guy I'd seen cooking. He must have seen us make a beeline for the photo.

"Come on," I said, throwing a thumb at it. "I thought chupacabra were, like, the size of goats or something."

Slowly the guy shook his head, staring hard at the photo. "My wife wanted to have this up in the restaurant. I despise it." He shrugged and told me his name was Eduardo. I introduced the two of us.

"If you hate it, why keep it up?" I asked.

"You must have missed the part where I said my wife wanted this up in the restaurant," Eduardo said with a half smile, showing off a row of nicotine-stained teeth. "This creature, it is out there. Do not stray into the desert at night."

That reminded me how low on time we were getting. I checked my phone. Twelve minutes.

"So it attacks at night?" I asked, suddenly wondering if the creatures were also affected by moonlight. I switched gears and kept things light. "So day trips are cool? We plan to do a little exploring."

Eduardo shook his head.

"Road workers, local men, went to get sand for the concrete. The best sand is several miles into the desert where it's cleaner. Less debris. They left around midday and did not return." His eyes went to the floor. "They used to come in here. Good men. They did not deserve this."

"I'm sorry about your friends."

"Customers," he said then bobbed his head. "But, yes, friends. Another tourist, he was taken at night. But the young boy and girl, this was also during the day. It is not safe at any time."

"What did the cops say?"

That got a dark laugh out of him. "Stories of monsters in the desert? They have little interest in our fairy tales."

Without a word, Kane crossed the room, scanning some of the other old photos.

I thanked Eduardo and told him I hoped his friends would return. He shrugged. I dug into my pocket, intending to grab my phone, when I felt the edges of the photo. I pulled it out and showed it to Eduardo.

"You might want to put this with your collection," I said. "It's from my granddad's old album. He won't be needing it anymore, and I've got no use for it."

Eduardo beamed as he took it. "The San Miguel! *Bueno*!" Holding the photo up, he traced his fingers around the front of the church. "When was this? Before the renovations?"

"It's old. That's all I know," I said, turning to join Kane. "It's all yours. I don't—"

The old cook grabbed my arm, and I saw his hand shaking as he held the photo. His lips pursed, and he looked like he wanted to spit on it.

"No," he said, shaking his head vigorously. "No, I do not want this photo. Not with that man."

"You knew my grandfather?"

He took a half step back. "Which is he?"

I pointed Granddad out, and Eduardo let out a breath. "No, not him. The fat man, here. I will not put any photo up of that man."

He'd referred to the smiling guy with his posse encircling him. It was the same man who had soured the woman at the church.

"Who is he?"

"No good, that man," Eduardo said, flicking the photo with his finger. "Old cartel boss before they were called such things. Gangs. Murderous gangs."

My mouth hung open. "What?" I flipped the photo back around to see it with new eyes. "No way. That big guy there?"

Eduardo said, throwing his hands up, "I hope he is in hell. That is what he brought to this world, and he deserves the same."

"He's dead?"

"Yes, Rafael Calva Zepeda died an old man, which says everything about justice around here. But his legacy," Eduardo said, his voice dripping with venom, "she is standing at the top of the stairs."

"The bride?"

Eduardo nodded. "This is husband one. I have heard she is now on husband three, but even now, she may be joining her father. Dying."

Wait. No way. No damn way.

"W-what's her name?"

"*Diablo*," Eduardo said then made a spitting sound and crossed himself. "That is what her name should be. This is the name she earned. Her parents christened her in that church, if you can believe such a thing. Rosa took that groom's name. When he died, she kept it."

"Rosa Nieto."

He nodded, his eyes fierce.

Oh shit.

Oh shit, oh shit.

My phone buzzed. Five-minute warning.

I peeled away from Eduardo and raced across the restaurant, grabbing Kane's arm. "We gotta go."

"Look."

"No, no," I said tugging. "We gotta find a place. No time to get back to the car, and we hafta—"

Kane slapped the wall next to an aerial shot of the town. Two of the tables next to us jumped at the noise. I glanced across the street and saw a sign out front.

Hotel.

A dash across the street, and we would be fine. I had a minute. Just the one.

The framed poster by Kane's hand showed the town in black and white. The date in writing from some kind of black pen on the original photo read 17 December, 1962. Next to that was a nearly identical shot showing how the town had grown around the old church.

The bottom left of both showed a big mountain ridge. One peak had collapsed. Maybe an old eruption? It looked like some angry god had reached down and punched the summit, caving it in.

The effect of this left a raised ridge all around, a small clearing below. Blocked from view on all sides.

I stepped back, waving Kane toward the door, a big smile on my face.

"That's it!" I said. "First thing in the morning, we're going up a mountain."

Chapter Twenty-Six

We bolted out of the café. Kane started running back toward where we'd parked the hearse, and I had to leap to grab his fluttering jacket.

"Nope," I said, tugging and dashing across the street. Well, not so much dashing as not going anywhere. Dude was a rock. "No time."

I'd spotted one hotel, and that was where we were going. I didn't even see a name—just a circular sign that with a slumbering stick figure. A universal depiction immune to language barriers.

As I dragged him inside, Kane pointed up at the sign. "This place offers lodging to very skinny people who float above beds. I do not trust such furniture."

I ignored him, which increasingly had become the best response to his weirdness.

Check-in was quick. In a tourist town battling neighbors for dollars, you don't mess around. Sixty seconds after the desk clerk swiped Kane's card, I had two key cards to our room.

My phone buzzed. We'd just made it.

Thanking the lovely woman at the reception desk, I rounded the corner to take the stairs one flight up. Found the room and pressed the white card to the black panel.

The door clicked open... and that was when I realized my mistake.

"I forgot to ask for two singles." I swallowed. "That's a big damn bed, but it'll probably just fit you."

Kane checked the bathroom, the tiny closet, then the sleeping area. I had no idea what he was looking for.

"Is fine," he said and grabbed two pillows, throwing them to the orange carpet. "I will sleep on floor."

"Man, you don't have to do that. Just keep your paws to yourself," I said and scrunched up my face at him so he knew I was teasing. I pulled my backpack off and chucked it where the pillows had been.

Dude left me with one. Wolves are pillow hogs.

I dug around in my pack and felt good about having my slingdart nearby. I only had three darts, so we would have to find someplace that carried stuff like that. At the very bottom was the second most precious possession I owned.

With that thought, I thumbed my grandmother's locket nestled under my shirt. That reminded me of something, and I unzipped one of the many pouches on the bag. I held up the tarnished piece of jewelry.

"We gotta get you a proper chain for this," I said, holding up his locket.

He turned and smiled, taking it from me. "And a very tiny picture, yes."

"Right."

Handing it back, he said, "I do not understand why it is so warm."

"It's been in my hot pack all day." I dropped the locket back in the pouch, zipping it up. "We'll find a trinket shop and get you a chain before we leave."

Kane put on a tiny smile that didn't reach his eyes. Neither of us said what we were both likely thinking.

I dug through my bundle of clothes in the main compartment. My fingers traced the edges of the box.

When the monsters were gone, we would use the serum. He would be a wolf again. He could go back home and back to his partner, his wolf wife. That thought filled me with joy and despair at the same time.

I'd never had a friend like Kane. Well, *no one* had ever had a friend like Kane.

And I would miss that friendship.

Pulling out a shirt for me to sleep in, I saw Kane chuck his jean jacket onto the single chair at the tiny round writing desk.

I looked down to the floor. "You want a blanket or something? Doesn't look comfortable."

He chuckled. "Before last year, I have slept on ground my entire life. So this I prefer."

When he stripped off his belt, I held up a hand.

"You don't sleep naked, do you?" I couldn't recall if he did. Anytime we'd shared a room, we'd always had two beds, and I'd been out before him.

Back at Miss Florida's farm, he'd slept in his clothes, but that was because I'd put him there that way.

He'd been too beat to hell to notice.

"People are troubled by nakedness. So strange," he said, tossing the belt onto the chair. "But, to be respectful, I will not sleep naked."

Then he dropped trou right in front of me.

Here was a fun fact about wolves. Apparently, underwear was not a thing. Probably not a surprise.

I spun around, feeling my cheeks redden, and held up a hand. "Was that supposed to be funny? Um, that's very naked."

"Not true," he said. "I am still wearing T-shirt."

Chapter Twenty-Seven

The next morning, we got up later than I'd hoped. But after driving across an entire country then halfway across another, I'd needed the sleep.

We grabbed some breakfast at a tiny open-air restaurant and made our plans for the day.

"No way we can take that beast of a car up the side of a mountain," I said, shoveling eggs into my mouth. "There'll be a place that has rentals. Let's go see what they've got."

"What do we do with Mercedes death car?" he asked, getting a bit of a look from the two women eating at the next table over.

"Yeah, we can't leave it there," I said. "The hotel reception lady gave me a chit that I can take to a garage up the road. Before we head up the mountain, we'll park it in there."

Kane nodded, chewing his breakfast steak. I'd made it very clear that we wanted it as rare as possible. That had gotten me an odd look until I explained that my big friend was on the BC Caveman Diet.

BC as in British Columbia, where he was born, but I didn't bother explaining. The BC kinda worked on its own.

Kane got a chunk of meat so raw, when he stuck it with a fork, I think it might have mooed.

I'd caught him sneaking glances at my backpack. I knew what was on his mind.

"The serum is totally safe," I said. "I got it wrapped up like a wineglass. It won't shatter, and I won't lose it."

Kane grunted and chewed his food. "It is how I return to my family."

"You don't think I know that?" I asked, wiping my hand with a napkin. "The moment we get rid of... our new friends, I'll jab you in the neck with it myself."

That got a smile out of him. Then it faded.

"You make it sound simple," he said and looked up at me for the first time in a long while. "It will not be. They are better and stronger than before. Perfect killers."

I shrugged. "Maybe."

"Of course they are," he said and stabbed his last piece of bloodied meat. "They are made from me."

After breakfast, we walked to the alleyway on the far side of the square. When we got back to where I'd parked the car, there was a Mercedes-size hole where it had been.

"Well, shit," I said, adjusting the backpack. It was ass-crack hot, and sweat was pooling where it touched my shoulder blades. "I guess they do tow in this town."

Kane walked around the car that had taken our place. It looked like an old Ford that had been built before my mom had been born. He peeked around the hood, as if our car might have somehow been hidden there. "Can we get it back?"

"Scan around for a sign," I said, glancing at the brick wall to my right. "There'll be a number for the tow company. It won't be cheap."

A craggy voice called down from above, "Car gone."

I looked up to see a man who was likely the same age as the car that was now sitting in the spot where we'd originally parked the hearse.

Fair enough, I guess. We'd taken his spot.

I used my hand to shield my eyes from the sun and squinted up at him. "Can you give me the number of the tow company so we can get it back?"

He shrugged and looked off into the distance.

I tried again. And added, "Please?"

"No tow."

I glanced over at Kane, who was bending down and looking at the ground. Did he think our car was *underneath* the old Ford?

"Right," I said, embarrassed that his broken English was the only way we could communicate. "Is that the name of the company that hauled our car away?"

"No tow," he said, waving his bony hand toward the space. "Take."

Ah shit. "Stolen?"

"Three people take. I hear them," the man said, searching for the words. "No see me," the man added and pulled a thin brown curtain in front of his face.

"Right," I said and turned toward Kane. "It got stolen."

Kane stood, dusting his hands off. "No broken glass."

"Maybe I didn't lock it."

"You did lock," Kane said, walking up next to me. Ah, good. Shade. "I heard the bird sound when you clicked the key fob. You always click too many times so it goes cheep-cheep-cheep. Cheep-cheep. Cheep-cheep-ch—"

"Got it." I sighed. "Well, we can't really go to the police. I mean, we kinda stole it first."

"This is a good point."

I called up to the man. "Did you happen to see who took it? Kids? How they were dressed?"

"No kids. Three people."

Right. He'd said that. "Any idea what they look like?"

The old man stared at me for a long, long moment. Then, he said, "No," and quickly slipped back inside. Before I could call up, he drew the curtain.

"He says no."

Kane grunted. "His lips say no, but his body says yes."

Shooting him a look, I said, "You gotta watch who you say that to, I think."

He ignored the comment. Hmm. I guess that went both ways.

"His face, expression," Kane said. "Arms pulling in as if to protect chest."

"He's old. Old people do that just to breathe."

Kane stepped out of the alley, looked up to the dark window, then to me. "He saw who it was. But is worried about danger for saying. Worried about saying who it might be."

It didn't matter. "Fine, fine. He doesn't want to get in trouble with the local crooks," I said, waving him after me. "Let's go find that rental. Maybe they've got jeeps."

Chapter Twenty-Eight

"You've got to be joking," I said to the skinny kid behind the fold-out camping table. "You don't have, like, a sedan or truck or anything?"

This rental shop, a sidewalk stand with a tin roof nailed to wood poles, had been the third we'd checked. All had the same answer—no one rented cars.

"Might have to go to the airport if you really want a car," the young man said in a west coast accent. West coast, United States. "But that's at least a two-hour drive from here."

"Great," I said.

"Maybe three."

"Wonderful."

"But you'd need a car to get there, so you are in a pickle, I think," he said and pointed to the multicolored machines in the racks next to his shack. "You can't take those out on the open highway. I mean you *can,* but you'd probably end up under a truck."

Kane ducked under the roof and stepped forward. "I prefer not to go under truck."

I held a hand up to him and looked back at the kid.

"Fine. Fine," I said, frowning at the scooters. "You got one in purple?"

I had to sign an insurance form but knew, if we damaged it, some eighties actress named Heather Thomas would get the bill.

Kane handed over his bank card for the very pricey deposit as I went into the market next door. I had to grab a few more things for our trek up the mountain.

Twenty minutes later, he shouted something over my shoulder. I half turned my head, not wanting to take my eyes off the road. Mainly because we'd left any real *road* behind nineteen minutes earlier.

"What?" I called back.

"This is n-n-n-not comfortable," he growled. Then he made a yipping sound when I hit a rock and we bounced. The scooter bottomed out for a moment, leaving a gouge in the dirt behind us.

Kane groaned. "That was the most not comfortable of all the uncomfortable so far."

"Sorry."

Back at the Scooter Shack, when the guy had seen us get on the moped, he'd balked, started to speak, then stopped. I knew he wanted to say, *"Put the guy twice your size at the front,"* but his California sensibilities forbade him from suggesting the man should drive.

Sure, I didn't have remotely the intuition that Kane had about what was going on in someone's head but took a devilish delight in the moral battle playing across the kid's face.

He'd handed us our helmets and, over the plaintive whine of the bike, said, "Be careful. That one's got a bit more pep than these others because your friend is..."

I helped him out. "Big?"

"Dude's a redwood."

An apt description. Anytime I leaned to turn, it felt like the big guy on the seat behind me was going to topple.

The four jugs of water I'd hung across the gas tank served as a type of ballast and helped keep us steadier. Because it was hot out in the open sun, the woman at the gas station had suggested we take the extra water with us.

More of a warning than a suggestion.

"Agua," she'd said, pointing toward the mountain. *"No agua... es muert*e.*"*

Got it. Don't wanna die, bring water.

I'd stopped by the gas station because the kid at the scooter rental said we would only get about seventy-five miles out of its tank. We would be heading up a crazy steep hill. That would burn through a bunch of extra fuel, so as a precaution, I bought a red can and filled that with gas.

The scooter had a cute basket on the back because usually tourists took the little motorbike out for picnics. Or maybe for a stop at some local gardens.

I'd put our big gas can in there.

And it was this basket that Kane held, arms behind his back, to keep steady.

At first, he'd gripped my backpack, but when we'd gone down into a divot and back up again, he'd damn near thrown me off the seat. After that, he rode the scooter bent forward, arms back, like an Olympic skier taking the biggest jump of their career.

The punishing sun was making my head swim. We'd pulled over twice to sit under the shade of a lonely tree to get out of the heat. We drank water, ate gas-station sandwiches, and talked about nothing important. During those brief respites, it felt like a mini holiday.

At the pace we were going, we would be near the lip of the mountaintop valley within a half hour. It had taken most of the afternoon to get that far. The scooter was slow, and with all our weight, I think it slid along rather than rolled most of the time.

When we were about a mile away, thankfully, the sun had crossed the sky far enough to where it wasn't sizzling us from above. Nighttime was closing in, but I had prepared for that this time.

I slowed the bike and wobbled it off the trail.

For one, I couldn't roll up with the scooter to where we needed to go— the damn thing was far too loud. I wasn't sure how well the sound would come up over the ridge, but I wasn't taking any chances.

Also, a wire fence had cut right across the trail. Chicken wire across the top. The barrier was sturdy and as tall as me.

It had a sign. Kane stood in front of it, arms crossed. When I came up beside him, I saw he was moving his lips.

"It's in Spanish," I said, and he lightened.

"Oh. I will need to learn Spanish."

"You don't have to," I said. He'd learned French and English pretty damn fast. If he put his mind to it, he would probably know my family's language better than me in a week. But reading? Nope. That still vexed him.

"It says Beware. Do not Enter. And something about military." I pointed at the words on the bottom. "Entry will be fatal."

"Okay," he said and sighed. "We should go back then."

"What?" I spun at him. "Are you—"

Then I caught the look on his face. He was terrible at hiding his smile. And to be honest, I was glad he was. Dude had a great smile.

"Pretty funny, yes?"

I shook my head. "Not really." I dropped my backpack next to the scooter, which I'd leaned against the only tree I could see for a mile. I stared at the fence, looking left and right. The barrier seemed to encircle the entire mountain top.

"We gotta work out how to get over that," I said, flapping my shirt to cool down. Reaching for one of the water bottles, I uncapped it and downed a few big gulps before I heard a thump.

Kane was on the other side of the fence.

"How the hell did you do that?" I asked.

Pleased with himself, Kane scanned the surroundings, walking about twenty feet to my right along the fence line.

"Dude! Is there a door?"

Not answering, he passed a couple yards to my left. He crossed his arms. "I do not see gate. But we saw vehicles in the video, yes?"

I blinked. "Uh, I dunno. I just saw the three curved buildings and monsters being wheeled around on gurneys by people in lab coats."

"Two vehicles out front," he said and closed his eyes. "White and green. Pill-shaped cars but big."

"Yeah, yeah. Vans probably. How the hell did you get over there?"

"I jumped."

"Over the fence?" I asked, and Kane cocked his head, still looking at the barrier. "Great. How the hell am I supposed to get over there?"

"Jump."

"Jump? How the hell am I supposed to jump that?"

He shrugged. "Jump high."

I frowned at him. He knew there was no way I could clear the fence. Not even with a boost.

"Very high, actually," he continued. "There is sharp wire at the top. Very slicey."

Before I could tell him where *he* could jump, he took two steps forward, bent down and launched himself over the fence. He cleared it easily and landed five feet in front of me with a thud. Then he spun around. "You could climb on back, and I will—"

"Uh, no. I'd lose my grip and get all"—I waved my hand toward the fence—"slicey."

Kane looked at the sky, tracing his hand up in a curve, and pointed toward the sun, which was now kissing the top of the mountain ridge above us.

"Sun will go down soon," he said, his eyes flitting left and right. "Night is coming."

"I got that covered. But first, I need to find a way past the fence."

I scanned the area but only saw a smile bend his bearded face.

"Ma mère, she would make *holopchi* in the winter," he said, walking over to the moped. "Is very good. You have had?"

Jesus, he could be so frustrating. I shook my hands out in the air. "No, I have no idea what that is."

"It is cabbage roll. My human mother called this 'broke food.' This means—"

"I know all about poor people food, man. I been there my whole life."

He turned his head to me. "No, not 'poor.' Poor is a way of living. A place where your head is and hard to escape this thought." Kane shifted the scooter out of the way, and for a moment, I thought he was going to set up a ramp so I could Evel Knievel over it.

Dunno where he might get a ramp from. Hell, he could be a ramp.

"Broke, ma mère would tell me, this is different," he said and laid the bike down. Then he moved my backpack over and placed it next to the bike. "You can still be wealthy in your heart if not in your wallet. This is 'broke.' Temporary state that you can change."

I huffed. "Doesn't always work that way. Sometimes life deals you your hand, and it's shit."

Kane leaned down and put both hands on the tree, shoulder length apart. "Then get new cards."

"I would," I said, hooding my eyes. "I'm just too broke to buy any."

He laughed then drew in a deep breath and grunted, flexing his arms. His legs spread, farther and farther apart, toes pressing into the ground. His face flushed, teeth brilliant white against pink skin.

"Ha, come on, man," I said. "You can't—"

Oh, but he could.

It sounded like a ponytail was being ripped from the back of someone's head as the tree shifted and the roots began to rise out of the ground. Kane grunted and twisted then grunted again, and the whole tree came out.

He lifted the twenty-five-foot tree like he was coming out of the batter's box. Balancing it on his shoulder, he swung toward me.

"Woah, shit," I said and ducked as the roots skittered across my back, peppering me with dirt and sand.

"My apologies."

Standing back up, I stared at him as he moved the tree backward, putting himself in the center of it so that it balanced on his shoulder.

"What the hell is that for?"

Staggering his legs, he swung it toward me. "Like the *holopchi*. When we serve, must use a ladle to put cabbage roll on plate." He slapped the log on his shoulder. "This is ladle."

"Wait." I frowned at him. "Am I the cabbage roll in this analogy?"

He furrowed his brow. "No, no. Is not like that."

"Right. You want me to sit on the end of it so you can ladle me over the fence and to the other side. That about right?"

Kane grinned weakly. He cleared his throat.

"Okay," he said. "It is exactly like that."

Chapter Twenty-Nine

It took us twenty minutes to walk to the top of the ridge. It probably should have taken half that, but I'd had to stop every other minute to pull slivers out of my thighs.

"Ow," I whispered and crouched down next to Kane. I found yet another tiny stick embedded in my skin, plucked it out, and flicked it at him. "No more ladling."

We kept our heads low as he swept his big sausage finger in front of us. "Three curved buildings. This is where they keep the monsters we saw."

"How they hell did they get those buildings up here?"

Kane pointed to our left, where a winding dirt road cut through some trees, heading to the other side of the rise. I nodded and motioned to the two vehicles, which were just like he'd said, vans with green-and-white stripes.

"Good memory," I said. "Those look like transports."

"For the abominations they create in those curved buildings." He grunted. "Why are there trees up here but not down side of mountain?"

He was right. A tiny, lush forest surrounded the hangars. A lot of saplings and more mature trees populated it but nothing as massive as a redwood.

"It's pretty good cover, but I can't imagine Covenant transported them up here," I said. "It looks like the mountaintop blew off eons ago, and they grew sometime after that."

Kane tapped the side of his head. "You are very smart."

"Duh," I said and rolled my eyes. "But, I mean, why do *you* think I'm very smart? Just to see if we're on the same page here."

"Volcanic soil. Very rich and fertile for trees," he said, nodding. "This I learned from a documentary show with an old, pasty English man who loves animals very much."

I chuckled. "Which is why you liked him, yeah?"

"Of course. We like those who favor us."

"Not always. You've never been in a dive bar at three a.m," I said. "Too much favoring."

I twisted away from the ridge to pull out another splinter and caught a glimpse of the sky. I saw the first hint of a star winking out from the heavens.

"Oh shit," I said and sat up quickly, handing him the bundle I'd taken from my backpack. "Here, put this stuff on."

"What is this?"

"I got it from that street market. It's covering, man," I said and shoved the clothes at him. "Get, you know, covered."

Kane already had jeans and a jean jacket on, but I wasn't taking any chances. Grumbling, he slipped on the black sweatpants and turtleneck. I'd gotten the biggest size I could find, and it still looked like he was going to burst out of the stuff.

"Is scratchy."

"You're gonna be scratchy if there's any hint of a moon tonight," I said and pulled out my phone. "That said, I think you might be in the clear. No moon."

His eyes got big. "No moon? Where would it go?"

As he slipped on the black ski mask and gloves, I pointed my phone screen at him, which showed a shaded-out circle. At the bottom of the screen, it had the date with the words New Moon.

He started to speak, made a spitting sound, then tried again. "Pfft. No mouth hole." He poked his tongue at the fabric.

"No, you need to be totally covered. Just in case. So yeah, no mouth hole."

Kane tilted his head, which looked like the top of a big burnt match. "Or is it *new* mouth hole?" He started chuckling. Nobody found Kane funnier than Kane.

After he slid on the cheap sunglasses, I leaned back to get a good look at him. Kane was covered in black, head to toe. *Except* for the toe part.

"Where are your damn shoes?"

"Hmm," he said with a shrug and looked at his bare feet. "New shoes."

"Stop that!"

I spun around and looked to where we'd left the scooter and backpack. Too far. I sighed, stripped off my shoes, and gave him what I'd been wearing.

He stared down at the pink knee highs and looked at me. Even with his face covered, I could sense the horror in his eyes.

"I cannot."

"You have to!" I said then lowered my voice. "They're sheer, so when it's hot they keep you cool."

"I will not look cool."

Holding them in my fist, I shook them in front of his face. Impressively, he scooted back using only his muscular buttocks, backing away from the floppy pink tubes. I threw them in his lap.

"Put 'em on, barefoot boy," I said. "I thought you weren't all hung up on stuff like pink for girls and blue for boys."

Sighing, he looked up to the ever-darkening sky. He grabbed the pink supersocks and began slipping them on.

"Is not concern over gender. That is a human thing. Wolf does not know pink," he said, tugging the second sock up and under his pants leg. "Food and fight, these are in shadow."

"What does that mean?"

"As wolf, easy to distinguish gray, black. See in the shadows within shadows after we have smelled prey or predator." He twiddled his toes and shrugged. "Blue, this I know. Yellow, yes. But red, green... These I recall as only variations of those other colors."

"And yet I know for a fact you love purple," I said, smiling. "Purple cars. Purple candy. You're a big purple-lovin' guy."

He slid back onto his knees, looking over the ridge again. "As human, yes, I can see purple. Ma mère was a fan."

"Of purple?"

"Of Prince."

I took one last glance at his feet, stifled a giggle, and slid up next to him.

The metallic clank of lights startled me, and I shrank back. Two of the hangars lit up from within. Light arrays flickering to life up near the ceiling. The third building was still dark.

Kane had his face down, shaking his head. I asked him what was wrong.

"That sound of light coming on," he said, distantly. "I do not like it. Bad memories."

From the dark building, two people in lab coats wheeled out a creature on a metal cart. We'd seen similar scenes in the few seconds of video back at the Covenant HQ. Except this one didn't have any IV bags. Not even restraints.

It didn't take long to work out what was going on.

"I think that one is dead," I said. "Maybe the treatment is too much for some of the, um, candidates. Kills them."

Kane glanced over then squinted toward another building. He said nothing.

"That would be a good thing, yeah?" I said. "Hell, maybe the new concoction is killing some."

"No," he said, inching forward then sweeping his hand toward where the dead creature lay on the gurney. "That one has slashes across its belly. Across its throat."

"Why would they—" I looked back to see if I could pick up what he had, but the light was too dim. "Wait. You think one attacked another?"

"Hmm." Kane looked over the edge. The very steep drop led down to the flat clearing. "That does seem possible."

The sky lit up, and we ducked. When we peeked over the ridge again, both of us stared. The creature on the gurney had been *fried*. All the way up here, we could hear the crackling of its skin as it smoldered.

One of the techs had burnt the dead creature. With a flamethrower.

"Holy hell," I whispered as the tech hung the tank and nozzle back up on a rack next to the hangar. "That was intense."

The guy in the lab coat parked the still-burning corpse at the far end of the walkway. He then stepped into building two, and a moment later, a pair of creatures were wheeled out on gurneys. Each had a tech hovering over them. These monsters were cuffed to their beds. Straps across their chests and legs.

Their electronic collars flickered, cycling through a series of lights. Blue, red, green.

"Doc Hammer controlled them through those collars with her tablet," I said to Kane as he leaned over the rock ledge. "Those guys likely have tablets like she had. That must be how they keep them in line."

Kane pointed toward the remains of the one on the metal cart. The smoldering husk lay there alone in the dark.

"One of them killed that one," he said, his voice distant.

"Explains why the ones still alive are strapped down like BDSM night at the Tickle Club."

Kane swung his head toward me. "Your human experience has been very different from mine."

I bopped him on the shoulder and was reminded of something I'd been meaning to ask. "Speaking of which, when did you get so damn strong?"

"Always have been strong. Powerful."

"Enough to jump over fences? Pull trees out of the ground or lift two-ton cars on their sides?" I shook my head. "Unless you've been a bit demure about your capabilities—not a thing with you—you're getting stronger."

"Maybe."

I snapped my fingers, which made him twitch.

"Sorry," I said. "Or maybe after Marata jammed you with the go juice, it amped you up."

"Maybe."

"I mean, that's a good thing, right? Free upgrade."

Kane positioned himself into a crouch and looked down at the insanely steep drop then back at the techs. "Nothing you get for free. Always a cost."

"What the hell does that—"

He leaped over the ridge and landed twenty feet below without a sound. I watched him creep toward the hangars then get totally swallowed by shadow. Except for the bright-pink socks, of course.

"Screw this," I muttered and scooted over to the tree closest to my side of the ridge. I'd done plenty of climbing in my house-thieving days.

Same thing, I thought, trying to convince myself.

Leaping over the edge, I stretched both hands out, reaching for the closest branch. I caught it and swayed in the air.

Holy shit!

The branch began to bend under my weight. I looked down, holding my breath so I wouldn't scream. Hand over hand, I moved toward the trunk and exhaled a shaky breath.

As quietly as I could, I dropped from branch to branch to branch until my feet hit the rock and grass of the mountaintop.

Twenty seconds later, gulping quiet breaths, I sidled up next to the man in black.

I punched him in the back, which hurt my hand a little. "Wanna tell me before you make a move like that?"

He looked back at where we'd been. "Maybe you should stay."

"No way, Wolfman," I said. "Pack of two, remember?"

Kane tilted his burnt-match head then nodded. Pulling away from the side of the van, where he'd been watching the techs, he sat back on his heels.

His *pink* heels.

"One more living creature is in that third building," he said. "There are three of the NextGen here."

"*NextGen?*"

"I could hear the two men with the creatures talking, so this how learned of the third one. And that they call these ones NextGen."

"Right," I said. "Okay, they're strapped down and may be sedated. Easy pickings for you."

He shrugged. "Still conscious, it seems. They will be very strong. Possibly too strong."

Maybe he was worried that I was there, in danger, but I'd heard something in Kane's voice I never had before.

Fear.

"This is our chance." I put a hand on the black fabric of his shoulder and squeezed. "Destroying these three means we have three less to deal with later."

"Exactly," he said and spun toward the edge of the vehicle. "You stay here."

Then he ran.

Chapter Thirty

Kane

Once again, I am on the hunt.

The strength within me, this is my power.

Keen intellect feeds my strength.

Yes, an intellect, in part, born from watching endless eighties and nineties television with ma mère on a comfy sofa in British Columbia.

Thus, my power is *The Dukes of Hazzard!*

My power is *The A-Team!*

It is also *Murder, She Wrote,* with demure-yet-alluring Jessica Fletcher, unraveling all the murders. Although I have always suspected she may be a serial killer.

Every dinner party she attends, someone dies.

You would have thought people would stop inviting her to dinner parties.

So clever, she!

With my muscular human legs, I crouch low and launch myself forward. I race to the cover of several tall skinny sheds, just to the right of the three hangars. When there, I stand erect, flattening my body against one of the strange tiny buildings.

Hmm.

Odd odor. Unpleasant. I peer up and see on the door someone has drawn a crescent moon in sharpie pen. A childlike drawing. No flair.

The drawing reminds me of the enchantress above, but when I look, I see nothing of her. Tonight, she does not dance among the stars. New moon is no moon.

Tonight, I am free of her curse.

Inside the nearest hangar, I hear a struggle between two people. One is a man, grunting. Much grunting and some cursing. The other sounds garbled, not quite—

"T-5," the man shouts, and I peer around the corner of the stinky little shed. It is one of the people in the lab coats. A tech, Emelda has called them. "This one is... She's still conscious!"

A dimmer voice calls out, "You use all of it?"

"Yes, goddamn it," Grunty Tech says. "And she's fighting me." His voice redirects, and he shouts, "Stop it!"

He gets two responses.

The first is from the man called T-5. This man calls from the other side of the shed. I cannot see him, but I believe he may be one of the two pushing the metal beds with NextGen creatures upon them.

T-5 says, "Jesus, man, it's strapped down. Get it sorted, mate!"

"She's struggling and squirming," Grunty Tech calls back. "I got half the damn dose squirted across the bindings."

The man called T-5 laughs and chatters to the tech nearest him. He says, "I got another dose. We gotta go. Come grab it."

I can see the silhouette of Grunty Tech cast upon the thin walls of this third hangar. He is snapping his arms away from a prone figure. He strikes down with a fist. As he turns to walk toward the two other techs, the shadow on the bed flexes upward like a spider caught in its own web.

This is when I hear the other response. It is a voice, desperate and pleading. Not quite human.

"No."

Mistaking this answer from Grunty Tech, T-5 replies, "Stop screwing around. Come grab this, or we're leaving you behind!"

The shadow tech backs away from the bed and stumbles. Recovering, he runs, and I see him appear in the gap between the two buildings. His hand is over his mouth, eyes wide behind wire glasses.

Even from a distance, I can read his face. The woman's utterance has shocked him.

This is my chance. I look left. Then I look right. Then I look behind because it feels like I should do this too.

Perplexing is such paranoid desire! Like some unnecessary ritual. I know in my wolf heart that this stain upon my psyche has come from being that wretched poodle.

I push the thought aside, my need to focus paramount. I race forward for the entryway closest to the stinky sheds. A flimsy orange construction fence cannot stop me, I leap it, silent and stealthy. Bursting inside the hangar, I hear the two men fumbling with glass and plastic outside.

This is my chance!

I race to the hospital bed, my fist high above my head, ready to strike.

However, I pause. Frozen.

The monster's features are so familiar. Its short muzzle has a bar between the back teeth, pinning it to the metal bed. Tufts of hair run up its sides, as it is forced to pull back its lips in a permanent snarl.

The NextGen woman—and it is a woman, for I can still see some human left in this creature—pricks up the wiry folds of her ears upon my approach. Alas, this is not a human quality.

Her ears rise higher on her head than they should for a person. Not curved, they are pointed. She turns to me and regards me with the black eyes of an Enhanced.

And yes, the man called Steve Janus was right. She is more than Enhanced. Much more. She is also part of me.

No, I cannot think this.

Through the thin material of the hangar walls, I can see the Grunty Tech is turning. I am out of time.

I look up to my fist, high above my head, but it will not move. My arm shakes. My vision blurs. How can I kill something born of my—

"P-por..." the creature says, its long tongue struggling with the rubber bar holding its mouth open. Its short snout twitches. The skin there wrinkles in undulating pink folds. "*Por favor.*"

She is pleading with me.

My body is frozen, but the creature is not. Her eyes flick toward a scalpel on a tray next to her head. A tear slips down the smooth, human-like skin of her cheek. It disappears into tufts of wiry black hair.

In my head, I hear the voice, imploring me, begging me. *Do it, Father. Please!*

"Y-yes," she says, forcing her head to bob. Nodding an affirmation despite the restraints. She locks those black eyes upon me and repeats, "Yes."

I grit my teeth, fighting back a sob. *She pleads for death.* Then in a crystal-clear, feminine voice, she begs me. "Please."

When I look to my hand, I am holding the scalpel. It is cold to the touch. So very cold. I do not remember picking it up.

My brain screams, instinct admonishing me for my unholy betrayal, and I slash with the blade, releasing the woman from her hell. Crimson erupts from the yawning gap in her throat. When her lifeblood sprays across me, it is a familiar scent.

It is my scent.

No, not mine. This is what they stole from me. The metallic taste of it is tainted. Distorted. Distorted to create this poor abomination before me.

Blood bubbles from the gash in her neck, and she looks to me, like a child, but her eyes are softer now.

Tenderly, I put my hand to the side of her face and feel the slick dampness of many tears. Shaking my head, I whisper, "I am sorry."

The light within her black eyes goes dark.

"Hey!" a voice shouts from the door. "Who the hell are you?"

Chapter Thirty-One

Shit!

I'd watched Kane race up next to a line of porta potties, trying to peek inside the hangar. I'd been a second away from chasing after him when one of the hospital gurneys bounced forward, pushed over uneven concrete pavers by the two techs.

That had put me in their line of sight. I was trapped behind the van.

When the tech inside the hangar came out, Kane had run in.

Through the translucent material of the wall, he'd been just shadow. I saw him raise his fist above one of the creatures. Then he froze!

"Do it," I muttered to myself. "Kane, do it!"

He stood there, frozen. My heart stopped beating. I was grinding my teeth so hard my jaw felt like it was going to crack.

Clasping my shaking hands together, I whispered, "Please."

When he struck the creature, it buckled briefly then stopped. I could only watch as his silhouette, strangely, reached down toward it in a slow, tender way.

That was when the tech returned, brandishing a new syringe, and spotted him. "Who the hell are you?"

Oh shit, oh shit!

Pandemonium. The tech called out, screaming, actually *screaming*, "Guard! Guard!"

Guard?

Inside the van I was hiding behind, I heard a fumbling, and then the door flew open. Jesus, there was a guy right inside the van! How did he not see Kane run across?

When I heard a clatter, I crouched down to look under the van. I saw a phone face down in the gravel. The guard had been on his phone. Playing Candy Crush or swiping through the local Tinder prospects.

From beneath the undercarriage, I saw the bottoms of the guard's shoes as he ran toward the two techs who'd put their gurneys between themselves and building three.

When he got onto the path, he slid the rifle off his back and raised it, ready to fire.

That elicited a yelp from the tech in wire glasses who burst through the door, fleeing from Kane. The guy stumbled and fell into the guard, nearly knocking the armed man over.

Movement on the opposite side drew my attention. Kane burst out, hooked a left, and disappeared into a dark copse of trees behind the hangars.

It seemed the entire mountaintop had once been covered in a tiny, isolated forest. To build its labs, Covenant had carved out an area the size of a football field right in the middle of it.

Glancing back and tracing my eyes along the high stone wall, I tried to gauge how much of the foliage he had to hide in.

"Not much," I mumbled, chewing on a nail.

The guard poked his head into building three and leaped back out.

"Who was in there?" he shouted at the tech who was picking himself up from the ground.

"I don't know," the man said, dusting off his lab coat. "He was dressed all in black!"

"Hold on," one of the other techs said, his voice dripping with disdain. "You saw a goddamn ninja?"

"No! I didn't say that!" the first guy shouted back. "He was huge. Biggest guy I've ever seen. Ninjas are tiny!"

The third tech shook his head. "That's kinda racist."

He laughed with the guy standing next to him. Clearly, they weren't buying the terrified dude's story. That was, until the guard stepped in, crossed into the hangar, then slowly walked backward. As his shadow retreated, the rifle barrel waved around like a conductor's baton.

Outside again, he growled, "Subject 17 is dead."

"What?" the pair of techs said in unison. One of them asked, "Are you serious? Dead?"

"Throat slashed," the guard said, his eyes never wavering from the entrance to hangar three.

"What? How?"

"I don't know!" the guard yelled, the light behind him illuminating the spittle bursting from his mouth with each syllable. "Maybe T-7's ninja did it?"

All three techs started to shrink away, but the guard wasn't having it. He slammed his meaty hand onto the shoulder of the tech who'd been in building three. The one he'd called T-7.

"You aren't going anywhere," he said, shooting a glance at the other two to make it clear he was in charge. To T-7, he barked, "Now tell me *exactly* what you saw."

"I-I-I don't... h-huge man dressed all black. Black ski mask. Eyes covered in some iridescent plastic or something."

"What does that mean?" the guard shouted, pulling the terrified tech closer to his face.

"It... His eyes were covered. Some specialized material," the man said, his words bursting like popping Bubble Wrap, "Goggles, maybe? They probably help him see in the dark or may be heat sensitive. They looked, um, very high tech."

The guard squeezed the guy's shoulder harder then pushed him back inside the hangar with the slain NextGen. He followed behind. Their two bodies elongated in shadow, and I saw him grab something out of his belt. He held it to his mouth. "Base, this is G-2."

A voice crackled over the radio. "Go, G-2."

"Trouble at the Camp. We've got an intruder. Geared up. T-7 thinks he might be a pro," he said and peeked toward the shadow bed. "Subject 17 is down. Dead."

After a two-second pause, the tinny voice returned. "Whereabouts of the intruder?"

"Don't know location. Subject is very large and wearing all black."

The other silhouette turned in profile. "And pink socks."

The guard waved him off. He'd definitely had enough of the guy. He keyed the radio again. "Base, do you copy?"

"Yep," the voice crackled back. "Five squad is two minutes out."

The guard nodded. "Is there a Primary?"

"Affirmative." On the radio, the voice cut in, sounding like it had clicked in halfway through a laugh. "Enzo. Enzo is leading."

"Jesus," the guard shot back. "*Enzo?*"

"Of course, Enzo," the voice on the radio said. "They all listen to him."

The guard's arm flexed, shaking, as he squeezed the handset. "That's the fucking problem!"

"No, it's not," the person back at Base said. "Enzo will listen to his collar, and the collar is controlled by the Maestro software. Get a tech to bring up the program on their tablet."

"Negative," the guard said. He sounded like he was speaking through a clenched jaw. "He acts like their damn alpha. Keep that monster locked up in his cage!"

Another pause, then, "Let's see how he and a squad do against *one* guy. Good test. Let us know how it goes. Over and out."

The guard shook the radio in his fist then jammed it back on his belt. Then he grabbed the collar of the squeaky tech, who was trying to head back out to join the other two.

"You're staying," he said. His shadow head appeared to look up. "Five of those things will be here in a minute. Get a tablet, keep them in line, and have them kill your big ninja!"

"But—"

"Go!" the guard yelled, more mist exploding from his lips.

The tech burst out and ran to the side of the hangar, digging in his pants pocket. He pulled out a small black device and pointed it at a metal box on a pole. Holding it like a car key fob, he thumbed it, shook it, and thumbed it again.

When the box clicked, T-7 threw its door open and dug inside.

The other two techs watched, slack-jawed. They flinched when the guard yelled at them.

"Get those two subjects to the Church!"

I put my fist to my mouth. Kane wouldn't ditch me, so he would be close by. Probably making his way around the side of—

A strange fluttering from above caught my attention. Familiar, but I couldn't place it at first. Then I could.

A helicopter.

I had to get out of there! Spinning around, I looked up to the ridge where we'd come down. Where I'd nearly broken my neck. Shit, it was way too steep to climb. Dammit, I'd have to scale back up the tree.

That was when another noise drew my attention. I crouched back down and saw two techs, each with a gurney, coming my way. Right toward the van I was hiding behind.

I was trapped.

Chapter Thirty-Two

Kane

A keen hunter knows when to attack and when to vanish. When to be the shadow of death and when to disappear to become a creature of the dark.

So I am hiding.

As a wolf, I was skilled at eluding predators and sneaking up on prey. Using the forest as a weapon. A tool of stealth. I could slither and slide like a snake in the trees.

Now, I hide behind one, staring at the man with the rifle. I can see him, but *ha!* He cannot—

"You there," he shouts at me. "Don't move."

Stupid skinny trees.

Alas, I do not heed his advice, and I run. Bark spits behind me as he fires his weapon, seeking to strike my flesh. I cut to my right, deeper into the darkness, and feel one of his stray bullets graze my leg.

Too close!

If he is hunting me, Emelda should be safe.

I am now running to escape. At least escape this man, who—

Crack!

A tree branch near my head shatters midshaft as a bullet slices it clean through. Splinters fall upon me like hot rain.

Remember the forest! Remember the wolf within!

I begin shifting and leaping left to right as I run, although this is much harder as a large human. Something sings past my face, ringing my ears. How is this man still seeing me in the total darkness of the woods?

I stop and hide behind a pair of trees. I am out of his sight lines.

How is he tracking me? I am the color of night! A shadow in the shadows!

Ah. No.

Staring down at the pink lady tights, I know this is what gives me away. I consider what this man must have seen as he aimed down his rifle barrel. A formless void flying through forest darkness, chased by two blobs of pink!

My footwear has betrayed me.

When I thought I was a creature of stealth, he could see me dodging. He could see me weaving. And as if being pursued by two hairless baby weasels!

Stupid weasel feet!

I attempt to remove the pink tights. However, when I pull the toe fabric, they seem to grow and grow and elongate. A crashing through the trees behind me. The man with the rifle is coming!

Still, I continue to pull on these tights, and there are only more tights. *Do they never end?*

Finally, I strip off the weasel feet and throw them to the ground. Then I kneel with plans to bury them but do not. Instead, I ball up the troublesome tights and stuff them into the pocket of my black sweatpants.

Crouching low, I run. More of a brisk jog, actually. Is very hard to run with knees bent. Fleeing my pursuer, I bank left and away. Another shot rings out, but no longer shooting at me, the man is firing wildly into the small forest.

And it is a very small forest.

I have reached its edge far faster than I hoped and now face the wall of rock. I look up, seeing a possible handhold. If I can get to the top and slide over the ridge, I can hide there. Slide around the edge and find Emelda once more.

Bending low, I explode upward, extend my body, and grab hold.

When I do, bits of the rock tumble away, and I slide back down. I have to snatch a large clump from the air before it hits the ground and reveals my position.

Stepping back, I peer up to gauge the distance. I may be able to jump five meters, but it is hard to see in the darkness. Stars above, yet no moon tonight. This makes it difficult to see. So very dark.

But I will use the blackest night to my advantage.

Moving down the edge of the tree line, I cut back and slip between the trunks. If I keep to the edge of the tiny forest, I may be able to return to our hiding spot behind the people van. Emelda would know what to do from there.

That is when I hear the engine of one of the vehicles start, rev, and spin its tires.

Peering between the trees, I see it shift and slide as it barrels out of the mountain valley. That way must be the exit. However, I do not see Emelda. She must be hiding behind the second van.

I hope this is the case.

That is my goal now. To make it to the—

The sound of the white-and-green van fades, and another takes its place. A thumping and whirring. This is a sound I know. This is the sound I heard when Covenant appeared with the duplicitous Doc Hammer and her lies.

A helicopter.

When I look to the dark sky, I see nothing. No lights. But the wind below stirs, kicking up dust and dirt and rock. Through the branches, I see one of the tiny smelly buildings shimmy then topple over.

The machine that lands looks like a long, skinny bug with big bibulous eyes. Is quite creepy.

A soldier dressed in camouflage jumps out and races to the rear of the helicopter. The tech who had been in the third building runs out, holding a rectangular computer device over his head. His wispy hair is being tousled by the helicopter wind.

He approaches the soldier. They speak, but I cannot hear over the whirring blades.

However, I can hear movement to my right. The man with the rifle is stalking closer to me, but wolf does not wait for a predator to strike.

I devise a plan. A very simple plan. These are the best. Or at least I convince myself of this truth.

Part one of plan enacted, I then reach up and grab a tree limb, pulling myself higher. My powerful thighs gripping either side of the tree, I reach up again and pull. Then— Wow, oh wow.

Splinters.

Very painful.

I do not make a sound despite their tiny bites on a place I do not want bites of any size. Slowly, I lift away then pull a bit higher until I am at least four meters up in the tree. Still, my predator moves closer. Not used to a fight in the forest, he is loud with his footfalls.

The crack of branches. The shuffle of leaves.

What a moron.

A snarling catches my attention, and I turn. In front of the hangars, the man dressed in camouflage fatigues is pulling on a long, thick cable, backing away from the rear of the helicopter.

I see feet. Then I see who those feet belong to.

A NextGen creature. Unlike the one I dispatched in the hangar, this one is dressed for combat. So is the one that follows. And the one after that.

As the camo man steps back, he jerks the thick wire, which is looped through manacles on each of the monsters. There are five of them.

They are here for me.

Camo Man shouts at the tech, whose fingers are moving wildly on his computer tablet. A moment later, the unruly group of five straighten as if electrified. One of the creatures is larger than the others. He is at the back.

The man with the tablet approaches this one, slowly. Tapping furiously on his device. If he continues in such a manner, he will crack the screen. One cannot make smart choices when emotions run so high. When one is as panicked as he.

Especially with electronics. Very costly to repair.

The largest of the monsters lifts its head toward the tech, stiffens with a shudder, then nods. Strangely, the other four do not look to the man with the tablet. Instead, they defer to this largest creature. It glares at each of them in turn.

I see no word spoken as they form a V-shape behind him.

Camo Man twists something on his thick wire, and the manacles fall to the gravel below. The tech's hands dance over the screen. The monsters are under his control.

"Gotcha!" I hear below me, and the man with the rifle jumps around the tree.

He is pointing at the two pink socks I laid on the ground before I climbed. His rifle downward, he expects to see the intruder in black.

Alas, he finds him as I leap from the tree, my fist in motion as I fall. It crashes into the shoulder of the arm hefting the rifle, and I hear the crack of bone. The man screams once. Before he can scream again, I twist his head so, if he chooses, he could for the first time, see his own lumpy backside.

If he isn't dead, of course.

I drop the body to the earth, but his scream has alerted the NextGen monsters. Fierce black eyes point in my direction. They are coming for me.

A good hunter knows when to flee.

I am a good hunter.

And I flee.

Running through the small copse of trees is far too slow! The creatures behind me snarl as they rip through branches and tear away limbs. My only hope is the rock wall. I do not know if I can make such a jump, but it is my only way out!

Ten seconds later, I am again staring up at the sheer face. So high!

Their snarling gets closer. Closer.

No time.

No other options.

I bend down deep and leap into the air, reaching and scrabbling, stretching my arms far, far, far! My knees collide with rock. My bare toes smash against stone. But I am no longer on the ground.

I look up to my grip upon the top of the ridge. My right hand swings wildly as I hold on with one arm. If I can pull up, I will be over...

My mind wobbles. The night around me flashes from black to brilliant white. The snarling in my ears goes silent and I hear... nothing.

Silence.

But I *know* this silence.

It is the quiet peace of home in the Canadian forest. I can see its leaves and rocks and hills. There! I can see my family! My pack. My wolf wife.

She turns her beautiful face toward me, yellow eyes warm and loving. My heart aches for her, but I cannot reach her. I run but do not move.

How is she here?

Or how am I there?

My pack begins to howl, in unison, the song I know well. One that is distinctive to my family. This is a warning. A call that there is danger.

Then I am back on the ridge, my grip slipping because my fingers do not curl anymore.

What is happening?

The flashing in my mind—from day to night, night to day—ceases, and I return to the Mexican mountaintop. I feel twisting within me—painful, unnerving.

My grip falters, and I fall, my eyes looking upward, my mind getting lost in a field of stars. I am changing! But how do I change when there is no moonlight kiss upon my human skin?

No, that is not right.

Emelda did not say there was no moon. Instead, she called it something else.

A new moon.

I hit the bottom of the rock wall, where it sharply curves toward the forest, and I roll and roll, my mind and body tumbling.

No!

I spread my paws out to stop the spinning and rise to my feet. Not two but four. I see the NextGen racing toward me, tearing through the brush, their dark eyes blazing wildly at me.

I snarl at them.

Four of the creatures hesitate and slow, but the largest of them turns back and growls at each. As he does, I look down at my body.

What is...

The alpha NextGen has gotten the others in line, and they pick up their pursuit. They are seconds away, but when I try to run, I stumble as my paws catch on fabric.

I step back from the black clothing and let it fall away. Then I look to my body. This is a body I know.

I am not a man.

Nor am I canine.

I am wolf once again.

Chapter Thirty-Three

"Hmm," T-7 said. "That's weird."

The tech glanced at the dense patch of woods, but from his vantage point between the stop hangars, his view was obstructed by leaves, branches, and tree trunks. G-2 looked back to the camera feed on the tablet in the tech's hand.

"It's like a dog, but it's too damn big. A wolf? Maybe the guy in black brought it with him?" the guard, G-2, said. "But even an animal wouldn't take on five of those creatures."

"Still, he looked like he was lining up on an attack vector." The other man shuffled the video back to the moment when it looked like there would be a bloody confrontation. "Then he just pricked his ears and backed down. Reassessed."

"How the hell do you know it's a he?"

T-7 pinch zoomed. "See that shadow?"

G-2 shook his head. "I really didn't need the close-up shot, man."

"No," the tech agreed, nodding and tapping the *live* button on the upper right. "You really don't."

"You," G-2 said, "are a lonely, lonely man."

The tech ignored him, flipping between the feeds of the cameras mounted on the vests of the NextGen creatures. The software worked to steady the images as they ran. The lenses bounced and shook.

All but the one on Enzo. That alpha ran like it was gliding across glass.

The guard had said something, which he missed. Turning his head slightly, but not looking away, he asked him to repeat it.

"I asked you if that wolf is following the guy in black. No way that thing got here on its own, right?"

"Exactly. And yes, I expect he's domesticated the animal somehow."

The guard spun and walked toward the half-circle parking lot. Trailing behind him, the tech switched from feed to feed.

G-2 squinted and wished he had brought night goggles with him. There were likely some in the helicopter, but the pilot had locked the cockpit up tight once the NextGen had been set loose.

Didn't matter. The creatures and their prey were already charging over the rise on the single road leading in and out. He would never see them.

"If that guy has a head start because your monsters were screwing around with the wolf, he could get through the goddamn gate!" The guard lifted his rifle to a shoulder to stare down the telescopic sight but only saw the wavy hills of the mountaintop encampment's west side.

"No, no," the tech said. "The gate slams shut the moment a vehicle passes through."

G-2 glanced at the screen. Five camera feeds all showed the ass end of a wolf as he leaped and bounced over a scrub-covered hill.

"No way we can let that guy leave. Any way he could climb it?"

"Ha, no chance," the tech said, shaking his head in rapid, birdlike twitches. "It's as tall as the ridgeline. That gate in the Jurassic Park movie was like a kiddie fence compared to our gate. Totally impenetrable."

"Right. Then how did the guy get in? How did his wolf get in?"

For the first time, the tech looked up from his computer tablet and scanned around the encampment. He licked his lips.

"Well, impenetrable from *this* side. A precaution if any of our subjects got free. We never considered," G-2 said, his words fumbling over one another, "that, I mean, anyone would try... ever try... to get in."

A strange keening split the air, triggering the guard to lift the rifle to his shoulder again. Seeing nothing but gravel, dirt, and grass, he looked back to the tech.

"Did that just come from your tablet?" The guard scanned all around them. The lab setup had always given him the creeps. So did the monsters this place created. "Where the hell did that come from?"

"Impossible to tell." The tech lifted a hand and spun it in the air. "We're in a huge bowl made of rock. It's just echoing around us."

Once again, the sound—a warbling animal call—rang all around them.

"What the fu—" the guard began to say.

"Shh!"

G-2 gritted his teeth together, spun around, and pointed the rifle barrel at the back of the tech's head. His finger danced over the trigger for a moment. He lowered it and spun to peer into the darkness.

Another sound. Or sounds. It was impossible to tell.

"Did you hear that other... Was that the echo?"

The tech furiously tapped between camera feeds. The creatures had reached the gate, all closing in at once as a pack, but their infrared showed nothing. The gate was closed. Secured.

No man in black.

No wolf.

The guard asked, "Did they get out?"

"Impossible," the other said. "But that first call was a wolf howl. Hmm. I wonder..."

"Wonder? Wonder what?"

The tech stepped into the driveway, staring in the direction of where the NextGen *should* be tearing apart the man and his pet wolf.

But the camera feed was static as only the creatures stood at the gate.

"Why are they just waiting there?" G-2 asked, jerking the tech's arm. "Why did they stop?"

"The collars give them commands, which they must follow to the letter." T-7 groaned in frustration. "I instructed them to pursue the intruders all the way to the gate. Once they got there, that command had been fulfilled. Now they're waiting."

"Waiting for what?"

"The next *command*. We deleted all improvisation out of their programming after that fiasco with the damn tourists," the tech said. Drawing his finger across a slider at the bottom of the device, the tech added, "We do not need any more trouble."

The guard swallowed. "Like those kids?"

"Exactly!" T-7 said and thumped the pad in three quick, successive taps. "Okay. I've got them on a search grid, fanning out and back on the hunt."

G-2 lifted his rifle again. "Goddamn it, I don't want them coming after us!"

The tech casually put his hand on the man's weapon, pressing it down. The guard snapped it from the other's grip.

"They can't. They're programmed to obey us, not eat us," he said, chuckling softly. "This entire area isn't even a mile across. There's no way the intruder could have gotten—"

"Hush!" The guard licked his lips. The rifle barrel swept left then right. "Did you hear that? What is that?"

"The wolf. Same as before."

"*Not* the same as before! Why does it... Is that all echo?"

T-7 sighed then listened if for no other reason than to appease the jittery guard. He understood the man's fear because he *had* felt the same. The moment he gripped the tablet and had the NextGen under his control, he didn't feel fear.

He felt like a god.

The guard took a half step closer to him and asked, "What *is* that? It's like a chittering sound."

"A wolf howls for two primary reasons." The tech closed his eyes to listen as the howl repeated. Then that queer echo again. "One is a warning to others. Establishing a pack's territory."

"There are more wolves out there?"

"Of *course* not," the tech said, his voice thick with derision. He watched on the screen as the camera marked Enzo rose skyward. On the feed, he could hear the NextGen alpha sniff the air. It then turned, stalking forward. "See? Enzo has picked up the scent."

The guard let out a long breath.

"Fine," he said. "You said there were two reasons why the wolf would howl like that."

"The other is a rallying call. But there's no— Oh, wait. Hot damn! They've found their target!"

On the screen, all five feeds showed virtually the same image, from slightly different angles. The wolf was coming up over a hill covered in scrub. In the distance, in the faint light, they could see the top of the stone wall, tree branches fluttering from the other side.

The wolf stood there as two, then three, smaller creatures came up beside him.

Enzo and the others stopped, their camera feeds swiping left. Then right.

Highlighting the alpha's feed, he began to type in a new command but thought better of it. He opened the microphone feature.

"Surround and destroy, Enzo," he said. "Then find the man in black and tear him apart!"

The alpha didn't move. Its gaze swept left and right. When T-7 triple tapped the alpha's feed, the yellow box glowed red. "Surround. And destroy!"

The camera feed dipped to the ground, and they heard Enzo groan in pain. When the camera rose again, it focused on the wolf and the other three creatures, a third its size.

"What the hell are those?"

"I think..." the tech said, laughing hard enough to momentarily lose his breath. "I think those are coyotes! A wolf and three coyotes versus five of our NextGen? Oh boy, this is going to be bloody."

"Coyotes?"

T-7 held the tablet to his face and barked into the mic, "Enzo, just kill the damn wolf and its pets already!"

G-2 pointed to the fluttering at the top of the screen. A fluttering from the top of the rock wall.

"It's a mountain!" the tech said. "The wind up here is just blowing the treetops."

"Trees? Those shadows are coming from the other side," the guard said, leaning in. "There ain't no trees on the other side."

"But..."

Then they saw.

The wolf stood, lifting its head in the air, howling a long call that rose and fell and rose again. On the hill, two more coyotes appeared next to the first three. On the left of the wolf, six more.

"Hold on," the tech said, his fingers zooming in on a NextGen feed focused on the area atop the mountain ridge. His brain couldn't comprehend exactly what he was seeing. It looked like a waterfall, a torrent of shadow, flowing over top of the wall and dropping from sight.

Tilting his head, he could hear a rumbling, growing louder and louder. A distant thunder rising in a place that almost never had thunderstorms.

When he pinched the screen, the scene on the hill had changed. Everything had changed.

"That," G-2 said then swallowed loudly. "I mean, that is a lot of coyotes."

Chapter Thirty-Four

Kane

Once again, the wolf has a pack.

Yes, they are like dogs. Dogs with long pointy ears, but I know how powerful dogs can be. I do not know if the pointy ears will help.

But these yipping dog creatures are brave. Each has the heart of a warrior. And, of course, the body of a border collie.

They are not wolf, but I can sense the wolf within!

Cousins.

They have embraced me as family. And are keen for a fight.

I howl again as more pour over the rock wall behind me, running and yip-yip-yipping, teeth bared. Before me, the monsters watch as my pack swells in number. Surveying the battlefield, I see my new pack has grown from dozens to what must be hundreds!

The cousin wolves look to me.

Time to fight.

Leaving the high ground, I skulk toward the closest of the monsters. One sees me, locks eyes, and I know it comes from my body. As if kin. Or something more.

No, I cannot think them thus.

They must be destroyed.

When I am only meters away, this lead creature bares its teeth. We both stare at an alpha.

Before I can launch myself, I am hit in the flank by another of the creatures, protecting its pack leader. We roll, and my vision goes from dirt to stars, dirt to stars. Even before I can stop our tumbling, the monster is ripped from my body by the cousin wolves.

First two then three. Then ten.

Getting to my feet, I see them tear and bite and claw. The monster beneath fights back, tossing one into the black, for it is far stronger. But as one is flung free, three more take its place!

The horde of cousin wolves engulfs the monsters, overwhelming them. Some run right over, charging down the path from where we came. Toward the light of the encampment.

I yearn to join the fight, but I must find Emelda. Once she is safe, I will join my cousins to defeat these abominations.

The NextGen blocks my return, and I must go another way.

Around me, the stone walls rise so high. I cannot climb. I spin to my rear, where more of the cousins leap from the wall, running vertically, rolling and getting to their feet once more.

This gives me an idea.

I charge toward the wall, seeing one of my cousins near the base, and I leap, landing on its back. The second I feel its fur beneath my paws, I leap to the next, moving higher. I search upward, seeking the next gray body, finding it and leaping again.

This is how I climb the unclimbable wall.

The power of my pack.

I stumble only once but grab the back of one of the gray cousins and pull myself up with my teeth, leaping from its haunches, propelling myself upward once again.

At last, one final leap, and I am at the top of the ridge.

Breathing heavily, I scan to see if I can spot Emelda. From here, I can see the white-coat-people's camp clearly. She is not behind the van. Nor is she near the helicopter. I search the darkness behind, near the curvature at the bottom of the wall.

Where is she?

Below, I see my cousins continue to pour over the wall and flood the battleground. I hear the screaming of the monsters, their plaintive cries. My wolf heart aches, but it is necessary.

Then I see him.

The alpha below.

He locks eyes with me, challenging me to the fight. The animal within wishes to take him on. To destroy this creature.

No. I must help Emelda!

I cannot see her.

The alpha roars, batting away the wolf cousins. Again, he calls, eyes blazing, challenging me. I have decided. He must die.

When I look to him once again, he lifts his head, preparing for another vocal challenge. He shivers and buckles as the cousin wolves flow around him. Gripping his skull, he squeezes his head. Then he spins *away* from the fight.

A new one has begun at the place they call the Camp.

Running across the mountain ridge, I scan the ground for any signs of my friend. In the light of the hangars, I see a thick wall of cousin wolves leap and shift and run. The guard who first chased me stands before them, bullets flying from his rifle.

There are too many. Far too many. He calls back to the man in the lab coat, but I cannot hear over the raging battle below me.

That tech turns and runs toward the still-smoldering corpse of the monster. Bending down, he lifts a tank to his back and grabs its hose apparatus. Sparks fly as before, then flame shoots from the end of the nozzle.

Howls, this time in pain. The lab coat man is burning my cousin wolves! As they try to approach, he washes them in flame. Some retreat. Many burn.

My howl is one of rage. This man is attacking my pack! Attacking... *cousin wolves*.

Yes!

The presence of my cousin wolves has awakened a memory. I have a plan now.

Yes. Yes.

I leap from the wall, away from the encampment and into the darkness beyond. Running as fast as I can—and I can run so very fast, for I am wolf once more.

This is what I have wanted for so long. My body returned to me so that I can rejoin my pack, my wolf wife who awaits me.

My legs moving quickly across the scrabble, down the hill to where we leaped the fence earlier that day. My heart races. My *wolf* heart races.

At the wire fence, I jump, clearing it easily.

Ha! I am an even stronger wolf than before. A fine, fine alpha I will be for my pack. Never second best. The most powerful alpha wolf there has ever been!

The thought propels me forward. I'm still running. Past where I pulled the tree from the ground. Where I'd lifted Emelda, my friend, over the fence.

I stop, breathing heavily.

Running would take me home. A very long journey but every step closer to home. Back to my pack. However, I have another. My pack of two, and I must ensure she is safe.

But also the cousin wolf pack that fights for me even now. The man with the flame stick is killing them.

This must stop.

I will stop him.

I race to the tiny motorcycle and rip through the basket for what I need. Gripping the handle in my teeth, I run again. Ungainly, my head lolls low, but I am stronger than any wolf before.

One leap, and I am over the hill, racing upward.

Above I can see the lights of the compound. The sounds of battle rage. Snarling and howling and yipping.

At the ridgeline, I arch to my right and then go over the top.

Wow, so very steep. It is almost straight down.

At the bottom, my shoulder smashes into the dirt, and I roll. The canister is very heavy. Back on my feet, I grip it once again. Pain there. Hmm. I may have lost a tooth.

As I race back to the hangars, I draw in air heavy with the stench of burning hair and flesh. The man in the lab coat is sweeping his flame across my cousins as they surround him. Dozens of them.

Two of them tear into a lump on the ground, ripping off pieces of flesh.

I see a rifle next to the bloodied clothes, the man within now just a meal for my cousins.

Releasing the handle in my mouth, I hear the container thud in the dirt. I call to my cousins a warning, hoping they understand. Some swivel their heads toward me. Some do not. I call again.

Others join my call, alerting the pack. As one, they race back down the gravel road to where their brothers and sisters continue the fight. The sounds of howling back there have diminished. The yipping and barking drowning out the cries of agony from the monsters.

Gripping the container handle again, I stalk forward. The man in the white coat sees me. His eyes are red-rimmed. Where I saw a coward before, I see that he now feels the power of the hunter.

And he turns toward me, scowling.

"Where is your master? *Huh?*" he screams at me, laughing in a strange, drunken way. This strange man has found a new fever. The fever of killing. And he enjoys it so.

All men are animals, deadly and fierce. In the world of humans, a brave man learns how to tame the beast inside his heart. The lesser ones do not. They embrace the monster within.

This is his moment.

I glare at this human monster, shifting left then right. When his eyes flutter downward toward my mouth to see what I am holding, I know he is blinded by his flame. And his rage. And his newly born thirst for blood.

As I run toward him, my eyes scan for my friend. Emelda. I pass between the people van and the helicopter. The pilot has his fingers splayed across the glass, staring at me wide-eyed.

But Emelda is not here.

This is good.

"Come on! Come on!" The man in the coat turns his fire stick toward me, flames dancing in his wild eyes, and challenges me. "You wanna eat me, don't you?"

Faster, I run toward him.

"Eat this!" he screams, gripping his weapon so hard it shakes in his hands.

I flick my head, releasing the handle of the red canister and smashing my front paws deep into the dirt and gravel. Bending down into a crouch, I push myself hard and rocket to my side and run fast, as fast as I can move, as the canister flips end over end toward the lab coat man.

The faster I run, the slower time moves, and mon père's deep voice fills my brain.

In that frozen moment, I recall the smell of grease. Dirt. And grass.

A fond memory.

Standing over the machine, mon père points out what all of the parts do.

"Below this is a blade that spins," he says to me, speaking in French, I believe. In my memory, both English and French sound the same. Human language, not wolf. "This is what slices the top of the grass. Then the cut grass, it is flung from this side."

"Is the flying grass dangerous?" I ask in a squeaky voice.

"Ha, no, Kane," he says. "But the blade is, so never reach beneath when the mower is running."

I nod my young-man head, my hair flopping down over my eyes. "All safe, but the blade is not. Yes, I understand."

He pulls the cap off the machine's small white tank. "Also, this is dangerous. I will do this, not you. Very dangerous."

Stepping back, I look down, ready for some snake or other dark creature to burst out, brandishing its teeth. This makes my human father laugh.

"No, no. Nothing will come out," he says, lifting the red can. A red can like the one I have thrown at the lab coat man. "But within, this is petrol. Very dangerous. If not handled right, yes, there is a chance of it to explode."

Furrowing my brow, I shake my head. I do not know this word.

"Explode?" mon père says as the pungent liquid flows from the red can into the tank. "This is like fast fire. Very, very fast. With a, um, blast, yes?"

I nod. Then frown. I don't get it.

"Petrol is very dangerous. This can here? It is like fourteen sticks of dynamite," he says. Then his eyes light up. "You know TNT, yes?"

"Oh, of course! TNT, this I have learned about," I declare. "The coyote who tries to catch and destroy the Road Runner bird. He uses TNT very much."

"Yes, yes," he says, laughing. "Coyote, of course! They are cousin to the wolf, do you know this?"

I shake my head.

"Now you do." He winks at me. "They can even mate with your kind and make what are called coywolves!"

His expression makes me laugh. But, alas, I have no interest in mating with any but my wolf wife. And, according to the cartoon, coyotes only come in males.

"But this is a lesson not about mating but danger," he says, capping the fuel container once again. "This can plus fire? Can you guess the sound it makes?"

Behind me, the lab coat man lifts his flame toward the spinning red canister, a knee-jerk reaction to a projectile he cannot identify.

The lab coat man discovers the answer I did as a boy.

Boom.

The blast lifts me from my feet, and I am flung into the air, rolling end over end again. I only stop when I feel the rock wall against my back.

A vast plume of light erupts into the sky, blotting out the night. Hiding the stars and the no-moon new moon, which has changed me in ways I do not understand.

Fire races around the encampment like a pack made of flame creatures. All three hangars burn. The black helicopter explodes.

In the quiet, I know that the battle of the NextGen and the cousin wolves, the coyote, is over. Gasping for breath, I feel the heat radiate across my fur.

The brilliant light spreads to the tiny forest behind the encampment as the trees begin to burn. A *crack* sound draws my attention. The tires on the van are popping. One of its side windows shatters then another. Material within begins to burn.

I sniff the air. Emelda is not here.

And neither is the other van.

Chapter Thirty-Five

I tried to focus on the beauty of the night sky's tapestry of stars.

"So pr-pr-pretty," I stammered as the van jostled over another rock or tree limb. Maybe a possum. Or was it opossum? Was there a difference? Maybe opossums were the ones from Ireland?

We hit another bump, a big one, and my body lifted off the roof of the van. I had to clench my hands so I didn't lose my grip on the luggage rails. My fingers strained as I hovered, suspended in air for a moment, then came right back down again.

I saw new stars. Musta banged my head.

"What the hell was that?" I heard the driver ask. My eyes got big.

"I don't know," the other tech said. "Might have been a possum."

That had been the first time either of the men had said a word since we'd rocketed out of the mountaintop encampment.

I'd looked everywhere for a quick place to run but came up empty. When they'd gone to the back of the van and flung open the doors, I was out of all the good options. So I picked a bad one. Swallowing down a lump of terror, I grabbed the side mirror and pulled myself onto the roof.

They hadn't seen me. Probably because they were focused on the two monsters they'd loaded in the back.

My plan had been to wait until they slowed down then roll off the back. It would hurt, but I knew how to take a fall. You did it enough, and you got good at it.

Problem was, they never slowed down. Two or three times, they turned into the dirt then back on the road, probably losing control, but I didn't think the driver touched the brake once.

Raising my head, I could see the mountaintop in silhouette against a field of stars. I hoped Kane had gotten away from—

The top of the mountain exploded.

A flash of light, then flames. Just over the sound of the screaming engine, I heard a low rumble.

"Jesus Christ," the tech in the passenger seat said. There was a squelching sound, then he spoke again. "T-7! T-7, what the hell is going on up there?"

A foot or two above the guy's head, I was asking myself the same question. Had Kane gotten caught up in that? It looked like a friggin' bomb had gone off.

Could he have survived that?

I turned my head, pressing my ear against the roof of the van, scrunching my eyes up, trying to listen closer. The tech below me called a few more times but got the same answer. Silence.

The radio ticked and squelched through a few bands of static. Again, the tech barked into the radio.

"Hello, Base? Um, Church base, this is T-4," he said. Even from here, I could hear his voice shaking. Or that might have been my head bouncing against the roof.

The squawk came back, "Go, T-4."

"I'm trying to, um, get a hold of the Camp," the passenger said. "There was an incident. It... They're not answering?"

"Is that a question? No, don't answer that. Hold on," the impatient voice said then huffed. A full minute later, the voice came back. Its asshole tone had evaporated, sounding as confused as the tech below me. "So all feeds and communication have gone dark. Do you have a visual?"

"Yeah," the guy said with a hiccup chuckle. "The visual I have is a big fireball where the camp is supposed to be."

Another minute went by. I could hear whispering between the passenger and driver, then the voice on the radio crackled.

Both men yelped, obviously surprised by the sound of it.

"We have lost the Camp. Any survivors?"

A pause. "I survived. T-5 is driving."

"No, not..." The radio voice sounded British. Not bippity-boppity-boo British. Like a crooked tollbooth operator from a Guy Ritchie movie. "Are all the subjects from the Camp lost?"

"We have two. Both are viable."

"Good. Okay, good," the voice on the radio said. "Drop them here, then hightail it to the Palace. Janus wants to talk to you guys."

A brief argument broke out below me. After a few fevered whispers, the driver spoke on the radio for the first time: "This is T-5. Janus wants to speak to us? Why?"

"Why do you *think?*" the voice yelled, frying the speaker. "The lab is gone, right?"

The two techs below me argued over who was going to answer that question. After a moment, the first guy answered, speaking in an overly official tone. "That is unclear at this time."

"Right," the radio guy said. "Is that because of all the smoke and fire? No, don't answer that. Just bring the two subjects to the Church, and get to the Palace."

There was another whispered exchange between the two guys below, then, "Roger. Two minutes out."

I just had to hold on a few minutes more. My back would be bruised, and I didn't know if I would ever be able to unfurl my fingers from the bars of the luggage rack.

Wherever we were approaching—this place they called the Church—would be my chance to get off the roller-coaster ride from hell. They would have to stop to drop off their cargo.

Unless they had monster drive-thru. I *really* hoped they didn't have monster drive-thru.

I lifted my head up and looked back to the mountaintop, the yellow-red glow already dimming. My eyes watered as I prayed that Kane was okay. For the next few minutes, I ran through countless scenarios in my head of how that might have happened.

Then I smiled.

Kane would have *caused* that. How? Dunno. But if anyone could create chaos in calm, it would definitely be him.

Still smiling, I bent my head around to peek forward to see how close we were to slowing down. And I nearly got smashed by Jesus.

Chapter Thirty-Six

The bottom of the stone cross caught the edge of my shirt, nearly ripping a hole in it. If I hadn't lowered my head, it would have torn a hole in me.

When I looked behind us, I saw the archway made of rock. The bottom of the huge stone crucifix poked below like baby's first tooth.

Weird. The Church was an actual church?

The van slowed *a little* when the dirt road became gravel again. But not much. This guy had a lead foot.

I twisted my head and saw heads. Well, not actual heads. The tops of statues. White stone, covered in dark stains and green grime. Leaning to my side, I caught sight of a massive brick fountain filled with dead, rotting leaves.

At least I hoped it was dead leaves. My only light was from the headlights, and when we passed, the world got swallowed back into darkness.

The driver bent the van left, and we finally slowed. For the first time since I'd climbed up top, I slowly pried open my hands. The pain of it shivered through my fingers, up my wrists, and twisted into my spine. My eyes watered.

As I was about to lift myself from the roof, a massive block of concrete came right at me. No Jesus this time. Just cold, angry gray rock.

I flattened myself to the roof—*again*—and we skidded to a stop. The two techs jumped out of either side and began pulling their two subjects out of the van's rear. I had about three inches of headroom, so I slowly slid to the side away from the building.

Once they went inside the Church, I was getting the hell out of there.

The back of the van slammed shut, and I braced for my shot at freedom. I listened.

Silence.

Did they go in already?

Below me somewhere, a scrabble of tires across rocks, then... an odd whirring sound. The whine rose and fell, ending in a click.

I heard the metal gurneys rattling but only for a second or two.

"That one there," another voice said. Hmm. Sounded like Guy Ritchie's tollbooth guy. "This one there. Come on, you!"

For the next minute, I tried to work out what in the world was going on below. The clatter of metal, the sounds of exertion. A few strained curses between grunts, but no other words were spoken.

Another click, then the whirring sound rose and faded away.

Okay. Now's my—

The doors to the van opened again, and the vehicle bobbled as the techs got back inside.

Not fair! Come on, you!

I had to stop myself from groaning as the doors thunked closed on either side. The passenger got back on the radio. "Base, T-4."

The van fired up and slowly backed out, and my view switched from concrete portico to a pinpricked sky once again.

"Base," the guy tried again. "This is T-4. We've now delivered the subjects."

The radio crackled as the voice on the other end hit the upper limits of the tiny speaker's capacity. "*I know!* I just bloody saw you!"

A pause, then, "Roger. 10-4."

"Just how dumb are you? No, don't answer that," the radio voice said, and he gulped loudly, like he'd taken a swig from a bottle. "Okay, Janus needs an incident report, so... you delivered two of what *should have been* four. That right?"

The van rumbled away, slower than before, crunching gravel beneath its tires.

"Affirmative," the passenger said then cleared his throat.

In a singsong tone, the radio voice said, as if writing as he spoke, "The two other subjects promised... got blowed up."

I nearly slid down the roof as the van came to a crunching halt. The driver got on the radio.

"No, Base. One was killed during..." He paused then continued, "The incident. The other had to be incinerated prior to tonight's events. Non-viable candidate."

Again, silence below me.

"Got it. Yeah," the voice said, stitching his last word into a long sigh. "What can they expect? The last lot had actual soldiers as candidates. They were a proper fit. Can't blame us when they give us street people to turn."

"Base, I don't think this is appropriate..." the driver said, clicked off, cursed, then clicked back on. "*Not* street people. Road workers. Laborers who toil in the sun ten hours a day. They're strong."

A throaty chuckle came over the radio's speaker. "They better be. Because now seven have to do the job a dozen were supposed to. From what? Twenty?"

"Copy," the driver said, and I heard him throw the radio handset up on the dash. The van started moving again, and neither man said another word as they headed to someplace called the Palace.

The road workers hadn't been killed.

They'd been taken. Kidnapped and turned into monsters.

And there are seven of them? Seven of those things?

I muttered, "Holy shit," then ducked as the bottom of stone cross breezed by my head.

Chapter Thirty-Seven

My back was screaming at me, but finally, I was off the damn van.

After the two guys got out, I'd waited a minute before I even moved a muscle. And, sure, I'd planned to be smart about it and wait at least another minute more, but I was tired of lying on cold aluminum.

I slid down the back, dropped to my feet, and drank in my new surroundings. "What Greek hell is this?"

"The Palace" was like some joke, and the only one not laughing was its owner.

While lying on my back, I'd seen the two light poles that stood like sentries on either side of the huge structure's front steps.

I saw now why it had taken the techs the best part of half a minute to get to the Palace's front entrance. There had to be thirty or forty steps. Starting wide at the base then slanting inward to a third the size. Their shape reminded me of a wine decanter.

"Wine," I whispered to myself. "First chance I get, I'm guzzling down a big glass of expensive wine. And by glass, I mean bottle."

From the circular drive out front, you couldn't fully see the Palace's first floor. Which meant whoever was inside couldn't see me. Light spilled out from one room on the ground level, but the second floor was totally dark.

A dozen skinny rectangular windows dotted that top floor. If that were Morse code, all those dashes probably spelled out a rude limerick.

But the entire building, I mean...

"It's the goddamn Parthenon," I muttered. "Built in the middle of the Mexican desert."

Four sets of double columns framed the entrance, capped by an elaborate and fancy-pants portico. And the columns were huge. Like the sort of concrete pylons you see on some bridges.

On either side of the steps, halfway up, a pair of horses and riders sat upon two massive stone plinths. Both seemed identical. I took a few steps closer. The horses didn't look like any I'd ever seen at a stable.

Not that I'd been to many stables. Or any.

They still looked like horses but those drawn from descriptions in the more terrifying parts of the Bible. Their manes flared out like flames. The open mouths of the beasts revealed teeth that curved into points. Their bodies were oddly muscular.

However, all the scary stuff ended at the saddles.

"Who puts jowls on a statue?"

The riders were in suits. Not suits of armor—actual suits. The weirdest part was that I recognized the identical faces of the riders. Couldn't place it, but I'd seen that guy somewhere.

From the front of the structure, another light flickered on. I slid up next to one of the statues and crawled a few more steps up to peek inside.

The light came from a room to the right of the front entryway, which was an open space all the way to the back. Through that passageway, I saw more stone structures but couldn't make them out.

The two men stepped into the room, which looked far more modern than the building's Gothic exterior.

Through the window, I saw one tech hand a bottle of water to the other. The second guy wiped his brow with its condensation. They stood at the edge of a big round table. I crept closer, keeping an eye out for anyone keeping an eye out for someone like me.

Weird. They were in a conference room.

To the left was the entryway. Above that was a carving depicting a creature that had the body of a lion and the head of a man. Once again, that same jowly face.

Who the hell—

Orange light glowed from the room, and I dropped lower, ready to run. Peeking up, I saw its source.

The techs stood at the edge of the round table. In the middle, a massive digitized head floated. It looked like a mini parade float. The head had video flames around it but not cool ones. Like clip art images that rotated back and forth.

I crept up the steps, hidden in shadow, and crossed under the weird lion-man relief art to take one step into the open-air entryway. I couldn't hear.

Damn.

Peeking around the corner out front again, I saw the two men nod in unison then begin speaking. I still couldn't hear, but as best as I could tell, this was like some gonzo augmented-reality Zoom call. Craziest damn thing.

The huge head turned. I recognized the face.

The same face on the two statues out by the steps and on the body of the lion above the door. And the very same one I'd seen days earlier back at the Covenant building when we'd killed the last of the Enhanced soldiers.

This was the asshole who'd told us where to find the last of the serum that would nullify the effects of their virus. He'd encouraged Kane to use it. Not out of kindness. He had simply wanted us to go away.

So he could grow his new batch of monsters, the NextGen, here in Mexico.

Right.

"Janus," I muttered. The techs had even said it back at the Church. I remembered the guy now. "Steve Janus."

What the hell was this guy up to?

Screw it. None of this mattered.

I had to get back to the hotel. When Kane had gotten away, he would head there. I looked back to the faint glow at the top of the mountain. The fire had nearly burned itself out.

At least I hoped Kane had gotten out of that.

Staring out at the massive courtyard, I saw the van. Despite how terrified I was, I smiled. If they'd left the keys behind, it would be good to see how it rode when you were *inside*.

I crossed out of the open-air entrance, my heartbeat thudding in my neck like my own personal soundtrack. The sort you heard in a sweaty spin class with a skinny, spandex chick barking into her wraparound mic, *"Faster!"*

Okay. Okay. It would be fine.

The keys would still be inside the vehicle. No use in pocketing them because there wasn't anyone around for twenty miles. This was me manifesting. Or just hoping.

The moment my foot hit the first step, a voice called out from the dark entryway, and I froze. She'd spoken in Spanish, but growing up in my house, it was a phrase I knew very well.

"What the hell are you doing?"

Chapter Thirty-Eight

The woman's harsh whisper launched my heart up into my throat, and my first thought was to run.

But where?

I had visions of myself lost in the desert scrub with my T-shirt tied around my head, surrounded by the shadows of vultures swooping overhead in lazy circles.

Turning slowly toward the silhouette of a small woman, her hair tied up in a kerchief, I tried to look calm.

"Oh, hello."

"Who are you?" she asked, this time speaking in English. She cast a look back over her shoulder. I worried she might call someone.

So I lied.

"I don't know," I said, keeping my voice low. "Hiking, right? Seems so good on TV and in the brochures."

She frowned, shaking her head. "You are not a hiker. Not in those shoes."

"They're expensive tennis shoes. Made to look cheap. It's a fashion thing."

"You want I should call the guard down at the gate? I bet they are looking for an excuse to shoot someone," she said, stepping forward, brandishing her broom like it was a sword. "And you are a *someone*, yes?"

"Correct."

The rattle of the conference room door opening rang down the hall as the orange light from the window extinguished. I could hear footfalls ring across the stone floor.

Done with their meeting, the techs were coming back out.

The woman took one look at me, back over her shoulder, then waved me forward. Shit! She was going to turn me in.

To buy time, time to think, I pointed at my chest. *Me?*

"*Rápidamente,*" she said. "Quickly!"

I moved toward the far side of the open-air entrance, opposite the wing with the conference room, but she whisked by me, her apron flapping behind her. She stuck out a hand, and I grabbed it.

There was the shuffle of shoes across stone, and a voice called out, "Miss Carminia? Is that you?"

She spun around and shoved me up against the stone wall, bathed in darkness. One of the techs stepped forward and lit a cigarette. The other stood only a few feet away. I was standing behind the statue of jowl-faced Steve Janus, portrayed as an Adonis wearing nothing but a fig leaf.

"Everything okay?" the man asked, stepping closer to her. I shrank back closer to the statue. I avoided the fig.

"*Si, señor,*" she said and nodded, clasping her hands together. "Just gathering some berries from the bushes. We have berry bushes. And it is from those that I was gathering."

Damn. The woman was worse than I was at bullshitting.

"At this hour?" The smoker took another step closer. I could see his shadow head looking left and right. "A bit late, yeah?"

The woman chuckled. "At this hour, there is no sun. And tonight, not even a moon," she said, forcing another laugh. "But no sun means no hot, yes? Best time to be outside."

He took another step, letting out a frustrated sigh. I could just see the edge of his white coat.

The man pulled out a box of matches and relit his cigarette. The tips of my tennis shoes glowed yellow, and I fought every urge inside me to squeeze farther behind the statue. If I moved, I would be spotted.

"Cooking during the day, gardening at night," the tech said, chuckling. "I envy you, Carminia. I wish I had it that simple."

"Yes, I am lucky," she said, but I'd heard that tone from women in low positions my whole life. Hell, I'd used it myself. She didn't feel lucky at all.

"Well, watch out in the dark. The prickles aren't the only things that bite," he said and started turning. He spun back. "Speaking of which, how are our... guests?"

The woman looked into the darkness then down at her hands.

"*No sé, señor,*" she said, shaking her head. "As good as can be expected, I think."

"Good," he said. "Good."

The tech turned and joined his buddy, both heading down the insanely long set of steps. When they got to the bottom, she scurried down the side of the building, flapping her right hand for me to follow.

As she hurried along, I kept pace. If either of the techs looked up, they would only see her. Carminia was blocking me from sight.

When we got to the corner, I went first. Then I kicked my leg out, ready to book it.

But she'd anticipated that and snatched the back of my shirt. This was a woman who'd raised kids. I spun around, scowling. She let go and lifted her hands in mock surrender. She crossed her arms.

"Okay," she said, grabbing a device off her belt. A radio. She held it in one hand, which rested on her other arm. "You tell me why you are here, or I call."

"How do you know I won't just clock you? Knock you out?"

She laughed. "I have known many people over the years who would do such things." Carminia looked me up and down. "You are not one of those people."

"Okay."

"But," she said, shaking the radio at me, "I am old, and my judgment not so good. So tell me, and maybe I don't call the guards."

Leaning against the wall, I looked skyward. Stars for days. I heard the van fire up and then the tires spit gravel across the concrete.

I laughed. "Those guys ever drive slow?"

"If you did the work they did," she said, dim starlight glinting off her eyes, "you would drive fast too. Now, you talk."

Within two seconds, I had a dozen lies spun up in my head. All of which I knew I could sell. Or felt pretty confident I could.

But something about this woman reminded me of a Mexican version of my dad's mother. Or my own mother in maybe twenty years.

No, not twenty. Ten now?

Wow, where had the time gone?

Sure, I could have pulled a story, several, that I knew I could make her believe. I didn't.

Tired and tired of running and being chased and being bounced on the van roofs, I caved. And told her the truth.

Mostly.

Chapter Thirty-Nine

After a minute of listening to my story, the woman held up a finger and walked us over to a circular table with four seats. It was made from chalky stone and big enough to fit ten people around it.

I sat down across from Carminia. She came around and parked her butt on the same bench as me.

That made me like her instantly.

It took about ten minutes to go through the whole story. Well, not the *whole* story. Just the stuff from Whitey the shopkeeper on, really. She didn't need to know about my friend's moonlight skin allergy.

Carminia listened without a word. Every now and then, she would gasp, close her eyes, and bring her hands to her mouth.

I'd told her about gangsters and monsters and secret mountain labs and driving a stolen hearse—all of that. When I finished, she asked me the only question I wasn't prepared for.

"Why?"

I blinked.

"*Why?* Because those creatures are dangerous, Carminia," I said, throwing a hand to the darkness. "Out there in the world? You can't imagine— Wait. You know about these NextGen, don't you?"

Carminia folded her hands in her lap and looked toward the house. Then her gaze drifted back toward the long garden behind it. There was a straight line, a hard edge, that suggested a steep drop.

However, her gaze had landed in the far corner. In the shadows, I could make out the shape of a shed or small cabin.

I asked, "You've seen them?"

She shook her head then shrugged. Before I could ask her what the hell that meant, she repeated her question, more specifically.

"Why you?" she asked in heavily accented English. "Why do you and your friend risk dying to do this?"

"Ha, I mean... You think we should call the police or something?"

She flapped her hand in the air in that way only older women can pull off. All the emotions and arguments, points and counterpoints dismissed in a bend of the wrist and waving fingers.

"No, this *palace* of theirs?" She motioned to the Greek mansion, a scowl bending her soft face. "It used to belong to a police chief, very corrupt, many years ago. After he died—and not well, this I will say—many thought it would be turned into a resort. Another company buys it, no one knows who, and now we have... this."

I looked at the massive wall next to us. It was almost as long as a football field, and there were columns and cornices and statues and topiaries all down the side. Everywhere you looked.

The design looked far less ancient Greek and more like a sociopath-multimillionaire fever dream.

When I asked her when the company, which I assumed was Covenant, had purchased the property, she told me it had been years earlier. Decades.

That didn't jibe with what I knew. Or thought I knew.

A parent company of Covenant, maybe?

I started to ask about it, but she shook her head, pointed at me, and crossed her arms. She still wanted her answer. I knew this woman would be watching me to tell the truth. So I told her the truth, wrapping it around a lie.

"I told you about Kane."

"Yes. Big Frenchman who likes blue jeans."

"Ha, right." I'd given her the basics. "His brother was killed by one of those creatures. An earlier version of them called Enhanced. This upgrade they've got... well, Kane is making sure they can't harm anyone else ever again."

She nodded, more satisfied. Then asked, "And you? Why are you helping this Kane?"

"Because he's my friend."

For a long, long moment, she stared at me. Then got a quirky smile and nodded.

Carminia proceeded to tell me that she'd been hired on to cook and take care of the house. Which was empty.

"Empty? Why do you have to take care of a house that no one uses?"

This got a laugh out of her. "Oh, the head man uses this house. He just never comes. Pops up on screens or in the conference room, which you saw, yes?"

"Yeah. Weird."

"Try walking through quiet house, and suddenly, the big head is up there on the screen."

"Why? What for?"

"He is some big, big boss," she said then lowered her voice and leaned in. "From what I overheard, he is only involved now because the person who was running this, she left suddenly. He was up higher, yes? All-the-way-up person?"

I nodded. "Like corporate or something? CEO?"

"Yes, CEO." She nodded and pointed at me with a big smile. "So he takes over."

"To do what?"

Carminia shuddered. "To make those things. That conference room also has meetings with guests that come." She pointed to the rear of the massive palace, hooking her hand up and over. "On the back, down more steps, there is a long, long strip of road."

"Long strip. A landing strip?"

"*Si*, yes, landing strip. For planes."

I stood to get a better look but only saw blackness out in the distance. Sitting again, I asked, "What are the meetings for?"

Carminia wrung her hands. "When they are here, I make the big dinners. And have to clean it all up after, which takes much longer."

"Dinner for who?"

"Money people. From all over. Different accents," she said, her voice lowering again. "They are buyers. They come to see the things."

I nodded. "Here? In this palace?"

She shook her head. "No. Other place, down the road, it is—"

"Right, the Church," I said, interrupting her. We'd already been out there too long, and I had to get back to find Kane. "I saw it earlier tonight."

"No, not church. Well, yes, they call it 'the Church,' but it is old convent. Closed many, many years ago and was supposed to be torn down. A few weeks ago, these people? They buy it."

"Why would they want a run-down convent?"

Carminia shrugged. "It has tunnels below. These were used many, many years ago, back in 1800s. The nuns used to hide escaped slaves from Texas and Louisiana. Part of the railroad."

I shook my head. "The Underground Railroad?"

"*Si*, that is it," she said proudly. "Mexico makes slavery illegal much earlier than the US. So escaped slaves cross border to start new lives. One of the places they went was the old convent. When authorities come to inspect, they find nothing. Because the people are below."

"Wow, that's pretty great."

"It *was* until someone finds out about the tunnels. There is a river, which the nuns used for milling. Bad people, they make water go down the hill," she said and sighed. "The people below did not survive. Convent was closed after that, but some believe their spirits remain."

"Spirits?"

"Haunted."

I closed my eyes, holding my hands to my chest. The light breeze around us felt like it had turned colder.

Carminia broke the silence.

"Yes, well, now, those tunnels are where they keep those things." She pointed back to the circular drive by the massive steps. "The money people come in here, they have dinner. The vans come and take them to the convent so they can see. When they return, who is interested go into room, one by one, and speak to the big head man."

"Why?"

"To *buy*, Emelda. These men are warlords and militia bosses, and they place orders, then"—she fluttered her hand and made a whoosh sound—"they get in planes and go."

I slumped back against the stone table. "Then we have to destroy them before they get out in the world."

"Two days," Carminia said.

"What?"

She nodded, looking at her hands again. "Yesterday, I am cleaning up after the meeting, and the head comes out of the conference room table, and he tells me. Friday, more planes coming. Six of them."

"Oh shit."

"I say to Mr. Janus, 'How many people do you expect for dinner?' But he says, no more dinners after Friday. Just make Palace extra tidy. These people will come through, go and come back, and go straight to the planes. He tells me that I am to go to my quarters when the first plane arrives and to not leave. To *not* look out the windows."

Standing, I walked toward where I knew the dark airstrip was. "It's Wednesday night. We have to take care of this tomorrow."

"How can you do this?"

I turned to her. "I don't know. My friend just blew up their mountain labs. Maybe we do the same with the old convent, if that's where all these monsters are."

The old woman rose slowly from the bench and walked toward the back of the property, but she didn't go toward the gaudy Greek home. She pointed ahead to the smaller stone building that had been hidden in shadow. I followed her.

"Not all there," she said, her voice so quiet I could barely hear her.

Carminia waved me over to the tiny cabin's one small square window. Behind the thick glass, iron bars blocked anyone from getting in.

Or out.

When I looked inside, my heart broke in a million pieces.

Chapter Forty

I looked at the boxy truck parked on the side of the dirt road. Couldn't help it. I stared.

"There was a time," Carminia said, fumbling with her apron, "I wanted to open a restaurant. But I started with this."

"A food truck?"

"Yes, food truck!" She said a bit too loudly then hushed herself. "After my husband was gone, I didn't have the money for a building. So this." Carminia smiled and stroked the side of the truck.

"It's nice," I said, feeling like crap. "And I'm sorry about your husband."

She laughed. "I'm not. He left."

"Oh."

Rubbing a spot on the side of her truck with her thumb, she said, "He leave me for a fifty-three-year-old Instagram lady foot model who has one of those porn pages with the fans."

"Oh."

"I hear he does the clipping now." She shrugged. "Her toes too."

I shook my head a few times. It didn't help. There was a *lot* to unpack there.

"But the business is on a break. Has been for a while." Carminia brightened and smiled at me. "One of the guards remembered my tacos! *Everyone* remembers my tacos."

She had taken me past her temporary home—she'd emphasized it was temporary—which was a tiny house on the far edge of the complex. About a quarter mile down a winding dirt road sat her food truck, pointing down the hill as if primed for a fast getaway.

The truck's red-and-white awning had been rolled up and secured with rope. At the top, the name of her business-on-wheels was written in painted script.

Tacos Locos.

"Your truck is called Crazy Tacos?"

"Marketing." She shrugged. "You have to find a way to stand out."

"I'll remember that."

Minutes earlier, I had told her I had to get out of there and asked if they kept any spare vans on the property. She'd been hesitant, but after hearing my story, she said she wanted to help.

That was when she'd led me to the van, making me promise to take care of it. I had and meant it.

"Is there a way I can reach you?" I asked after she'd pushed the keys at me. "Can I get your cell number?"

"They made me put my phone in a metal box when I got here."

Nodding, I popped open the door. I had to grip its handle and lift myself to get up into the truck. "That makes sense."

"Most upsetting is that I have farms I must tend to."

"Oh," I said, looking around in the distance as if crops would suddenly spring from the desert scrub. "You make your own ingredients? For the taco truck?"

Shaking her head, she mumbled, "Farmville."

Ah. Right.

In a few hours, the morning sun would be blinking at the horizon. Hopefully, Kane made it back to the hotel before that happened. A big naked dude wandering through town would attract attention we didn't need.

I hopped onto the raised driver's seat and banged into the other door, nearly falling off. When I looked underneath, it was basically attached to a fat, coiled spring.

It reminded me of the old junky playground near my grandmother's house that had these animals you could ride when I was a kid. A lion, a duck, and a horse. Originally, the horse had been a unicorn. Danny Slathery had tried bending the big spring all the way down so he could ride the horn. We all watched. Danny lost his grip.

He'd moved out of the neighborhood after that. Sometime later, they'd snapped off the horn.

Settling myself on the food truck's seat, I jammed the key in to fire up the ignition. It did not fire.

"It's dead," I said, calling out the window.

She pointed down the road.

"Starter is no good. This is why it is pointing toward the downhill." Carminia swept her hand low and out. "Roll down and start."

I nodded. "Gotcha."

"Always park somewhere uphill to roll and start. *Comprende?*"

I did comprende.

In a decade of driving, I'd never once owned a new vehicle. The asking price on every car I'd purchased had been followed by the letters OBO. I had popped many, many clutches over the years.

Releasing the parking brake, I shifted the gear stick—a long, bent pipe jutting from the floor—into Neutral. The moment I pulled my foot off the brake, the big, boxy truck began to roll. Carminia walked alongside for a few moments and touched the side of the vehicle gently.

"I'll take care of it," I called out the window. "Promise."

The truck picked up speed, leaving her behind. She called after me.

"*Buena suerte,*" she said. "Good luck, Emelda Thorne."

I watched the speedometer climb and climb, feeling my hands get a bit damp. How was I going so fast already?

Ah, right.

The gauge was in kilometers, not miles. Unfortunately, it didn't also have the miles-per-hour conversion. I didn't know how fast fifty kilometers per hour was, but that felt like a good round number to pop the clutch.

"Okay, Crazy Taco," I said because I'd always felt talking to vehicles got them on your side. "Ready?"

My sweaty fingers gripping the key in the ignition, I released the clutch and twisted. "Fire in the hole!"

I should have been wearing the seat belt.

The vehicle bucked and rocked and *futt-futt-futted,* knocking me around. I twisted the wheel as I nearly tumbled out of the too-high, spring-loaded seat. Then suddenly—

Vrroom!

The Crazy Taco came to life and rocketed forward. I'd been pointing at an angle so had to quickly cut the wheel to get back onto the dirt-and-gravel road. I fishtailed left and right for about thirty feet, then I got control.

When I looked at the large wing mirror, I could see Carminia had covered her eyes.

"It's all good," I yelled out the window. "Thank you!"

Time to get to the hotel. And find a steep hill to park my ride.

Chapter Forty-One

B y the time I finally rolled into town, it was dawn. I'd gone up and down roads that turned into desert all night. In the end, I found the pink spires on the horizon and used that as my guide.

I drove past the hotel to mentally drop a pin in my mind map. Not willing to slow too much because I worried about the damn Crazy Taco conking out, I flew past.

Out of the corner of my eye, a block past the hotel, I saw a huge black Mercedes.

"Shit," I said to the truck. "Kinda looks like our hearse."

That didn't make sense.

We'd parked the vehicle on the other side of the square, and some local thieves had boosted it. There was no way someone would park a stolen vehicle within a few hundred yards of where they had taken it.

Right?

I put that thought of my mind, hooked a right, and eventually found a steep enough incline to ensure I could get the Crazy Taco cooking again. I did a three-point turn in the road to turn around.

Which turned into a thirteen-point turn, blocking traffic on both sides of the skinny road.

After a few long minutes of blaring horns, waggling fingers, and angry Spanish words—where I'd heard the word for "mother" at least half a dozen times—I finally got the van parked. After a small prayer, I flicked the engine off.

Leaning over to the dash, I rubbed my hand gently across the cracked vinyl.

"Thank you, Crazy Taco. Please start when I come back, 'k?"

I heard knocking on the side of the van. Hard. Insistent. *Shit, if that's the cops...*

In the wing mirror, I saw a man and a woman come up, staring at the truck then at me.

"*¿Estás abierta hoy?*" the woman asked, eyes wide.

It took me a second to process the words. In my best Spanish, which was awful, I told them that, no, I wasn't open today.

The man mumbled something softly, which I didn't pick up. He then turned to the woman and, with a half smile, spoke again. She furrowed her brow and smacked him playfully.

They walked off, arm in arm.

I hadn't understood a word they'd said to each other but knew exactly what the exchange was about.

"*I guess I'll have to eat your cooking, then?*"

Smack.

Either I'd subconsciously picked up the too quickly spoken words, or I'd just read their body language. A deep French-Canadian voice rang in my memory.

Furrow and frown. Twitch and shift.

"He's becoming more human, and I'm becoming more wolf," I said, shrugging, as I opened the creaking door and hopped out. "I think I'm getting the better deal."

* * *

Ten minutes later, I walked into the blissfully cool air of the hotel lobby. Breezing past the front desk, I took two steps at a time and then realized that I didn't have my bag.

No room key.

And worse—the Covenant-made serum had been in my bag.

"Stupid," I said, smacking the heel of my palm on my forehead. Kane would have picked it up because it was the key to him getting back to his family. I couldn't drag that stuff around anymore.

When I got to the room, a cleaning woman was standing at our door, peeking in. A cart with towels was parked a few feet away.

"Excuse me," I said, but when she saw me, she brushed past, saying, "No English." I turned to watch her disappear down the hall when I heard a familiar voice.

"Emelda? Is this you?"

My heart sang. *Thank God.* I grabbed the door before it closed and pushed it wide but didn't see him. The bed was as messy as I'd left it the day before.

Kane's voice came from the bathroom. "Emelda?"

"You made it!"

His deep baritone rattled through the door: "Yes, come in."

As I opened the door, I said, "I'm so happy— Yow!"

I closed the door again, scrunching my eyes closed and shaking my head from side to side. After a few seconds, he called my name again.

"Um," I said. "You could have warned me you were in the tub, man."

"Okay," he said. "I am in the tub."

"Did you invite the housekeeper into the bathroom too?"

"House... keeper?" His voice brightened. "This is like Mrs. Garrett of the Life Facts show, yes?"

"I have no idea what that means," I said and told him to draw the curtain and cover up. I opened the door, and he welcomed me with a warm smile from the edge of a sheet of plastic covered in yellow flowers.

"I am very happy you are okay, Emelda."

His head swiveled back to stare at the water. I wanted to hear about how he'd blown up the mountain, sure, but we had very little time and had to make plans. That said, I could tell something was bothering him. When I asked him about it, he told me.

I sat on the toilet seat. I asked him to repeat what he'd said. When he did, I still couldn't believe it.

"You became a wolf again?" I asked, a smile tugging at my lips. "You're serious."

"Yes."

In the space of five seconds, I'd asked ten different questions. At no time did he even look in my direction. Finally, I settled on the most important one.

"How?" I asked and sat on the floor. Sitting on the toilet felt gross. "How did that happen?"

He shrugged then motioned down to his body. A group of bubbles drifted off his fingertips and floated behind the curtain.

"Alas, I am a human man again," he said. "Only a small taste of the world I crave, and this is stolen from me when the sun comes up."

I blinked. "Wait. When the sun came up? So you changed because of—"

"Yes, even with no moon, I changed."

Shaking my head slowly, it started to make sense. Well, as much as this sort of stuff could make sense.

"It's not no moon, Kane. Not really," I said, looking at the ceiling. "New moon just means the Earth is blocking the sun. The moon's still up there. We just can't see it."

He lifted a dripping hand and waved it in the air. Bubbles fell to the floor. "All of this means little. I have no control. And now it is worse."

"No, Kane. No, not at all."

He turned to me, catching the tone of my voice.

I spoke the thoughts as they raced through my brain. "Remember how we were worried about the serum we got from Covenant?"

"The one that killed Gregor. Yes."

"Right, right," I said. "But he was *already* dying. When the serum entered his body, the virus that changed him into an Enhanced became dormant. He reverted back to being human."

"Which I do not want, yes." Kane shook his head slowly and started to rise.

I threw a hand out. "No, no. Don't get up."

He slid back down, but his eyes were closed. I'd never seen him so down.

"So we were worried that you might take the stuff, and poof, no more Wolfwere. But, like Gregor, you stayed human. But now..." I trailed off, waiting for him to finish the sentence.

He blinked and looked at me. I rolled my hand, egging him on to finish the thought.

"But now..." he said slowly. Pensively. I nodded excitedly, and he added, "Now, you are going to tell me why this is good?"

I sighed but smiled through it. I snatched a sliver of soap off the side of the tub and chucked it at his hairy chest.

"If the new moon changes you into a wolf," I said, back on track, "we wait until it comes back, and *then* we give you the serum. That way, I think, you would stay a wolf."

In his eyes, I could see the wheels turning. They picked up speed, and he snapped his head toward me.

"Yes. *Yes*, Emelda," he said and slammed his hand down, splashing water. I laughed. He continued, "I am so lucky to have a smart human with me. Yes! That is it!"

As quickly as the joy had come, it was replaced by an electric trill of fear.

"Wait," I said, swallowing. "You did bring the bag back, right?"

He nodded. "Yes, I wore it like a headband, for I was very much sweating as I pedaled the moped bike."

"Pedaled? It's got a motor."

Kane stood, pulling the curtain closed for my benefit. But not totally closed. And I looked away far slower than I should have.

"Ran out of gas," he said, reaching around the curtain's other side and grabbing a towel.

"That's why we had the extra fuel can in the basket, man," I said and left the bathroom. On the writing table, I saw my bag and smiled. I called through the wall, "There had to be at least a gallon of gas in there. Did you use it?"

"Oh, yes. I did use," he said, and I heard him chuckling. "Just not for the moped bike."

Chapter Forty-Two

As Kane dressed, he told me what had happened at the top of the mountain the night before. I'd seen the craziest shit in my life since I'd met him. This was a whole new level.

"You called for help," I said, laughing, "and got coyotes?"

He frowned at me.

"Do not disparage the cousin wolf," he said, pulling on his T-shirt and buckling his pants. "I think many of them sacrificed their lives to help me."

Putting on my serious face, I nodded and apologized.

I'd put the bag up on the bed. I unzipped it and pulled out the book-sized box. Flicking the clasp, I opened it up. The syringe with the serum was intact.

Good.

Closing the box, I shoved it back into the sack. I would have to find somewhere much safer to store it. Maybe the hotel had a safe?

"Here's the plan, then," I said. "Once we're done here, we wait until the next new moon then give you the shot."

"Here?"

"No, not here, man. We'll get you back home to Canada." I pointed north.

He smiled and gestured in the opposite direction.

"Whatever. In the meantime, we can chill. Have a few weeks of rest."

"After we kill the monsters."

"Yes, of course," I said, blowing out a breath. "After that. Or... we could just go now?"

He shook his head slowly. I sighed.

"Fine. I had to try. But this is going to be so much harder than anything we've done before. They'll be much stronger."

"Which is why I must destroy them. My responsibility."

Before I could say anything else, a knock came at the door. Probably the housekeeper checking to see if the room was clear now. Or so she could take another peek at the guy in the tub.

I crossed the room and turned the handle.

"Emelda, wait! Do not—"

The door was shoved from the other side, knocking me back. Standing in the doorway was a man dressed in a suit. Behind his left shoulder was another man, at least a head taller. Over his left?

The woman I'd seen leaving the room.

I said to her, "Don't need housekeeping. Can you come back later?"

When she smiled, it made the hairs on my arms prickle.

The man in front stepped forward and put a hand on my shoulder, which triggered Kane. He jumped toward us, fist already raised. He stopped when the taller man rested his hand on the shoulder of the man in front of me.

He leveled a pistol at my head.

Suit Guy laughed and clasped his hands together then said, "Everyone friends?" He bent down to my ear. "Tell your large friend to take a seat."

I frowned. "Do it, Kane."

The three of them piled in and closed the door. The woman blocked the exit, still dressed in her fake housekeeping outfit. The taller man checked the bathroom then stood in that door. Dude was big. Only a few inches shorter than my French-Canadian friend.

The guy running the show introduced himself as Carlo. He did not introduce his two friends. Both had pistols out. Not directly pointing them at us, but the threat was there.

Carlo stood at the wall and motioned for me to sit on the bed, keeping me between him and Kane. I didn't, and he grinned.

"You have sent us on quite a chase, Emelda Thorne," he said, flashing a set of crooked teeth at me. "We have Miss Rosa's hearse, which she will be happy about. Has a few dings, sure, but there is something missing."

I crossed my arms. "Her Nickelback CD? Yeah, I chucked that out the window."

This got a laugh from Carlo. "No. And so much hate for Nickelback. They are not so bad."

"I would have to agree," Kane said, speaking for the first time. "Unfair, so much hate. Very good Canadian band. They have won several Juno awards."

Carlo kept his eyes on me but spoke to Kane. "No one knows what those are." He leaned forward, his smile falling like a house collapse. "Where are the caskets?"

What?

I mean, I knew what he'd meant when he said something was missing. But what the hell did they want the coffins for?

Stalling for time, I asked, "What coffins?"

I would have to work on my stalling-for-time tactics. Even I let out a small groan. Carlo leaned back against the wall, but I couldn't help but notice he'd started to clench and unclench his fists.

Whatever. I'd had far tougher guys than this loser try to intimidate me.

"The moment the vehicle you stole stopped," he said, waving to the other three, "we took a flight down. A chance to see a bit of the homeland. It has been too long. For you, never, yes?"

I pursed my lips, not giving him anything.

"Such a shame. Your mother, born here. Your *abuelo,* also born and lived here," he said, the side of his mouth twitching upward. "That means grandfather in Spanish."

"I know what it means!"

Shuffling back, I sat on the bed. He lifted his hands and tilted his head, eyes closed, in a mock apology.

"Depending on what you say next," Carlo said, "you will claim a piece of Mexico that neither of them have."

"Oh?"

He bent down on one knee and put a hand next to me on the bed. "You will be buried here."

Kane rose behind me, growling, but I turned my head to the side. I knew he could read my expression. He sat back down at the writing table. I could feel the heat of his anger on my back.

Carlo asked, "Where are they? Tell us, and you can both go free."

I didn't need to be able to read the guy to know that wasn't true. The only thing keeping us alive at that moment was that he didn't know where to find the coffins.

But I was still perplexed. "Your boss is worth millions, right?"

He shrugged, and his hand slid closer to my leg.

"She can buy a hundred coffins," I continued. "Why those two?"

"Rosa is sentimental."

"No, I wanna know," I said, looking around and trying to look casual. We had three people between us and the door. How the hell were we going to get out alive? "Why those coffins?"

He stood straight and put his hands on his hips, which tugged his coat back and exposed the butt of his pistol. Then he nodded toward Kane. "Does *he* know where they are?"

I shrugged.

"Okay," he said, pulling out the gun and pointing it at Kane. "I know that you do. So why don't we shoot him?"

"Do it," I said. "Fine."

He glanced down at me then raised his gun higher. "Fine? What fine? I said I will shoot him if you don't tell me!"

I stood and crossed in front of the nose of his pistol, resisting the urge to flick it.

"But if you kill him, where's the incentive for me to tell you after that? You can't shoot him, Carlo."

The woman at the door chuckled and muttered something under her breath.

"I can," Carlo said, stepping closer to me. "I shoot him, and then Carlita takes little pieces off you. She starts at your toes and works her way up until you tell us."

Carlita took a step forward and purred. She actually purred at the very thought of cutting pieces off my body.

I tried to swallow, but my mouth had gone dry. Although the factory in my brain that made asshole juice was still cranking.

"Wait. Carlo and Carlita?" I tried to control the shaking in my voice. "Are you guys related?"

"It is all family. Rosa is my great-aunt and Carlita a cousin. Several times removed, I think. We like to keep it in the family." Carlo's smile deepened in a way that made me ill. "Which is why it hurts so much to think that you, Emelda, would betray us."

I was ready to hit him with another snarky remark, but... *what did he just say?* That factory in my brain clanked to a stop.

"Yes. Oh yes, but this was nothing new," he said, speaking slowly. "The granddaughter of Nicolas Zaragoza is known to us. In the past, you have worked for our competitors but always such little jobs. Petty house thief. Inconsequential. Until a few days ago, of course, which has finally reunited us."

My head spun. These assholes knew me. *Knew* my grandfather?

"You're full of crap," I said, my voice trembling. "Granddad was a *miner*. Not a crook."

Carlo shrugged, clearly enjoying my discomfort. "You are partially right. Nico was not a very good crook, no. But always very 'full of crap,' yes? Which is why Rosa set him up in that shop many, many years ago."

I shook my head. "No way. No way!"

"We knew all about our competitor's operations, thanks to him. A dutiful soldier spy."

"That can't be true," I said. The denial felt hollow even to me. "He only went to Minneapolis because my mother lived there."

That made Carlo laugh. "And why is that? Because she got a very nice job at a florist in Minneapolis, yes? Emelda, who do you think owned that flower shop?"

I sat back down on the bed, staring at the wall. I said nothing.

"Nico's daughter meets some white boy and wants to move to America. So many young people want to go north, but the paperwork? Impossible. So he asks Rosa for help," Carlo said and opened his hands to the ceiling. "Miraculously, she has a job and residency and—this is important—Nico has a debt."

"To spy on the Family," I said in a whisper. I thought about the figurine, my grandfather's wood carving, in Whitey's shop. It was true. I knew it was true.

Carlo snapped his fingers in front of my face, bringing me back. But when I came back, I'd brought something with me.

Rage.

Full-on, eye-watering rage.

"Old news, all of this," Carlo said, lifting the gun from his belt. "Tell us where—"

I dropped to the floor.

Before my hands even touched the carpet, Kane was up and hurling the chair at Carlo. It smacked the man in the chest, and his gun went flying.

Kane rolled forward, leaping over top of me, and rose up, clocking the tall man on the chin and lifting the guy off his feet.

When he began to fold, Kane threw the big man at the woman before she could get a lock on him with her pistol. The unconscious man's body smashed her against the door, and the two of them rolled deeper into the room.

A second later, Carlita recovered, raised herself onto her knees and lifted the gun toward me.

The door slammed open, smacking the weapon from her hand.

In the gap, a white-haired man in a crisp gray suit and expensive sunglasses looked around. He pointed his own pistol around the room, heard the woman behind the door groan, and smashed it into her again.

I jumped to my feet, unsure what to do next. Kane stepped between me and this new threat.

The man in the gray suit held the door open wider, waving us forward.

"Come quickly," he said in a Spanish accent. But not Mexican Spanish. Different. "We must go!"

Chapter Forty-Three

I could hear Kane's big feet stomping down the hall behind me and feel the labored breath of the man in the gray suit on my neck.

Who was this guy?

Hooking a left to take the stairs down, I felt a hard yank on my right arm.

"No, no," he said, his eyes inscrutable behind the brown sunglasses. "Up."

"Up?"

"Yes, yes. They have more of their people waiting by the exits."

Of course they did.

Kane stopped at the stairwell and looked at me. Then we both heard the shouting coming from our room. Before they could come out, I bolted after Gray Suit up the stairs, which shook with the big guy's pounding feet behind me.

It wasn't like we could go far. The hotel only had three floors, and I'd run out of stairs. I looked down the empty corridor.

More shouting below. They were coming.

A head popped out of a door halfway down the hall. I knew this guy was with Gray Suit. Not only because the white-haired man was running toward him, but the dude was wearing the exact pair of brown-tinted sunglasses.

I could taste acid on the back of my tongue, swallowed it down, and with no other options, raced toward the open door and ducked inside. Kane was right on my heels.

The suite was similar to the one we'd just left, with an extra room through a door between the two single beds. These guys had gone for the upgrade.

And just who were *these guys*?

I could see another two men in that second room. One stood near a window. Both were wearing the same damn sunglasses.

Like these guys all went on afternoon shopping sprees together.

Gray Suit had crossed the room and peeked over the rail of the tiny balcony. He pulled the curtains closed, and they waved lazily in the breeze.

"Please sit," he said.

Huh. They'd gotten a double.

I glanced at one of the beds and—nope—so I strode over to the table by the balcony, crossing between him and one of the beds. Kane stood in the short hallway next to the bathroom.

The guy who'd waved us in was attempting to close the door but struggling to get around my friend. He placed a gentle hand on Kane's back to move the big man and—nope. *Good luck with that, buddy.*

"Please, sir," he finally said in an accent like the first guy's, extending his hand deeper into the room.

The shouting outside was growing louder. Kane looked toward me, and I nodded. He took one step forward. The door closed.

"Sir?" Gray Suit said and let his hand drift to the other chair at the table.

Kane's gaze locked on the man's face. Kane glanced at me then went into the adjoining room.

"What is your friend doing?" Gray Suit asked.

"What are *you* doing?" I asked, hoping he would pull out a badge or something. "What the hell is going on here?"

The tall man slipped off his dark sunglasses and put them in his breast pocket. He introduced himself as Gabriel.

"Okay, Gabe," I said. "Who are you?"

He smiled. "Would you rather we give you back to Rosa's people? I can have my man call for them." Gabriel took a few steps toward the door, extending his hand, his long fingers fluttering in the air.

"Are you the police?" I nodded to his coat pocket. "Or, like, Feds?"

"Of a sort," he said with a wide grin, showing off perfectly capped teeth. "Are you okay? I expect that was a traumatic experience."

I sighed. "I'm fine. We're fine." I relaxed my shoulders and slumped against the wooden chair. "And thank you for helping. I got the feeling we weren't getting out of there alive."

"You were not."

Gabriel said it with such finality, such assurance, I felt the panic well up in me all over again. I guess he'd read it on my face.

"Don't worry, Emelda," he said with a warm smile. "They would not expect you to come up to the third floor."

"I didn't expect it!"

"Exactly," he said and sat on the corner of the bed. He faced me and crossed one leg over the other. He tugged on his pants leg to straighten it. "You are in danger in this city. Rosa has sent her people to retrieve what you have taken, They won't stop until they have it."

"I should have taken the damn jeep. Even if it didn't have wheels, the ride would have been smoother than this."

He frowned at me and asked, "¿*Qué?*"

I waved him off. The dude's Spanish sounded so... lyrical. A bit proper. Musta went to some fancy school. Do fancy schoolkids become cops? Or whatever he was?

"We can offer you protection." Gabriel looked to the adjoining door and frowned. "Both of you. Eventually Rosa's people will leave this hotel to search the city. It is then that we can get you to a safe house."

I liked hearing the word safe because I hadn't felt that way in a very long time. We still had to get to the Church, but the priority was leaving the hotel. Alive, preferably.

"Okay," I said.

Gabriel turned to his man in the leather jacket at the door and spoke in rapid Spanish. Too fast for me to catch all the words. I was pretty sure I heard the words for "telephone" and "quickly" and maybe "chicken."

Not so sure about that last one.

I really needed to bone up on my Spanish.

But I'd grown up with two native speakers. And a number of times, my mother had waved me into the room to talk with family down in Mexico. And she'd had Spanish-speaking friends.

None of their accents sounded quite like Gabriel's.

Something was off. Or maybe I was being paranoid.

"The arrangements are being made, Emelda," he said. "It will only be a few minutes."

"Arrangements? That sounds ominous."

He laughed. "Transport to the safe house. Stay as long as you like."

I looked to find Kane, but he was still in the other room.

"What is your role in all of this, Gabriel?"

The thin man entwined his fingers. "We are only seeking the return of the stolen items."

My world dropped into a lower gear, slowing down all around me. I looked at the door again. Where was Kane?

"The *what?*"

Gabriel leaned forward. "Where are the coffins?"

I couldn't take it and jumped up from my chair. The leather-jacket guy by the door shifted his feet.

"Why is everyone asking about two damn death boxes?" I shouted. "Rosa can take her last ride in a cardboard box. It ain't gonna change where she's going to end up."

"Yes, of course, but—"

"Hell. I was implying she was going to hell."

Gabriel nodded. "I gathered that."

"Great. Good. It was, you know, kind of a nice line, and I wanted to make sure that was clear."

"It was."

Kane poked his head in from the other room and raised his eyebrows. I nodded. He disappeared again. What the hell was he doing?

Gabriel's face turned serious, and he spoke softly.

"Within those 'death boxes,' as you call them, are two old artifacts, very old, that mean very much to our employer." He tilted his head to the side as if considering something. "We have business connections with friends in Minneapolis. As a favor to us, the Family tasked your boyfriend with stealing the plates from Rosa Nieto's warehouse. Which you did when you took the caskets."

"That wasn't the... I mean, they're *empty*. We looked," I said, growling my words. "And it's *ex*-boyfriend. Very ex, now."

The man in the gray suit shook his head and held his hand out to indicate I should sit again. When I did, he slid a few inches closer.

"From what we understand," the man said, pressing a few strands of his gray hair behind his ear, "the disks are hidden in a false bottom within the caskets."

Groaning, I shot to my feet again and leaned against the sliding glass door. I ignored the frown from Gabriel. It had all become clear to me.

Whitey had sent us on the warehouse job to find some gold and silver artwork. Disks. But we hadn't found them in the warehouse because they'd been hidden. Hidden in the car we'd used to escape.

Taking a half step onto the tiny concrete balcony, I looked down. I felt a pang of jealousy. Families. Couples. People sunbathing by a crystal-blue pool. It didn't look like any of them had had guns pointed at them all day.

"I should have taken the damn jeep." I chuckled darkly. "Even if it didn't have wheels, the ride would have been smoother than this."

The man in the leather jacket exchanged a few words with Gabriel as I stared at the serene scene below. I wished I was down there.

"Rosa's people have left the hotel. Shortly, we can leave, too, but I must know where the caskets are, Emelda. We must have those plates back."

I threw my hands up. "You're not cops."

"No."

"So this is about money?"

He shrugged. "Oh, they are very valuable, but my employer doesn't want to sell them for profit. His family has had them in its possession for generations They are a piece of history, hidden for centuries."

"History?"

Gabriel smiled and sat down in the chair I'd vacated. He looked up to me.

"When the great General Cortez came to this part of the world in the seventeenth century, he elevated the people he met. The Aztecs were primitive. Tribal. He enlightened them."

I had heard a very different version of that encounter. Sure, I wasn't any sort of history buff, but to my family, Cortez had been an asshole. An asshole in a shiny hat that looked like a spittoon.

"The leader of the Aztecs," the white-haired man continued, "thankful for enlightenment of his new Spanish benefactors, bequeathed gifts to Cortez. You know Montezuma, yes?"

"Sure," I said and leaned against the sliding door, exhausted. "Something about not drinking the tap water."

"Among those gifts were a gold disk and a silver disk. A gift to the Spanish people," he said and spread his arms, palms open. "My employer wants these returned to Spain, where they belong."

"And Rosa wants to sell them for millions?"

He chuckled. "She could get far more, but no. Both represent deities to the Mexican people who feel they hold power."

"What? You mean like everlasting life?"

"Nothing so ghoulish," he said and made a smacking sound with his lips like he'd bitten into a lemon. "Rosa sees herself as a queen, a ruler, in this life. Now that she is close to dying, she wants to be a queen in the afterlife as well."

"You have *got* to be joking."

"As I said, old Mexican beliefs. These people are very simplistic."

I felt an anger bubble up in me. One that I hadn't even known I had, but in an instant, I knew exactly where it came from.

"You're talking about *my* people," I said. "So maybe watch your damn mouth, yeah?"

He lifted his hands to me, the palms almost bleach white against his olive skin.

"No offense meant. I am only explaining."

Then it all made sense. "You came all the way from Spain? Here?"

He nodded.

That explained his odd accent. Dude was old-school Spanish. Not new-cool Mexican Spanish.

I looked back down at the lush, perfect courtyard below. Two families splashed away in a circular pool without a care in the world. If I gave the coffins over, at least this part of my crazy life would be done.

Yeah, we still had a small army of monsters to kill, but you should take the wins where you can.

But not this time.

"I dunno, Gabe," I said, looking to the door between the rooms. I really wanted to talk with Kane alone. He had great intuition about these things. But, then, so did I. "Maybe those old disks should go to the people of Mexico? From what I know of it, ol' Monte had been basically enslaved by Cortez, right?"

"Emelda, we both know you have left your past in the past," he said, grinning with those perfect teeth, but the smile didn't make it higher than his thin top lip. "You don't even speak Spanish."

"I know a few words," I said, shrugging. "You know *pendejo*? That's a good word."

In that moment, all his playfulness fell away. I didn't know if the word for asshole was the same in Mexican Spanish and, um, Spanish Spanish, but it seemed like it might be.

He steeled me with a hard look. "Give us the caskets."

I heard a thud in the next room, but Gabriel drew my attention back with a snap of his fingers. Glaring at me, he said, "If you return them to us, we will take you to the safe house."

"And if we don't?"

He shrugged, and I realized he hadn't even reacted to the thump in the next room. They'd done something to my friend, and Gabriel hadn't been surprised by it at all.

However, he certainly had to be surprised to see my big friend burst through the connecting door and launch himself over the bed at him.

Hell, I was surprised.

But not as surprised as I was when, after driving a knee to the head of Gabriel and climbing over the man, Kane grabbed me and kept running.

"Ooof!" I said as my friend lifted me, took one step onto the stone balcony, and leaped over the rail.

We were three stories up.

As I fell to the ground below, I got the idea that Kane had indeed seen something I hadn't.

Chapter Forty-Four

Kane

Ten minutes earlier

When I walk into the adjoining room of the fancy hotel suite, it smells like cleaning solution and fresh sheets. No one slept in this place last night.

This room does not belong to these men.

It also smells like Cheetos.

However, I do not see the package with the cartoon cat anywhere in this part of the suite. It may be in the next room, where Emelda is.

Here, I see two men. One staring out the window. The other at me. Neither says a word. But they do not have to.

On the man facing me, I see distrust. His eyes flicker to the other at the window, down, then back to me. Deception. He feigns a smile, a casual expression he does not feel. He fears being discovered. For he is hiding something.

And it is not tasty snacks.

In an attempt to look casual, the man puts his hands on his hips. When his jacket presses tighter to his waist, I see a bulge. For a moment, I stare at his bulge.

He shifts as he sees me stare at his bulge.

I think to reach out and grab it, but I know what it is. He has a weapon. If these men are authorities, as they pretend, this should not surprise me. However, he is nervous when I regard his bulge.

For the next few minutes, I stare at it. This is so he knows I know about his bulge. When he shifts to turn, I walk a few paces and continue to stare.

Emelda is shouting, so I go to the door between the rooms and look in. She is fine. Angry, but she likes being angry.

I step back into the room and see that the two men are sharing a glance. The movements of their limbs reveal nervous tension. Jerky. Twitching. Halting.

These men are not who they pretend to be.

When the man at the window turns, he sees me standing there and flashes an expression at his partner. The double wrinkle at the corner of his eye flicks. The dimple in his chin deepens. His lips, though, they tell me the real story.

Two very important pieces of information.

First, the unspoken question that hides behind his teeth. *Do we need to subdue this man?* That tells me the most important thing I need to know.

Like Carlo in the room below, these men will not let us leave until they get what they want. And, possibly, not even after that.

The second piece of information is what I see on his lips, and I now also have a question.

"Where is it that you are keeping your tasty Cheetos snacks?"

The man at the window looks to his partner then to me then back to his partner. Still facing his counterpart, his eyes flicker to me.

He is preparing himself to attack.

"Wha'?" he says.

Smiling—my expression also false, but fair is fair—I point at his face.

"Your lips, they have the orange dust. Some on your collar as well. It is very difficult to wash out of clothes. I recommend hot, not cold, water. And you may have to shout it out."

The man's concentration breaks, and he laughs incredulously. His friend shrugs and looks to the other. It is then that I grab the Bulging Man and hurl him toward his friend. The two smash into each other and collapse to the floor.

A second later, I am on top of them, and I slam my fist into the Bulging Man's face. The other, struggling beneath his friend, cannot punch and instead tries to push my face away. His pinky ring clacks against my teeth as his finger pulls at the corner of my mouth.

"*Alors!* It is the Flamin' Hot ones!" I pull his orange-dusted hand away. "So spicy."

Then I smash him in the face as well.

I twist to run away then spin back, rifle through his sports jacket, and find a single-serving bag of the tasty snacks with the troublesome orange fairy dust. I pocket these.

Back on my feet, I run from this room to the next and see Gabriel reaching toward Emelda. This angers me so. Shoving off with my left leg, I launch over the bed and drive a knee into his shoulder.

A reflection in the mirror spins. This is the woman blocking the room's exit. She is raising her weapon once again.

Can't go that way.

So I choose another.

I grab Emelda and take one stride across the balcony. I jump.

She shouts in my ear, "Holy sh—" but the second word, a favorite of hers, gets drowned out. Ha. Later, I will have to tell her of that thought.

Irony?

I don't know. The concept is still so confusing.

The pool's water is surprisingly cold, and I feel my body tense as we land between two elderly ladies on brightly colored and oversized floating donuts. They are both sent across the pool in waves, screaming.

I get to my feet, dripping with water that stings my eyes. A strange chemical smell.

Lifting Emelda because it is too deep for her to stand, I attempt to run to the far side of the pool.

"Ugh!" I bellow. "Cannot run. Water slowing me. Must move... faster!"

"Stop talking like that!" She pounds me on the shoulder and yells in my ear, "Put me down!"

But the man and the woman are at the window now, so I toss her out of the pool onto an inflatable lounger in the shape of a pink bird. She lands and bounces. The impact folds the bird's head downward, and she gets a big yellow beak to the head.

I leap out of the pool, into the air, and land next to her.

"You *jumped* out the window! How did you even know," Emelda says, struggling to get up from the deflating water fowl, "that would work?"

"Quickly, Emelda," I say, sticking my hand out but keeping my legs back. "The pink bird is trying to consume you!"

She smacks my hand out of the way and screams at me, "Flamingo!"

Such a good word! *Flamingo!* An exclamation of surprise, yes?

I love this word.

In the second window, one of the men I knocked down is standing and shouting and making strange finger gestures.

"That dude is pissed," she says, running toward the road along the back of the complex.

Following, I say, "I think he is very mad about the Cheetos."

When we get to the road, Emelda steps onto the blacktop. I see her seek out the church's pink spires then look to her right.

I spin back to the hotel. They are no longer in the windows. They are coming.

Damp sloshing tells me Emelda is running up the street. Water is still dripping off her, splashing out every time her pack smacks her back.

Horns blare as she crosses the street, and cars skid to a halt. I leap on top of a vehicle that comes within inches of smashing into her, glaring into the car.

"We need a vehicle," I shout to her, squinting at the driver. His goes slack, and I see a little part of his throat bob up and down. "This one will do."

She shouts over her shoulder, running faster, "I've got something better!"

Chapter Forty-Five

"This is not better," Kane said as he tumbled into the rear of the Crazy Taco and smashed into something that should not have been smashed into. The sounds of falling and clanging metal rang out behind me.

"Sorry," I said.

I'd taken the corner too fast, but we were running out of time. And, of course, running from not one group of murderous assholes but two.

The big French Canadian had been in a crabby mood even before we'd gotten to our ride. I'd asked him about it, and he'd been cryptic.

"Tasty snacks," he'd said. "Now soggy snacks."

His mood had not improved after I had him get out and push the taco truck. He had been unimpressed by it when he'd first seen the big boxy vehicle. The three twenty-something tourists didn't help.

"Are you open?" a woman asked in a European accent that sounded a bit like the Muppet chef.

Kane was leaning against the rear door, ready to push. I watched him in the side mirror as he straightened to face them.

He answered, "Open to what?"

A skinny blond man laughed. "A taco, mate!"

"Hmm. I have seen this thing on the Internet web," he said, shaking his head. "However, there are three of you. One too many, I think."

"What?"

I shouted out the window, "Kane! Gotta go!" He'd spun away from the pasty, confused people and had started pushing.

Parking on the hill would have worked just fine, but the moment I'd pulled out, another car crossed in front of us, and I had to slam on the brakes. It was a big black Mercedes. When I turned to get a better look, it had banked left and out of view.

Finally rolling, I was racing through the streets. My cell had been in my pocket when we'd gone for the impromptu swim, so I had it drying in the door handle.

So I had to use nineteenth-century GPS.

I scanned the tops of buildings to find the pink spires. They were especially majestic, with fluffy white clouds forming in the sky. After that, I drew a mental line to the mountaintop where the lab had been. On the opposite side would be the road that would take us to the convent.

After a five-minute detour, I headed toward the Church. I'd gone down a few streets that ended at the edge of town. There weren't any roads heading in the direction I needed to go.

"Hold on!"

So I made my own road.

To be honest, the desert was a bit smoother than the road. Fewer potholes.

After another half hour, pushing the Crazy Taco as fast as it would go, we began to rise up the slope. I cut left and rode along the mountainside, leaning but nowhere near tipping.

I headed straight and found the road.

Which, to be honest, kind of left me amazed. I felt like a tracker. Yeah, there was just the one road. but dammit, I found it! That made me a bit happy.

Kane was still grumpy. More so after I made the sharp turn from desert scrub to road.

"I think maybe I should drive," he grumbled as he stumbled up to the front compartment for the eleventh time. Maybe twelfth? I'd lost count. "Most of time in Crazy Taco truck has *not* been on road."

"This will take us where we need to go," I said. "Just relax."

"That is not possible when you drive."

"Hush."

At the first *Camino Cerrado* sign, something I'd wondered about the night before finally made sense. The sign hung from a metal crossbeam strung between two poles, which had been dug deep into the ground.

"Maybe we are not supposed to go this way," Kane said, looking in the wing mirror.

"It says Road Closed, but it's not," I said. "Or maybe it is, but this is the way to the convent. Last night, the driver of the van slowed three times, went onto the scrub, then got back onto the road."

Kane nodded, looking up at the sky. He sighed, draped his arm out the window, and stared at the desert. He fell silent.

I asked, "You okay?"

"I am fine," he said, sighing. "Tired. You must be very tired as well. No sleep."

"I'm running on adrenaline right now. And we're about to get into some subbasement full of monsters, so I'm thinking that'll be better than a triple espresso."

He turned to me. "Thank you for doing this."

"Doing what?"

"You are risking your life to do this thing. Monsters and gang people," he said. "Is very dangerous."

"I'm trying to help you, man. We need this, right?"

He nodded, tilted his head, and for the first time in hours, smiled.

"I think you are a good person, Emelda."

Swallowing down a lump of something in my throat, I stared at the dusty road, unsure what to say. I had been called many things in my life. The only person who'd ever said I was "good" had been my grandmother. I pulled her locket out of my shirt, kissed it, and tucked it back in.

"And you would have made a fine hunter," he added when I went quiet. "Which is the very best compliment."

"Hunter?"

He nodded to the back, and I checked the rearview. One of the caskets was on its side. Damn. He'd bashed into them pretty hard. The other looked jammed under a prep station. They were our insurance policy. If we did get caught by either of the asshole crews, we could drop the caskets and run.

To be honest, I had been kinda proud that I had wound around the streets and driven us right to where we'd stashed them. Not just proud but, as Kane had run to grab them, kind of astonished I'd done it.

No one who'd known me in the past would have ever described me as someone who was any good with directions. But that was before, and I guess this was now.

New and improved Emelda?

The jury was still out on that one.

After we went around the third roadblock, I told him my idea about killing the monsters. I always thought better while driving, and this trek through the desert had helped me come up with a plan that might work.

Maybe.

Chapter Forty-Six

I stopped the taco truck just before the big stone gate. The one that had nearly taken my head off when the van had sped under it.

The old convent appeared like something from a horror film. Somehow that felt sacrilegious to even think, so I looked up to the cross and whispered an apology. Kane saw this and laughed.

Just beyond the gate was a courtyard made up of rock that looked like busted-up brick. The path leading to it, the same sort of material. The walls of the convent were twenty feet high and solid stone. Black streaks dripped down from the roof.

In the middle of all the red gravel was the fountain I'd seen the night before. It might have been beautiful at one time. Now, it was full of leaves and branches from nearby trees. And, for being in the middle of the desert, the place had a lot of trees.

I knew the reason for that was to our right down a short road.

The courtyard was nestled in the gap left by the two front walls joining at a perpendicular angle. On the right, I saw two doors. Both had boards across the front. Spray-painted across the splitting gray wood was a word I didn't know.

But the message was clear enough.

Don't go in here.

"What is the black up by the roof?" Kane asked, pointing through the windshield.

"Mold, I think."

He turned to me, frowning. "In the desert?"

"Yeah," I said. "When you smell the air, what do you pick up?"

Kane sniffed and went through a list so long—wood, leaves, rot, decaying flowers, dirt, clay—I had to interrupt him.

"What about water?"

He frowned and nodded. I pointed to a part of the roof that jutted upward and was capped by another cross. I didn't know much about the architecture of covenants or churches, but it looked like a gazebo that you could access via stairs to look out at the grounds.

"Somewhere on the other side, around back, is where the nuns used to make bread," I said and told him the story that Carminia had told me. "It was how they paid for upkeep. The place was controversial because it had housed escaped slaves from the north. I guess the church didn't want to get into local politics."

"They needed the river for bread?"

"Yeah. There was a mill there they used to grind the flour. And to irrigate crops," I said and waved my arm around. "This spot is like an oasis. The river that comes through here is one of the few in the region."

He nodded. "An oasis. This is metaphor, yes?"

"I suppose you're right."

Then I explained what I wanted to do. Inspired by a moment that had closed the place more than a hundred and fifty years earlier.

Kane looked away. I threw my hands up.

"Well?" I asked and got a shrug in return. "That's all I got, man. If it works—"

"The plan used by bad men to kill others?"

"Um, yeah. But, you know, they were bad, and we are good." I gave him a crooked grin. "You even said so yourself."

Kane pointed to his right, indicating that he could smell the river on that side of the complex. As we drove, the red gravel turned to dirt then back to gravel again. Up a low rise were the busted-up remains of the old mill.

Its roof had long since deteriorated and fallen away. Three of the four stone walls had crumbled, dropping its stones around the outside.

"She's a fixer-upper," I said.

The dirt road ended in a circle. A long grass clearing led to the river, but being so close to the water, I didn't know if the vehicle might get stuck, so I parked.

Before I turned off the taco truck, I considered leaving the engine on. Kane would have to push us again to get it going. But the gas gauge was busted. Carminia had told me that she thought there was plenty of fuel on board, but the thing was a beast.

I had no idea how much gas I'd chewed through getting into town and all the way out here to the convent. I didn't want to, you know, save the world and end up stranded.

At the top was rubble. Just big rocks, small rocks, and rotten wood. The only thing left standing was a stone bridge that allowed you to cross from the other side. I didn't see anything of interest over there.

Standing on the stone bridge, I could see how the water passed beneath it through a series of channels cut out in the base of the wall.

"At one point, I think they had a system for closing up some of these holes to force the river toward the mill house to turn the wheel," I said. "But that's long gone now."

Kane looked at me and shrugged. "What can I do?"

"Nothing. I mean, if we had a few hours, we might be able to block some of these holes," I said and looked up and down the bridge. "But we just don't have—"

Crash!

I spun around in time to get the splash square in the face. On one side of the bridge, the river boiled as the last standing wall came crashing down. The massive bits of boulders tumbled and rolled as the water shot up all around them.

Stumbling off the stone bridge, I looked down at my pants. They were soaked.

"Coulda warned me!" I shouted at him.

For the next few minutes, I watched as the massive clumps of rock broke into smaller pieces. They rolled and tumbled and slid toward the channels that I'd hoped we could block to redirect some of the river. But the water levels weren't rising.

It hadn't worked.

"Ah, well," I said and waved Kane back the way we'd come.

As we ran past the van, he asked, "Plan A, then?"

"What is Plan A?"

He threw a thumb over his shoulder toward the river. "Biblical flood was Plan B, yes?"

"Sure, I guess so."

"Right," he said, trotting ahead. "Plan A is go down and kill the monsters."

I jogged after him.

"Yeah, I don't love Plan A."

Chapter Forty-Seven

"This place," Kane said as we crept through the abandoned convent, "is very spooky."

Thumping his back with my palm, I chuckled.

"Man, you're the scariest thing in here," I said softly. "There's nothing to be afraid of."

He stopped, spun toward me, then bent down, putting his nose a few inches away from mine. "Then why are you whispering?"

"Setting the mood." I brushed past him. "When they dropped off the NextGen creatures, I'm pretty sure it was on the far side."

Kane rotated in a circle. "Which is far side? All sides can be far depending where you are standing."

We walked down a long hallway that ran past the inner courtyard. I'd remembered some Jane Austen movie where someone had called it a cloister. Actually, that might have been the name of one of the main character's sisters.

At the corner, we passed room after room, filled with small piles of junk. No beer cans or wrappers that teenagers might have left behind. Just clumps of unidentifiable stuff that had been there for decades. Or, given the convent's age, maybe a century.

I saw an entryway at the end of the hall. On either side, where there once had been tall vases that held reeds or plants, lay broken shards of ceramic. The edges were as sharp as if they'd been shattered.

"Vandals, maybe," I said, bending down to pick up one of the pieces then chucked it back. I pointed at the door. Like the others we'd seen, this one was boarded up too. Except the boards here were on the inside.

Kane walked up and peered through the tiny window. "They could not have come in here. These boards smell dusty and damp. Nails were driven in long ago."

I nodded.

"There was this whirring sound," I said, trying to recall what I'd heard. "Like maybe a winch. It sounded familiar, but I couldn't place it."

"Out there?" Kane asked, pointing at the door.

Shrugging, I said, "Had to be, but that door isn't—"

Kane punched at two of the boards near the top and the one around the middle then kicked the bottommost barrier. Dust and dirt and mold spores flew through the air, and I had to roll back to stop from choking.

"Jeez, man."

I looked at him, standing there in his jean jacket, jean pants, and long hair. Surrounded by smoke, he looked like an extra in an eighties Whitesnake video. He jiggled the long handle.

"It's locked," he said then punched a hole just above the handle and ripped the entire apparatus out. "It is no longer locked."

Standing, I waved my hand through the dusty air as it floated outside. That struck me as odd.

"The wind blows out the door, not in?"

He'd stepped onto the threshold and looked back at me. "Is very spooky place."

"Will you cut it out!"

The patio was merely a section of stones, but off to the right, there were two grooves in the grass that exposed some dirt below.

"We drove up to this patio part," I said and craned my neck upward and saw the portico I'd nearly been squished by. "But I know they didn't go inside here. Not through that door."

"You said they would go below, yes?"

"Right, but I don't see... Hold on. Look at that." I bent down where skinny stone pillars jutted up from the patio's corners. Next to one of them was a shiny metal pole about ten inches long with a box on top.

I examined the box on both sides. The top had hinges, so I grabbed the bottom and pulled upward.

"It's an outlet," I said, running my fingers over the plastic indentations. "Three-prong."

"Maybe for music system when convent had picnic parties?"

"Don't be weird," I said. "It's new."

The big guy stepped off the stone patio and examined the nearby grass. He bent down, and I heard his knees pop a few times but didn't say anything about it.

"At end of two tracks, there are four dents in ground," he said. "Wheels, yes?"

"Right. It's a charging station," I said, motioning to the long patch of lawn that abutted the side of the convent. "Probably for some type of golf cart. And those tracks lead around back."

Behind the convent was a huge courtyard of long grass. In a region that was basically desert, the nearby river kept this little slice of heaven thriving. And overgrown. The foliage had been left to go wild and unmolested by people.

The only hint people had been here before was what looked like six long stone slabs. I envisioned the nuns working there, rolling dough into bread. Well, that wasn't the only hint.

A concrete ramp had been cut into the earth behind the convent. It led down.

Kane started walking toward it, but I shot my hand out and stopped him. Then I pointed above to the big rectangular door at the bottom of the ramp.

He saw it. "Camera."

"Right." I put my hands on my hips.

Lying flat against the back wall, I slid closer to the cement ramp. The door looked like what you might see on a double garage, except it was made from thick metal. Not aluminum.

I pointed back the way we'd come. "The golf cart tracks lead to the top of that ramp. I can't see a way in there."

Kane sighed. "If we try to break the door, this will alert people inside."

"Definitely," I said then jutted my chin at him. "You really think you could break that door? It looks like solid steel."

He stood to his full height and clenched his fists. "I would like to try."

"No, no," I said and waved him back down. "There's gotta be another way in."

"This place before was where they hide people from the bad men. Beneath the convent church, yes?" he asked, rubbing his hairy chin.

I nodded. "At least that's what Carminia told me."

"Would not the nuns have had a secret way for the hidden people to get in and out?"

"Sure," I said, smiling at him. "Your logic is sound."

Kane took a few steps into the lush green yard but far enough back where he was clear of the camera. At least, I hoped he was. He shook his head.

"You would not put secret entrance in a place so clearly seen, I do not think," he said.

We spent the next fifteen minutes circumnavigating the entire stone building, making sure to keep clear of any cameras. We saw two in the courtyard, two in the back, and another that pointed back to the old mill. With the cover of the trees, that last one *might* not have caught us walking back. Maybe.

At the rear of the convent, farther in the distance, the remnants of a fence gave way to a long rolling field. I could still see divots where the rows of crops had once been planted.

"I bet that was once wheat back there," I said to Kane. I turned, and he wasn't there. I spun in a low circle.

How the hell could a guy that big move so fast?

Along the wall were piles of wood, moldy bales of hay, and what looked like old, rusted chains. This latter darkened my heart. I had no idea if those had come from the onetime residents here, but I had to look away.

Kane came around the next corner, scratching his beard. He did that a lot. I didn't know if his skin was dry or if it was some holdover from when he'd been an animal. Or part of his thinking process. I walked toward him.

"The nuns made bread, yes?" he asked softly. "The police, when they come to search, if they see something they did not expect, this would make them curious. They would inspect."

I waved my hand to encourage him to get to the point.

He pointed to the field. "Wheat grown there." He gestured toward the river then at the six rock slabs nestled in the tall grass. "It is milled up there, and at tables, they make the dough. Then they bake."

"Right. And?"

"All of these things, police would expect," he said. "So entrance would be hidden by one of those things."

I stepped deeper into the dirt garden. "You think they've got a tunnel way out there that leads inside?"

He shrugged. "Maybe. But even better would be an entrance that police do not want to touch."

"Enough with the Sherlock stuff, man. What's your idea?"

Kane laughed and tugged on my arm, nearly knocking me down. At the corner, he peeked around then waved me forward.

In this space was a patio area like we'd seen by the side door, except much larger and cylindrical. Four small stone tables crumbled under the weight of years and weather. Benches on either side hadn't fared much better.

Up against the wall, though, were what looked like three chimneys that some old builder had never bothered finishing. About an arm's length across—Kane's, not mine—they were only a little shorter than I was. At the top of all three was a cement cylinder in the middle.

In the front, each had a mouth blackened like much of the building, but this wasn't mold. It was soot.

I nodded as a smile grew on my face. "Ovens."

Kane went to the oven on the far left. This one had considerably less soot on its opening than the others. He gripped its side, grunted, and pulled.

Brick ground against rock as the oven shifted and revealed a dark passage beyond. Kane bent down, grabbed one of the rocks, and tossed it over to me. I caught it with my right hand and looked at it.

The edges of the stones had been smoothed to make it easier to move the oven to the side.

Holding up the rock, I said, "Holy balls."

I chucked it over my shoulder, walked over, and peered into the ink-black void.

Kane asked, "Do you want I should go first?"

"No, I can do it," I said then took a step forward. I felt something nip at the skin of my arm, unnaturally cool in the hot, humid air. Brushing it off—I didn't want to get bitten by any desert bug—my finger came away slightly damp.

I sniffed it, but it had no smell. I looked up and saw the white fluffy clouds had darkened.

"Do you want I should—"

"I got it, I got it," I said and slipped into the dark hole.

Chapter Forty-Eight

G-4 saw something flicker across monitor seventeen. That wasn't supposed to happen. But since working for Covenant, a lot of stuff that wasn't supposed to happen had.

This job was far better than the warehouse security he'd done the past three years. When the recruiter had approached him in his work's parking lot, he'd been intrigued.

Hourly wage, thirty-five dollars.

Birthdays, paid double.

Free room and board on site, required.

Hazard pay, one hundred dollars per day.

That had all sounded sweet. Although that last item had given him pause. However, when they'd mentioned there were also free sodas in the break room, he'd signed on the dotted line.

The sticky wicket, as his grandfather might have called it, was that *free room and board* meant he would have to live on campus. And that campus was underneath a creepy old convent.

On that first night in the convent—"the Church," as the bosses called it—he'd searched his employment contract's fine print for how he could get out. The fine print was twenty-two pages long, and he'd fallen back asleep after page three. He'd awoken three times to the noises.

Only the fine-print document helped him get back to sleep.

That had been three weeks earlier. And he'd almost gotten used to the ethereal groaning ("It's just the wind, mate"), the morose singing ("local radio resonating through the pipes, mate"), and the strange clinking of chains ("probably the ghosts, mate").

However, the things in cages?

That had taken far longer to get used to. The way they would snarl and slash at their bars when he slid their food through the slots. Well, if you could call uncooked dead animals food.

But after a few weeks, it almost became routine.

What wasn't routine were the motion detectors on the cameras pinging and sending images. That had never happened before.

"G-3!" he shouted, elbowing his counterpart awake. "Did G-5 go walking through the tunnels?"

The other man opened his bloodshot eyes and scratched his short dark curls. "What?"

"Where did G-5 go?" G-4 tapped monitor seventeen, which was now showing an empty passageway. "Did she go wandering the tunnels? Something tripped the cam."

"Not unless she was sleepwalking," G-3 said, grabbing his coffee cup, seeing it was empty, and standing to get a refill. "Doesn't she usually find somewhere to crash this time of night?"

G-4 felt an electric buzz roll through him. Some sixth sense pinging like the flashing red dot on camera seventeen. After he banged away on his Dr. Pepper-stained keyboard, Cam 17's feed appeared on the main screen, and he shuttled the video in reverse. His heart skipped a beat, maybe several, when he saw two people fly backward, left to right on his screen.

He hit Play.

"Jesus, look at the size of that guy."

G-3 chuckled. "You better watch that kind of talk in here, mate. Convent, yeah? The ghosties don't like that."

"Shut up and look!" The other guard banged his fist on the desktop then rewound the feed and played it again for his coworker. "That huge dude and the woman. Where the hell did they come from?"

Now G-3 was fully awake. He tapped away on his own keyboard and checked the logs. Nothing.

"Doors haven't been opened, and no one's crossed the lasers," he said, rubbing his three-day growth of beard. "They didn't come in through the bay door."

"That's the only way in!"

G-4 leaned forward, putting his nose almost to the screen. "Apparently not. And now I can't pick them up on any of the cams. Where did they go?"

They both jumped when a clang rang out. Not over the monitors. Close by. Too close.

"We need to call this in," G-4 said, his voice trembling. "We have to—"

The other man threw a stapler at him. "What? And say we let two people in and don't know where they are?"

"No, we—"

"We call a higher-up, and the first thing they'll do is blame us for leaving a door open for some hikers to wander in. You know what happens then?"

G-4 did not.

G-3 sighed. "Didn't you read the fine print? Page twenty-one?"

"Uh, I haven't got to page twenty-one yet."

There were no more staplers to throw, so G-3 instead threw him his best disdainful look. Then a new look crossed his face. He got to work on the keyboard again, and a new alarm sounded in the control room.

The other man looked up at the pulsing red light. "W-w-what are you doing?"

"Don't worry. It'll be fine."

"No, it won't be *fine*. You can't do this!"

The tone rose, and the flashing light quickened. The camera feeds came to life, showing all seven cages, each with a creature inside. They were stirring. They knew what the sound meant.

"You heard G-2, mate! Enzo got killed up on the mountain," G-3 said and thumped the final key. "He'd been the problem. Before that the beasties took their instructions from their collars and did as they were told."

"Well, we can't confirm with G-2, can we? They're still unpredictable. You can't!" G-4 shouted, leaping for the keyboard and getting the back of a palm to his face.

"Enzo was their alpha," G-3 said, folding his fingers behind his head and settling deeper into his chair. "Now that he's gone, they're totally under our control again. And tonight, they get a midnight snack."

G-3 took a deep, satisfying breath and considered going to get one of those free sodas. Then he looked at the secure door. *Yeah, not going out there. Not now.*

He grinned, ready for the big show.

Chapter Forty-Nine

"*E*nzo *was their alpha. Now that he's gone, they're totally under our control again. And tonight, they get a midnight snack.*"

I turned to Kane, my mouth hanging down. "They let them out?"

His face was stone, and his eyes cut toward the secret hatchway we'd climbed through.

He asked me, "Do you want to go back?"

After we'd slipped into the gap behind the old stone oven, I'd made sure my slingdart was still secure in the waistband of my pants. Check. And the steel arrows in my back pocket? Check, check.

We'd stepped into total darkness.

"I can't see for shit down here," I said, my hand on Kane's back as we crept through the passageway. "What do you see?"

"I also see the same."

"What?" I tugged on his jean jacket, stopping him. "If you can't see, we need to go back and find a flashlight or something."

"No, I am saying that there are droppings. Mostly rat, I think," he said then grunted. "Big rats."

Kane reached back and put his hand on my arm. Just a twitch of his finger told me to stop. *Quiet.*

I felt him slide to the wall and could hear his coarse palms searching the stone walls. It sounded like sandpaper on rough concrete.

"There is breeze here." He grunted again. "I can feel edges of…"

There was the sound of metal grinding against rock, and then I heard him grunt with exertion. As he pushed, a thin line of light grew from a line to a rectangle to a square. He bent down and poked his head through the hole, which was about the size of a fifty-inch flat-screen.

"Another passage on other side. This one has light," he said and lifted his foot to step through. "Follow."

From one spooky tunnel into another spooky tunnel. What was the harm? When I looked at the square of wall that had been pushed away, there was a frame, but instead of a picture within, it had pieces of glass, pottery, and small stones fashioned into flowers.

In the center was a crucifix.

Kane had spun the cross sideways. That had been the first grinding sound I'd heard.

Stepping through, I said, "That's got to be left over from the nuns. I bet the guys running this place now have no idea they're even here."

Light in this new passage made it easier to see, but it was intermittent. A pulsing red light.

Ahead, where the passage turned left, we saw more light, much brighter. Slowly we crept closer. We were moving forward on cat feet, quiet as the night, but I worried the sound of my hammering heart would give me away.

Ten feet from the corner, I could see Kane much more clearly now. He stopped and turned to me.

"Fear is good," he said, putting his large hand on my chest. "Fear sharpens the senses, strengthens the muscles, and quickens reflexes. Embrace this gift, and it will make you powerful."

I gritted my teeth. "Fear is gonna make me shit my drawers!"

"Ah, yes. Good defense. The smell will drive our enemies away," he said, grinning at me. "You are prepared for the hunt."

Before I could hit him with my own snarky comeback, we heard voices rising. Two men arguing. Well, one guy shouting and the other one laughing.

"Enzo was their alpha. Now that he's gone, they're totally under our control again. And tonight, they get a midnight snack."

"Why the hell would they let them out?" I asked, flattening my hands on top of my head. I felt it was the only thing keeping my skull from exploding.

"Guards have seen us on their TVs."

"Damn. Damn, damn, damn," I said. "I was hoping..."

My voice trailed off, and I looked at the slingdart in my hands. I didn't even remember pulling it out. My big friend bumped his knee into it softly.

"To kill them in cages?"

Ashamed, I stared at the stone wall ahead of me. It had stood for more than a century, but time had taken its toll. Chips, cracks, and discolorations marred it, but all this time later, I knew it was as strong as it had been when first installed.

Or maybe with all the pressure of the building above, compacting the stone just a little, it had become a bit stronger.

"It doesn't matter. They're out now," I whispered to him, nodding to the light in the adjoining tunnel. Then I had a thought. "Remember when we were at Covenant and the Enhanced came out and they were all wearing those collars?"

"Of course."

"We saw those same collars on the NextGen," I said, speaking more rapidly now that a plan, finally, was coming together in my brain. Sort of. "It sounds like they can control these creatures from inside that control room. If we can get in there—"

Kane shook his head. "The alpha."

"You heard them!" I said, pointing at the next hallway. "That alpha's dead, so now they can get the NextGen monsters to do whatever they want. They've got full control, and they're using it to hunt us in these tunnels!"

"No, their logic is"—he grinned at me sadly—"not sound."

I took a step back, too many thoughts racing through my head to pick one. Shrugging, I said, "Fine. Tell me why."

Bending down, he spread his huge palm atop the dirt and stone floor, clutched his hand, and rubbed the dirt between his fingers. "These creatures come from me, yes?"

"Right. So?"

"My blood?"

"Yes!"

He stood, rising to his full height, towering over me.

"I am wolf," he said then extended his arm and rolled his fingers, letting the bits of dirt and rock fall from his hand. "Some part of them is wolf."

Then I got it.

"Oh shit," I said, putting a hand to my mouth. "There's another alpha."

His smile grew, and he nodded. "Always two in a pack. Male and female."

Before I could say another word, an earsplitting howl rang off the walls all around us.

Chapter Fifty

We had a new plan.

Plan C? I couldn't keep track anymore.

"If we can get into the bunker, there may be some kill switch or something," I said, my hands so damp I had to keep rubbing them on my pants.

Kane didn't seem so sure. "That would be efficient."

I peeked around the corner and pulled back again.

"Right? That would solve all our problems. These are bloodthirsty monsters, so they have to have some nuclear option that, I dunno, kills them. Right?"

Kane stared at me for a long moment. He nodded then got a queer look on his face.

"Okay," I said, taking a deep breath and blowing it out slowly. "Here we go—"

I had stepped forward to round the corner when Kane yanked me back so hard, my chin banged against my throat.

Before I could say a word—and I had a lot of words I wanted to share with him in that moment—he spun, wrapped an arm around my chest, and started running in the opposite direction than we'd planned. So *new* new plan?

Standing at the framed relief, he fumbled around, searching for the way to open it.

I gritted my teeth. "What's going on?"

After a glance down the hall, the light twinkling off his eyes, he said, "They are coming."

That was all the info I needed. Yep, new plan. Get the hell out. I elbowed him out of the way and put my fingers on the cross to turn it. It wouldn't budge. I tried again.

Nothing.

The echoes of snarling and claws clacking across stone grew louder. The damp exhalations of what sounded like predatory dogs, all trying to beat one another to their prey.

"This goddamn thing won't—"

Kane put a gentle hand on my wrist. "I would not use such language in here." His hand went to my cheek, and he leaned in closer. My eyes stayed locked on the immovable cross. "One cannot think with panic juices running through brain. Calm, yes?"

That broke my anxiety fever, and I laughed. "Panic juices?"

He shrugged and gave me a wan smile. But I knew he was worried too. The grunts and sounds of chasing feet and the snapping of claws grew louder.

Inching my face closer to the centuries-old wall art, I traced my finger around the edges of the cross. I drew a finger through dirt and grit and silt. Just above the cross, where the man hanging there gazed, I felt the hint of a line.

I slid my fingernail across this spot, and it ticked over two parallel grooves.

A smash of glass drew my attention, and I turned, my eyes so wide, I was sure I could poke my tongue out and lick the eyelash.

"Calm heart, calm mind," Kane said slowly, like an intonation. "Observe and act."

My head snapped back to the relief, and I put both thumbs on the bottom of the cross. It gave a little then stopped. Kane grunted.

Lowering to a knee, I pushed harder until the cross snapped upward. But the sound of it, stone against stone, was so loud it was like a pistol had gone off. To my left, I saw a shadow grow.

The silhouette of a NextGen monster moved closer to the corner. It had heard us.

We were out of time.

Pushing on the artwork didn't work. I tried to lift the cross higher. Nothing. Frustrated, I slapped at the stone crucifix, and its bottom tilted a little to the right. I pressed it higher to where the man on the cross looked as though he were lying down for a nap.

The wall relief clicked free.

In one quick move, Kane palmed the hatchway open, revealing the black void beyond, and lifted me through the hole. I tumbled to the ground, sucking in dirt and grit. I had to hold my breath so I didn't cough and give us away.

The big man landed next to my head, and he pushed the hatch closed. But not all the way. A sliver of light remained. Kane peered through the gap.

He stepped back, falling deeper into the shadow of the secret tunnel. I stood just in front of him and could feel the scruff of his beard brush against the top of my head.

Through the gap, we saw her.

The NextGen stalked right past the spot where we'd been only seconds before. Her short snout lifted into the air, and she sniffed, drawing in a long breath. Squinting, she tried peering deeper into the darkness, searching for the source of the scent she'd picked up.

Kane extended his arm and slid his fingers behind the cross on this side of the trapdoor. If she got too close, he could shove it closed.

I hoped.

This was the remaining alpha. And she was hunting us.

As she stepped forward, her long arms swept left and right. It was such a queer motion but familiar in some way. Like a carnival magician gearing up to delight and enchant their audience.

As she moved, I could see the coarse black hairs on her arms glisten in the light, as if they'd stood to attention. Sniffing the air again, she took another step closer.

With his free hand, Kane tried to pull me back, but I shrugged him off.

A few feet away, she continued to slide her arms back and forth through the air. One hand stopped. Then the other. The pulsing light sparkled off the tips of her extended claws.

Then the screaming began. Glass breaking.

The NextGen alpha spun on her heel, took one quick look back at what had to be an odd black line on the wall, our gap to see her, and bolted down the hall from view.

I reached forward to widen the gap, but Kane didn't release his grip on the cross, holding it firm. Snarling and howling rang out through the passageway. Shadows played across the wall like a black-and-white horror film.

Large, impossibly large, creatures swung their claws and chomped down on flesh and bone. I heard a cracking sound. Then another. More howls.

Grunting and growling and what sounded like an argument but with grunts and short barks. Were they fighting over the kill?

My stomach turned at the very thought of it. I looked at my hand, still holding the trapdoor, and saw it twitching. I was trembling.

That surprised me.

In that moment, I didn't feel the fear as I had before. The trepidation was still there, of course, but that near-paralyzing panic had become a memory. It seemed my body hadn't gotten that memo from my brain.

The damp cacophony of gnashing teeth and tearing claws was joined by a new sound. Mechanical, not animal.

I whispered, "What is that?"

Kane grunted, and my neck hairs shook. He didn't know either.

The sound repeated in short bursts. A new alarm had sounded. Had one of the guards hit the panic button? That didn't seem right because, judging by the sounds one hallway away, those guys were already dead. The screaming had stopped. The feeding had begun.

Glass shattered again, not as much as before, then the slapping of feet on stone returned.

In less than five seconds, the banquet only twenty feet away had ended. The sounds of damp footfalls got quieter and quieter.

I elbowed Kane's arm away and pushed the stone relief open. I crawled over and through and stood on the other side. He followed.

Looking back at him for a read, I waited. He nodded. The monsters, for now, had left.

I jogged back to the corner and peered around it. Glass and blood covered the floor and the opposite stone wall. The sight of it raised something up in my throat that I had to swallow down.

Throwing caution to the wind, I rounded the bend and strode forward. Within reach of the bunker's door, something squished under my foot. I looked down and pulled my shoe back. I'd stepped on an ear.

The smell hit me all at once, and I had to put my hand over my mouth.

"Hurry," Kane said and slid around me. His fingers flew to the handle of the control room bunker, and he shook it. Locked.

We didn't need a door. Kane hopped up, and I watched as the toes of his bare feet curled over the metal lip that had once held the thick glass of the window. He bent down to avoid the jagged shards and leaped inside.

Deeper within the convent, I heard the snarling and howling erupt once again. I only prayed they hadn't heard us and were not racing back.

Slower than Kane, I lifted myself through the busted glass, stepped across the bloodied console, and dropped down inside.

Chaos.

Smashed monitors. Three office chairs had been overturned, the stuffing of one torn out and spread around it like an April snow. One of the men had hidden beneath the counter where their keyboards had sat. His arm was twisted at a queer angle, back and around as if he were aggressively scratching his back.

His chest had been clawed out. I could see the white of rib bone and the smooth of muscle, frayed and dripping with blood.

The other man lay across an open office drawer, his back broken over the top of it. He lay staring up at the ceiling, eyes wide, a forever expression on his face. A question that had no answer. At least not for him.

Sharp odors assaulted my nostrils. Blood and metal and sweat. Smoke rose in small wisps from one of the computers. A computer tablet had a chunk missing because it had been bitten.

Of the dozen or so monitors, only three showed any sort of picture. Of those, two of the feeds rolled, making it hard to discern what was happening. Movement on one of them. The creatures racing down one hallway then another.

Were they trying to escape?

Kane spun, his arms raised, hands clenched. Eyes locked on an area on the far side of a cabinet, he stalked forward.

Then I heard a bump. A shuffle of feet.

Kane leaped forward, raising a fist, and smashed the skinny door. It went right through, and with both hands, he ripped it off its hinges and threw it behind him.

"No!" a voice called out, ragged and harsh.

He reached inside and pulled out a woman so fast her glasses flew from her head and clattered to the floor. Kane held her up by the white lapels, bringing her face closer to his.

Terrified, she asked, "Who are—"

She turned away from him, squinting as if awaiting the blow she knew was coming. Then she opened her eyes, and her gaze fell upon her comrades.

When she opened her mouth to scream, Kane's hand flew up and covered her lips. It covered half her face.

As he pulled the woman deeper into the room, I turned over one of the office chairs that still had padding. Kane dropped her in the seat.

I jammed a finger at her. "Who are you?"

"What? Who the hell are *you*?" she asked then wrapped her arms around herself, as if scared by her own volume. "What is going on?"

Stepping back, I swept my hand toward what was left of the two men. One was smashed into a spot under the desk. The other was draped unnaturally over an open filing cabinet like a discarded coat.

"Oh." Her hand went to her mouth. "Oh my God."

I had a deep desire to smack her back to her senses like they do in the movies. I resisted. But that option wasn't off the table.

She stared at the dead men. "How did they get out?"

For the next few minutes, I told her what we'd heard and seen. What we'd gleaned from listening in on the conversation from the neighboring hallway.

She put her head in her hands and rocked, making the chair squeak. Kane reached out and stopped it from moving.

He asked her, "You were hiding in there?"

The woman looked up at him, as if seeing him for the first time. She blinked away some dampness then shook her head.

"It's... I mean," she said, struggling to find her words. "I crawled in there to sleep for a few hours. I woke up to... all that noise and just froze. I knew it, though. Knew what was happening."

I growled at her. "And you did nothing?"

"What could I do? Those things are unstoppable. We made them that way!" Again, she blanched at how loud she'd been. Casting a glance at the blood-spattered far wall, she said, "They said we'd be able to get them under control again. There was one—"

I cut her off. We didn't have time for this. "The alpha. Yes, we know about that."

"But there is another," Kane added. "She is leading them now."

Her eyes vacant, she nodded. Lost in her own world of misery and regret.

I had my slingdart and a few arrows. Kane had, well, Kane. Could we really take on seven of those things?

Kane led her to what was left of the smashed console and let her sit. He knelt before her. "What is your name?"

"It... I'm G-5. Guard number five. We're not allowed to use names."

"Really?" I asked and motioned to the busted glass, smashed monitors, and all the blood. "You're worried about getting pulled in to HR? *Now?*"

"A-Adriana," she said, almost as if she were unsure of her own name. "My name is Adriana."

"Good. Adriana," Kane said, smiling kindly. "Can you turn off alarms? I must listen for the creatures."

As if snapping from a trance, she rose to her feet, spun, and grabbed a computer keyboard.

"Darn it. It's... This is useless," she said then went to the wall. She flipped up a plastic cover with red hash marks across its plastic front. She pulled the recessed switch beneath it, and the noise quieted. But not all of it.

"The *other* alarm," I said. All the racket was making it hard to think.

Adriana got a strange look on her face. She glanced around, stepped to the keyboard again, then backed away. She looked at a smaller monitor to the left of the bank of computers. It hadn't been smashed because it had been covered with a metal hood.

"Why is that...?" she asked then backed up. She put a hand to her chest. "I don't know if that's a good thing or a bad thing."

I stepped over to the screen. The readout said something about a proximity warning. The number nine flashed in the upper right corner with the letter E next to it.

I spun to her. "What does that mean?"

"That's the dual lasers by the entrances. The big door by the ramp to get in and out," Adriana said. "It indicates they've... left."

"*Left?*" I asked, spinning back to the small monitor. "That's definitely a bad thing, Adriana! The last thing we need is those things out on the loose. If they get—"

"Hold on," she said, shaking her head. "Wait. That doesn't make sense. It says nine. There are seven."

I looked at Kane, but his face was unreadable. Turning back to Adriana, I asked, "Are there more? More of those?"

Her eyes flitted between me and my big friend. "You mean the NextGen soldiers?"

"Of course."

She shook her head. "We'd had more, but..." Her voice trailed off. "Thirteen at one point. Back when we had them all in one pen. One morning, three were dead. Enzo did that."

Kane grunted. "Fighting. Kill until you are alpha."

"After that, we separated them into individual cages," she said and closed her eyes, leaning against the smoldering console. "Last night, they brought two new ones from the Camp. But the five they'd sent out on some mission, some hunt... Something happened up at the mountaintop lab and—"

"Yeah, yeah, we know all about that," I said, waving my hand in the air. "We need to know if they've gotten loose."

"Wait, *wait*," Kane said, looking down at his twiddling fingers. "Very troublesome math problem. Like train with oranges that stops in Vancouver—"

"Kane!"

"But then it picks more up in Ottawa. How many oranges left? I don't know! Is so confusing!" He laughed nervously and looked at the guard. "How many NextGen creatures are left now?"

"Seven," Adriana said and shook her head. "But it said nine exited the Church, so I don't..." She bent down and tried the keyboard, but again, nothing. She banged it lightly with a fist. "No. No, I got that wrong."

"No, you didn't!" I pointed at the monitor. "I can see the number nine right there!"

She stood and looked up at the screens above. Three cameras were in order, but two of the screens fuzzed and flipped, making them virtually useless.

"That letter E means entry," she said, shaking her head. "That doesn't make sense. Nine didn't leave. Nine came in. Five, then a minute later another four. But it's all busted up. Could be malfunctioning."

Before I could ask what the hell she was talking about, Kane stepped forward and leaped over the desk and computers, through a ragged hole in the glass, and landed back in the hallway.

"Is that door still open?"

Adriana shrugged, distant. "Possibly."

"You must close that," Kane said. "The monsters cannot leave. If we fail, we fail. But they must never leave this place."

"Look." Adriana pointed, her voice a raspy whisper. She indicated one of the flipping monitors. On that one, through the static, I could see the NextGen creatures stalking through the passageways. They turned a corner, and the motion detection camera showed the adjacent feed.

They walked forward, led by the one we'd seen in the hall. The alpha.

Kane looked left and right then took a few steps closer to the red wall behind him. "I must leave."

"Not by yourself," I said and put a foot up on the console. He shook his head.

"You stay here," he said. "You must get the door closed."

I growled. "Kane, you can't protect me from them. I'm going to have to face off against the monsters sooner or later."

"Yes, I know. But most important is for you and Guard Five Adriana to get door closed. That is most important thing."

"Kane, n—"

"Yes, Emelda Thorne," he said, a smile tugging at his lip. "Closed case. Trap them in here for good. I will destroy them."

My voice cracking, I leaned forward, shaking my head. "You can't take on seven of those things."

He took a deep breath and banged his fists together, hopping up and down in place.

"Warming up. Do not want to pull a muscle," he said, his smile full. "And I do not have to kill all seven. Just the alpha. Then I am the new alpha."

"Are you sure?"

He tilted his head, cocking an eyebrow at me.

"Mostly sure," he said and raced down the hall toward the monsters.

Chapter Fifty-One

Kane

I run down the damp corridors, the smell of rot and blood in the air. The sounds of snarling grow louder. I am close to them! This realization fills me with both anticipation and trepidation.

It is these creatures that I have to remove from the world. However, they are also from me. Not my cubs, no, but born from me.

No matter.

If I am to return to my family, my pack, they must first be destroyed.

But a sadness, one I cannot shake, fills my legs with rock and grit. I run slower but not on purpose. It is like I am running on sand.

Always seems like such a pleasant way to run. But very difficult. Not pleasant at all.

Television commercials lie.

I shake my head to clear my thoughts then round the next corner. They hear me coming. They are waiting.

In an alcove, all of the NextGen creatures encircle another. The alpha. It is her I must take down to win their allegiance. I can do this for—

Two of the NextGen come for me, claws out, teeth bared, but I watch their musculature, how they move, and I anticipate. I twist left then right and bend as they leap toward me. Both fly over my head, but one does get a hand out, slashing across my back.

"Aaaagh!" I call out.

That hurt.

The alpha tilts her head sideways. I can see from her movements that she is testing me. Seeing what this man before her can do. I am a curiosity. She sniffs the air, and recognition passes over her face.

With a small gesture, she commands another two to charge. I had heard the snarling behind me, and those NextGen are up on their feet once again. She wants to see what these two can do.

Instead of both leaping at me simultaneously, one advances while the other trails.

I know this predatory move. I have used the same.

They wish me to dodge away from the first attacker, and once I do, the one behind will already be moving in that direction. Simple creatures.

I do not duck. I do not dodge.

Instead, I run directly at the NextGen creature. It lets out a throaty howl, and I can hear the human beneath the twisted dark fur. As I close the distance, faster than he had anticipated, his eyes flicker slightly. I have confused and confounded him.

Which are both likely the same thing but sounds better in my brain when said twice with different words.

Running like an American football person racing for the white stripe, I am lifting my knees high as I race forward. What is the word for that? I do not recall.

Faster and faster, I push my muscles, knowing that, yes, I am still a man. I do not have fur nor claws nor gnashing teeth. I cannot let the monster lay a hand on me. The gash across my back stings as sweat pours into it.

Just a few paces away now, and I—

High-stepping. Yes. This is what I heard the football announcer man call it.

I lift my trailing knee higher than before and plant my bare foot in the middle of the creature's chest. It lets out a very human "ooof," and with my momentum and mass, I stop it midrun. Bending my knee, I bring the other foot up and spin around, facing the floor, then leap.

This launches the first creature into the second, sending both clattering to the ground. I also fall but anticipate and land on all fours.

As wolf does.

I spin back, up on my hind legs—feet!—and curve my muscular arms and bellow at the alpha. I am challenging her now. This is the fight I want. Me versus their leader.

The alpha huffs.

She then raises her arms slightly, waving them back and forth as she did earlier. Such a strange move, this. Her head tilts slightly, and she sniffs the air. She senses something I do not.

Or is this a feint to confuse me?

It may be. She is clever. Trying to confound.

Hmm. Single word also very effective.

The slightest flicker of two left claws and the pack of NextGen begin to huff-huff-huff in unison. I recognize this. Planned charge. Not two at a time but all—

From behind, I feel the swipe of claws. Then the impact between my shoulder blades, and I am launched through the air, flying past the alpha, who only watches as I pass. I roll and roll, smashing my head twice, then crash against the far wall.

I am dazed. And confused. And also confounded.

However, I prefer it when *they* are the ones those things can describe. Not me.

The seven of them stand, three on either side of the alpha. Where two passageways join, I slowly wobble up to my feet and raise my bleeding fists. My head swims, and the gashes on my back feel like I'm being bitten.

The alpha only. This is what I need. I cannot take all—

A spark against the rock, just behind my head. It flashes white like a tiny crack of lightning.

I hear movement to my left, down the adjoining passageway, but I cannot turn from my predators. That would mean my death. There is no fighting fair in the animal world.

There is only the vanquished and victorious.

"There you are, my friend," a voice rings out. I stare at the alpha, and she locks me with her eyes. It is not she who spoke these words. I risk a slight turn to my left, keeping the creatures in my peripheral vision.

I recognize this face.

It is the man who calls himself Carlo. Rosa's cartel man who tried to kill us in our room. There are others with him, some in shadow. They stalk closer. Like a pack.

"We only want the caskets. Return them, and you'll walk out of here," he says. "If you don't—"

Another gunshot, but the flash is just off the shoulder of Carlo. He is surrounded by his people, but why would they shoot at him?

The cartel man spins away from me, as do the rest of his crew. The NextGen stand in the hall before me. I am cornered! Monsters in front, mobsters to my left.

But there are... others now.

"That is *our* property, my friend."

Who is this?

This voice did not come from Carlo or his crew but from farther down the tunnel. When the cartel man moves closer to the wall, flattening himself, I see another group of people walking closer. Weapons raised.

Three men and a woman. Of course. The Spanish people who also tried to kill us but in a different hotel room. Gabriel and his people have come as well. Following Carlos, who followed us?

I do not know.

And it does not matter. Not now.

The four men with Carlo lift their weapons as they split, hugging the walls. They fire their weapons back at Gabriel and his people, who are scattering like rats in the dark. More sparks erupt off the stone.

I draw in a long, full breath. Calming, this is. Also, it centers my thoughts, slowing time around me. I see movement from the NextGen, legs pumping forward. Three creatures on the left, three on the right. Only the alpha remains still.

Rosa's cartel guys scatter and fire. The Spanish people, they are peeking and pointing their weapons around the corner.

There is a human expression that, for the first time, feels appropriate to me.

Between a rock and a hard place.

Of course, my rock is seven killer monsters. The hard place, two groups of killer gang people all firing weapons.

I do not recall if the rock-and-hard-place maxim has any solution. I believe it is a fancy manner of saying, "You are in deep doo-doo either way."

But wolves find other ways. Ways that other creatures, lesser creatures, could never conceive of.

Aha! I will use rock to get *out* of hard place!

Sort of.

Upon the wall, to my left, I see my salvation. Ma mère would say this was both figurative and literal. She was clever like that. I miss her and her tenderness.

A stone-art picture with a cross hangs on the wall, only a few paces away. Through there, I can get to an adjoining hall. Before I can move, I hear NextGen stalk forward.

The slow click and clatter of claws across stone floor. The labored, hungry breathing. The song of the hunt in raspy exhalation and snarling grunts.

I cannot reach the passageway before the creatures strike.

Also, about thirty feet down from the wall art, Carlo is pointing his weapon at me and will fire if I attempt to flee. Farther down the darkened hall, Spanish Gabriel's crew members aim their weapons at Carlo's people. A standoff.

The NextGen are closing in. Grunting, growling, snorting. They are coming for my blood.

"You can get out of here, free and clear. We just want the caskets," Carlo says, his gun hand trembling, fire rising in his eyes. Ah! He thinks the snarling sounds are coming from me. "Don't you dare run. Don't move a muscle, Kane."

I disobey.

Dropping to the floor, flat like mat, I hear Carlo fire his weapon. The bullet flies over my head.

Many years ago, my human parents were having a "healthy disagreement" over which Christmas film to watch. Ma mère wanted to watch an old film about a man who dies but does not die and then... angels with bells or something. Confusing.

Mon père insisted—but did not argue; they made it clear they were not arguing—that his movie choice was, in fact, the greatest Christmas movie ever. Watched both.

But I did not say that, secretly, I liked mon père's movie better. More explosions. And the bad guy dies because all good stories should end this way.

The NextGen had been staring at me, and when the bullet strikes the wall, turn to regard the humans. Carlo's people stare back. And Gabriel's crew, who had been staring at Carlo's people, now also stares at the monsters.

It is then I recall my favorite line from mon père's Christmas film.

From the floor, I yell, "Welcome to the party, pal!"

The flash of bullets explodes like angry iron fireflies, and blood spits down upon me. From the floor, I see the six NextGen lift their heads from me and toward the gunshots.

They twitch and flinch as each bullet pierces. There is blood but also something else.

Rage.

They roar in unison and race toward the shooters, who in turn fire faster. Screams join this strange song.

As they step into a new fight, I have my own. I stand and turn as the alpha rounds the corner. She ignores the blood fight down the hall, only seeing me. Her prey.

She howls, baring her teeth, brandishing her claws, which extend from her fingers, growing longer and longer. The nails on her feet extend. The collar on her neck begins to twinkle, lights moving faster and faster, rotating around the metal ring.

The alpha grips her head, shaking it from side to side. Down on one knee, she grabs a stone near the wall as I hear a horrifying scream, then another, erupt from behind. But I cannot turn from her.

She begins smashing at the collar with the rock, but it's a flailing motion. Erratic. She draws as much blood from her neck as sparks from her collar. However, I do see that for each cut she endures upon her skin, the wound fuses closed almost immediately.

As she continues to bash, I spin around and see the two gangs of humans firing and fighting against the NextGen. One of the creatures is beating one man with the arm of another it has torn free.

"Okay," I say to myself. "Bye-bye."

As the alpha struggles with the collar, I leap to the wall.

When I reach for the stone painting, a bullet pings near my hand and slices a gash across my forearm. The pain centers my mind.

Pushing up on the cross, I twist it to the side and push open the trapdoor and launch myself into the void on the other side.

When I jump up to close it, a clawed hand reaches into the gap and holds me in an iron grip.

Chapter Fifty-Two

"Who the hell are those guys?" Adriana asked me, furiously searching for another keyboard. I walked over to the dead guard draped over the open cabinet, shoved him to the floor, and looked inside. After a few seconds of digging, I came out with a long, snaking cord.

"Heads up," I said and chucked the new keyboard her way. Adriana wasn't a sporty type. The keyboard smacked her in the solar plexus, and she made a "gluuung" sound. One hand went to her chest as she bent down and grabbed the keyboard.

"We've got so many people after us right now," I said, trying to work out what was happening on the camera feed. "Might be the Mexican cartel. Might be the Spanish mob."

Adriana let out a whoop as she typed away. "It's working again!"

On the feed, I saw the alpha's collar flash with light. "Shut that one down, man!"

"There," she said triumphantly. Then her computer sparked, and flames burst from its casing.

Adriana dropped down onto her chair, too quickly, and nearly spun out of it. I stepped forward and put my hand out, stopping her from tumbling to the floor.

"That computer's dead," she said.

"What about the door?" I asked, shaking her shoulders. "Those assholes got it open. We have to close it!"

She nodded, leaned forward to unhook the keyboard, and slid under the console. I looked up at the two screens.

Two of them showed a fight between the humans and monsters. She peeked up, frowned, and rested the keyboard on the floor.

"Those guns won't do a damn thing," she said, snapping the cord in place. "They'll barely slow the NextGen down, and they heal in seconds."

I looked up on the console to make sure my slingdart was still within reach. It was. "What about a shot to the head?"

She laughed darkly. "Their skulls are like iron. Thick bone so strong, bullets just ring off. We found that out the hard way."

"So nothing will kill them?"

Adriana peeked over the desk and looked at the small monitor with the metal hood. She shifted through screens, but without a mouse, it was slow going. Instead of getting angry, she started chuckling.

"You know the funniest part? The techs I talked to said they had no idea what they were even working with," she said, tabbing from field to field. "They were creating those things from this substance. One of the techs..." She muttered under her breath as I looked between the small monitor and the screens above. "He told me they ran every test on it. They weren't supposed to, but they did anyhow. He was so sweet. He didn't belong here. I don't belong here."

Yep, my girl was checking out.

"Hey, man," I said. "You gotta close that door."

Her eyes came back into focus, and she smiled. "Milton. His name was Milton."

"Uh huh," I said and looked at the green indicator light that meant the door to the underground tunnels was still open.

Calm heart, calm head.

"Okay, Adriana." I sat on the floor next to her. "Close up that door as you tell me all about Milton."

She blinked a couple times and looked at the tiny screen.

"He told me his name," she said softly, and her fingers moved across the keyboard again. Then they stopped, and she folded her hands in her lap. "I never told him mine."

I was about to say something when the light flicked from green to red. The door was closed.

"Great. That's so great," I said and let out a long breath. "Milton didn't also happen to tell you how to kill those monsters out there, did he?"

Adriana shook her head. "They had no idea. They made those things and had no idea what they were even creating."

I laughed darkly, leaning my head back against the edge of the counter. For a moment. I knew what they'd created, and I had to do something. I couldn't let Kane fight them alone.

"Part human, part wolf." I stood and grabbed my slingdart off the console. It looked so small in my hand. "And, hell, part werewolf, I suppose."

That got a weird, choking laugh out of her. Girl had really lost it. She dug in her coat pocket and pointed up at the battle raging on the monitors.

"Then those guys don't have the right kind of bullets."

Loading one of my bolts into the slingdart, I took a deep breath and stared down the hall. Yeah. I was about to run into a fight with monsters and mobsters. With a slingshot and a few darts.

"Well, then." I chuckled. "You don't happen to have the *right* kind of bullets, do you?"

She pulled out a crumpled pack of cigarettes, lit one, and took a long, long drag.

"For friggin' *werewolves*?" she asked, blowing out a breath that had no smoke. "No, I'm all out of silver bullets."

Something clicked in my head.

Without another word, I jumped through the gap, but instead of running toward the fight, I ran in the other direction.

Toward the secret passageway that led back outside.

Chapter Fifty-Three

I tore open the rear doors to the Crazy Taco as a crack of lightning turned the night sky to day.

The sound made my already hammering heart bang harder, but that wink of light had been perfect timing. I saw both caskets inside.

When I went to hop into the back, my foot slipped, and I smacked my knee on the trailer hitch. The rain was coming down like a river.

I didn't have to open the coffins. Well, not in the traditional way. Kane and I had already looked inside and saw nothing.

Carlo—or had it been the Spanish dude?—said the disks were hidden in a false bottom. On the coffin nearest the door, I ran my hand along the lowest edge of the black lacquer exterior. It all felt like one piece.

I looked at the casket that had gotten wedged beneath the ovens. When that had happened, it squeezed one side, separating the end pointing at me. I saw the hidden compartment.

Moving slower this time, I hoisted myself into the back of the Crazy Taco, climbed over casket one, and knelt next to the other. I jammed my fingers into the gap and pulled. A drawer slid out as long as my arm.

Lying there was a golden sun. I gawked. This had been what the Aztecs had given Cortez five hundred years ago. It had been lost—or stolen—and now it was sitting in the back of a food truck. The disk was beautiful and haunting.

But not the one I needed.

When I tried to close the shallow drawer, it jammed against something. I reached my arm deep inside and pulled out a black box the size of an eyeglass case. Solid plastic, except for a rectangular cutout with a white tab. A USB port.

I knew what the box was because Covenant had used similar devices.

"Dammit, that's how they tracked us," I muttered. "But why didn't they just grab them from the old butcher's shop? They'd have had—"

Right. We'd put the caskets in the old walk-in cooler, and the thick metal walls must have blocked GPS signals. When we'd pulled them out again, they'd tracked us to the convent.

Didn't matter anymore.

It took me a minute to find the hidden compartment on the other casket, but when I did, it didn't want to open. I needed something to wedge it free.

That wouldn't be a problem.

Jumping up, I unlatched a half-dozen metal drawers. I found spatulas and whisks and knives. A steel mallet that looked like it had been stolen off some medieval battleground.

I jammed one of the spatulas into the gap, dragged open the compartment, and stared.

"Of course," I said, chuckling. "Of course it's a moon."

The shimmering metal revealed a strange depiction of some woman. A goddess, I guessed. She stared skyward, her arms and legs pointing at odd angles. Then I realized her limbs had been separated from the body.

If we got out of this, I wanted to find out more about what the art meant. Actually, if we got out of this, I needed to properly learn about my own heritage.

If we got out of this.

Whatever had happened to this goddess, I wasn't about to make things much better. Around the edges of the disk, like the sun, were metal spikes that depicted radiating light. Moonlight, in this case.

And more importantly, the shiny metal appeared to be silver.

"I hope this works."

The next part took a few minutes. I had to prop the ancient piece of *invaluable* art on the ground behind the truck. I needed to get as many of the spikes off as I could. But I wasn't Kane—I couldn't just snap them off. But I did have something that could.

"*And my axe!*" I screamed up into the pouring rain, ran inside, and grabbed the murderous medieval mallet. Yeah, it wasn't an axe, but whatever.

The thing was heavy, and I would need two hands to really get a good swing. When I jumped back down, I splashed in the water, soaking any dry spot I had left on my pants.

That was when I realized something.

"That can't all be from the rain. Where did..."

Peering around the truck, I looked up toward the river and saw water rushing down its bank. In the few seconds I stared, the flow got stronger and stronger.

Oh, damn.

I had to hurry.

Chapter Fifty-Four

Kane

I try to pull the stone hatch closed, but the alpha has both hands wrapped around the side. She yanks it from my hands.

The sheer strength of the creature stuns me.

She reaches through the hole, grabs me by my jean jacket, and drags me through. As I am extricated, my head bashes against the upper lip of the stone, sending stars into my brain.

Dazed and my mind spinning, I feel the impact, but it does not fully register in my mind.

She is in front of me, stalking back and forth. To her pack, she calls out in a raspy voice, "Here now."

Lying on the floor, I glance down the hallway, which is painted red. The bodies of the two gangs lie in crumpled heaps, limbs torn from torsos. I can't even see how many people there are. But they are all dead.

The creatures hesitantly rise from their prey, drinking in the blood from their prizes. This will aid their healing and only make them stronger.

Alas, I am just a human man.

And I feel broken.

The alpha stalks over, grasping my long hair and lifting me off the ground. Taller than I am, she raises me up with her outstretched arm, and my head brushes the ceiling. The alpha laughs in my face. Spittle flecks pepper my face.

I hang limp. My head lolls forward as if my neck were made from summer reeds. With her other hand, she pierces my chin with a claw and lifts my head to face her.

"Weak," she snarls. "So weak."

My lips trembling, soft words fall from my mouth, blood bubbling on my lips.

"The weak speaks," she says and pulls me closer. "Dying words. Say them louder so I may enjoy."

The NextGen creatures creep closer, snickering. This is fine. They are far enough back.

My eyes rise languidly, liquidly, and I repeat my words. The alpha pulls me closer to hear so she may revel in my dying breath.

I say, "Flamingo."

Her head snaps back, and in that instant, I bring both my knees up and smash her under the rib cage. The creature's grip slackens, and she drops me, but I am ready for this and land on my bare feet.

As she struggles to draw in a breath, I slam her with a fist in the same spot I pummeled with my knees. Her eyes roll briefly, and she staggers back, arms outstretched.

Launching forward, I push back against the blackness at the edges of my vision and deliver a punch with the other hand, which was already in motion before the first landed. I smack the alpha on the chin, spinning her head sideways.

I must take the head from its neck.

Their injuries heal too fast, but ripping her skull from the body? No one can heal from that.

My knee rises again in the same spot as before, and she arches forward, gasping for air. I wrap an arm around her neck, but she gets a claw into my back and sinks the nails deep. I stifle a cry and begin to bend her in half, wrapping my powerful thigh around her lower body.

I will pluck her head off like a flower.

Screaming and smashing me with her claws, she expels a breath from her lungs and with it a single utterance.

"¡Ayuda!"

I am unfamiliar with the word but instantly know the meaning. The NextGen advance toward me, claws raised.

But if I can kill the alpha before they strike, I can claim to be the new alpha! Would killing her be enough?

When I wrench and pull, twisting as I grip her lower body, I feel the first slice of new talons, which split the skin on my side. My hip warms with blood.

Every instinct commands me to protect my flank, but no, I must kill the alpha. I hear the throaty inhale at my back and prepare for the strike.

However, as the grunt of exertion erupts behind me, the creature, visible out of the corner of my eye, bursts into white light. Bits of its burnt flesh splatter across me and the alpha.

It exploded.

Two others advance, and I spin to put the alpha between us. This loosens my grip, and she sinks her teeth deep into my forearm. I cry out in pain so complete, my vision turns white.

No.

That flash was not in my brain.

Another of the NextGen has... exploded.

This new chaos has the alpha's attention now. She turns from my arm, so I bring an elbow down on top of her head, and she falls to my feet.

Another burst of light, and a third NextGen vaporizes.

Then I catch the familiar scent on the air. I turn to the black square, the hole in the wall, and call out.

"Emelda! What are you—"

"Get back," she shouts from the void. "I've only got one more!"

Three NextGen are left. Two have retreated, wary of what took down their comrades. This third, seemingly oblivious, leaps toward me.

I hear the zing of her slingshot bolt as another white streak rockets toward the creature. No, not white. It's a reflection.

Silver.

But the creature is baiting her. He spins and grabs the silver spike before it can split his skin, continues spinning, leaps in the air, and drives it deep into my chest.

Burning and white-hot, my skin feels like it's on fire, and I crumple on top of the alpha, who is pulsing with ragged breaths.

The creature closest to me barks something to the other two, and they split off. One running past me, the other around the far corner.

"Oh shit!" I hear Emelda cry out then the pounding of feet.

The NextGen stalks to the hole and launches itself through, never touching the sides. I hear his splashing feet take up the chase.

I try to raise myself, but my body has been immobilized. My vision rolls like the computer screens in the control room. Flip, flip, flip. Through the flashes, I see the alpha push me aside and leap to her feet.

I cannot breathe. Water rushes past my head, or is this in my mind?

The silver spike is burrowing deeper into my chest, burning my flesh, and the white of my vision snaps away to black. My last moments will be watching my only human friend get chased down by one of those creatures!

I must fight against the black.

Push it away from my vision. A dark forest arises around me. Did I die and go to my ancestors?

No!

Not yet!

I grit my teeth and can feel blood, taste its savor in my mouth.

No!

I cannot let Emelda die. Not like this! Not in the jaws of such creatures.

Ahead, I see eyes in the dark forest, stalking toward me. Is this a new foe? In my mind, I turn my head to the side, trying to get a look at it. The creature copies my moves. I tilt my head down, and it does the same.

I call out, scream, and howl, but no sound comes from me.

The red-eyed creature before me lifts its head, a mirror of my own actions, but it does scream. It does howl.

Then the dark turns to light, and I am back in the tunnel once more. The alpha stands over me, blood and spittle dripping from its mouth onto my face. It steps on my chest, driving me deeper into rising water.

"No, this is mine to kill," it growls. In the creature's hand, the silver spike begins to smoke. It barks in pain and chucks it away.

I try to reach up, but when I see my hand rise, it is bubbling and melting and reforming, pale skin to purple-black fur.

Pain shoots through my body, and when I call out, it is the roar of the Wolfwere.

Chapter Fifty-Five

M y heart pounded against my chest as I raced through the hidden tunnel system. I cursed myself for not being able to snap off a few more of the silver spikes, but I'd run out of time.

The river had burst its banks, and the gushing, angry froth was already rising past my ankles.

As I ran through the tunnels, each step got harder and harder as the water climbed up the wall. My lungs burned as I sucked in breath. I was growing weak with exhaustion.

I tried to map the layout in my mind as I ran, my hands in front of me, feeling for the walls in the near total darkness. If I kept running at full steam, I would smash right into a frigging wall!

On my left, I heard the scream of one of the NextGen. Its fist punched through the wall, and chunks of rock tumbled into the rushing water ahead. A beam of light from the other side pierced the darkness.

Nope.

I wove around its claws and smashed down on the creature's hand with the handle of my slingdart.

However, the busted-out hole did light up my passageway, just a little, and I saw the turn ahead. I banked hard to the right, and the moment I did, another burst of light flashed as the other NextGen bashed its fist into the wall and reached for me.

How were they tracking me so easily? It couldn't be by scent, not with all the water.

Ah. Right.

The water. They could hear me splashing through the damn tunnels. Nothing I could do about that.

The creature swiped its claws, coming inches from my arm. Throwing myself toward the opposite wall, I bounced off and kept running. Fleeing my predators. I was their prey.

Oh, wait.

The thought hit me a half a second too late. They weren't trying to catch me. These creatures weren't mindless. They were cunning. Whether that came from the animal part or the human, it didn't matter.

The NextGen were corralling me. I realized this when I took the next sharp turn and got a fist to the chest. I flew back, fell with a splash, and a torrent filled my ears.

Nope and nope.

I emerged from the water, held up my slingdart, and drew back the snaking yellow band. The monster halted its advance, hesitation playing across its face in the faint light. Then it grinned. Long, sharp teeth. Its tongue flicked the tips of its long incisors.

"No more," it said, pointing at my empty slingdart.

Yep. Busted.

I grabbed the rubber band of the slingdart and twirled it around like I was going to bonk it on the head. It must have looked absolutely pathetic because the NextGen laughed.

It almost sounded human.

"Nowhere left to run," it said as I pressed my back against the stone wall. It stalked closer. "No more silver."

But then I realized something.

That?

That wasn't entirely true.

Chapter Fifty-Six

Kane

The alpha regards me as I stand anew.

Her eyes widen as I rise, and her jaw slackens. I am reminded this NextGen is part human, for these are human gestures.

She is also part of me.

I pause. Before me, this is not just a monster. It is more.

My hesitation was a mistake. The momentary flicker of doubt, she would read this on my face. Instinct commands her to strike.

The blow catches me in the stomach, and I double over. A second powerful fist smashes me down onto the floor.

But not floor.

I am in... a pool?

How is this?

I spin to my back, and when I look up, she is above me, shimmering and warbling. Strange. My nostrils burn. The taste in my mouth is rock and dirt. And river.

Clever, she.

So clever!

By hitting my chest, she stole my breath. Very little oxygen left in my lungs and none beneath the water flooding the tunnel. I reach up to strike, but it is slow, and she dodges easily. So hard to see, and my movements stir the water.

My vision of her comes to me in pieces.

I see the human. I see the creature. I see the wolf within.

Another blow strikes my chest, squeezing out what little air I have left. She is trying to drown me. A pitiful part of me thinks this might be better. But I cannot.

I have my pack to return to. My wolf wife.

And my friend who is being chased by the beasts within the inner tunnels.

Through fractal visions, I see another strike coming, this time claws extended. She has made a mistake of her own. This not her fault. She could not see me shift my legs for they are hidden beneath the water.

This is not her fault.

I strike out with my feet, connecting midcalf, and the snap of bones cracks off the walls like a gunshot. Falling, she reaches forward to break her fall, and I grab her hand in mine. For a moment, I hold it.

Then I squeeze hard and roll, lifting myself from the water and submerging the creature below.

A froth of bubbles turns the water white as the alpha cries out in pain.

Chapter Fifty-Seven

The monster stalked closer, and to buy myself a second or two, I threw my slingdart at it. It raised its forearm, and my flimsy weapon bounced off, splashing and disappearing in the black water.

The creature stalked closer, raising both arms.

I put my hand to my throat, grasped the thin chain around my neck, snapped it, and wrapped it around my trembling fingers.

Its body marched toward me. Even in the dim light, I could see its muscles twitch and tense. Tendons stretched, and bones moved beneath its thick hide.

I knew where it would hit before it struck and instinctively ducked from its blow. The creature's fist smashed through the wall behind me. A brilliant beam of light burst through the hole. It struggled to pull its arm free.

Above me, I saw its throat.

I pressed my palm at the flesh there, and where the chain touched skin, it sizzled, smoked, and began to burn.

The NextGen *screamed*.

It flailed in pain, still trying to remove its fist from the wall, but in its panic only wedged itself closer toward me.

Wrapping my other hand around the back of its head, I pressed my palm harder, deeper, gritting my teeth. Its other arm came up to slash at me. But, as before, something in my brain anticipated the move, and I twisted my body away.

Its second fist passed through the wall.

With both of its hands caught in the stone, it hung on the wall like a man in stocks. I slipped out from beneath it and grabbed the thick hair on the back of its neck. In my other hand, I gripped the chain of my grandmother's locket tighter and growled at the monster.

I smashed my fist down on its skull.

Sparks and flame erupted. I struck it again and again and again until I felt its skull give way and my hand smash into mush.

The creature was dead.

And I had killed it. One of the most powerful beasts that had ever walked the planet.

Me.

I felt a tickle on my neck and looked down. A spider had fallen from the ceiling, landing on my shoulder.

"Oh my God!" I screamed. "Get off, get off, get off!"

The NextGen collapsed and took the crumbing wall with it. A torrent of water rushed in. We had to get out of the tunnels, or we would drown.

I ran to find Kane. And, sure, to get away from the damn spider.

Chapter Fifty-Eight

Kane

Water rolls across my thick hide and fur as I stand over the alpha, one foot pressing hard upon her chest. She struggles to lift herself, seeking air that will never come. With broken limbs, she cannot free herself from this water grave.

Through the shimmering surface, she glares up at me with those all-black eyes. A brave hunter still.

She strikes out with her claws but weakens with each effort. I feel them slice across my shin and calf but do not notice the pain.

No.

The pain is within for I know what I must do.

She is drowning, but this is not a hunter's death. When I raise my hand and extend my own claws, she sees her fate. When she roars for the final time, no bubbles escape her dark lips. The alpha is defiant until the end.

Like a wolf.

Like a child of Kane.

The only gift I can give her is to make it quick. I do.

Near death from asphyxiation, she is weak, and I slash her throat deeply. The alpha's eyes roll back into her skull, and she is gone. My heart wants to break, but not yet. I will endure this pain later. For now, it sits like a stone in my chest, growing heavier with each breath.

However, my body is slashed. My bones also cracked.

I know what I must do, but in this I will honor the fine hunter before me. I lift her dead body from the water and open my mouth to take her blood.

Chapter Fifty-Nine

"Here!" I shouted down the tunnel as I ran toward Kane.

Even over the roar of the water and the splashing of my feet, I could hear that his voice was deeper, raspier. I knew what I would see when I laid eyes on him again.

The river had breached the tunnels, bubbling in froth and dirt and branches. By the time I turned the next corner, the water had risen above my knees. As I passed the busted-out holes in the walls, I was wary of a claw reaching in, trying to grasp me.

But the remaining NextGen weren't interested in me anymore. They were now howling, not in rage or even primal hunger. It was fear.

I trudged through the water, swinging my arms in the air, fighting upstream. Rounding the next corner, I saw the square of light and the massive head of the Wolfwere peering down the passageway.

"Come now, we must go!" he shouted.

I breezed past him.

"Not that way," I called over my shoulder. "I closed the main door."

I heard the splash behind me as he squeezed through the hole.

"Very good! I am proud of you."

The torrent of water had risen to my hips, and I struggled to push through it. Then I felt two powerful hands grasp under my arms, lift, and carry me. Ahead, I could see the gray light of night at the top half of our exit.

The bottom half was river.

Over the rush of water, I yelled out, "Stop. Kane, stop!"

"Cannot stop," he growled in my ear.

I shot an elbow into his side, which I knew wouldn't hurt him. Hell, it wouldn't even bruise him, but he would get the message. Who needed words?

Furrowing and frowning *and* elbowing to the ribs did the job.

At the first hidden trapdoor we went through, I twisted the cross and pushed the hatch open and stuck my head through. Lights were flickering, and electric arc light filled the next hallway.

I took a deep breath to shout for Adriana, the guard I'd left in the control room, to come our way.

Then I heard the snarling. The growling. The feeding.

The NextGen creatures had discovered her, and their hunger overtook any instinct they had to escape the flood.

I closed my eyes, pulled back out, and closed the hidden door once again.

Ahead, the water was now two-thirds filling the gap. Kane had to lift me to the ceiling so I could breathe in the pocket of air. He grunted and growled, fighting the raging river.

The water fought back.

My body was being battered by the flow and branches and floating debris. A flash of yellow whipped past my head. A Styrofoam taco, smiling and bug-eyed, headed to its watery grave.

A few feet away, all light winked out.

We were underwater. As powerful as Kane was as the Wolfwere, I could feel his body trembling, shaking with the exertion to keep us from being sucked back. If we fell, if he lost his footing, we would die.

The convent would be our tomb.

My vision darkened as my lungs screamed for oxygen. But Kane couldn't move a step farther. Each time he lifted his foot, he would slide back. His grip on my torso was so tight, even if there were air to breath, I would not be able to take a lungful.

With my last seconds of air, I reached forward, seeking some sort of handhold, anything.

My fingertips touched stone to my left. We were right at the exit!

Wiggling and squirming, I slid his grip lower down my hips. My fingers back on the stone, I walked them, digging my nails into grit. I felt the far edge. The outside wall. I pulled. Twisting sideways—either Kane was weakening, or he had a sense of what I was trying—I put my other hand out to join the first.

I pulled.

And pulled.

Slowly, so slowly, we began to inch forward. My eyes were slammed shut, and I knew if I were to pass out from oxygen deprivation, I would never even know. I focused on my hands and pulled with every ounce of strength left in me.

Then I felt one of Kane's arms pull away.

Jesus, he was losing his grip!

With only one of his arms around me, the water coming even faster now, I was seconds away from being dragged out of his grasp.

I felt a massive hand on top of mine. He'd reached out, copying my grip on the wall, and began to pull with me.

We tugged and pulled until, finally, the tops of our heads broke water. I felt a cool breeze on my forehead, my nose, and—sweet relief—my mouth.

I sucked in a huge breath, taking in some water, and coughed.

Kane pulled us up and around the corner. Even outside the tunnel, the water was still up around our knees. A storm raged above us, which had sent the river into a fury, seeking prey of its own.

"Hold on," he shouted over the symphony of rain and rushing water. "Throwing you!"

"What?"

An instant later, I was in the air, flipping once and landing on my stomach, smashing some of the rounded red clay roof tiles. The thud that shook my body told me Kane had jumped up.

He helped me to my feet, and on wobbly legs, I looked down at the chaos. Water churned all around the abandoned convent like we were standing in the middle of the river. Swirling and snaking, seeking out all that had been hidden.

The Church's secret revealed itself to the rush of water then was lost forever.

I turned to Kane then—*yikes*—spun away.

"What?"

"Dude." Holding a palm to him, I said, "You need more fur on your full frontal."

He laughed. "I just saved your life, Emelda!"

Turning back and looking at his face—mostly his face—I pointed at his long snout.

"Um, hello? Who told you to get in the tunnel?" I inched closer. "Who pulled us out?"

The purple-black skin between his eyes furrowed. He nodded.

"I helped."

"Yes, you did, Wolfman," I said and patted his arm. A crash behind us made me jump, and he reached for my arm, but I batted him away.

When I looked down, I saw the Crazy Taco truck floating, banging into trees, knocking down topiary, and spilling out wrappers and bottles from its open rear doors. I saw my pink backpack and felt an electric bolt rattle my bones.

"Go," I said, pushing him. "Go get that! Your serum is in there."

Kane leaped from the top of the building and hit the water running. A massive log rolled as it came close, and he slashed it with his claws, cutting it to splinters.

He snatched my pack, trudged back through the water, and jumped back up beside me. With furious fingers, I ripped the main zipper open and shoved my hand inside. The clothes were soaked, and I dug through them. My hands brushed up against the interior, and I felt a hard edge. When I unzipped that pocket, I found Kane's passport wallet and the passport with my face under the name of some TV actress I think my friend had a thing for. Thankfully, the rubber lining had kept them dry.

But where was the damn box?

Panicking, I just wanted to upend the backpack and spill everything out. But we were on a roof in the middle of a rain storm. Bad idea, panic brain.

I squeezed the bottom of the pack and felt hard edges.

My heart leaped.

Chucking damp clothes all around me, I finally spotted the case. I carefully reached inside and pulled it out. With a silent prayer, I flipped the clasp and peered inside.

The capped syringe was still intact, its queer liquid still encased within the glass. I breathed a sigh of relief then heard another crash as the Crazy Taco smashed into the black Mercedes. A glimmer of chrome twinkled from just beyond the exterior fence. That had to be whatever the Spanish crew had driven here.

The occupants of both of those vehicles were now entombed below.

The truck careened and bent, smashed another of the hearse's windows, and kept going. As it passed trees and slipped through debris, I watched it disappear to wherever it was headed next.

"Um," I said, pointing down, "we may have to buy a new truck."

"What about priceless disks?" He took a step forward. "Should I get?"

I sighed. "Nah. Some things are meant to stay lost."

We stood and watched for a few minutes to see if the two remaining NextGen had found a way to scrabble out. Kane ran the perimeter of the roof, leaping over the gaps with ease. When he had completed a few circuits, he stopped next to me.

I caught the expression on his face.

"What's wrong?"

He shrugged. "Is good. They are gone."

"But?"

Kane looked toward the moon, the tiniest sliver of a crescent in the sky. The beginning of some things. The end of others.

"They came from me. Not their fault."

"I don't think they were soldiers like the Enhanced," I said.

He told me about the woman back on the mountaintop. The NextGen who'd begged for death. Kane had granted her wish.

"My guess is these NextGen were the road workers who went missing," I said. "They twisted them up and made them into monster soldiers. Or tried."

"These creatures were..." He stopped, struggling to find the words. "From me. Like offspring. In some manner."

I tried to think of something to comfort him. To tell him we had done the right thing. And we had. But I knew nothing I could say would make that unique ache, that hole in his chest, feel any less painful.

He blinked a few times, took a deep breath, let it out, and hit me with a smile. A big monster smile that I actually found charming. In a way.

"You have my serum," Kane said. "It is over?"

As he said it, I could tell even he knew that we weren't done.

"There are two more," I said, my voice a whisper.

"Yes. Marata will be difficult," he said and sighed. "Doc Hammer will be easy to dispose of in the warehouse."

"Harsh."

He shrugged. "She made the bed to lie in."

"Close, Wolfman," I said and smiled, but my smile fell away quickly.

"What?"

The image of what Carminia had shown me back at the Palace flashed to mind. I looked up at his amber eyes.

"Those aren't the two I'm talking about."

Chapter Sixty

W e waited for the storm to pass, and within the hour, the rain slowed to a sprinkle. There wasn't much we could do about the river while it was still so high.

We slept in the roofed lookout spot on top of the convent. There was a hatch at the bottom, but the idea of opening it felt like prying open a grave.

By morning, the water had receded. I'd laid out a pair of sweatpants to dry over the rounded brick wall of the outlook. The sweatpants would be tight on Kane, but it was all I had until we got back to the hotel.

My legs still ached from my trek through the underground river, so I rode on Kane's back all the way to the Palace.

Halfway there, I laughed and bent down close to his ear. "Canadian Uber?"

He let out a call that I was pretty sure was supposed to sound like a moose. It didn't sound like any moose I'd ever heard.

I'd heard one, by the way. Just the one, so who was I to judge?

As we stepped onto the rear of the Palace grounds, I looked to the far corner and saw Carminia's cabin. No lights were on inside.

The soil here wasn't wet, which was odd. Of course, the river wouldn't have flowed all the way to the Palace, but the storm had been so intense! Surely it would have soaked here as much as back at the convent.

I shooed those thoughts away. Clearly, I was trying to distract myself.

When we got to the stone house, I led him down the short passageway as Carminia had led me. When he entered, his huge eyes got even bigger. He smelled them before he saw them.

At the barred window, I peeked inside. Then stood back so he could see. "Who are they?"

I placed a hand on my chest and drew in a shaky breath.

"A few of the early NextGen escaped. Covenant must have tracked them down but only after those tourists had been mauled," I said, my voice phlegmy. "For whatever reason, the creatures attacked two kids but stopped before killing them."

"But they were bitten."

He didn't say that as a question because he'd picked up their scent the moment the front door had come open.

"Yes. Carminia has been feeding them, but that can't continue," I said. "Especially after tonight."

"I see."

He turned away from the window and leaned against the door. Inside, I heard the heavy breathing of the children. Although I didn't know how much "child" was left in either of them.

I put my hand on his bare arm. "I don't know if we should take them to a hospital or..." My voice trailed off.

"No. No hospital can cure."

He nodded to the backpack over my shoulder. I sighed and weakly tried to protest. "But that's yours, Kane. That syringe with the serum is the only one left."

"Enough for big man like me, yes?" he asked, grinning sadly. "Enough for two little ones."

I nodded. Of course, I'd had the same thought, but the decision had to be his. This was his life, what we had risked everything for. And we would be throwing it aside.

"Give it to the children," he said, placing a hand on my shoulder. "We will find another way."

I wiped away the dampness in my eyes, sniffed, and nodded.

"But how? This was the only—"

"No, maybe not only," he said. "Last night, I become the creature not because of moon but because of your spike."

"Silver."

"Yes, silver," he said, "but I do believe it would have killed me if the alpha had not removed it so that she could kill me herself."

I laughed and sobbed at the same time. "Selfish."

"But so much of this we do not understand. Why did I change after silver was removed?"

"And when you got jabbed by Marata with her go juice. You changed then too."

"Exactly," he said and placed his hands on either side of my face. He'd intended it to be a comforting gesture, but his massive palms and fingers enveloped my head. He pulled his hands away. "Sorry."

Pretending to spit out hair, I said, "Don't worry about it."

Chapter Sixty-One

Three days later, we were rolling up to the St. Louis warehouse where we'd dumped Doc Hammer. Had that been only a week earlier? It felt like a lifetime ago.

Before leaving the Palace, Kane had given a half dose of his serum to each of the kids. They were feverish and trembling as they slept, but within minutes, their fevers broke.

Kane and I waited a few minutes more, and when we looked back in, they, well, looked like kids again.

I went inside to leave Carminia a note to tell her to check on them the moment she awoke, which I expected she would anyhow. I also had to leave her an email address, one of my old ones, so she could give us a way to pay her back for the Crazy Taco truck.

Searching around for something to write on, I went into the Palace conference room because it was the only place I'd seen anyone use.

Banging through drawers and opening cabinets, I came away empty-handed.

Kane stood at the door, watching me.

"This damn company is worth millions," I said, slamming another drawer, "and they don't have a single pen."

"Billions, my dear," the voice bellowed from behind me, and the floating head rose from the table. I didn't know what sort of augmented reality tech this guy had on his Zoom call, but it was next-level.

I jumped at his sudden appearance. Kane shifted his feet, ready for a fight. I really think he wanted to punch the digital head.

Steve Janus waved a hand in my big friend's direction. At least, I think it was his hand. The dude looked like a head. No shoulders. No arms. Then a flappy hand came up beside his head.

"Oh, calm down," he said in a weird singsong voice. "What a mess you have made, yes? So much time and effort gone to waste. Hmm..." He turned and called to someone off camera. "See if we can get a tax write-off for this whole thing. There must be some way. And if there's not... just... find someone to change a law or just make a new one."

I stood with my arms crossed. Part of me wanted to bolt from the room. Another nastier part wanted to gloat that we'd shut him down.

"Sorry your drug lords and warlords won't be getting their super soldiers. I feel"—I fanned my eyes and adopted a mock expression—"bad about that."

Janus's eyes shot back to me, like he'd been listening to someone else. Then he waved his hand dismissively.

"Yes, yes and no, no," he said. "But yes and no, sure."

I looked at Kane. He looked at me and shrugged.

"Bit of a funding thing, that whole business. This was a billion-dollar project, yes," Janus said then muttered something off screen about his accountant. "Eventually, yes, yes, terrifying monster soldiers unleashed upon the world. Boo-hoo. But I had other plans first. Big moves. I only do big moves."

"Not this time."

Janus laughed too hard. "Yes. Well, if you have a better idea about how to fight an army of demons, I'd like to hear it."

Kane looked at me. I looked at him and shrugged.

"Listen, the two of you," Janus said, sounding distracted as his eyes drifted between us and, I guessed, others in his room, "if you could stay there, I would appreciate it. I'm sending someone to kill you both. Tying up loose ends."

I laughed. "You've got no one left! They're either eaten, drowned, or blown up."

Actually, I didn't know if that was true.

"Ah. Right," he said, leaning forward. I heard the sound of pen scribbling on paper. "There is the housekeeper. Carmen or whatever."

"Carminia's a cook," I said. "Not a killer."

"Obviously..." Still writing, Janus cocked an eyebrow at me. "You've never had her lasagna."

With that, the big head blipped away without another word.

"Do you think the children are okay?" Kane said, nudging me as I drove, bringing me back to the present. "They are home back with family?"

A sadness rolled over me. *That* was exactly what the serum was supposed to do for Kane. He'd given it up for two little strangers. I nodded to him, my lips pressed together.

"Also, we need to fix my chain, yes?" he asked, digging the locket out of his leather coat. The one *good* thing that happened in Mexico? The denim jacket had burned to a crisp on top of the mountain.

"You still want to wear the locket? We know why it's warm to you now," I said as he rolled it around his hands. "It's silver, which could make you, you know, explode."

He held it between two fingers. "No exploding. Maybe because of tarnish?"

"Maybe, but do you really want to risk it?"

"I do," he said, tucking it back in his pocket. "Its warmth will remind me of you. And we will both have lockets. This is called twinsies."

I had to give it to him, Kane knew how to make me smile. Reaching up to my neck, I caressed my own locket and thought of my grandmother. Then my thoughts drifted to my mother's dad.

"Do you think my granddad really worked for Rosa years ago?" I asked, pulling into the parking lot of the run-down warehouse. "He was a drunk, sure, but I never thought of him as a bad man."

"Bad?" Kane asked, hitting me with a warm smile. "Working in one gang's shop, spying for another gang. No killing, I would think. Some stocking of shelves, yes. Very little murder in such tasks."

"Don't bet on it. You've never worked in retail," I said and smiled to let him know I was joking. "But I can't get my head around the idea that he worked for, you know, criminals. That just doesn't seem like him."

I opened the squeaky door to our rental car and stumbled out into the parking lot of the St. Louis warehouse. When I slammed the door, the rearview mirror shook and fell onto the dash. When it disappeared down in the footwell, I chuckled.

We'd been lucky to get *any* car back in Mexico. That had been due in large part to an older couple who'd been standing behind us when we'd hurriedly checked out of our hotel. The moment I heard the Minnesota accent and their plans about heading home, I gave them my biggest smile and a story that was at least ten percent true.

They'd given us a ride to the airport, and we tracked down the very tiny rental lot. We had a choice between an old Honda hatchback and something called a Hyundai Citroen. Kane nixed the latter.

"Sounds very much like citron," he said, grimacing. "This means lemon in French."

We'd gone with the Honda. It was older than me but, my best guess, had far fewer hard miles than I had. We'd driven all the way to Missouri without a problem. Except the problem of *technically* we had, sort of, stolen it.

Kane's bank card would take the hit, but he didn't seem too worried about it.

As I stared up at the derelict warehouse, I walked around the rusted back bumper and nearly smacked into my big friend. He'd bent down on one knee so we were nearly face-to-face. He placed a hand on my shoulder.

"From what you say, Grandfather Nicholas did what he felt he must to help his daughter," he said. "She wanted to come to America, so he put his own needs aside to make it so."

I thought about it for a moment, and the more I did, the more I liked that thought.

"Your logic is..." I said and grinned at him, "sound."

"And your grand-père might have been a better man than you are giving him credit for."

"Maybe." I nodded. "I wish I'd known him better. I guess I'll have to ask Mom about my—my *abuelo*."

"Yes, yes," he said. "And your grandfather too."

Laughing, I grabbed a crowbar out of the trunk and pointed at the door to the warehouse.

If he'd been the Wolfwere, he could have simply smashed it open with a fist. Hell, he seemed to have gotten stronger in recent days. He could probably do it as a human.

Kane wedged the crowbar between the huge metal door and the jamb and yanked until the triple locks busted from the inside. The door flew wide.

We listened for a moment, expecting Doc Hammer would have heard the clatter and started snarling. She didn't.

He stepped forward, and I put a hand on his shoulder.

Whispering, I said, "If she's gotten out of that collar and she's running around in here, that could be trouble. Trust me, you don't want to be chased around this place."

We wove around the upended machines and overturned tables and strewn boxes from when Marata had been hunting me. That had been before she'd picked up Kane's scent on my neck. Had it not been for that, I would have become a Marata snack.

Would there be some way to use Kane's scent to help track down the Enhanced woman?

Maybe.

First things first.

We still had the gruesome task of cutting the remaining Enhanced population by half. Hammer was an asshole. She'd tortured Kane and tried to kill me. Still, I wasn't a murderer.

Or was I?

During Kane's quest to find home, I'd done things I would never have dreamed I was capable of. And I'd done some real awful stuff over the years.

The image of my hand smashing the NextGen flashed before my eyes. The moment when my fist penetrated his skull, I'd felt so powerful. So alive!

Thinking back now, that made me feel ill.

Walking ahead of me, Kane turned, noticing my silence. He stared for a moment then stopped.

"When you must kill, you must kill," he said. Somehow, he'd known exactly what I'd been thinking. "When it is to survive, this is just."

"Is that the animal way?"

He shrugged. "It is the living way."

Kane walked up to the huge wall, climbed onto the cement podium holding the vat, gripped the brick, and vaulted over the top.

I didn't know if I bought his logic.

The living way.

For now, it would do. But would I look back one day and regret all I had done? Would I see the faces of those I'd killed?

Hell, would I live *long* enough to be troubled by the faces of the dead?

Kane tapped me on the shoulder, and I flinched. I'd been so lost in my thoughts, I hadn't even heard him do... what he'd had to do. And I was glad for that.

I had enough angry demons running through my head already, I didn't need to add the screams of Doc Hammer to my orchestra of regret.

I asked him, "Is it done?"

Without answering, Kane wrapped an arm around my ribs and scaled the wall once again. I was beginning to feel like Jessica what's her name in that old King Kong movie.

When we landed on the other side, I nearly covered my eyes. I didn't need to see her remains.

But I didn't.

All I saw was the tether on the floor.

And no Doc Hammer.

Not a dead or a live one.

"Where the hell is she?"

Kane walked over and grabbed the end of the chain, holding it up. It had been cut right through. Glancing around, I searched for a discarded axe or saw or blowtorch. Anything.

"How did she break that collar? It was designed to hold the Enhanced!"

"I do not know," he said, lowering it.

I put my hands on top of my head. Our final fight had just doubled in size.

Then I remembered that Marata had gotten free from her chains too. Of course, she hadn't had a collar like Hammer had.

I snatched the chain from Kane's hand and examined it.

"Look at this," I said, holding it up to his face and pointing. "It's been *bitten*. Bitten in half."

"It is stronger than steel, yes?" Kane asked, his bushy eyebrows knitting together. "In my beast form, I do not know if I could do this!"

Examining the break, I looked closer at the bite mark. A line of jagged tears cut right through the supposedly uncuttable metal.

In the middle of the mark, there was one space without an indentation. A blank spot.

"The person who bit this had a gap in their front teeth." I closed my eyes and dropped the chain. "Marata. Marata is the one who freed her."

Kane looked to the chain then to me.

"We knew we had to destroy both," he said and shrugged. "Nothing has changed."

I turned away and swallowed when I saw the wall we'd just climbed and what had been written on this side. No, not written but *carved* into the brick.

"Everything has changed, Wolfman," I said and headed toward a hole in the wall that had been bashed out by the feral woman months earlier.

"What?" he called after me. "What has changed?"

I pointed up at the gouged-out lettering across the top of the brick. Then I remembered he wouldn't be able to read it. So I read it for him.

"It says Animals First." Before climbing through the hole, I turned back to him. "They're working together now."

#

Chapter Sixty-Two

Acknowledgements

T his book would have been an absolute mess without my lovely Beta readers: Claire Armstrong-Brealey, Peggy Hackett, Donna Cronin, Chris Robinson, Joe McCormick, Michael Pelto, Bill Thompson, Megan Rang and Steve Lewis. I appreciate your insight and that using up your valuable time to join me on this wayward adventure. Thank you, thank you, thank you.

Thank you to the Red Adept editors for helping make me sound like I know proper English.

And to my alpha in our pack of two, my lovely wife Tiffany.

Chapter Sixty-Three

The end is near!

Pre-order the final book in the series, *Kane Unmanned* on Amazon.

Coming soon!